Sophie's House of Cards

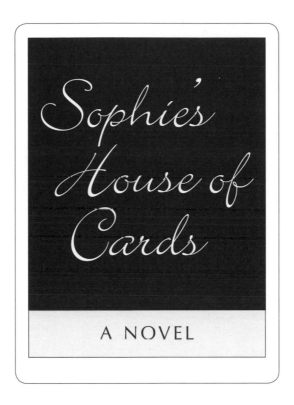

Sophie's
House of
Cards

A NOVEL

SHARON OARD WARNER

UNIVERSITY OF NEW MEXICO PRESS • ALBUQUERQUE

Library of Congress Cataloging-in-Publication Data

Warner, Sharon Oard.
  Sophie's house of cards : a novel / Sharon Oard Warner.
     pages cm
    ISBN 978-0-8263-3077-2 (paperback) — ISBN 978-0-8263-3078-9 (electronic)
   1. Mothers and daughters—Fiction. 2. Tarot cards—Fiction. 3. Fortune—Fiction.
4. New Mexico—Fiction. 5. Domestic fiction. I. Title.
  PS3573.A7675S67 2014
  813'.54—dc23
                                   2014007131

"There Is a Mountain" by Donovan Leitch
Copyright 1967 by Donovan (Music) Limited
Administered by Peer International Corporation
Copyright Renewed
International Copyright Secured. Used by Permission
All Rights Reserved

COVER PHOTOGRAPH: Lisa Tremaine
BOOK DESIGN: Catherine Leonardo
Composed in Sabon LT Std Roman 9.75/14
Display type is Bickley Script

For my sons, Corey and Devin

Don't we require, finally, a place in our thinking for fortune, or destiny, or whatever we choose to call what will happen to us, how the avalanche will break over us.

—Mark Doty, *Heaven's Coast*

February 13, 2008

Dearest Sophie:

Most of what I know about the cards I learned from a woman named Serafina. Back in 1968, the year I ran away from home, I enrolled in her class with the express purpose of becoming a fortune-teller. Of course you'll laugh at this, but at the time I thought I was doing something practical. Gaining a job skill! By then I was sick of panhandling, but I lacked both a high school diploma and reputable references, so I was shit out of luck when it came to most jobs.

Serafina's husband owned a pawnshop on the edge of the Haight, and she conducted her classes around a card table in the back room. If you leaned on the table, it was apt to collapse. The walls of the room were lined with pawn too big to go out front: a unicycle, a gun rack, and, if I remember correctly, a stuffed grizzly bear. I was seventeen years old and most nights I went to sleep hungry. My plan was to learn as much as I could as fast as I could.

One of the things my teacher insisted on was "making the cards your own." For her, that meant coloring a black-and-white deck using colored pencils. I completed the task—all seventy-eight cards, thank you very much—but my first spring in Taos someone stole that deck. Swiped them right out of my backpack, along with a pair of embroidered cutoffs and a tube of red lipstick. Stealing tarot cards is bad juju. Which is why I want to be clear that these cards are a gift.

This deck, called the Albano-Waite, was printed in 1968. Today, it's Antiques Roadshow–worthy. Take care of the cards, Sophie. Keep them in a pine box or wrapped in a silk scarf. Don't let other people handle them! If by chance someone does use your cards, I suggest smudging them. Fortunately, we live in Indian country and smudge sticks are easy to come by.

My favorite spread is the Celtic Cross. When I read for you, that's the spread I used. If you look closely you'll see that there's a small cross (cards 1–2) at the center of the larger one (cards 1–6). The interior cross concerns the heart of the matter, and the larger one predicts the

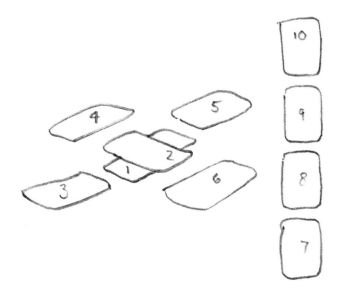

Celtic Cross—Staff

outlook over time. The staff (cards 7–10) gives the seeker guidance on surrounding circumstances, with the last card as the possible outcome. The perspective of the drawing is skewed, but that's your mother for you.

In my green trunk, you'll find a sign I fashioned from the flap of a cardboard box. Using colored pencils, I shaded the letters in every color of the rainbow: TAROT CARD READER. With that sign, I created an identity for myself, one that has proven more durable than I could have imagined.

All my love,

Your mother, Peggy

~ The Seeker ~

PAGE of CUPS.

The Celtic Cross spread requires a significator, a card chosen in advance to represent the questioner or seeker. Most often, court cards are used for this purpose: a Page is used for children and teens, a Knight for young adults of either sex, a Queen for a mature woman, a King for a mature man. The easiest method for selecting a card is to assign a suit based on the seeker's astrological sign. Because you're a young person and a Pisces, the Page of Cups is your card. Fire signs (Aries, Leo, and Sagittarius) are associated with Wands, Earth signs (Taurus, Virgo, and Capricorn) with Pentacles, Air signs (Gemini, Libra, and Aquarius) with Swords, and Water signs (Cancer, Scorpio, and Pisces) with Cups. It's really quite that simple.

FROM HER UPSTAIRS bedroom window, Sophie watches her father amble out to the hives. Jack is wearing coveralls and carrying his smoker in one hand and the veiled hat he calls his "bee bonnet" in the other. It's a Sunday morning at the beginning of September, and Sophie is up early, on the lookout for just such an opportunity. Right now Jack is furious with her. She knows he is, but Sophie is confident that he doesn't want to stay mad. She is and always has been his adoring daughter, after all, and she's determined to prove it to him.

The open field Jack crosses is covered with brushy sage and rabbit bush or chamisa. From Sophie's vantage point the hive boxes look like small chests of drawers and are all the more arresting because they're painted not white but primary colors: red, yellow, and two shades of bright blue. The view from her windows is expansive. Past the hives, beyond the Bosque and the river, the Sleeping Sisters bump up on the horizon, five volcanoes that have been dormant for thousands of years but are still not extinct.

Within a minute or two she is down the stairs and out the door, having made a brief stop in the kitchen, where she doused her tongue with honey from the jar on the dining room table. Above her, clouds billow and scud across a vast blue surface before disappearing to the west. Striding toward her father, Sophie reaches out to finger the tops of the brushy sage, covered now with tiny purple flowers. They're like straw to the touch, so dry they crumble into the beds of her nails, and when she thrusts her hands into the pockets of her jeans she deposits papery, purple specks into the white seams.

Jack takes no notice of his daughter's approach. He's busy searching for his queen. "Where are you, little lady?" he mutters, head bent to the frame of brood, which bustles with the brown bodies of hundreds of worker bees. His bee overalls trail the ground. Bought to accommodate his belly, they don't fit him anywhere else. He doesn't wear the veil, though he keeps it handy on the ground beside him in case the bees are out of sorts. Just now he finds it difficult to gauge their mood because he can't see them well enough—they're little more than a blurry mass of movement. Even holding the frame at arm's length, he can't see for shit. "I need elbow extenders," he mutters to himself.

A few feet from the hives, Sophie stops and stands motionless. The air is still, but an occasional breeze tousles her brownish-black curls, covering and uncovering a startling lock of white. She waits for her father to take notice. When he doesn't, she attempts the word "Jack." The single syllable comes out slurred, the "J" sound missing. She's trying not to flatten the honey against the roof of her mouth.

The bees continue to boil over the surface of the frame. Most don't notice the change of situation, but a few rise into the air. Inevitably, one or two drift toward Sophie. To the bees, her red T-shirt resembles some impossibly large flower. She is the sort of miracle bees don't think to question. Sophie opens her mouth wide and sticks out her tongue, allowing the golden sweetness to dribble over her chapped lips and pointed chin.

For a moment Jack suspects she's been smoking dope again. Pot reduces her to mindless hilarity; to use sixties lingo, she finds it impossible to "maintain." Jack blames marijuana for the recent stunt at Movies West, which cost Sophie her job. He's readying a reprimand when he spots the first bee hovering in the air about her face, homing in on her tongue. Instead of scolding her, he laughs, a huge guffaw he reserves for what truly delights him.

There Sophie stands, shoulders thrust back, mouth open wide. Her tongue is a landing pad for bees! They float about her face, alight, and gather on her cheeks, lips, and even the tip of her nose—five, ten, then twenty or more until the lower part of her face is bearded by their brown, bustling bodies.

She's fearless, his daughter—it's both her boon and her bane—and Jack's heart swells with love. "I wish I had my camera," he exclaims, a feeble gesture since they both know he isn't the sort to document family life. Still, Sophie is pleased with herself. She wishes he had a camera, too. No one will ever believe she managed such a feat. The very idea of a bee beard would give her brother Ian a heart attack.

After the honey is gone and the last of the bees have departed for other flowers, Sophie allows herself a nervous shake of the shoulders. Then she raises the hem of her T-shirt to her mouth and scrubs her lips until they turn a rosy red. Catching Jack's eye, she grins. "I know: they're cleaner than we are. But damn, their feet itch." A second later, she adds, "I know, they don't have feet, but it sure feels like they do."

The lean expanse of her belly is visible, and as she resumes rubbing, the shirt hikes higher, exposing the bright white of her bra. At least she's wearing one, he thinks, but he wishes she wouldn't insist on such intimacy. It's the way she runs to the bathroom in her underwear, for instance, or curls, some nights, into a single bed with her brother, who is too old now for that sort of thing.

"Where is Ian?" Jack asks when Sophie has smoothed her shirt back into place.

"Ian the Terrible is still snoozing, but not to worry. I'm going to wake him and hustle him into the shower."

"Ian the Terrible? What's that about?"

She shrugs. "Wishful thinking. You know. He's such a wuss."

Jack hunches his broad shoulders and squints off into the distance. "Bully problems at school again?"

Sophie shrugs. "Maybe. Probably." She folds her arms across her chest and regards him seriously. "We never see you anymore. You're at work or you're at the fixer-upper. I'm fixing Sunday breakfast: eggs and sausage."

He frowns. "Nice try, but I'm pissed, Sophie. You've made a mess of things, and you know it."

"I didn't do it all by myself. I had some help from my stupid boss."

"This isn't the time to talk about it. Bees don't like an argument. . . ."

Sophie moderates her tone: "I can get another job, Jack. Now that I'm going to be driving—"

He puts up a hand to stop her. "I definitely don't want to talk about driving. But you can help me out here. Go get my glasses out of the glove compartment of the car."

"Okay."

She backs off a safe distance, then turns and runs through the brush in the direction of the low-slung adobe house, its pitched metal roof gleaming in the sun. Jack's dusty green Taurus station wagon is parked in the gravel wash behind Peggy's Toyota. Sophie throws open the Taurus's driver's-side door and disappears inside. When she emerges, she's pulled a grimy khaki bucket cap over her wild head of hair. She doesn't want him to see her tears.

As soon as Sophie hands him his glasses, Jack returns to business. He holds up another frame, eyes scanning the comb for the queen, who is bigger than the workers, with a long, pointed abdomen. She moves slowly, her carriage dignified and, yes, royal. Still, she is a bee like the others and therefore difficult to pick out, which is why some beekeepers glue a colored disk to her thorax. Not Jack. He's contemptuous of such measures, likening them to painting the backs of turtles, something pet stores did when he was a boy. It's not natural, he has explained to Sophie on a number of occasions; nor is it necessary. The trick to finding the queen is not to look for her.

"Scan the surface," he reminds her now. "Don't look at the parts. We're talking gestalt here, Sophie."

She is only half-listening. Her father has been schooling her in bees since she was a little girl. She knows more about bees than she does about the Revolutionary War or algebraic formulas, more about bees than about similes and syllogisms. Too bad bees don't show up on the SATs, she thinks. She'd ace that section for sure.

And then he finds what he's looking for. "Come here," he says quietly. "There's my little lady."

Sophie sidles up beside him and watches as Jack plucks the queen out of the mass of worker bees, the better to examine her. It's just as he expected, and he knows what has to be done. He doesn't hesitate. He smashes her between his thumb and index finger, then flicks her to the ground at his feet.

"What the hell, Jack!" Sophie cries. She doesn't give him a chance to explain; instead, she whirls around and stomps off to the house, kicking up sand as she goes.

High overhead, clouds billow and sweep across a smooth, blue surface, passing one after another. At this rate they'll reach the Colorado Rockies by nightfall.

Half an hour later, Peggy arrives in the kitchen, dressed for work in a red printed sarong skirt and a matching sleeveless leotard. Her long, unruly, mostly gray hair is pulled up off her neck and clipped with a silver barrette shaped like a feather. She sells both the barrette and the sarong at the shop she runs in Old Town. This time of year, Peggy does her best business on Sundays, so she wants to get an early start.

When she asks if there's something she can do to help, Sophie motions to the orange linoleum counter, where the eggs are assembled next to a large green bowl. "I thought we'd have scrambled eggs."

Peggy asks, "Do we have Egg Beaters for Jack?"

Sophie nods emphatically. "I checked." She is busy breaking up chunks of chorizo sausage with a table fork. She stands, stork-like, one bare foot propped on top of the other. Even in the halflight, her red toenails gleam. During the summer—and in New Mexico, September certainly qualifies—Sophie goes barefoot in the house. They all do. No matter how hot it may be outside, the brick floors retain a comfortable chill that cools the body from the ground up.

Together, mother and daughter peer into the soupy contents of the cast-iron skillet, a bubbling cauldron of crumbly meat and fat, all of it stained a brilliant, peppery red.

"Good lord," Peggy murmurs. "I've never seen so much grease in my life. . . . Where's Jack?"

"He's out at the hives."

Peggy picks up an egg and gets down to business. These are free-range chicken eggs, brown-shelled, with tough exteriors. She whacks them once, or occasionally twice, against the hard edge of the bowl before they give way. Over the years she has quieted many of her frustrations in just this fashion. As a little girl, she cracked eggs for her mother, and given all the foods needed for the continual round of church activities—cakes for birthdays, casseroles for Friday-night socials, cookies for Sunday school—they went through several dozen a week. She recalls the shells of those Waco eggs as having been white and paper-thin. If she gripped too tightly, they gave way, plunging the ends of her small fingers into cold yellow goo.

A minute later the back door shudders open with a loud, creaking complaint, and Jack shoulders his way inside. He's just struggled out of his bee overalls, and the effort of removing them has left him winded. He carries his work boots, one under each arm.

Seeing him, their elderly golden retriever, Lucy, lurches to her feet and clatters across the brick floor, barking ecstatically. These days, only something truly exciting draws her out—the bone from a pot roast, say, or a visit from the FedEx deliveryman. Evidently Jack's appearance has made the short list of major events in Lucy's life.

It's embarrassing the way she greets him, wagging her tail so strenuously that her backside sways. To keep from flopping over, she has to plant her legs and extend her claws. Jack leans down and gives her a pat on the head. "Hiddy ho, Mother's Farm Lucille Ball," he croons, calling her by her complete name, the one they used to register her. Years ago,

Peggy intended to breed golden retrievers. It was one of her projects that went by the wayside. All that's left of the scheme is this elderly dog.

Jack calls out, "Morning, all!"

"Morning," Peggy replies. She whacks the last egg so hard that the shell shatters on impact. Several bits wash into the bowl along with the whites and the quivering yellow yolk. Rather than pick out the shell bits, Peggy takes the whisk and whips the content into a froth.

"Where's Ian?" Jack asks.

As though in response to a summons, the boy appears in the doorway, clad in baggy green sweat pants and a white T-shirt stretched at the neck and hem. It looks as though someone grabbed and held on tight, while the boy inside squirmed his way loose. "Here I am," he says, and yawns.

"It's almost ready," Sophie calls over her shoulder. She's busy dumping warmed tortillas from a foil packet into a pottery warmer. The dining table has been hastily covered with a white cloth and is anchored in place by a large bowl of oranges, apples, and speckled bananas. The Grangers aren't really fruit eaters, but they know they should be, so Peggy keeps buying the stuff. Most often, the apples develop dark sores, the bananas go soft and smelly, and the kiwis shrink to hairy pebbles.

They take their traditional places, Jack at one end of the table and Peggy at the other. Lucy tries to reestablish her outpost underneath, but Sophie sits down and nudges the dog aside with her foot. In recent months they've had fewer meals as a family, and Lucy has gotten used to the extra space. She gives it up grudgingly.

"Tortillas?" Sophie asks, hefting the heavy warmer and passing it to Peggy, who receives it with both hands, then sets it down to remove the lid. After peeling away one floury disk, she returns the lid and passes the warmer to Ian, who takes two tortillas and offers it to Jack.

The eggs come around next, heaped on an earthenware platter, yellow clumps that Peggy categorically refuses. She hates eggs, and they all know it.

Ian asks whether the eggs have cheese in them, and when Sophie admits that she forgot the cheese, he takes only one modest clump and passes the plate to Jack, who is unsure how to proceed. His expression is pained. When Peggy notices, she remembers the Egg Beaters. They're still in the refrigerator. Sophie and Peggy both offer to fix them, but Jack won't hear of it.

"It's not a big deal," he says, serving himself an ample portion. "I've been good all week. A little splurge never hurt anyone."

"We forgot the chorizo!" Sophie exclaims. She gets up and looks for a slotted spoon, then lugs the skillet around the table and doles out the greasy meat. Even Lucy gets a bite or two. When the chorizo has been distributed more or less evenly, Sophie dumps the saturated paper towels in the trash and returns to her seat, wearing a bright smile. "Let's eat!"

Peggy has never cared for chorizo—the meat is both grisly and fatty. It's the butcher's worst, she thinks, and then she imagines some frontier wife dosing the only meat she has on hand, graying stuff that's begun to stink, with ground red pepper. If it wasn't fresh, the wife would make it look fresh, by god. And so she did.

As though to reproach her thoughts, Ian, sitting to Peggy's left, thanks his sister for fixing chorizo. "We haven't had it in ages," he says as he raises a bulky tortilla stuffed with mostly sausage to his mouth.

The bright morning light pours into the room through the west windows, and Peggy now sees something she hadn't noticed before: a bluish-gray bruise on the inside of Ian's wrist. He's had trouble over the years with bullies, mostly Hispanic boys who have taken a dislike to him on account of his towhead and ivory complexion. They've actually called him "Whitey" on occasion, and have tried to make the nickname stick. Ian won't answer to it, though; he won't even turn his head. "Reverse discrimination," a counselor called it. "Pure D meanness" is the way Peggy thinks of it. She asks him how school is going.

He offers a wan smile colored by cayenne. Even his teeth are orange. "Okay," he replies with a shrug.

"Middle school sucks," Sophie says with surprising vehemence.

Peggy tries to soften the remark. "It's just something you have to live through—like purgatory."

"What's purgatory?" Ian asks.

Peggy purses her lips. She herself was raised Baptist—Southern Baptist, in fact—but church was something she shrugged off in adolescence and never took up again.

"Correct me if I'm wrong," she says to Jack, "but isn't purgatory a way station? A place for people who aren't bad enough for hell or good enough for heaven?"

"Temporary suffering," Jack says, recalling the way his priest lisped the words.

A lapsed Catholic, Jack was not inclined to incorporate religion into the life of the family, but he wouldn't have objected if Peggy had done so. In fact, he would have been relieved. The two of them are pushovers as parents, and he wonders now whether they would have done better if they had been lectured from the pulpit, cajoled and pushed into doing the hard things.

"Don't quote me on this," he says, "but I believe purgatory is for those who've committed venial sins—the lesser transgressions. Hell is reserved for those who've indulged in at least the occasional mortal sin." He smiles to himself. He was a good catechism student, but they were all fairly good back then. Children wanted so badly to please their elders. What had become of that sort of adulation? He rarely sees it anymore, and certainly not in his own kids.

Sophie clears her throat and asks, "What's the difference?" Jack looks at her blankly. She struggles to clarify. "Between the two kinds of sins, mortal and what-do-you-call-it, verbal."

Ian laughs loudly, assuming his sister is intending mockery. But seeing her outthrust chin, he abruptly goes silent.

Jack shrugs. "Forgivable and unforgivable, I guess you could say." And then he returns to the topic of middle school. "In my day, we called it junior high, but it did feel like some sort of holding pen." He scoots his chair back. "Anyone else want a glass of milk?"

They all shake their heads. Ian is chewing, but when he's swallowed, he asks why it's necessary to suffer through middle school. Why not just skip over it? How about homeschooling? "Didn't the hippies homeschool their kids?"

Jack circles back to the table and stands holding his empty glass. "We aren't hippies, Ian."

Ian turns to Peggy. "Mom used to be." He runs his hands through his straw-like hair.

Peggy recognizes the gesture. She does it herself. "Used to be," she echoes.

"When you lived in the commune, were there kids?"

Peggy nods. She remembers several children, but in the years she lived at Morningstar, none were school-age. Jimbo and Denise had a baby who screamed so relentlessly that the other members of the household nicknamed him Banshee. And there was the little girl who couldn't stop twirling. Every morning she would stand in the courtyard and spin until she toppled over. No one seemed to think much of it, but in retrospect Peggy realizes that the girl's behavior was obsessive and clearly symptomatic. The child was asking for help or attention, and the rest of them subverted her attempts to get it by joining in, twirling and laughing as they passed by.

Peggy frowns. "It wasn't paradise, Ian. We had problems, too."

"But were those kids homeschooled?"

It's coming back to her now, a school held in a small adobe house in Arroyo Hondo: TLC, Taos Learning Center. She stalls as she tries to think of how to tell the truth without making matters worse. Jack is already frowning at her from the kitchen.

"The hippies had their own school," she says.

"Like a charter school?" Ian asks. Albuquerque has a number of these, some of them geared to problem students, others focused on technology or even media arts. The graduation rate in Albuquerque is absolutely abysmal—47 percent of those who begin high school actually finish it—and in such a dismal academic climate, any alternatives that can be fostered are. Peggy smiles. "Exactly like that, Ian."

Having refilled his glass, Jack rejoins them. "This is 2007, Ian. We aren't living in a commune."

"I wish we were!" Ian replies. "I'd sleep in a teepee."

"Me, too," Sophie chimes in.

Peggy's curiosity—and concern—get the best of her. "Ian, is that a bruise on your wrist?"

"Just dirt," Ian replies quickly, dropping the offending wrist out of sight. He picks up the stuffed tortilla with his other hand and awkwardly brings the floury package to his mouth. As he takes a bite, bits of chorizo drop into his lap and rain down on the floor. Lucy moves quickly, knocking Sophie's knees as she passes. They listen to the slurp of her tongue on the floor.

"More eggs, anyone?" Sophie asks. She picks up the platter and passes it around again.

Peggy asks what Jack was up to with the bees.

He replies without thinking, "Requeening." He gets up and pours himself another glass of milk, then sits down again, casting a sidelong look at Sophie, who appears to be concentrating on her plate.

"What's requeening?" Peggy asks.

His end of the room is banked with shadows, and Jack has to squint to get a better look at his wife, whose earrings shimmer in the morning light, long dangly things that resemble chandeliers. He is taken aback by the question. Surely she can't be serious, he thinks. Can it be that she doesn't know the answer to her question? For years, the air in this room has buzzed with bee facts and lore. Until the fixer-upper, bees were the one subject he was truly passionate about. Is it possible that she never heard a word of his talk?

They all sit expectantly, and finally Jack decides to take the question at face value. "What it sounds like," he says. "Replacing the queen." An uneasy silence follows, which Jack feels duty-bound to fill. "Has to be done from time to time," he explains. "The queen gets old or injured— loses part of a hind leg, say—and the egg-laying suffers. Puts the whole colony in jeopardy."

"So you play God?" Sophie asks.

Was it the talk of purgatory that led her in that direction? For the life of him, Jack can't figure it out. Their forks poised mid-air, the rest of the family waits for his response. "God doesn't meddle in the lives of bees, Sophie," he responds patiently. "Nature takes care of itself. If I didn't replace the queen, the bees would get around to it. They might swarm first, though, or the hive might die off afterward. Nature takes its chances, but beekeepers don't. We can't afford to. Let nine days go by and I'll introduce a new queen. Most of the hive won't notice the difference."

"You don't feel bad about it?" Sophie asks.

He shakes his head. "It's doing the greater good."

"What's best for the individual may not be best for the group," Peggy puts in. Inside, she's smarting. It's hard not to take the conversation personally, though identifying with an insect is a new low for her. Still, she feels so useless these days, useless and unattractive, unsuccessful and unloved, for heaven's sake. How did it happen?

"Is it a sin to kill a bee?" Sophie asks.

Jack pushes away his clean plate. "Well, wasting food is a sin, if you believe my mother, but I don't know about killing a bee." He doesn't consider it a serious question and is surprised when Sophie follows up by asking whether it's a sin to kill something larger than a bee, whether size has something to do with it.

He shakes his head. "I don't really believe in sin these days, verbal or otherwise." He smiles, hoping to coax a grin from her, but she looks pretty serious. He'd like to reach over and tousle her hair. Instead, he changes the subject. "Good breakfast, darlin', but Ian and I need to head over to the fixer-upper."

From the other side of the table, Ian sighs and quickly pretends to concentrate on his remaining food. He wishes Jack would let him stay home for once, but Ian knows better than to ask for the day off. Such a request would only lead to a lecture in the car on the way over to the fixer-upper, with Jack expounding on how lucky Ian is to have a father who cares enough to teach him valuable skills. Ian knows that already, but he doesn't much care.

Everything about the fixer-upper is borrowed: the plans for the renovation, the money for the down payment, the tools Jack uses to make the repairs. But the time he spends there is all his, or so he likes to say. The address is on Guadalupe Trail, although from the street the house itself is all but invisible. If it weren't for the number painted on the mailbox along the street, no one would ever find the place. Even so, Jack often has to take calls from harried deliverymen, especially if they're new to town. In Albuquerque most everyone is used to this sort of thing—houses are often stacked up back to front rather than side by side. But this casita is more hidden than most. Seventy-five years ago, it would have been a medium-sized house; now it is dwarfed by the stucco mansions surrounding it.

Back when it was built, the front of the casita probably faced the street. In the decades since, the neighborhood has grown in unpredictable ways. The current façade is hidden behind a taller-than-average coyote fence. The cedar *latillas* are nearly seven feet tall. Jack supposes that the former owner must have lashed the damn things together himself. The backyard is a patch of dirt dwarfed by a stucco monstrosity, home to a family of six. Jack likes to point out to Ian that six people used to live in the casita. "Those were different times," he muses to his son. "People believed in togetherness."

Jack bought the casita from one of the night janitors at Central New Mexico Community College (CNM), a fellow named Felix Apodaca. When Felix started telling Jack about the property, the plan was for Felix to renovate the place. The casita had been left to Felix's wife by an uncle who drank too much but was a decent-enough man and was fond of his niece. "It's small," Felix told Jack one evening. "Two bedrooms, one on either end of the house, and between them a kitchen, a bathroom, and a small sitting area with enough room for a La-Z-Boy and a small table and chairs."

Off and on for months Felix would stop by to empty Jack's trash and shoot the bull about the casita and his remodeling plans for a minute or two. But the plan wasn't realized. Felix's wife finished her degree in hospitality and took a job in Pennsylvania managing a bed-and-breakfast. Felix was hired as a maintenance technician. He would be doing fix-up work, all right, but not for himself; he'd be under the employ of his wife. "But you know," he said with a shrug, "it's better than emptying trash cans—a step in the right direction, don't you think?" And Jack agreed. Within a day or two, Jack had decided to remodel Uncle Melvin's casita himself.

In the months since the closing, Jack and Ian have spent every Sunday there. During the week Jack goes over sometimes in the evenings. And he's been known to sneak off on Saturday afternoons for a few hours.

As soon as the rest of the family is out of the house, Sophie calls her boyfriend, offering leftovers. Will says he's famished; he'll be right over. Although Sophie planned to shower, she is still clearing the table when she hears a short rap on the side door. Almost immediately, her boyfriend raps again, harder this time.

"Coming!" she cries, tossing a handful of cloth napkins into the air and darting across the floor. She throws open the door and invites him inside, but she doesn't meet his eyes. Instead, she studies his feet, clad in yellow-and-white running shoes. As soon as Sophie and Will reach the kitchen, she rushes off to the bathroom without a word of explanation.

It doesn't matter. Will is used to the unpredictable female. He's the son of a single mother. So he simply steps over the threshold, wanders into the kitchen, and drops into a chair at the dining table. Lucy is there to greet him. Will bends to run his fingers through the golden-red fur of her haunches. Will has never had a dog of his own, and Lucy is yet another reason to envy his girlfriend's homelife.

Having indulged a few tears, Sophie stands before the bathroom sink. She is irked at the shiny state of her nose and cheeks. Have the bees left some sort of insect goo on her skin? She tugs a Kleenex from a box on the counter and rubs it roughly across the bridge of her nose. If she were to look closely, she would notice a few small blackheads along the ridge of her nostrils, but Sophie is not the sort to scrutinize; she will step back rather than lean in.

By the time she returns to the kitchen, Will has helped himself to eggs and chorizo, which he's scooping off the plate with a cold tortilla. He isn't picky—he doesn't insist on warm food or deep kisses. He's happy with whatever he gets. Right now he's draped over the table, shoveling food into his mouth, but when Sophie walks up to him, he straightens and slides back in his chair, offering her a sly smile.

"Hey," he says. "These eggs have shell in them." He opens his mouth and sticks out his tongue, and Sophie sees it there, a hard brown fragment against a pink background. He wags his tongue and she's suddenly embarrassed, which is why she doesn't throw herself onto his lap or lean over and thrust her tongue in his mouth, or do any of the other things she might ordinarily do. Instead, she simply plucks away the shell, flicking it on the floor or, in this case, into Lucy's fur.

Will bends to the plate again. For him, eating is serious business. "I wish my mom would cook like this on Sunday mornings," he says.

"Peggy didn't cook this," Sophie replies. "Since when does Peggy cook?" In fact, Peggy does cook several times a week, but that's dinner.

Will eyes her warily. "I wouldn't know," he says, "because I don't live here."

But Sophie is pursuing her own argument. "That's part of the problem, in my opinion."

Will stifles a laugh and does his best to follow Sophie down this bumpy road. The truth is, he'd follow her anywhere, even when it makes no sense to go there, as seems to be the case now. "What problem?" he asks.

"Men are happiest when women cook for them. For instance, look at you. You're happy, aren't you?"

He takes a bite and chews slowly and, he hopes, thoughtfully. After swallowing, he gives her his best smile. "I'm delirious, Sophie. Cook like this for me and I'll never leave you."

"I *did* cook like this, Will," she says, bending to grab a napkin off the floor.

"But you didn't cook for me."

"I called you." Her hands have arrived on her hips. "You're here eating, aren't you?"

"These are leftovers, Sophie. Don't get me wrong. I'm happy to have them, but you cooked for your dad. Where is he, anyway?"

"Gone," Sophie answers bitterly. "Working at the fixer-upper. I never see him anymore." She is feeling good and sorry for herself, and she wants Will to pity her, too. So she's taken aback by his response.

"What the fuck? He lives right here in this house, Sophie. How would you feel if he lived in Lubbock?"

Sophie stops fiddling with the napkin and drops it into the seat of the chair beside him. "I'm sorry, Will," she says earnestly. "I know you miss your dad. And your mom is pretty much a bitch, so there's that, too."

"I'm used to it," he replies. He returns his attention to the plate. But he has lost track of his hunger, so he merely picks at the eggs and spears the last crumbles of chorizo.

"Isn't your dad Catholic?" Sophie asks. She is smoothing the napkin on the table. Her face is flushed. She has never done anything even half this hard, and it isn't in her nature to state things directly. She isn't a blurter. It would be easier if she were.

"Yep. His whole family is Catholic, especially *mi abuela*. She's crazy Catholic."

Sophie thought as much. "We were talking about sin at the breakfast table. You know about the two kinds of sins—"

"Yeah, sure," Will replies. He looks up at her, curious, but she is still smoothing the checkered napkin. "Mortal and—"

Sophie snickers. "Verbal," she puts in, and she is surprised when he doesn't laugh. "A verbal sin," she says.

"What's a verbal sin?" He pushes the plate away.

"I guess telling a lie would be a verbal sin. But it isn't real, Will. It's a mistake I made. The term is 'venial.'"

He nods. "Yeah, that's it. Those are the small sins."

"Exactly! So, my dad killed a bee this morning, and I was asking him whether that's a sin."

"Your dad's Catholic?"

Sophie shrugs. Her hands are shaking a little. She presses the napkin firmly against the surface of the table to make them stop, then asks Will what he thinks about killing a bee.

"Insects are insects," he says. "You have to kill them. How could it be a sin to kill an insect? *No one* would ever make it to heaven. You can kill an insect without even knowing it. Dozens of them even, every day."

Sophie takes a deep breath and glances his way, one quick look to gauge his mood. Is he getting irritable? It's so easy to frustrate him. She knows she should get to the point, but she can't bring herself to do anything more than circle it. She spots Lucy sitting at the kitchen door. The dog wants out. Sophie gets up and opens the door. When she returns, she asks Will about putting down a dog.

"What if Lucy had cancer, say, and she was in pain and needed out of it?"

And Will responds as she expects, by saying, "Of course not. It would be a sin to let her suffer. Surely." None of this is in the Bible, of course, but Will is pretty sure God would go along with his reasoning.

"What about abortion then?" Sophie asks. She gets up and circles the room, arms crossed over her chest. Her face is hot, and she starts to feel a little sick again. It has only been a few minutes since she threw up; her stomach is entirely empty. Maybe that's the problem. Maybe she should drink a Dr Pepper or something. She wanders over to the refrigerator and is peering into the crowded space when Will responds.

"Is this a test or something? Abortion is different. You're not killing something by accident or because it's in pain. And you're not killing an insect or a dog. You're snuffing out the life of a *person*." He goes on to tell her that he wrote a paper on the subject just a semester or two ago. It was for his junior-year English class, and he made a B+ on it.

"So, that's your opinion or the Catholic Church's opinion?"

He shrugs. "Both, I guess. If you're getting yourself a Dr Pepper, will you get me one, too?"

"There's only one. We can split it." She suppresses a belch and turns back to him. "I'm not feeling so great," she says. She holds the cold can to one cheek and then the other.

Will's young face softens, and he reaches out his arms. "Come here, Sophie," he says, his voice a warble of desire. "I'll make you feel better."

In a few minutes they're climbing the stairs to her bedroom. Most often, they make love at his house, while his mother is away at work or school, or, on occasion, in the backseat of his car. Once, earlier in the summer, they slipped onto the University of New Mexico campus with an old quilt and managed a quick fuck near the duck pond. That's his favorite sex memory. He replays it in his mind nearly every night before going to sleep.

Will has never been up to Sophie's room before, and for a minute or two he simply looks around. A bank of windows along the south wall lets in all the available light, which in New Mexico amounts to brilliance. What furniture there is—a mattress on the floor, a chest of drawers, an overstuffed chair—has been pushed against the walls. The long rectangular space is empty in the middle, revealing a stretch of scarred and faded hardwood floor. The sharp, sweet smell of patchouli lingers in the air.

"This is where I dance," Sophie tells him, and to demonstrate, she twirls across the floor. Although light on her feet and graceful, she's also reckless and a little woozy. On her twelfth revolution, her feet tangle and she collapses, laughing. She's not hurt. Anyone can see that. But she's not in control either.

Will stands over her and watches her convulse. He's noticed this before, the way Sophie loses herself in laughter, taking it from giddy to goofy, then beyond, to something that looks like grief. He recognizes this behavior—his mother described it to him when she got home from work at Movies West the night she fired Sophie. For a split second, he pities his girlfriend, but soon he has shrugged off his discomfort. He kneels to embrace her. They kiss, their bodies twining tightly, before Sophie breaks away and scrambles up, retreating to the windows. Will is startled, but he doesn't take offense. Instead, he sits and watches her reverie.

Finally it occurs to him that he's supposed to be the pursuer, so he raises himself to a standing position in one long, fluid movement. He edges up behind her and presses his groin against her buttocks. At first she doesn't respond, and so he waits, staring over the top of her head at the Sleeping Sisters.

Since boyhood, Will has wanted to see a real live volcano. He prefers not to believe what he's heard about the inertness of those five humps. They're sleeping, he tells himself, and what's sleeping can certainly awaken. It could happen; one day, they could just boil over. Aroused, he runs his hands down the sides of Sophie's jeans before working his wide, flat fingers into her pockets, caressing the insides of her thighs through the soft white cotton and, in the process, embedding a few purple specks of straw flower under his nails.

Sooner or later—they have time, plenty of time—the two will find their way to the mattress, where they will tumble down and make long, satisfying, and unprotected love.

"We don't need one," Sophie will tell him when he reaches into his pocket for a condom. That afternoon, on his way to work as a busboy at Garduños, it will cross his mind briefly: Did Sophie start taking the pill or something? He'll have to remember to ask. But he won't. Not for some weeks, anyway. All evening long he'll be filled with her sweetness. He'll carry it away with him; he'll taste it on his lips.

These days, bees can be ordered via the Internet and delivered through the U.S. Postal Service. Jack orders his from Zia Bees, a business out of Truchas, New Mexico. Rightly or wrongly, he believes that bees bred in the Southwest are more likely to stay healthy, because they are acclimated. Another plus: the queen doesn't have to spend as much time in transit. She travels no more than a day or two, without the expense of express mail.

It didn't occur to Jack to tell anyone else that he's expecting a new queen, not that it would have mattered much. Most often, Ian is the only one home when the mail arrives. Such is the case on the Friday afternoon when the postwoman delivers the padded envelope. Sophie is at Tam's, Peggy is still at the shop, and Jack is getting in an extra hour or two at the fixer-upper.

Ian doesn't hear the first or second ring, but he's on his way down the stairs to the bathroom as the third ring—which is really more like a buzz—wafts through the house. Ian freezes on the next-to-last step, not sure of what he's hearing. Then recognition kicks in and he lopes through the kitchen and down the hallway, an exhilarating experience that ends with his body thudding against the front door, which is locked. He has a little trouble releasing the deadbolt, and he is breathing heavily when he finally opens the door.

The middle-aged postwoman is standing on the welcome mat, her wide face rosy from the heat. She doesn't look perturbed by the long wait. Instead, she's pressing the puffy envelope to her ear. When she sees Ian, she feels the need to explain herself: "I thought maybe she'd be buzzing, but I don't hear a thing." She lowers the envelope—a bit reluctantly, it appears—and holds it out to him. "I brought you your queen. Couldn't just leave her in the hot old mailbox, now could I?"

"Thanks," Ian says, adding, "She's my dad's."

He wonders briefly if it would be too weird to ask the postwoman to carry the mailer a few steps farther, down the hall and into the kitchen. He can see himself pointing to the china hutch, its surface already piled with unprocessed mail: circulars, solicitations, and a fair number of unpaid bills. *Just leave her right there*, he can imagine himself saying.

But that would be so cowardly that he might as well curl up in a ball and wait for the first of several thousand kicks to come his way. "You can decide to be brave," Jack has told him. So Ian holds out his hand and accepts both the mailer and the bundled regular mail.

His hand trembles, and the postwoman takes note. "There's not a thing in the world to be frightened of, son!"

She's dead wrong, of course. There are thousands of things to be scared of in this world, and lots of them are smaller and deadlier than bees. Even Ian knows as much. But he simply nods and thanks her for taking the time to come to the door.

Half an hour later, Sophie finds her brother at the kitchen table, gingerly examining the mailer. He's drinking a glass of milk as he studies the large black-and-yellow sticker: LIVE QUEEN BEES! KEEP WELL-VENTILATED, OUT OF THE SUN, AT ROOM TEMPERATURE, AWAY FROM INSECTICIDES.

"The new and improved queen is here!" she shouts.

Ian turns and frowns at her. "No need to yell," he says mildly.

Sophie shrugs. She's a little sweaty from the walk home. Her face glows warmly, and she's pushed up the short sleeves of her red T-shirt so they're bunched under her bra straps. "Shall we have a look at her?"

Ian nods. He's delighted with the way things are turning out. His sister is here to do what he wouldn't have had the nerve to do, both because bees make him nervous and because his father might not like it. Ian tries to stay on Jack's good side. Sophie doesn't have to try, or hasn't had to until recently anyway.

She pads over to the drawer nearest the sink and rummages around until she finds the kitchen scissors. Her plastic flip-flops make a definitive slapping sound each time she takes a step.

"Give," she says, brandishing the scissors. Ian hands the mailer over and watches Sophie neatly slice off the top, then tip the contents into her open palm. The queen has arrived in a rectangular plastic cage, along with several worker bees and a plug of candy that serves to feed her and her attendants.

"Why, hello there, little lady!" she says in a much quieter voice, holding the cage up close to her face. Then she does what Ian hoped she would: she pulls out the chair next to his, takes a seat, and proffers the cage. "Want to hold her?" she asks. "She can't sting, Ian. Don't worry."

When he offers his palm, Sophie gently transfers the plastic cage from her hand to his. She offers a little lesson on the difference between the queen and the worker bees. "She's bigger than her attendants. Do you see that?"

The cage is a little longer than the width of Ian's palm. It holds four regular bees and the queen, who resembles a cross between a cockroach and a bee. Unlike her attendants, she isn't striped. Her larger size seems caused entirely by the size of her abdomen.

"She has ovaries," Sophie tells him. "Which is why her belly is bigger than theirs. It's probably too late for her to lay eggs this year, but come springtime she'll be working her little ass off. Queens can lay two thousand eggs a day." Being a guy, Ian isn't overly impressed by this statistic, but it blows Sophie away.

The mailer includes instructions, and Sophie reads through them while Ian continues to examine the insects. He's only half-listening as she explains the process of introducing the new queen to the hive. "Jack won't let them out of the cage, you see. That would be disastrous because the workers would kill her and her attendants as intruders. It's kind of cool, the way this works."

She goes on to explain the process: Jack will wedge the cage between two frames of brood, but before he does, he will pierce the candy plug to make it easier for the worker bees to eat their way through the plug and free the queen. By the time they complete the task, the workers will be pleasantly satiated and familiar with the queen's scent. She will seem like one of their own, so much so that they will experience this first meeting as a reunion. "Pretty cool, huh?" she concludes.

Ian nods and gazes down at the insects in his palm. "Awesome," he agrees.

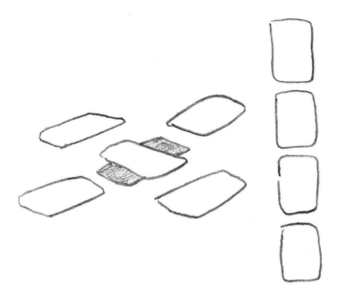

Position #1—"What Covers Her"

*What's the heart of the matter? The first card covers the significator and
provides insight into the basic situation.*

～ *Ace of Cups* (reversed) ～

In its upright position, the Ace of Cups promises new love and blessings from above (symbolized by the dove), including the possible conception of a child. When it's reversed, the message is muted. In the face of overwhelming emotions, gifts can feel like burdens.

PEGGY SITS CROSS-LEGGED on the bathroom floor, phone receiver in one hand and a jug-sized bottle of rum in the other. She has just emptied the cabinet of a dozen or so rolls of toilet paper, and now she is surrounded by them. Peggy buys their toilet paper in bulk at Costco. Whatever they have on hand is stored under the sink. Their rum comes from Costco, too, a bottle of Bacardi big enough to last a year—until, that is, Sophie started partaking. Judging from the Sharpie mark on the rim of the bottle and the empty Coke cans in the recycling bin, Sophie is back to playing bartender for her friend Tam.

At dinner it occurred to Peggy that the girls were a little too giddy for a routine Saturday-night sleepover. But it wasn't until she spotted the discarded Coke cans that Peggy put two and two together: it was time to check the rum. Only she couldn't remember where Jack had hidden it.

On this first Saturday in October, he is in Vermont, having flown out on short notice to check on his elderly mother. Bored by the nursing home, Vernie has been slipping out and wandering the streets of Brattleboro. In cases like this one, the social worker explained, family members must take an active role. At first Jack's daily calls did the trick, but as soon as he slacked off for a day or two, Vernie went missing again. Thus he had no choice but to reiterate his message in person.

Peggy doesn't want to call Jack—certainly not after the talk they'd had on the eve of his departure—but she needs his help finding the bottle. Once she has him on the phone, he directs her to the bathroom, where he has stashed the bottle behind several stacks of toilet paper. Sure enough, Sophie's been draining it.

"Oh Jack, this is a lousy hiding place."

"Since when?" he replies crossly. "I'm the only one who replaces empty rolls, so it seemed foolproof to me." He goes silent for a second, then adds: "And *you* couldn't find it."

About a year ago, Sophie and Tam's sleepovers began including a mixed drink or two, and for a while, Jack and Peggy chose to look the other way. "Once a pushover, always a pushover," Jack said, but Peggy protested: "We aren't so much pushovers as we are *permissive*." "Permissive" might be a dirty word in some circles, but Peggy does her best to steer clear of those. People who sneer at permissive parents are generally Republicans. In Peggy's opinion, they worry about all the wrong things.

Only now that Sophie has her learner's permit, Jack seems to be siding with the Republicans. No looking the other way, no behaving like the French. At a recent family meeting, he made himself very clear: no drinking whatsoever. Sophie had said she understood, but evidently that does not mean she agrees. Or maybe she assumes that since Jack is out of town, the rule doesn't apply. That could be it, Peggy thinks. But she keeps this observation to herself, knowing, of course, what Jack would say: *You're making excuses for her. At the very least, you should leave that task to her because she's better at it than you are.*

"Are you going to hide it again?" Jack asks. "And in a better place this time?"

"You hid it behind the toilet paper, Jack," Peggy reminds him. There's a limit to how much responsibility she's going to accept. Yet Sophie's transgressions appear to be linked to Peggy's own history of reckless juvenile behavior. Clearly her genes are responsible.

"We don't need to assign blame. . . ." His voice trails off. In Brattleboro it's after eleven at night, and Jack is bone-tired. He wouldn't mind a rum and Coke himself, but he's already undressed and stretched out on the surprisingly comfortable hotel mattress. All day his body has been propelled through space; now that his surroundings are stable and static, he can finally relax. He sighs deeply and allows his limbs to go limp—first his feet, then his legs, his arms, his hands. Peggy taught him this trick. She's still offering assurances, but he's only half-listening to them. She promises that the girls won't have another drink. She is seeing to it, she says. He's not to give it another thought.

The trip was particularly wearying because it required a plane change between Albuquerque and Hartford, Connecticut, the closest airport. From there Jack had to rent a car and drive the hour and a half to Brattleboro. Cautiously, so as to avoid a leg cramp, he stretches his calves and circles his feet, trying to undo the effects of the cramped posture he's been forced to hold for most of the day, first in business class on the McDonnell Douglas MD-80, then on the Cessna commuter plane, and finally in the crappy compact car that carried him from Hartford to Brattleboro.

"What worries me," Jack says, "is Sophie getting behind the wheel. She wanted to drive me to the airport for heaven's sake. She's liable to sneak out, Peggy. You know damn well she is."

"She doesn't have a driver's license, Jack. She has a learner's permit. There's a difference. She's allowed to drive *if and only if* there's an adult in the car. Please stop worrying. It's not good for you."

"Sophie pays no attention to our rules. Do you really think she has more regard for the Motor Vehicle Division? What matters is that she *thinks* she can drive. And she has a piece of paper in her wallet to confirm that misapprehension."

"Okay then," Peggy tells him. "I'll sleep with the keys."

He doesn't answer, and after a second or two, Peggy hears a snuffle and the beginning of a snore. Rather than wake him, she simply hangs up. She decides to stow both the bottle and the keys under Jack's pillow. She can figure out something better tomorrow. Finally, as she restocks the toilet paper and gets ready for bed, Peggy rehashes the talk with Jack from the night before. Her feelings are hurt. She likens the sensation to a sunburn; she is hot and sensitive to the touch.

For a solid hour Peggy had sat on the front porch and listened—or pretended to listen—even as the air cooled and darkness settled around them. Jack has a tendency to lecture. He is a teacher after all, so long-winded rumination comes naturally to him. In the six months or so since his heart attack, he's become even more loquacious. "Thinking out loud," he called it.

Last night the sky had been as black as she'd ever seen it, the stars mere pinpoints of light. For once they really appeared to be hurtling away from, and not toward, the earth. Would she feel more grounded here on Earth if she knew a thing or two about the stars? During her year at the commune, she'd had her chance to learn the constellations. Her lover Beau had tried to teach her, but she'd been a lousy student, too besotted to bother with astronomy or even astrology.

In the warmer months the two of them had regularly slipped out of the main house in the middle of the night and wandered off into the sage, Beau with a threadbare quilt tucked under his arm. Once he'd found a spot he liked, he would spread the quilt out on the ground. After they made love, he wanted to talk, most often to share his knowledge of the stars. At the time she wanted a declaration of love, but Beau was more intent on pointing out Orion's Belt. She smiled to herself, thinking that Beau and Jack had at least one trait in common. Both liked to hear themselves talk. Not Peggy. Even then, she'd kept her observations to herself. She pretended to see the patterns Beau traced for her, but the truth was that she needed glasses to make out anything that far away.

"Are you listening, Peggy?"

"Yes, Jack," she replied, pushing the past out of her mind. Beau was dead, for god's sake. She sighed. He'd been gone for over a year now, yet she still felt a wave of guilt and grief each time she thought of his passing. Beau had died in the dark, not knowing. She'd been selfish and had kept what was best for herself. Now she would just have to live with that fact.

When Jack finally got to the point—that he was returning to the classroom, that he had given up the administrative appointment and the extra money that went with it—Peggy was jarred back into the present. What did he want her to do? *Rob a bank?* They'd already gone out on a financial limb to buy the fixer-upper. Jack had wanted a diversion; he needed a refuge. And now he was carving out time to complete the remodeling. She understood the logic but not the math. How would they pay the bills?

"Right now, your shop is more retreat than retail establishment," Jack went on. "We haven't seen black on the place in at least a year. But the space is worth something. The space may be worth twice as much now as what I paid for it."

When the two of them had met, Peggy was hoping to start a business, and Jack was hoping to rent the space he owned in Old Town. One of them got what she wanted. As soon as they married, Peggy stopped paying rent. They've owned the house on Guadalupe Trail for nearly fifteen years, but they have two mortgages on it. They took out the second one maybe seven years ago, when the adjoining acre came on the market. It was Jack's turn to satisfy a dream. Since childhood, he'd wanted to keep bees, and the acre afforded him the space.

"You want me to close my shop?"

She expected him to say no, to reassure her somehow, but she was wrong. He had his answer ready: "Either that, or find a way to make a profit."

Peggy was shocked, though she shouldn't have been. Fleetingly, on days when an hour or more passed without a customer darkening the doorway, she considered the possibility herself. In the early years she was lucky not to have much competition. Most of the other retailers sold pottery, jewelry, baskets, and the like. But nearly a year ago a shopkeeper from Santa Fe had decided to open a second store in Old Town, just a few doors down from Everyday Satin. The Santa Fe location was called "The Red Rose"; the shopkeeper dubbed the one in

Old Town "The Red, Red Rose." Advertised as having "Santa Fe chic at Old Town prices," the shop drew both tourist traffic and local clientele.

Jack continued, "I'm tired, and I want to get out from under some of the stress. No, not stress. *Bullshit.* I want out from under the bullshit. It stinks! If I don't take the time, I may not *get* the time." He didn't have to mention the heart attack. The last sentence might as well have been prefaced, *Before I die, I deserve a little time to do as I like.*

Peggy didn't disagree, but she was frightened nonetheless. Jack didn't want to go to work. Ian didn't want to go to school. Sophie had been fired from her first job and hadn't bothered to look for another. What on earth was to become of them? Even more than feeling frightened, Peggy felt shaken. "Are you sure about all of this?"

He sat slouched in the rocking chair on the other side of the door. All this time, they'd been speaking to one another while looking away, him at the ground and her at the stars. Now, at the same moment, the old marrieds turned to each another in the darkness.

"Quite sure," he replied.

Upstairs, Saturday night is spinning into Sunday morning. Tam has finished off her own rum and Coke and Sophie's, too. Because they're at Sophie's house, Sophie is in charge of entertainment. Earlier she'd promised Tamara a *par-tee*, but that's not going to happen. Evidently Peggy has rehidden the bottle of rum and gone off to bed. Too much rummaging around and they're bound to wake her.

"So if we can't drink, let's call the 1-900-PSYCHIC number. Please!" Tam begs. She's not above begging; in fact, she seems to enjoy it. She puckers her lips and makes little smacking noises in Sophie's direction. Tam is pretty in a Jennifer Aniston sort of way. She's not *as* pretty as Aniston, certainly, but she's pretty enough, especially if you look just at her face and not at her flatter-than-she'd-like chest and heavy legs.

"We've been all through this," Sophie replies. "We've been all through this" is one of her mother's retorts, and the realization makes Sophie want to hit something. She leans across the mattress and jabs her friend in the shoulder, knocking Tam off balance so that she topples face-first into the mattress, a sheath of blonde hair spilling across the spread. She might be a carnival target—that's how hard Tam falls.

But even outright assault doesn't deter her. Tam is used to her impetuous friend. "Please, Sophie!" she wheedles in a muffled voice, lips pressed to the purple Indian bedspread, which smells strongly of patchouli and faintly of mold. Before Sophie dug it out and put it back into service, the spread had spent years folded neatly in Peggy's army locker.

"Don't you want to find out what's going to happen between you and Will?"

"I know what's going to happen between me and Will." But she doesn't and it's killing her.

"Are you breaking up?" Tam asks.

"No!"

"But you can't go over to his house anymore, right?"

"So?" It wasn't enough for Will's mother to have fired Sophie. Now Laurel has actually barred her from the house. "I may sue her," Sophie says. "She shouldn't have fired me for laughing."

"I thought she fired you for throwing a drink in a customer's face."

"No," Sophie says, affronted. "Why are you taking her side, anyway?"

"I'm not," Tam replies. "I'm just trying to point out that your future is every bit as unpredictable as mine. Seems like you'd want a heads-up from the psychic."

For weeks now Sophie has been hearing about Tam's calls. The first psychic declared Tam's old boyfriend to be a jerk. No news in that. But the second one promised that a Prince Charming was on the horizon and told Tam to wear pink every day. Her prince would recognize her that way. Last Saturday the girls took a trip to Cottonwood Mall to buy pink socks, pink T-shirts, and pink underwear, all charged to Tam's mom's Visa. No prince yet, but Tam isn't taking chances. She's wearing the panties even as they speak.

Sophie sighs and fingers the pimple on her chin. She could swear it's larger now than it was an hour ago. "I promised my dad I wouldn't make any more calls."

Tam nods. Now she understands. "How is your dad, anyway?"

"Okay, I guess. He left yesterday for Vermont, to see his mom and stuff. It's good for him to get away." Here, too, she is echoing her mother.

Tam leans forward and pats Sophie's knee. They've been friends for years. They met as middle-schoolers, playing softball on a Little League team. Jack was their coach.

"He's going to be fine," Tam soothes. She sounds motherly, older than her years, and for the most part, she is. She's been raised by a single mother who counts on her daughter—even leans on her occasionally—and Tam has done her best to live up to her mother's expectations. "Is that why you don't want to know your future? Because you're worried about your dad?"

Jack's not the same person he was before the heart attack. He's preoccupied these days; when Sophie talks to him, most often he looks past her rather than at her. She misses the man he used to be. But it isn't her dad she's worried about, not now anyway. Tam has a point: a heads-up on the future wouldn't be a bad idea.

"When I was going through Peggy's army locker, I found her cards," Sophie says slowly. Sophie's been snooping into her mother's past, and she's found a thing or two of interest, including the bedspread they're sitting on and a second one she gave to Will a few weeks back.

Tam's eyes widen. "Tarot cards?"

Sophie nods. She can see them now, wrapped in a blue silk scarf for safekeeping and stowed in a pine box. They're in the army locker in the storage shed. Sophie stands up and looks around for her flip-flops.

"I'll be right back," she says.

"I'll go with you," Tam offers quickly. "I can hold the flashlight."

Turns out that reading the cards isn't as easy as finding them. Without a book to go by—and she ransacked the army locker looking for instructions—Sophie has had to resort to studying the images and intuiting what they mean. The two of them have been at this for hours, lighting candles and incense (the room positively reeks of sweet jasmine), shuffling the cards, and laying them out in circles, in squares, in crosses.

Sophie is miserable. When they started the session, she felt pretty sure of herself. After all, her mother is a psychic, or used to be, so Sophie assumed she'd inherited the gene, or the predisposition, or the magical third eye. Whatever. Now her hopes are dimming. From one minute to the next, she can't decide what to say. The pimple on her chin seems to pulse. She's fingered it so often that it's getting infected.

"It's not fair!" Tam cries, indignant over Sophie's wishy-washy stance on the Page of Wands. First the card was a new boyfriend. Now Sophie has changed her mind and is insisting that it represents Tam's stepfather, Tom. "Make up your mind, for god's sake!"

"I'm trying," Sophie mutters. She's sitting cross-legged on the wooden floor; her butt's gone numb and prickly. Tam faces her from the edge of the mattress, pink panties glowing between her legs.

"Looks like your stepdad, Tam," Sophie persists. "I can't help what I see, can I?" Ever since Tam's stepfather took off for Alaska, Tam has been something of a mess. Tom's leaving is a big mystery. Not even Tam's mother, Belinda, knows what he's doing or when he's coming back.

Tam gnaws at a hangnail on her index finger. "You haven't really told me what you see."

Sophie is bent double, peering at the card. The Page of Wands looks like a man, but even gender seems up for grabs. He/she is dressed entirely in burgundy, including cape and hat, and clutched in his/her hand is a staff from which buds sprout. Across the top of the card stretches a row of mountain peaks capped in purple. The Page looks intent on discovering the New World, or at least some portion of the Alaskan pipeline. "Basically," Sophie says slowly, "I don't see Tom coming back anytime soon. Sorry, Tam. I know you really liked the guy."

"He's not my boyfriend," Tam grumbles, "which was, after all, the whole point of this reading."

"You have to understand that this isn't real, Tam. I don't have the first fucking idea what I'm doing."

"Oh, it's real all right," Tam insists. "I believe in it." She swallows with difficulty. "I need a drink of water before we go to bed."

"Sure." Sophie leans forward and scoops up nearly a dozen brightly colored scraps of pasteboard.

They tell stories, these cards. On the one under her finger, a man lies prone under a black sky, ten swords piercing him from neck to hip. He appears to be dead, but Sophie suspects he's alive, although he's in terrible pain and stuck in some unbearable situation. On another card, labeled "Temperance," an angel with red wings walks on water while pouring liquid from one golden chalice into another. Over her head, a rainbow arcs.

Before she gathers up these last two, Sophie slides them together so that their sides touch, willing the angel to rise up and pour the contents of her chalice over the man's wounds. It could happen, she thinks. But it doesn't. Instead, Tam calls from the doorway. "Are you thirsty? Do you want a glass of water?"

Early on Sunday morning, Jack calls again. Startled awake, Peggy gropes for the phone. If it weren't for the daylight seeping through the curtains, she would swear it's still the middle of the night. She's groggy, and it's all she can do not to react grumpily. Jack has a small favor to ask: Would Peggy mind zipping over to the fixer-upper to open the door for the electrician? The word "zip" speaks to her of his discomfort. Ever since the ultimatum, they're barely on speaking terms, so Jack wants to diminish the errand.

Even as she agrees, Peggy wonders aloud: "Do you remember that it's Sunday?" She turns over to check the alarm clock on the bedside table. Not only is it Sunday, but it's not even seven in the morning on Sunday. But Jack has not lost track of the days. A little grudgingly, he explains that the fellow he hired works another job during the week.

"Like you," Peggy says. "Okay, so what time will he be there?"

Jack reassures her that the guy won't show up until at least eight, so she has time for coffee and even a shower if she wants to take one. Then he makes a joke: "Jesse is just your type—long hair and a tattoo on his bicep."

"Very funny," Peggy says.

When they got together, Jack was (and still is) short and a little squat, dark-haired but fair-skinned. Back then he'd resembled a banker, whereas her type had tended to play guitar or straddle a motorcycle. But she was burning out on bad boys, and it didn't take all that long for Jack to convince her of the value of devotion. "Love those guys all you want," he said. "But just remember that they'll always love themselves more than they love you." True enough. She'd known he was right. Ultimately she'd been persuaded by his persistence and patience.

All these years he's loved her more than he's loved himself. But all that changed with the heart attack. Since he came home from the hospital, they haven't made love. It's an aberration in their relationship, and Peggy, for one, doesn't know what it means. Surely he isn't afraid of the exertion. As myocardial infarctions go, Jack's was mild. It occurred as he was leaving work, so he simply drove himself to the emergency room and announced his symptoms to the nurses at the desk. "You've heard of walking pneumonia," he told Peggy when he called her from the hospital. "This was a walking heart attack." The joke represented Jack's attempt to play down the seriousness of the situation, but his brush with fate has left him bruised and vulnerable.

Finally she says what she's thinking: "Do you still love me?"

Even as she says it, she realizes it's his physical distance that allows her to speak freely. And that gives him leave to stop speaking at all. She can hear him sigh, then laugh. Is it a laugh or a cough? More quiet.

"Loving you is hard work, Peggy," he finally says, "and I'm awfully tired these days."

"I'm not talking about sex, Jack," she puts in, though she is, at least in part. Peggy has always wanted what she can't have. She knows this about herself, but she has yet to make much use of the knowledge.

"I'm not either," he replies.

Every morning, Jack pours a cup of coffee, then reaches for the vials of pills he keeps nearby. In addition to Crestor he now takes a beta-blocker and an ACE inhibitor, as well as a prophylactic aspirin. It's not unusual for Peggy to enter the kitchen just as Jack has assembled the whole lineup in the palm of his hand. "White pill, blue-and-pink capsules, itty-bitty aspirin," he mutters to himself, a hangdog expression on his face. *Middle age is a surprise to all of us*, Peggy wants to tell him, but she doesn't, or hasn't yet.

When they hang up, Peggy slips on a robe and pads down the long hallway to the kitchen. She puts on the coffee, then stands at the narrow window beside the door. As the sky brightens, the cholla outside the door takes on shape and color. Tall and contorted, the cactus resembles an ancient and arthritic man wielding several broken canes. Sometimes the man appears furious, on the verge of striking a blow at an innocent passerby—one of the children maybe. But he has his spells of happiness, too. In early May he celebrates spring. Flowers the color of fruit punch emerge from his joints, and he turns downright jaunty. By fall the flowers have shriveled and blown away; he is weary, at death's door, which, as it happens, is also Peggy's kitchen door.

Now it is the beginning of October in a dry year, and he's thirsty. Just a minute, Mr. Bojangles, Peggy thinks. She's been referring to him this way for years, but only in her head.

Before she leaves for the fixer-upper, Peggy fills a green glass pitcher with water and carries it out to splash at the cactus's feet. Afterward she waits on the square of concrete that passes for a porch and watches the water soak into the ground. Yes, there it is. She could swear that Mr. Bojangles sighs with relief. Naturally, it's not the sort of thing you can see. His limbs are rigid, after all. But when Peggy listens carefully, she swears she hears it: a slight expulsion of breath. She reasons that other things breathe. Life is all around us, and it's best to keep that fact firmly in mind.

Peggy has been home for hours before Sophie stirs, then wakes to a room suffused with late-morning light. When she opens her eyes, Sophie finds herself staring at the back of Tam's head, which is only partially covered by a lumpy pillow. Long blonde locks crisscross the white cotton sham. Dazzled by the sight, Sophie reaches out and gently fingers a strand. Tam has amazing hair, purely golden and so soft. The lace sheers on the four windows filter the New Mexican sunshine into brilliant patterns that wash across the bare white walls, the hardwood floor, and the two girls huddled under the Indian-print bedspread.

October mornings can be downright cold, but the afternoons are perfect. All over town, people remember why they love Albuquerque. Autumn weather is glorious.

Despite Peggy's pleas, Sophie resists putting up real curtains, the kind that provide what her mother calls a modicum of privacy. Sophie doesn't like curtains. Sophie doesn't *believe* in curtains. That's the way she talks these days. Recently she's announced that she doesn't believe in automobiles or political candidates, and she isn't sure about God. She's decisive in her opinions, and she needs very little in the way of facts to form them. Information gets in the way, makes it harder for her to come to a clear conclusion. As Peggy might say, Sophie *eschews* information.

The cards are wrapped in the silk scarf and tucked under Sophie's pillow. While she strokes Tam's hair, Sophie rolls her cheek back and forth over the discernible lump, visualizing purple peaks, enormous eight-sided stars, and somber-faced suns. No one is more interested in the future than a teenage girl. Than *this* teenage girl. Within minutes, she'll be tiptoeing down the stairs, heart pounding in the narrow cage of her chest, wearing a lavender terrycloth robe over her T-shirt. She'll stow the cards in the patchwork pocket of her robe, where they will form a weighty little package that jostles against her thigh as she descends.

Downstairs Peggy huddles over the *Albuquerque Journal*, sipping cold coffee. Her toes curl into the warm flanks of their fat old golden retriever. Lucy knows her duty. When Peggy called, Lucy lumbered down the stairs from Ian's room and, sighing, dropped her rump onto the chilly bricks in front of Peggy's chair.

Sophie sneaks up behind her mother and peers down at Peggy's wild mane of grayish-brown hair, piled now into something resembling a bird's nest. Over the past few months Peggy has lost the weight the doctor ordered Jack to lose. She appears very thin; the notches of her spine are clearly visible through the cotton of her lavender T-shirt. Sophie reaches out and slides her hand along the curve of her mother's neck.

"Who is it?" Peggy asks, not that she needs to. Ian goes out of his way to avoid contact. He shies away from hugs and kisses. It's Sophie who can't keep her hands off things: paintings in museums, stalactites at Carlsbad Caverns, young men she thinks she loves. Her hands reach out and probe whatever is under her gaze. It's not enough to see something; no, she must feel it, too.

"Will you read my cards?" Sophie whispers.

"What?" Peggy asks. The deck arrives over her shoulder with a loud pop, then scatters across the real estate section. "And here I thought I'd hidden the intoxicants," she mutters. With a deft movement of her left hand, she sweeps the cards into a stack.

When Peggy was only a little older than Sophie is now, she read these cards for her dinner, for a place to crash, for a little pocket money. But it's been maybe a dozen years since she's had her hands on them. Even so, they feel familiar—the resistance of the edges, the sheer size of the cards, which are bigger than regular playing cards and a little unwieldy. After handling them a minute, she raises the stack to her nose and takes a deep whiff. They smell faintly of their pine box and of something else forgotten and sweet.

"I hope you and Tam haven't been playing with these," she says. "A deck of cards belongs to one person and one person only."

"Playing?" Sophie is offended, and also a little guilty. She worries that she may have ruined the cards, though her concern is entirely self-interested. She wants to know her future; she *needs* to know her future.

Peggy has already shifted the cards into her lap and begun a fumbling shuffle. "We respect each other's privacy in this house. You have your things, and I have mine." This is the same weary sermon she gave the little girl who scribbled in open books and bathed the dog in her mother's sweet-scented bath oil. It didn't work then, and it certainly won't work now.

Sophie leaves her post behind the chair and arrives on the other side of the table. Her hands are on her hips. She looks serious, ready to drive a bargain. "I want you to read my cards." Her hair is a storm of brownish-black curls, with that one lock of white hanging across her left eye. Back in February she began bleaching a handful of hair a shocking shade of platinum, and now she's reminiscent of Lily in the old sixties show *The Munsters*. Sophie could be the daughter Lily never had, all grown up now and sporting her mother's severe hairdo.

"I don't do readings for free, you know," Peggy says.

It's a stalling tactic, and Sophie knows it. "Charge my account," she replies. Sophie has kept one card back. She holds it up now, the face hidden from view, recalling for her mother their endless games of old maid. Sophie loved the game but abhorred the old maid card. Each time she drew it, she'd place the card exactly in the middle of her fan, holding it up for her mother to choose, a grimace of concentration on her small face. Peggy couldn't bear to disappoint her little girl; she took the old maid every time. No harm in letting the child win, she used to think, secretly pleased to have raised a daughter who was so recklessly in favor of her own happiness. Now she's not so sure.

Today Sophie holds the Page of Cups. After revealing it, she brushes aside the newspaper, sweeping it to one end of the long table. "This is my significator," she says, pushing the card between them, then plopping down in a chair. "I'm ready when you are."

Peggy's brow furrows. "How do you know about significators?"

The information came from Tam, but Sophie doesn't want to invite more questions, so she changes the subject. Out of the blue, she asks about her lost cat: "Have you seen Alex? I haven't seen her in days." Alexandra is a sleek black cat with a white star tucked under her chin. She is wild and defiant—as apt to scratch as she is to purr—but she generally stays close to home. Usually she's curled up in a rocker on the porch—that is, when she's not chasing lizards.

Sophie is concerned about her missing cat, afraid, really, that a coyote might have snatched her up. Ever since she turned sixteen, her worries seem to be multiplying. A new one appears every month. This morning she feels absolutely burdened, laden with a proverbial weight on her shoulders that causes her to slouch into her robe.

"Maybe we should do a reading about your cat."

"Not now, please. This is important."

"Really? And Alex isn't important?" Peggy reaches out and runs a finger over the Page of Cups. "All right then," she agrees, hoping she still remembers the Celtic Cross. "Frame the question carefully. Make sure it's clear in your head. Then shuffle."

For once Sophie does as she's asked, awkwardly rearranging the deck, mixing up the cards on the tabletop, then returning them to her mother, silently, her green eyes evasive. "Do I need to tell you my question?" she asks.

Peggy shakes her head. "You're communicating with the cards, not with me." Sophie's timidity is unexpected but not surprising; Peggy has seen it dozens of times. First readings are always a little scary.

Immediately Peggy begins laying out the cards with sharp little pops, keeping the cross she creates large and using all the available space. She mutters the words to remind herself: "*Covers* her. *Crosses* her. *Beneath* her. *Behind* her. What *may* come. *Before* her. *Herself.* Her *house.* Her *hopes and fears.* What *will* come."

Sophie scoots back, startled.

Peggy's hands sweep across the table, slapping the cards face up, one after another. She doesn't hesitate or hold back. Once the cards are down, she glances first at them and then at Sophie. All the energy of the last few seconds is gone. Suddenly she's a rag doll of a mother.

"You okay?" Sophie asks, her heart pounding.

"I'm sorry," her mother says, shrinking back and folding her hands in her lap. Underneath the table, Peggy jabs Lucy's side with her toes, again and again. She can feel the poor old dog flinching. To stop, she has to move her feet out from under the table, and once she's done that, she shifts her stance, turning her body away from Sophie and toward the door.

"Guess I'm not up to this," she says quietly.

"Try! Won't you just try?"

The pleading confirms it. How simpleminded mothers are, Peggy thinks. We imagine we can hide a bottle and that our duty is done. "Sophie, don't let's do this, please, sweetie."

"I have to," Sophie replies.

Other people forget what they don't use, but Peggy remembers every blessed thing: the Celtic Cross, the faces of the cards, the deepest desires of all the desperate souls who have ever sought her counsel. Most often, their questions were about love or money, or sometimes love *and* money. Cups or Pentacles, Pentacles and Cups. In Peggy's experience, you can toss out the Wands and Swords. Sophie's question is Cups, of course. Three in a row straight up.

Recklessly in favor of her own happiness, Peggy thinks. *My daughter is recklessly in favor of her own happiness. Is this my fault too, then? Will Jack blame me for this as well?*

"Please, Peggy. Please, please!" Sophie knows she's begging, but she can't help it. That's her future in front of her, so close she can practically smell it. If it's necessary, she'll bend over and press her chest to the table, intuit the cards' meanings using only her heart.

"What about this one?" Sophie points to the number nine card, which signifies hopes and fears. The Fool sallies forth, his gaze on the bright yellow sky, his feet on the edge of a cliff. Another step and he'll plummet to his death, but he never takes it; eternally, he's on the verge. "Does this mean I've been foolish?"

Peggy's been asked that question before. She glances at the Empress and sighs deeply. "Not necessarily," she replies slowly. "The Fool's about expectations and impossible goals. He's hope, baby." Reaching a hand over the spread, she squeezes Sophie's arm.

Across from the Fool, in the number-six spot, is the Knight of Swords. "The decision," Peggy says slowly, "has to do with a young man."

Sophie gazes at the Knight on his horse, his sword upraised as he rushes headlong into battle. Behind him the sky is streaked with dark clouds, and in the distance, a heavy wind bends the cypress trees.

"He has a strong . . . *will*," Peggy adds. The word hangs in the air between them.

"You know my question, don't you?" Sophie insists. "Just say it, why don't you?"

But Peggy won't. She can't. Instead, she sweeps her hand across the table, scattering the cards. Several lift briefly into the air before drifting to the floor—the Fool and the Empress, still insisting on their due—but Peggy refuses to look at them or at Sophie. "I had no business doing this," she says. "It's been too long, and besides, I need to get to the shop. It's Balloon Fiesta time. You know that."

"You can't do this to me, goddamn it!" Sophie cries out.

In her rush to get away, Peggy kicks Lucy in the side, raising a howl of protest. "I'm so sorry," Peggy calls over her shoulder, a blanket apology. She's flying down the hallway to the bathroom, where she turns on the shower. She can weep in private, and pretend later that she hasn't wept at all.

By the time Peggy returns, dressed in a long-sleeved green tunic and matching slacks, Sophie is hunched at the end of the table, her back to the door and her head bent forward. All that wild hair hides the movement of her hands. She's concentrating, doing something that requires all of her attention. Briefly, Peggy watches from across the room. When she calls out good-bye, Sophie straightens and turns, revealing a house of cards.

Peggy shouldn't be surprised, and she isn't, not really. After all, she taught her daughter this trick many years ago, using the old maid deck. On those rare occasions when little Sophie lost in spite of her mother's best efforts, Peggy would console her by building a house of cards, saving the old maid for last. "Look, sweetie," she'd say, balancing the cards against each other, like a line of hands raised in prayer.

To the outsider, the structure probably appears delicate, but the first story is sturdy. Blow as hard as you like; you won't knock it down. The second is another matter. It's as apt to collapse as it is to stand. Already, Sophie has finished the first two floors. The tarot cards make a large and handsome house of bright colors: red, green, yellow, and blue.

As she attempts the third story, Sophie bites her lip. She holds four cards, two in either hand. To stand, they must be planted at the same instant. "Steady," Peggy says, or maybe she doesn't say it. Maybe she's just thinking it.

Once the cards are in place, Sophie leans back and takes a ragged breath. "This next is the hardest," she says.

"I know."

"You chickened out on me, Peggy."

"I wanted to protect you," her mother admits, bending to collect the Empress and the Fool from the floor, then handing them off to her daughter. For now, neither notices the loss of the Knight of Swords, which has been carried away in Lucy's mouth. The Lord of Winds and Breezes, as he's called, is already buried in the depths of Ian's cluttered closet and, like the cat Alexandra, won't be seen again.

"Protect me from the truth? Is that possible?"

Scattering the cards didn't change a thing. Peggy sees that now. The Empress is still in her all-important number-ten spot, portending what will come. A large and lovely woman, she sits regally on her throne, the very vision of fecundity—another of Peggy's favorite words. Later today she'll turn it over in her head—*fecundity, fecundity*—but she won't say it aloud just yet.

Perhaps it's a trick of the imagination, but the house of cards seems to glow, filling the murky room with all the available light. Peggy sighs. Life is sweeter, she thinks, when you take it one day at a time, one hour at a time, this moment and then the next. No one is less interested in the future than a middle-aged woman. Than this middle-aged woman. Still, her heart lifts a little as she says the words: "If I had to guess, I'd say you're pregnant."

Sophie pinches the cards, yellow sky to yellow sky, and holds them, trembling, above a fragile foundation. She doesn't look up, but she gives a slight nod. "I think you're right," she replies.

Peggy wants nothing more than to rush from the house, shut herself inside her car, and wail, but she resists the impulse. Instead, she sinks into the chair nearest her daughter and buys herself time by studying the structure on the table. She inhales deeply and tells herself to take it easy. They don't need a shouting match. Seeing who can yell the loudest won't help anything.

"How long since you've made one of these?" Peggy asks.

Sophie shrugs and shakes her head. She hasn't the faintest idea. "The last time we played old maid?"

"But that would have been years and years ago."

"Are you saying it requires practice or something? It doesn't. All it requires is a steady hand."

"And good eyes," Peggy adds. "I've never seen one made of tarot cards. It's so big and colorful." The symmetry draws her eye—three triangles support two and two support one. It reminds her of the Eiffel Tower, minus the tall spire.

Sophie points at the Empress, bringing her finger as close to the card as she dares. "So, who is she?"

Peggy shakes her head. She doesn't understand the question.

Sophie goes so far as to touch the card gently with the edge of her nail. "Is she a real person?"

"You mean does she represent someone in real life?"

Sophie nods. "Duh," she says drolly.

"Duh yourself," Peggy shoots back. Everyone in the family enjoys making jokes at the mother's expense, and Mom is rather thin-skinned about it these days. "Not necessarily. The Empress is the third card in the major arcana, and she embodies fertility and creativity. The number three signifies creation, as in two plus one equals three. Get it?"

Sophie shakes her head.

"*One* man and *one* woman make *one* baby," Peggy says softly. She reaches out and touches her daughter's knee. "What do you want to do?"

They have to talk about it sooner or later, so it might as well be sooner. If she doesn't confront it now, she may never. Peggy has learned this much about herself. She avoids as much conflict as she can. She's a turtle when it comes to problems; she withdraws into her shop. And this thought brings with it a realization: that's what Jack is doing with his fixer-upper. He's evading the discomfort of confronting his mortality. Isn't that it, really? The rest of them are aware of his fragility, so he avoids them. For a second or two, anyway, she feels better.

Sophie doesn't know what she wants to do. It hasn't sunk in. "I didn't really believe the tests, but I do believe the cards." She sweeps a hand but stops just short of demolition.

"So you've taken a test?"

Sophie nods. She bought one at Walgreens, then, broke but still not convinced of her fate, walked into Target and stole a second one, not that she'd tell her mother that part of the story. She knows better than to try and shoplift at Target—they prosecute every offense. But the store is in the same shopping center as Movies West, and opportunity trumped caution. In the end, she was nearly nabbed. She had to run like hell and hide behind a dumpster, then sneak into work late. In any case, it didn't matter. It was a different box with the same outcome.

"When did you take the test?"

Sophie knows precisely when, but she doesn't want to say. So she shrugs her shoulders and offers a vague response: "A month ago, maybe?"

"Are you kidding me, Sophie? You've known you're pregnant for a month now?"

Sophie isn't nearly as calm as she tries to appear. She can feel the contents of her stomach roiling. "Don't make me throw up, Peggy. I'm pretty good at upchucking these days."

"Have you made an appointment at Planned Parenthood? Have you been to see a doctor?"

"No and no. I've been hoping it would go away, frankly. Sometimes it doesn't take, you know. So I've tried a few things, nothing drastic."

"What sort of things?" Peggy is feeling sick herself. How could she be so dense?

Sophie shrugs again. "Vitamin C first. But that didn't work."

So that's what became of the bottle in the kitchen cabinet. "How much did you take?"

"I didn't count, but not enough. It upset my stomach." Sophie hesitates. "So then I tried putting parsley up my pussy."

"Are you kidding me? Who told you to do such a thing?"

"There's lots of information on the Internet, Peggy. At first I was pretty sure I could take care of it myself. But I was wrong. Guess it's time for a family meeting, eh?"

Peggy doesn't think they should tell Jack, and she tells Sophie so. "Your father is recovering from a heart attack. Big revelations aren't part of the recovery plan. Have you told Will yet, by the way?"

Sophie shakes her head.

"Well, I think you should start there. Will needs to know, first of all."

"Why? Why does he need to know?"

Peggy refrains from the obvious reply: *DUH*. Instead, she tries to remember what it felt like to be Sophie's age, how she thought and what she overlooked.

Oh lord, she thinks. If Sophie doesn't have more sense than she did, they are all in for a very bumpy ride. Peggy left home at sixteen. She ran away on impulse, and stayed away for over a year. There was no real rhyme or reason to any of it. If Peggy is honest with herself, she knows that others her age behaved similarly. They were like puppies slipping under a hole in the fence, tumbling over each other in their rush to get somewhere, anywhere they hadn't been before.

The precarious nature of the moment takes her breath away.

Sophie is leaning eagerly toward her mother, and Peggy seizes the opportunity. She reaches out and grabs Sophie's arm, shakes it a little just to force her daughter to pay attention. She knows that what she plans to say next will make a hopeless hypocrite of her, but there it is, and here she goes: "Will is the father, which means he has a nearly equal stake in the matter. I'm saying *nearly* equal because he doesn't have to carry the child to term. It's your decision first of all." The cost of an abortion crosses her mind. She wonders how much the procedure costs these days.

Sophie shakes her head wildly, and reaches out to knock blindly at the cards. They tumble around her outstretched hand.

"I can't. I can't. I can't," she chants.

Later, driving to work, Peggy will wonder what Sophie was saying. Was it that she couldn't make a decision, couldn't have a child, couldn't tell Will? What was it, finally, that Sophie couldn't do? But in the moment, Peggy retreats. "I have to go," she says quietly. "I'm late already." She kisses the top of her daughter's prone head and takes just long enough to collect the cards and scarf, before heading out the door.

Once she's in the driver's seat, she gathers the cards and wraps them in the scarf. Her hands are shaking as she finishes the task. She sits silently for a moment to calm herself. Her gaze goes to the storage shed behind the house, a sturdier structure than its name would suggest. The building is a catchall for Jack's tools, his beekeeping paraphernalia, and whatever else no longer has a place in the house. That includes Peggy's old green trunk, which is where Sophie found the cards.

I should have hidden them better, she thinks, as though it's the cards that are at fault.

Used to be, Jack's mother lived in a small brick row house off the main street in Brattleboro. Now she resides in a nursing home called River View Manor, on the edge of town. The white frame building is long and meandering—the result of several additions—but it still extends along one central hallway, and each of the rooms looks out onto a bank of trees. Jack has heard people ask, "Where's the river view?" He wondered himself until he discovered that there is one. You just have to know where to look for it. From a certain vantage point in the gravel lot it's possible to see a swatch of the Connecticut River. Even on an overcast day, the flowing water shimmers mysteriously through the trees. It's moving; it's going somewhere.

His mother's name is Veronica, but that name has never suited her, and most of her life she's answered to Vernie or Mom. Now she's no longer addressed in either familiar—she is known in the nursing home as Mrs. Granger. Even Jack has to refer to her in this distant manner because his mother no longer recognizes him. She is less senile than she is simply stuck in a different place and time. If the forty-year-old version of her son were to enter the room, she'd know him in an instant. But this big, slack man with his reading glasses and shuffling gait? She doesn't have the heart to call him her own.

Each time they meet, she asks the same question: "And who might you be?"

He could ask the same of her. He can never get over how white her hair is, how blue her eyes, or the coquettish way she cocks her head and smiles dreamily into his face. It's an odd thing: he prefers this version of his mother to the earlier versions. It seems to Jack that we all have some phase of life when we are most genuinely ourselves. For his mother, it took losing everything closest to her. First a daughter, then a husband, and finally the house that held them. Now she is free to embrace her own unadulterated self.

Mrs. Granger is gracious, but she doesn't mince words. He likes the way she phrases the inquiry. "Who might you be?" It gives him leave to be anyone he wants to be. So a few visits back, he gave up trying to answer honestly. When he claimed to be Jack, her response was one of confusion and even alarm. She considered him an imposter, an intruder, and once she even picked up the phone and called the front desk for assistance. "This man won't leave my room," she reported in a firm voice. Vernie has always been firm. Even now, her grip is tight, her opinions unwavering. "I know right from wrong," she likes to say. To make matters easier, Jack has settled for being an emissary, someone sent by Mrs. Granger's son to check on her well-being. It's a pleasant ruse that puts them both at ease.

After all these years, Jack still misses Vermont and eagerly anticipates what Albuquerque residents refer to as his "green fix." For the first two days of his visit, he is pleasantly stupefied by his verdant surround-ings. Even fall looks lush to him. But on the last two days he finds himself dazed by remorse. How can he return to the desert? On Sunday night he drifts off to sleep while imagining a phone call to his family back home. *I've decided to stay*, he thinks of saying. He briefly consid-ers the clamor his announcement would cause: beseeching by his wife, wailing by his daughter, polite entreaties from his son. Even to him, it isn't clear what he wants more: the familiar beauty of Vermont or relief from the burdens of family life.

By Monday morning the weather has turned cold enough for a heavy jacket. He walks from the motel, and by the time he approaches the River View he is hurrying in anticipation of a heated interior. He doesn't head straight to his mother, though he feels the pull of her presence. Instead, he stops at the front office, which was closed over the weekend, and asks for Lynette Penser. A girl who looks to be barely out of high school greets him and nods eagerly as he introduces himself.

"We've been stressing out about your mom," she says. He senses re-proof in her tone, though he realizes he may be imagining things. He feels unaccountably guilty, as though he's abandoned his mother to strangers. "Stay right here," she tells him. "I'll be back."

Perhaps the girl is concerned that wandering runs in the family. If so, she doesn't have the first idea of how tired Jack is. As soon as she turns her back, he looks for a place to sit down.

The dayroom, just across the hall from the front office, is a comfort-able space lined with window seats and furnished with several over-stuffed couches. The television is on, but someone has muted it, which Jack appreciates. A little peace and quiet, a few minutes of relaxation, he thinks. He drops onto the nearest couch, and is pleasantly surprised by the softness of the cushions and the fresh scent they emit. People always complain that nursing homes smell like piss, but this one doesn't, at least not that he's noticed.

On the other side of the room, an elderly couple is playing cards. The woman laughs loudly and calls out, "Uno!" The man shakes his head in mock distress. After dropping a card on the discard pile, he reaches over and briefly covers her hand. He says something Jack can't hear; whatever it is brings a shy smile to the woman's face. They're flirting, Jack thinks as he settles his head against the cushions. Maybe his mother is having a better time than he supposed. Maybe it isn't misery that's been propelling her into the streets. He'd imagined that she's been fleeing, but he doubts that now. Goodness knows, *he* doesn't feel like fleeing. He feels like cozying up on the couch and letting the morning slip away.

When she arrives, the social worker is pleasantly informal. Instead of escorting him into an office, she strides into the sitting room and settles herself on the cushion next to him.

"Good morning, Mr. Granger," she says, extending her hand and shaking his firmly. "Thank you so much for coming."

He tries to rouse himself. He guesses he dozed off just before she sat down next to him. He hopes so anyway. "Thanks for getting in touch with me," he begins haltingly. "I adore my mother, and it's hard to be such a great distance from her."

The social worker must be his age, he thinks, or maybe even a little older. She wears her gray hair in one long braid down her back, and is dressed in a red corduroy jumper over a white turtleneck. Although she looks familiar, Jack suspects that it's not the woman he recognizes but her style of dress and no-nonsense grooming. He recalls girls dressing exactly this way when he was in high school. Likely the woman wouldn't find a thing to wear in Peggy's shop. Or would she? What the hell does he know?

They discuss his mother's new habit of taking walks around town. Ms. Penser explains that it wouldn't be so bad if Jack's mother could find her way back, but she can't. "Fortunately for everyone, lots of folks in town know Mrs. Granger, and several different people have been kind enough to return her to us."

He hears himself launching into an unnecessary explanation, but what the hell? Isn't this woman paid to listen to people's troubles?

"Honestly," he says, "I've wondered if it wouldn't be better to move her to a facility in Albuquerque. I would prefer that really, but back when she could still sort through the options, we discussed it and she nixed the idea. Said she wanted to stay here in Brattleboro, where she's lived all her life."

Ms. Penser nods. "Most people prefer familiar surroundings. Likely Mrs. Granger wouldn't know what to make of New Mexico."

He's isn't sure what she's referring to, but he is used to people in New England equating New Mexico with the Wild West. Back when he accepted a scholarship to study at New Mexico State in Las Cruces, he imagined he would have to learn Spanish right away, simply to communicate his most basic needs. So he smiles indulgently and offers the observation that his mother would hardly know where she was, given that she spends nearly all her time indoors. Besides, the very problem they're discussing might go away if Vernie were relocated. She might not have any interest in venturing out onto the strange streets of Albuquerque—assuming, of course, that she recognized the change of scene.

But if she *did* decide to leave the facility, those she encountered might not be so kind. In some respects, Albuquerque is a dangerous place to live. Certainly the risks are fewer here in Brattleboro, though he does have a fleeting thought about Gwendolyn, his younger sister, who lost her life to a drunk driver right here in small-town Vermont. Bad luck can strike anywhere.

"Do you want me to talk to her?" Jack asks.

"Well, you can try that. And we will want to go over some of the other alternatives while you're here. But why don't you go see her now? They'll be serving lunch in a half hour, and you'll want to get in a little visit before then."

His mother is napping, and Jack doesn't wake her. Instead, he settles into the armchair by the window and drifts off to sleep himself, trying to finish the nap interrupted by Ms. Penser. Mother and son doze together until Mrs. Granger's lunch tray is delivered. Jack sits with her while she eats. She accepts his presence with equanimity. This is his third day in Vermont, and she is more or less used to him. She smiles shyly in his direction and takes up her fork. Perhaps he is a remnant of her dream; perhaps she is a remnant of his. He is too weary to insert himself in any way. After she has finished her dessert, a scoop of vanilla ice cream, he collects her tray and, in the midst of the effort, bends down and gives her a quick peck on the forehead.

"Will you be back?" she asks.

"Certainly," he replies.

He returns to his hotel room in the middle of the afternoon and sees that he left his cell phone in the bedcovers. The maid was good enough to retrieve it and leave it for him on the pillow. The red light is blinking. He has two messages, one from Peggy and the other from work. Peggy reports that she spoke with the electrician, and the news on that front is good. The problem with the circuitry in the kitchen is fixed. The fellow wanted a check, so he came by the house to get it. Peggy wrote one from the household account, but at work this morning she checked the balance online and was surprised to find that they don't have enough money to cover it. Should she call the guy and ask him not to cash it?

She sounds flustered. Jack knows it's his job to shield her from this sort of distress. The message meanders, and at the end of it she has a question for him: "Where's all our money?"

"What universe are you living in?" he mutters into the receiver. He decides then and there to take the rest of his meals at the River View. On the first day of his visit, they offered him a tray, but he turned them down, preferring the local restaurant. He checks his wallet, counts a hundred dollars, and calculates that the end of the month is less than a week away. He calls Peggy back and is relieved when she doesn't pick up. "Don't worry," he tells her. "I've still got a hundred bucks. But don't write any more checks, please."

The other message is from one of the administrative assistants in the dean's office, politely requesting that Jack vacate his office as soon as possible. Now that he's returning to teaching, they need him to move his things to a cubicle over in Building C. They hope he can complete the task by the end of the week. Jack doesn't bother to answer this one. Pro forma is the way he thinks of it. They just want to remind him that he isn't one of them anymore. Surely they haven't identified his replacement yet, he thinks, though it will turn out that they have.

Jack likes to refer to himself as a "recovering administrator," and it's more or less true. He has served at CNM for five years, first as the associate dean of instruction, then as the dean of instruction. He began his career in administration under duress. Back when he started down that difficult road, he had a different name for himself: "reluctant administrator." He didn't covet the post. He didn't enjoy the authority, and he certainly disliked a lot of the duties that went with the job. But he'd more or less gotten used to them, and his family had gotten used to the extra money.

Jack likes to think of himself as serving the good of the whole. His is a beekeeper's perspective, and generally it has served him well. Like people, bees are social creatures. They don't operate independently; rather, they do what's best for the hive. Jack embraces the concept of the greater good, and in the past he has acted on it, assuming that others will do so as well. But they don't, he has realized at long last. Often enough, they just don't. Unlike bees, people most frequently do what is in their own best interest. Now that he is on the cusp of sixty, Jack wonders whether he's been sacrificing himself for naught.

On Tuesday Jack brings his mother a pot of begonias from the kitchen window of one of her former neighbors.

"How's Vernie doing?" the neighbor had asked Jack in the checkout line at the grocery store.

He whirled around, surprised. "You know me?" he exclaimed. He'd come to feel anonymous in Vermont, even downright invisible.

She laughed out loud. "We went to school together, Jack!" she says. "Margaret, remember? I lived right down the street from you the whole time we were growing up."

Unlike the social worker, Margaret was the sort to hide her age as best she could, by dyeing her hair and wearing baggy clothes and big, framed glasses. She had an open smile and she talked quickly, words spilling out of her mouth. She still lived in the neighborhood, though not in the same house.

She tried to tell Jack the location of her new home, mentioning crossroads and a nearby park. Finally he had to admit that he hadn't been to that part of town since they'd sold the house. They'd needed the money to pay for his mother's care.

He confided in her about Vernie's recent penchant for leaving the nursing home and meandering around town.

"She's looking for something, don't you think?" Margaret asked. "Trying to find her way back home, perhaps?"

Jack shook his head. "Maybe, but if so, she won't tell me." He had asked his mother why she left her cozy room to roam the streets, and had tried to impress upon her the necessity of staying indoors unless someone from the staff could accompany her. Vernie had listened quietly, without offering any sort of response. At the end of his little speech, she'd simply turned and stared out the window.

He shook his head sadly. "I have to go home tomorrow," he told Margaret, hoping she would volunteer to check in on Vernie from time to time. But she didn't bring it up—and Jack didn't have the heart to ask—though she did ask where he was staying. She wanted to drop off a little gift for Vernie.

He carries Margaret's blooms down the long hallway, past door after door, moving slowly and occasionally looking down to make sure he isn't jostling the delicate blossoms. Beekeepers appreciate flowers nearly as much as florists do.

As Jack passes by the nurse's station, a fellow in a wheelchair calls out in a falsetto voice, "Here comes the bride!" One of the nursing assistants, the youngest and cutest one, titters, and the old man grins broadly. He hasn't bothered with his dentures, so he has the happy face of an ancient baby. "Those for your mamma?"

Jack nods and feels a blush coming on—something that hasn't happened to him in many years.

"You're a mighty good son," the man notes, "but a mighty ugly bride." And then he guffaws.

Jack stops long enough to slap the fellow's outstretched hand. He's absolutely right. Jack prides himself on being a good son, a good father, a good husband, and an all-around decent human being. In keeping with this, he tries not to burden Vernie. Most often, he reports only good news to his mother, but this time he does something he didn't plan to do: he shares something about his own situation.

On this last full day of his visit, when the conversation has lulled; when Jack has carried his mother's lunch tray out to the main desk; when he has taken a bathroom break; when he has ventured out the back door and stood with his hands in his pockets, staring off into the trees, searching for the shimmer of the passing river, he returns to her shady room, with its one window to the outside world. He sits down and sighs.

"So, I've been meaning to tell you something," he says, then waits until his mother turns her gaze to him.

She's wearing a thin red cardigan, the same red as the social worker's jumper. The sweater is buttoned up over her white blouse, but whoever did the buttoning missed one of the holes, causing the front of the sweater to bunch. In his absence Vernie has picked up her crochet work, but she drops it into her lap, folds her hands over the project, and focuses her eyes on his face. That's one of the things he's come to expect from these visits, one of the things he yearns for when he returns home: the undivided attention of another human being. Peggy is not a good listener; he can tell the precise moment when she tunes him out.

"I don't want you to worry about him," Jack begins, "but your son has had something of a mild heart attack."

She blinks several times in quick succession and clasps her hands, but she doesn't seem unduly alarmed. Jack is relieved by her reaction. Evidently she isn't worried about his demise. Even so, he seeks to reassure her. "He's entirely recovered."

She shakes her head. "No, not entirely," she corrects. "It leaves a little scare." She lifts a hand and traces a line on her chest with one trailing thumb.

"Scar?" Jack wonders aloud. Did she mean to say "scar"? Vernie doesn't reply.

When he leaves she insists on kissing his forehead. "Give Jack my love," she says. "Does he still keep his bees?"

Jack assures her that he does.

She takes up her crochet, a silken, multicolored web. "He loved insects from the time he was a boy. I always wanted to swat those wasps, but he wouldn't let me. Do you know, he'd grab the swatter right out of my hand?" She laughs. "His daddy thought he was a bit of a sissy, but me, I was always glad he had a soft heart."

Jack doesn't remember this, but he doesn't doubt that it's true. On the plane returning to Albuquerque, he thinks about a soft heart. He wonders whether soft hearts go first, like ripe peaches or pears—they're sweet, certainly, but not long for this world. If that's the case, he has good reason to put himself first for once in his life. Or if not first, then at least a close second.

So he drives directly from the airport to the casita. He won't share with Peggy that he chose to visit the fixer-upper before going home to his family. Even to himself he has to create an excuse. He wants to check and make sure the circuitry is fixed. God knows he'd be devastated if the little place burned down.

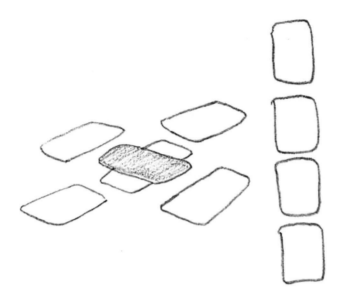

Position #2—"What Crosses Her"

Here's the rub. Whatever the situation, we will always face resistance or complications. The card in this position offers guidance on the obstacles you will encounter.

~ Three of Cups ~

Three women dance, their cups raised in celebration. One is grasping a fistful of grapes, an indication that the drink of the moment is wine. The setting is a garden, and the season is fall.

The Three of Cups is a card of family and friendship. Get ready for a party! Friends are on the way!

Unlike in New England, where fall is extravagant but fleeting, or Texas, where it scarcely makes a showing at all, in New Mexico autumn is leisurely and lovely. For weeks at a time, the air is refreshingly cool but not cold, and along the Bosque, the leaves of the cottonwoods turn several splendid shades of yellow. All through October, they glow golden.

And if the colorful cottonwoods aren't enough to raise spirits, the morning skies are decorated extravagantly with hot air balloons that grow in number as the weeks pass. They hang over the highway during the morning rush hour, buoyant baubles that belie the urgency of the hour. The season of balloons culminates in the Albuquerque International Balloon Fiesta, when as many as eight hundred of them drift lazily across the landscape, touching down on empty acreage, in parking lots, and occasionally in the middle of intersections.

As soon as the balloonists are finished with their fun and games, as soon as they've packed up their trucks and hit the road, the skies are filled with migrating birds—thousands of them. Sandhill cranes fly so high that their wavery Vs look like pencil marks in the sky; their throaty calls fill the morning air, and walkers and bikers stop in their tracks to search the heavens for evidence of them. The cranes and the geese, the mallards and the herons are on their way to the Bosque del Apache Refuge in central New Mexico. As they travel, any number of them will take a long sojourn along the banks of the Rio Grande.

The Balloon Fiesta attracts a hundred thousand sightseers, many of whom will spend an afternoon or two visiting Old Town. The early morning ascension is over before nine thirty, and the Balloon Glow begins after dark, when pilots light up the chilly desert floor with hundreds of tethered balloons. Tourists have the rest of the day free for shopping and sightseeing. The shopkeepers in Old Town count on the yearly influx of fall visitors. This year Peggy has stapled strings of balloon lights around the edges of the store's front windows. She purchased the lights on the web, and they do the trick. Many more passersby have entered the store, and quite a few have asked about buying the lights. Does she have any for sale? She doesn't, but, realizing that she could have more if she acts quickly, Peggy puts in a rush order for four dozen boxes, and on the day they're due—Friday, October 12—she arrives to work early. It is in this way that she discovers a young homeless man who has taken to slumbering in the alleyway behind her store. Homeless *boy*, she thinks to herself, because he doesn't appear to be out of his teens. He's not much older than Sophie, Peggy realizes as she approaches. And he's evidently dead tired. He doesn't stir, even when she's standing over him.

The young man's brown hair is long and matted. He wears it in the dreadlocks of disenfranchised, middle-class white kids. Recently Sophie regaled her mother with the recipe for dreadlocks. Peggy doesn't remember how they got on the subject, but she does recall the particulars. Mayonnaise is a popular ingredient, and so is peanut butter. Some use honey, Sophie said, and others swear by candle wax. "Is it possible to undo what's been done?" Peggy had asked. Sophie shook her head firmly. Dreadlocks have to be cut out, she explained. They're not reversible. "It's a commitment—less than a tattoo, but more than a pierced nose," Sophie said.

The homeless boy wears a tattered, filthy black sweat shirt and jeans. The soles of his feet are black. They call themselves "crust punks," Sophie has explained. The filthier they are, the *crustier*, the better. Peggy has seen these young people congregating outside the Winning Coffee shop near the university. They seem aggressively dirty—and charmingly carefree. She can imagine them clustered around Winning's cast-iron tables, oblivious to the discomfort of the chairs, chattering about nothing at all from early morning until noon or later.

The crust punk sleeps on. Already, the sun has risen high enough to reach into the corners of the alley. He's bedded down on the cardboard boxes Peggy had flattened and put out for recycling the day before. Briefly she's irritated by the fact that he's ruined them. They'll stink, she thinks, but then she's ashamed of herself. This is recycling, too, she tells herself. He's making good use of the boxes, and what more could she want?

The truth is that Albuquerque has more than its share of homelessness. The climate is mild, the citizens tolerant. Over the years Peggy has gotten used to these sad souls stationed at the corners of intersections, clutching battered cardboard signs: *Spare change? Will work for food!! Hungry vet.* Living ghosts is what she thinks of them. Most are harmless, although they do hector passersby for spare change, reminding everyone of the tenuous nature of existence.

The crust punks, in particular, remind Peggy of the hippies she lived with in the late sixties and early seventies, some of whom were pretty dirty, too. Hermit Henry comes to mind. He had taken a vow of silence, and rather than utter a word, he would scrawl notes on a child's chalkboard. She remembers one morning when she made pancakes on the camp stove. After filling his plate, Henry had scrawled GOD on his little green board and held it up for her to read. Did he mean GOOD? she'd wondered.

Though it's been years since Peggy has thought of Hermit Henry, she recalls now that his eccentricities were not only tolerated but accepted.

Hermit Henry's stench was legendary—sometimes they would chase him into the yard and douse him with dirty dishwater—but that didn't mean they rejected him. Certainly, then, she can muster a little compassion for this interloper.

So it isn't her intention to wake the fellow. She feels awkward, as though she's inadvertently trespassed, but she has to open the metal door, installed last year to deter burglars, and it's a bitch to unlock. The young man stirs and sits up just as she's managed to shove her way inside.

"Hey!" he says groggily. And then again, "Hey!"

Now she really does feel like an intruder, guilty and a little irritated. Reluctantly, she puts down her lunch sack and purse, then returns to the doorway. "Yes?"

He sits cross-legged on the nest of boxes. Seeing that he has her attention, he brings his hands together at his chest and bows. "Do you have anything I can eat?"

She's surprised. She was prepared to offer him money, but not her lunch. Namaste, Peggy thinks. *The god in me bows to the god in you.* He certainly seems to be paying his respects—that is, until he gathers his matted clumps of hair and, still bent forward, captures the messy mass in a rubber band. Like bundling straw, Peggy thinks. When he straightens again and looks at her, she can see the pale blue of his eyes. He has scant eyebrows and thin lips. Could his hair be blonde, and not the mousey brown it seems to be?

She sighs and turns back inside. In the darkness of the storeroom, she reaches for the sack she's left on the seat of a chair, plucks it up, and carries it out to him. "Tuna fish sandwich," she says. "And an orange."

"Cool," he breathes, opening the sack and peering in. "No cookie?"

He's making a joke. She knows this because Sophie has a similar sense of humor. When he grins up at her, she notes that his teeth are white. Apparently he brushes them on a regular basis, which gives her hope.

"Thanks!" he says, then: "I'm Donald."

She tells him her name before closing the door. When she checks an hour or two later, all traces of Donald are gone. He's restacked the boxes and stowed them in the space between the dumpster and the lumpy adobe wall. Tonight, when she is lying in bed trying to sleep, Peggy will wonder whether the appearance of the crust punk stirred up the spirits of the past. She will wonder, too, where Donald is and whether he's sleeping behind her shop again. Where did he come from, and who are his parents? Do they miss him?

For now she attends to the task of switching on a half dozen floor lamps, all of them faux Tiffany—"well-made plastic," as Jack puts it. Her shop space is narrow and dark. To brighten the interior, she recently repainted the walls a shade of peach, sponging on the color using a method she read about in *Sunset* magazine. She had imagined the result would be glowing, that the color would reflect light. But there is so little light that the orange walls seem to breathe rather than glow. Ensconced in her shop, Peggy feels as though she's hiding in a pumpkin, like a character from a Mother Goose rhyme.

The FedEx man arrives with the box of balloon lights just before nine o'clock. Peggy quickly unpacks the box and arranges its contents on a table up front. She makes a sign for the window, an enjoyable task, and she is actually humming as she opens the store to business at ten.

By the time one o'clock rolls around, she has sold several strands of lights and two broomstick skirts. It's been a busy morning, and Peggy regrets having given away her lunch. For months now she has been indifferent to food, but today she's ravenous. Though she rarely goes out to eat—it's too expensive, especially after factoring in the lost sales—she's tempted to run down the sidewalk to Church Street. She decides against it though, because she can't afford to miss even one customer.

She keeps granola bars and bags of peanuts in a desk drawer in the back room, for emergencies like this one. A mini-fridge is stocked with bottled water and cans of Dr Pepper. "You'll make it to six," she tells herself as she reaches for the storeroom light. The first thing she sees is the deck of the cards, wrapped in the blue silk scarf and lying in the middle of the desk. Last Sunday she left them in plain sight, as a reminder to take some notes. No time like the present, she thinks, so, along with a Dr Pepper and a bag of nuts, she scoops up the cards and carries them out to the counter.

The shop is quiet, which allows Peggy to reconstruct the reading on the glass countertop, laying out the cards as she remembers them and whispering the words to remind herself: *Covers her. Crosses her. Beneath her. Behind her. What may come. Before her. Herself. Her house. Her hopes and fears. What will come.*

Sophie's reading seems even more important now than it did then. Peggy wants to give the task her best effort, which means opening herself up to the universe. She returns to the desk for a legal pad and pen, to make a few quick notes on each of the cards. For nearly an hour, she concentrates on the spread, all the while sipping Dr Pepper and nibbling peanuts. When one bag is empty, she goes back to her desk for another.

As she is closing the drawer, the phone begins to ring, and Peggy has to rush to catch it, hurrying through the tiny storeroom, skirting boxes and an armless mannequin to make it on the fourth ring, a little breathless. "Good afternoon! Everyday Satin." When she tucks the receiver into the nook between her raised shoulder and lowered head, Peggy registers the stiffness of her neck. Does it always hurt these days? It certainly seems to.

"You named that store for me. I know you did."

Peggy makes an effort to slow her breathing. She doesn't want to gasp in response. "Candace, is that you?"

"Candace from the commune," the woman replies. "But you won't catch me in satin these days. That's a young woman's fabric, don't you think?" Evidently this call is the consequence of Peggy's having opened herself to the universe.

Peggy considers the long rack of handmade broomstick skirts, the shorter rack of cap-sleeved satin blouses, and, underneath the glass countertop, the case of necklaces—silver milagros strung on leather cords. She reaches in and fingers a wishbone crafted by a Taos artisan, one of the silversmiths Beau lived with at Mabel's. Candace and Peggy have had this conversation before, of course. They are sisters of a sort—of the competitive sort, who hold grudges and size each other up each time they meet.

"All right, all right! I might have had you in mind," Peggy admits.

Candace laughs loudly. "No doubt!"

Back in the day, Candace from the commune routinely wore a bit of velvet, a snatch of satin, and something leather to hold it all together, despite the fact that their home had neither electricity nor running water. "The hippie clotheshorse," they'd called her. Years later it finally occurred to Peggy that Candace must have trundled her things to a cleaner in Taos, though she kept her visits a deep, dark secret, disposing of any plastic wrapping or metal hangers before returning to Morningstar. There, she kept her clothes neatly folded in trunks that lined a wall of her bedroom. Candace was that rare bird: a trust-fund hippie.

Today her voice is a little hoarse. "This time I'm going to see for myself."

"You're coming to Albuquerque?" Agitated, Peggy reaches for the cards; her eyes alight on the Empress in her place of honor. *What will come.* The Empress wears a diadem of twelve stars. Even in the dim light, her crown glows. As Candace prattles on, Peggy rubs a finger over the card.

"This may be my last chance to meet those children of yours—before they're grown, that is."

Peggy scoops the cards into a pile as she responds, "Last time you were here—"

"I wasn't in good shape to meet anyone, Peggy," Candace cuts in.

"No, we were both of us messes."

Hard to believe, but it's been over a year since a small group from Morningstar scattered Beau's ashes on the mesa, in full view of Taos Mountain. While black-and-white magpies shrieked and swooped above their heads, Candace and Peggy had clung to one another and watched as their mutual love was reduced to a tiny gray sandstorm swirling around clumps of silvery sage. *Is that it?* Which of them had said it? *Is that it?* Crazy how quickly they had lost sight of him!

The next afternoon, they'd said their good-byes at Albuquerque's airport, the Sunport. They were spent, both of them, utterly spent, but they were still sentimental enough to kiss each other on the lips. A good-bye kiss, Peggy had thought of it. She'd never expected to see Candace again. "What's gone is gone." Her mother used to say it—*what's gone is gone*—every time a holiday gathering broke up. Sometimes it's easier to love family from a distance. Candace was family of a sort.

"I was wondering if I might impose," Candace is saying, "just for the night. I'll be coming into Albuquerque on Sunday afternoon, the fourteenth. I'll pick up the rental and drive straight to your place." Candace drops the r's in "Albuquerque" and "afternoon." Back at Morningstar, they used to tease her about the way she said "stah" instead of "star."

"This Sunday?" Peggy asks. Inside her clogs, her toes clench and unclench until a streak of pain races up the inside of her calf.

"Yep!"

"You're welcome, of course, but we don't have a guest room."

"I'm not fussy. I can sleep on the couch. Really, I'd just enjoy a little time with your family." Candace pauses, then admits that she's been lonely these last few months. Although she's lived a rather solitary life— as an only child, a childless wife, and now a middle-aged widow— Candace isn't an introvert by temperament. Unlike Peggy, she relishes the company of others. At Morningstar she welcomed everyone, even Hermit Henry.

"Of course," Peggy replies. "I should have been in touch."

"You're busy, of course you are. And it's not as though we've been close all these years."

"But still," Peggy says, "we do go back."

"Indeed we do, my dear."

"All right, then. If you don't mind not having your own room, we'll figure something out."

"Thank you, Peggy," Candace gushes. "I can't wait. Really, it will be such a treat."

After she hangs up, Peggy feels positively sick. She locks the front door, then hurries back to the cramped little bathroom, threading her way around stacked boxes, a discarded mannequin that Sophie used to enjoy dressing and undressing, and a display table Peggy has never gotten around to painting. The bathroom wasn't so much added on as crammed in. The door has to be kept closed because it blocks the passageway to the storeroom. A plumber she consulted had speculated that the building was plumbed shortly after Peggy was born, give or take a few years. As he said, no one was even dreaming of toilets and sinks when the building was constructed.

The toilet rocks whenever anyone sits on it—anyone except Peggy, that is. She has mastered the task of seating herself. She positions her buttocks over the bowl, bends her knees, and dips gingerly onto the seat, first the right bun, then the left. It helps that she weighs less than a hundred pounds and is able to deliver her weight accurately. But this time she doesn't sit. She lifts the lid and bends over the bowl, holding her white blouse to her chest with the back of her arm. One quick retch, and the peanuts and Pepper are history. What's gone is gone, Peggy thinks as she flushes.

Straightening, smoothing the front of her blouse, she edges over to the sink, where she wipes her mouth with a damp paper towel. The act of vomiting has brought tears to her eyes. Peggy blinks them away. For the first time in years, she sees, really sees, the poster of Taos Pueblo that hangs where a mirror should be, where a mirror once was. The poster depicts an artist's rendering of the historic, endlessly photographed north house. She chose the poster not for its accurate depiction of that iconic adobe high-rise, but for the looming mountain behind it, Taos Mountain, dusted by snow and ringed by ragged clouds, exactly as Peggy prefers to remember it.

Now what? Peggy wonders whether Beau can hear her thoughts, and if so, whether he is sympathetic or amused. Probably amused. But it's not Beau's voice that returns to her from the beyond. Instead, it's Peggy's mother again, and she's singing a ditty Peggy hasn't heard in oh-so-many years: "*Oh what a tangled web we weave when first we practice to deceive.*"

"Why don't we hoist a teepee?" Sophie asks on Sunday morning. "You know, in lieu of a guest room. Wouldn't that be awesome?"

The questions are for Peggy, who is busy stripping sheets. Since Sophie's bed is a mattress on the floor, the task entails crawling around on hands and knees. It occurs to Peggy that she's getting too old for this sort of thing. Perhaps she should delegate this particular task to her daughter. She is about to say something of the sort when she discovers a purple Indian-print bedspread wadded up inside the top sheet. It's familiar, but she doesn't place it right away. Instead, she wonders aloud: "What's up with the teepees? Just the other day, Ian asked if he could have a teepee for Christmas."

"Didn't you live in a teepee, way back when?" Sophie asks.

"Not that I remember," Peggy replies. She intends sarcasm, but Sophie snickers and makes a comment about too many acid trips.

By this time Peggy has untangled the top sheet from the bedspread, and now that she has her hands on it, she knows where it came from. "Isn't this mine?" she asks Sophie. "Did you filch this out of my trunk?"

"You weren't using it," Sophie says. "I found three of them: an orange one, a red one, and a purple one. Seems like you'd want me to get some use out of them. What good do they do anyone in a trunk? Anyway, what's up with the 'I, me, mine' all the time?"

Sophie has always been a handful. When she was little, she was too cute to reprimand, and later, she was too prone to tears. Now she's too smart. Peggy sits back on her heels and squeezes the spread to her chest. "I don't mind, I suppose, as long as you take care of it. But Sophie, you should have asked me." Peggy considers the purple spread, then wonders aloud: "Isn't red your favorite color?"

The red one is doing duty on Will's bed, but Sophie knows better than to say so. "I just grabbed the one on top," she lies.

Already Sophie has wandered away from her chore—dusting the chest of drawers—and is instead peering out the second-story window. Her eyes worry the line of bee boxes, one cheerful color after another, all of them glowing in the morning light. "There's plenty of room out there for a teepee," she continues. "The bees wouldn't even know we're there. I'd sleep outside. Ian would, too. Then you guys could have the house all to yourselves." The teepee was Ian's idea, and at first Sophie had scoffed. But that was before he showed her the Internet printouts. "Majorly cool," she told him.

"Who said we want the house to ourselves?" Peggy asks, though that's precisely what she's hoping for, at least where Sophie is concerned. It's all been arranged: Peggy's friend Candace will sleep in Sophie's room tonight, and Sophie will spend the night with Tam. Tomorrow morning Tam will drive them both to school. Peggy's shop is closed on Mondays, so she may or may not make the trip to Taos with her old friend.

But it's dawned on Sophie that Sunday night is a school night, which means Tam's mom will enforce an early bedtime, something Sophie's parents never bother to do. For Sophie the arrangement is an imposition; even worse, it's a raw deal. She'd like to weasel out of it, and though she knows a teepee isn't going to materialize—she told Ian as much just ten minutes before—it offers an excuse to grouse, to show her dissatisfaction. She pushes the subject: "Do you know how much they cost?"

"Teepees?" Peggy sits back on her haunches and considers. "Well, they aren't cheap, Sophie. You can't pick one up at Walmart or Home Depot. There's a company in Taos, Taos Teepees and Drums, something like that. Maybe a thousand dollars, more or less."

"I looked on the web," Sophie says, "or rather Ian did. The company he found is in Oregon. They made the teepees for *Dances with Wolves*. Awesome, huh?"

Peggy grunts. She wishes Sophie had a bed frame. Why doesn't Sophie have a bed frame?

Sophie persists: "Didn't you sleep in a teepee at Woodstock?"

Peggy sighs. "I didn't make it to Woodstock," she admits. She reaches for one of Sophie's pillows, flattened dingy things she should have replaced long ago. Peggy is wondering whether the pillows in her room are any better. Perhaps she should switch them out, at least for tonight.

Sophie is incredulous. "No way. That can't be. I remember you telling me about the Rolling Stones."

"The Rolling Stones didn't perform at Woodstock. That was Altamont."

"Did you go to Altamont?"

Peggy did not. She wasn't in California at the time.

"I could swear you went to Woodstock," Sophie says. "I've bragged about it. Tam thinks you were at Woodstock, and don't you dare tell her you weren't." She swings the dustrag in the air for emphasis. "What sort of hippie were you, anyway?"

Peggy sits back on the mattress. "Here are the facts: I was not present at Woodstock, nor were the Rolling Stones. On the other hand, our soon-to-be houseguest *was* in attendance, and so were Sly and the Family Stone." Peggy lingers on the final word, pleased with herself for thinking of it—rolling stone, family stone. She waits for Sophie's loud laugh, her usual reward for such wit.

Instead, she is confronted with teenage indignation. "So, Candace got to go and you didn't? What the fuck was that about?"

Automatically, Peggy's hands reach for the solace of her hair. She spends a soothing moment extracting the chopsticks from her hurried bun, releasing a coil of hair, then twisting the bun back into place again. While she is replacing the chopsticks, she slips and pokes the soft spot at the base of her skull, thereby losing whatever composure she has managed to attain.

"Money, Sophie," she explains. "I didn't have a cent to my name. No job, no car, no dinero." Peggy reaches for the laundry basket and, after dragging it closer, removes the top sheet, which she proceeds to shake out over the mattress. The sheet's white background is sprinkled with tiny pink flowers. She enjoys the task of smoothing it into place. For a second or two, she is lost in the smell of clean cotton enhanced with fabric softener.

Sophie isn't satisfied. "I'd have gone," she says grimly. "I wouldn't have let a little cash flow problem deter *me*."

"I'm sure you would have found a way," Peggy replies, though she doesn't believe it, not for an instant. Not this Sophie, a hothouse child if ever there was one, sheltered, coddled, allowed to believe first, last, and always in her own superiority. Sophie is special. But here's the irony: they all are. The whole generation is special, each and every one of them, and they have the trophies to prove it.

As it happens, Sophie is halfheartedly dusting one of her own trophies, a squat, plastic, mass-produced thing. If Peggy remembers correctly, the award was bestowed for a season of softball poorly played. Jack was the team's manager. Little League games were played on the fields behind the mission church, Our Lady of Guadalupe, and Peggy recalls that a girl on the team started each game by making the sign of the cross over her chest. Pretty soon, she had all of them doing it, even Sophie. Peggy advised Jack to put a stop to the ritual, but he declined. "We need all the help we can get," he had explained.

Tam had been on the team, too. She played second base to Sophie's outfield. Tam was the better athlete, but at the end of the season the girls received identical trophies. In what now strikes Peggy as a large-scale social experiment, her daughter's generation has been shielded from competition and encouraged not to keep score. At school it's much the same. Because of grade inflation, nearly all of them have managed their fair share of As. Last year's graduating class lauded seven valedictorians; the number was considered proof of a brainy bounty, not a sign of an educational system in distress. So what does "special" mean, Peggy wonders, if the term is sprinkled like sugar over the heads of one and all?

As Peggy shakes the flat pillows into pink pillowcases, Sophie is still grumbling about Woodstock. She seems to feel that she's been misled in the past, or that Peggy has made false claims. Sophie wonders aloud whether it's possible to address the deficiency, to rewind the tape. If so, she has a solution for her mother.

"Hitchhike! Why didn't you hitchhike?" If only Peggy had done so, Sophie could brag about it. "I can just see you holding up your cardboard sign!" She hesitates, then asks, "What state is Woodstock in, anyway?"

"New York," Peggy replies. "It's a challenge to get there if you don't know where it is."

"I'd have found it."

Life can be hard, darling, Peggy wants to say. But she doesn't.

A week has passed since the reading. Sophie is now about eight weeks pregnant. Still, nothing has been decided; nothing has been done. Earlier in the week Peggy had waited until Sophie finished up in the bathroom, called "Good night" down the hallway, then climbed the stairs quickly: thud, thud, thud. Peggy got out of bed and smiled faintly in her husband's direction. He was reading the newspaper, shuffling pages in the dim light. She doesn't know how he can see to read. More than once, she's asked him if he's nocturnal, part bat, maybe.

"Be right back," she told him. He didn't have any response.

Peggy climbed the stairs herself, quietly, and stood on the landing. She knew she should knock, but she didn't because she wasn't sure what to say or how to say it. What if Sophie raised her voice? What if Jack came upstairs and asked what was going on? Was it Jack whom Peggy feared, or Sophie? Was it the future or the past? Now the past is coming to visit. Peggy tosses the dirty sheets into the laundry basket, then, straightening up, basket in her arms, asks Sophie straight out: "Have you thought about what you want to do?"

Sophie is turned away again, peering out the window. "I've thought about it," she says. "Aside from the nausea, I don't feel that different.

It's weird because everything seems normal. But in the back of my mind, I'm dreading something—like I'm gonna get back a test, something I screwed up royally. I'm waiting to see that big, scrawled F across the top of the page, you know?"

Fucked, Peggy thinks. That's what the F stands for. "This isn't a test, Sophie," she says quietly, coming up behind her daughter. Brushing aside Sophie's thick, tangled curls, Peggy caresses her daughter's neck.

"Maybe it's not a test." Sophie twists away. "Maybe it's a bad dream. You know how when you have an awful dream, it's hard to shake? How it keeps surfacing at the oddest moments? That's the way this is. I'm having a decent day, walking from one class to the next, and I'm thinking about homework or something stupid Tam just told me and then all the sudden, *boom*, I remember: *Jesus, I'm pregnant.*"

They are both silent. Peggy hasn't stood this way, lined up behind her daughter, for some time, and she realizes that Sophie has grown at least a couple of inches in the last six months. She is now taller than her mother. Soon they won't be able to wear one another's clothes—or rather, Sophie won't be able to wear Peggy's clothes. With a jolt Peggy realizes that it isn't just her daughter's height that's changing.

"What does Will say?"

Sophie moans. "I put out some feelers, Peggy. I wanted to see where he'd come down. His dad's family is Catholic, so . . ."

"Maybe you shouldn't tell him, then, if you think he's not going to support your decision." Peggy isn't sure of what she's saying. She isn't sure of what she's doing, leaving out first Jack and now Will. But she doesn't see how sharing this news could improve the picture.

"If I go to Planned Parenthood," Sophie says softly, "will you go with me?"

Peggy resists the impulse to touch her again. "Of course I will," she replies.

"I'll call to make an appointment for counseling," Sophie says. "I'll probably have to miss my first and second classes. . . ."

"I'll write you a note," Peggy offers, then rushes on, reassessing, "It's a doctor's appointment, or it might as well be. Here's the thing, Sophie: I would rather not worry your dad, and that means I'll need to figure out the money. But I will. Leave it to me."

Sophie is sniffling. Within a few seconds, she's sobbing, using the dustrag to blow her nose. "I wish this weren't so hard," she says. "It's making me emo, Peggy. I'm turning into some kind of freak."

By the time Candace is due to arrive, Peggy is tired, but the house is cleaner than it has been in months, maybe years. The brick floors have been vacuumed and wet-mopped, the bathroom cleaned, the cobwebs swept out of the corners of rooms. The orange counters in the kitchen have been wiped down, the dining table sprayed with Pledge, the front porch swept. The trees are just beginning to drop their leaves, but in the corners of the porch Peggy discovered drifts with more leaves than she could account for by looking around the yard. Is it possible, she'd wondered, that she had let more than a year go by without sweeping the porch?

This last year has been such a trial. Peggy's mother was hospitalized twice, with symptoms that defied any sort of diagnosis. Twice in one month the Granger household had been turned upside down, first by Sophie's sixteenth birthday on March 13, then again, a short week later, by Jack's walking heart attack. Nothing went according to plan that month, not even the emergence of the spring bulbs.

Six months earlier, in a mood of optimism and even gratitude, Peggy had spent an entire solitary Saturday digging holes all over the front lawn and filling them with bulbs and a pinch of manure. The grass was spotty anyway, so why not create a spring garden? The idea had come from *Sunset* magazine. Occasionally Peggy rouses herself to try the magazine's recipes or modest home-improvement projects. A can of yellow paint and five evenly spaced towel hooks were all she needed to perk up the bathroom. Why not perk up the front yard?

Sophie has loved daffodils since childhood, and the flowers would be a surprise, something she would always remember as a harbinger of her sixteenth birthday. Peggy went all out, planting several different varieties: Thalia, yellow hoop petticoats, and a miniature version called tête-à-tête. On the day she planted them, Ian was the only person home. He was entirely indifferent to yard work. She could scratch about in the dirt all day, and he'd never ask a single question. In fact, he would pretend not to notice, in order not to be asked to assist.

February of 2007 had turned out to be colder than usual, but Peggy was actually grateful for the unseasonable chill. The later the warm weather arrived, the closer the daffodils would come to blooming on Sophie's birthday. Once March first rolled around, the weather seemed auspicious. A rise in temperature coaxed sharp tips of green to puncture the hard ground, and the stems followed. She kept a close eye on the flowers' progress, surprised but not displeased that no one else noticed the front lawn's new look. Most often, the Grangers use the side door that opens onto the kitchen. They drive right past the front of the house and park on the side. Even when they're walking—and Sophie and Ian are often on foot—they enter through the kitchen. That door opens and shuts all day, but unless a visitor or, rarely, a solicitor rings the bell, the front door remains closed.

Then there was a bit of bad luck in the weather department. On the very afternoon when the first buds were set to unfurl, winds blew in from the north. They held the city captive for days on end. In Albuquerque, mornings and evenings are usually calm, but for two days and two nights, the wind persisted, and everything and everyone—plants, animals, and the unfortunate landscaper or road worker—was pelted with sand. Only a few of the daffodils ever opened. The petals were fresh for an hour or so, before they were shredded into delicate yellow confetti.

Peggy never bothered to mention the flowers to Sophie. All she could hope for was that the bulbs would have enough energy to bloom again.

She would be the first to admit that these days it takes a visitor to motivate any sort of wholesale cleaning. Her daughter and son will help, but only if they are pressed to do so. Both supervision and some sort of reward are necessary. Money is best, though now that Sophie has a learner's permit she is also motivated by the chance to drive, to accrue fifty hours in the presence of a licensed driver over the age of twenty-one. This morning, Sophie even deigned to accompany her mother to Whole Foods for avocadoes and onions, cheese and tortillas, cilantro and tomatoes. She drove back home as well, proceeding slowly and cautiously down Carlisle Boulevard to Menaul. Sophie insisted on recording the drive as an hour, when it was certainly a good deal less than that, but Peggy was willing to fudge it a little. In return, Sophie made the guacamole. Now, with a minimum of grousing, she has been dispensed to Tam's house.

Because Jack and Ian are still at the fixer-upper, it appears Peggy and Candace will have time alone. For a minute or two, Peggy stands and tries to see her little kingdom from Candace's eyes. No doubt it's obvious that the kitchen is badly in need of an update. The orange Formica counters date back to the sixties, and the scarred and dusty cabinets are a disgrace. Then there's the dishwasher, or rather the empty space where a dishwasher used to be. It gave up the ghost a good year ago, and they have yet to replace it. On the plus side, she can point to a nearly new stainless-steel refrigerator. Appliances always go in threes; the refrigerator broke down shortly after the hot-water heater and dishwasher.

Peggy is proud of the china hutch on the other side of the dining table. It's a Southwestern piece, handmade by someone she used to know in Taos. While it took him a helluva long time to grow up and settle down, the guy has become a skilled craftsman. Peggy is reasonably sure Candace will have the good sense to admire the hutch, though this need for affirmation from a friend she rarely sees makes Peggy squirm. Why is she so self-conscious at such an advanced age? What difference does it make if Candace approves of her house or her housekeeping or her marriage, for Christ's sake? But for some reason, it does make a difference.

In the years since she returned to Boston, Candace has devoted herself to the world of antiques. She's a buyer at estate sales; her expertise is in French furniture. Her aunt Agnes, with whom she lived for years, had a whole houseful of French furniture. After Agnes passed away, the task of cleaning out the house and selling most of its furniture fell to Candace. She found that she enjoyed it. "I like old things, I like old people, I like old music," she's fond of saying. And by "old" she doesn't mean classic rock. She prefers Lena Horne to Carol King, Nat King Cole to Neil Young.

Although the calendar says it's October 14, the weather is unseasonably warm—it feels more like summer than fall—and therefore glorious. Peggy has thrown open the front door. When she hears the crunch of gravel, she goes out to the porch and waits as a small white Chevrolet approaches.

"Good grief!" Peggy says aloud. "You drive like an old woman!"

Candace is peering through the windshield, hands gripping the steering wheel. At the sight of Peggy, she brakes and stops the car right there on the gravel road, turns off the ignition, and steps out. "I'm not used to driving," she says. "It's not really necessary in Boston."

She's dressed for New England, in a loose-weave, red-and-gray poncho; black corduroy slacks; and red cowboy boots. Candace's look has changed over the years, but evidently her penchant for dressing up hasn't. It used to be that some of them would tease her about it, but in a good-natured way. No one wanted to alienate her—no one who might need her help, that is. And most of them did, or would, or might.

In a group photo from that period, taken outside the Mabel Dodge Luhan House, Candace is seated with her back against a post. Nearly twenty of the town's leading hippies posed for the photo, and no one else held a candle to Candace, not when it came to couture. She's wearing a ruffled skirt, a concho belt, and a fitted velvet vest over a white blouse with full sleeves. She's the only woman in the picture to don a hat; hers is a black beret carefully arranged on the back of her head, the part in her long blonde hair clearly visible.

Peggy doesn't remember the occasion, though she's in the photo, too. Like Candace, Peggy wore her hair long and straight back then, parted down the middle and tucked behind her ears. The shot must have been taken either in late fall or early spring—some are wearing short sleeves, whereas others have on jackets and ponchos. Peggy is sporting the Frye boots that got her through three winters in Taos. They were virtually indestructible, and good thing. She couldn't have afforded to replace them.

Beau is in the photo, too. He stands in the back row, a cowboy hat cocked on his head. The brim casts a shadow over his eyes, making it impossible to judge his expression.

After the two friends hug, Candace steps back and stands blinking and peering about. "I always forget how brilliant it is here!" she exclaims. "So bright you could swear heaven is just over the horizon. Do you ever feel that way?"

Peggy smiles and ushers Candace inside. "Not really," she says. "I'm used to it. But Jack was in Vermont a week or so ago, and he had something of the same reaction there. 'Dazed,' he said. 'Drunk on the greenery.'"

They pause in the hallway. Candace throws out her arms as though for balance. "Goodness," she says. "Now I can't see a thing."

"We'll just stay here while your eyes adjust," Peggy replies, patting Candace's shoulder. She is struck by the soft weave of the poncho, the silky feel of it beneath her fingers. Like most beautiful things, it's fragile.

"It's good to see you!" Candace blurts out, then: "Well, it *will* be good to see you, once my eyes adjust. I had the odd sense as the plane was landing that I was coming home. Isn't that strange?"

Peggy takes her friend's hand, dry to the touch and warm, and leads her down the hallway.

"Sometimes I've been thrilled by the sheer immensity of this part of the country," Candace continues, "and sometimes I've been scared out of my wits by the sheer emptiness of it. But it's never been home to me, not even when I lived here."

Quickly, Peggy remembers how much Candace likes to talk; they're well-suited because Peggy prefers to listen. She sits her friend down at one end of the long wooden table, asks whether Candace prefers white or red, then pours a glass of sauvignon blanc. After a few minutes of chitchat, she gets busy preparing dinner. As usual she's lost track of time, forgotten how long it takes to assemble enchiladas and prepare them for the oven. If they aren't baking when Jack gets home, he'll be pissy. He hates to eat late, says it gives him heartburn. Peggy has her own theory: she thinks he'd be fine if he just stopped grousing and grumping so much. "Try serenity," she's suggested, but she might as well prescribe a joint before dinner. These days he turns his nose up at anything hippy-dippy, and serenity certainly qualifies.

Within the hour, Candace has shed the poncho and slung it on the back of a chair. She's busy describing an estate sale she attended recently, a charity event that featured some of Caroline Kennedy's cast-offs. When Peggy turns around to comment, she notices that the poncho has slid to the floor—and that Lucy is preparing to curl up on top of it. The dog is circling meditatively. Before Peggy can act, Lucy sighs and drops her haunches.

"Oh, for heaven's sake!" Peggy cries.

Leave it to Lucy to make the most of the moment. As Peggy approaches, waving her arms, the golden retriever yelps like she's been hit. But she doesn't move an inch. She seems too confused, too frightened to heed the instructions Peggy is shouting in her direction. "Lucille Ball, get up!" Hearing her full name, the dog cowers, but that is the extent of her response.

Absently, Candace leans over and strokes Lucy's velvety ear. "Don't worry, Peggy," she says amiably. "You know how I love dogs." Once the poncho has been extricated, more or less covered with dog hair, Peggy suggests that Candace hang the elegantly woven garment on the coatrack in the corner. She gestures in the general direction, then returns to the cutting board and the onions she's lined up, one purple and two Vidalia.

During the two years Peggy spent at Morningstar, any number of dogs roamed the premises. The most memorable was Beau's three-legged border collie, a black-and-white wonder named Moby. It was amazing what an animal without a limb could get away with. Moby had shadowed Beau's loping figure into grocery stores and restaurants, through doorways ordinary dogs never darkened. Occasionally a manager or waiter would chase him out, but most often they simply looked the other way.

At night Moby slept next to Beau on a lumpy mattress in the back of a rusty VW bus. That ruin of a vehicle—Beau's home away from home—had been permanently parked at a drunken angle only a few feet from the front door of Morningstar's main building. It looked as though the van had run out of gas just as it was about to batter the wall. Remembering all of this and more, Peggy pauses halfway through chopping, drops the knife on the cutting board, and turns around. She's weeping, and though she swears it's just the pungent onions, Candace isn't so sure.

"What?" Candace asks, her eyes shining. "What? What? Tell me!" She is more than ready to take a trip back in time, and Peggy is the perfect companion.

"I was just thinking about Moby." They both know what that means:

she is thinking about Beau, too. Dog and young man were inseparable, in life and now in death.

Candace sighs. "So, I still haven't told you why I'm here, have I?"

"No, you haven't."

"Someone wants to buy my land."

Peggy is taken aback. She's quiet for a moment, having resumed her chopping. Then she manages to ask her question: "Did you have it up for sale?"

"No! That's the crazy, out-of-the-blue part. What do you think? I can't make this decision by myself, Peg."

"You're not planning to come back here, are you?"

Candace shrugs. "I've thought of summering in Taos, building a casita somewhere close to where the main building used to be."

"That thing just melted away, didn't it?"

"Yeah, it did. Just goes to show that there's more to making adobe bricks than we might have imagined."

Peggy smiles to herself, recalling the scene: the beautiful, long-haired, bare-chested men toiling, the young women clutching raised skirts as they danced barefoot in the mud pits. Had it actually been that sexy, or was that simply the way the whole world appeared to her then? She remembers the squish of the red mud between her toes and one of the other women—Candace?—pouring buckets of water, while three or four friends twirled and laughed and toppled into the muddy mess. "Is this what it's like to make wine?" someone had asked, which led to a discussion of grape vines and the suitability of both the climate and the soil. "We could start a winery," Jimbo said, to which everyone responded in unison: "FAR OUT!"

Back in the day, the main house had resembled an outpost, a set for a John Wayne movie. Having lived her whole life in Waco, Texas, Peggy had been astonished by the enormity of northern New Mexico. So beautiful and unforgiving, she thought. It was the sort of place Wayne would attempt to tame, battling Indians and inclement weather and cattle rustlers. She didn't need to see the movie; it didn't need to exist. She knew just how it would end: Wayne would die in the arms of his sobbing costar, a woman with breasts ample enough to cradle his hard head.

Evidently John Wayne was stubborn to a fault, like most of the men Peggy has known in real life.

Time changes everything, Peggy thinks. On the cold March day when the group of mourners hiked up to scatter Beau's ashes, Jimbo and Denise had lagged behind, both of them hopelessly out of shape. Peggy and Candace arrived well ahead of the others and had time to survey the remains of the main building, which by then was little more than a mound of mud. Even the best adobe requires maintenance, and they'd abandoned the place, all of them.

Candace has an announcement to make. "Would you believe a movie star wants the land?"

"No!" Peggy cries. Here she was just thinking of John Wayne, though it can't be him; he's been dead for years. Of course, she shouldn't be surprised. Taos has always drawn its fair share of luminaries. "Who is it?" she asks. Some people would be better than others, certainly.

But Candace doesn't know. She hasn't yet weaseled that information out of the cagey real estate agent. "He was so smug, Peg. He said, 'We'll reveal names when the time comes.'"

"Well, you can't possibly sell to just any old celebrity!"

The wine has emboldened Candace—that and her indignation. She's ready to call the agent and demand some answers, but Peggy deters her. She needs Candace to sauté the onions. "Jack will be here any minute," she says quietly, "and I promised I'd have the enchiladas in the oven by the time he got home."

Candace hasn't heard about Jack's heart attack, and Peggy fills her in, giving her a little background information as the two of them move about the kitchen. It feels good to talk, to share her worries and frustration. Generally she muses on these things alone, and it's hard to get perspective that way.

"Jack has been going through a rough patch at work," she says. She heats the griddle on the stovetop and begins lining the rectangular space with corn tortillas. Then she heads to the refrigerator and digs around in one of the drawers for the bags of shredded cheese. She's glad now that she didn't opt to do the shredding herself. They'd be eating at midnight if she hadn't cut a few corners.

"Is he okay?"

Peggy shrugs. "I guess so, but he's had it. He stepped down from his administrative job and he's back in the classroom." She holds up a hand, fingers splayed. "Five classes, he's teaching. It's not exactly optimal, you know, not for someone who's sixty and recovering from a heart attack. He wants out. Or anyway, he wants me to shoulder more of the load."

Candace has sidled back over to the table, where she is nursing her wine. "Anything else I can do?" she asks.

She's talking about dinner preparations, but Peggy can't help thinking in larger terms. During her whole life, Candace has never faced a similar situation. If she doesn't want to work, she doesn't. If she wants to get on a plane and fly to Albuquerque, she does. She doesn't have to worry about keeping a job that offers health insurance, nor does she need to plan for retirement. She can sell her land, or she can hold onto it. She is free to choose. Peggy takes a slug of her wine, swallowing the bitterness she tastes, willing herself to remember that Candace may have money but she doesn't have family. And which would you rather have? The answer should be easy, but envy gets in the way of equanimity. Candace often has this effect on her, Peggy tells herself. She has to get past it.

Candace fills the tortillas with a cheese-and-onion mixture and rolls them tight, whereupon Peggy douses them with green chile sauce. By the time Jack and Ian arrive, dinner is well in hand. The two women have poured second glasses, and they're laughing about the way waiters describe wine. Peggy has just given her favorite example: a young man at Seasons, a trendy upscale place in Old Town, described a pinot grigio the way someone else might expound on the view from a cabin window. There were rocks, flowers, a babbling brook. "Autumn in the air!" Peggy exclaims. "If I'm not mistaken, he actually included the quality of the light."

"I've had wine that good," Candace replies, "the sort that transports you elsewhere. In France. In France the wine is sometimes that good."

Peggy frowns. "But you were already transported, by airplane. You were there, someplace wonderful, drinking wine." She has never been to France. She has never been anywhere, really, certainly not anywhere outside the United States. "Wine would always taste better in France, don't you think?"

Candace shakes her head, but before she can elaborate, Ian pushes open the door and enters. He appears disgruntled. His jaw is set, his pale skin flushed with anger. When he takes note of his mother and her friend at the table, their eyes on him, he smiles ruefully.

"Hey!" he says.

Underneath the table, Lucy stirs, then heaves herself to her feet. Her wagging tail hits the table leg—whap, whap, whap.

"Hey!" Candace echoes. "You must be Ian."

"Good guess," he replies. He comes closer but halts a few feet from the table. He's wearing sweat pants and a forest-green T-shirt that advertises the UNIVERSITY OF VERMONT. "I'm dirty," he says. "I may have black widows in my pockets." Before they can inquire, he heads down the hall to the bathroom.

"Are you two drunk?" Jack asks. His overalls are stained, his work boots unlaced. His steel-gray hair is brushed back from his broad, lined forehead. He looks weary but satisfied with the day's work.

Candace replies that they're not drunk. "We waited for you," she says.

"Well, you can wait for me a little longer while I go move your car. You left it in the middle of the road!" He holds out a hand for the keys. Candace retrieves them from her bag and tosses them in his direction. He shakes his head as he retreats down the hallway.

As soon as he's gone, the two women burst out laughing. Neither of them gave the car another thought once they got inside the house.

When Jack returns a few minutes later, he drops into a chair by the door and begins the task of removing his boots. Over the years, Peggy has tried to discourage this habit, instilled in him by his mother. Jack was raised in a house with a mudroom or winter porch, rooms with lines of hooks for coats and scarves, open floors for boots and skis, benches for sitting, and boxes or baskets for holding gloves and hats. But this is New Mexico, where the only thing Jack is likely to track into the house is sand, of the same texture and color as the stuff Peggy played with as a child. Jack lived out his whole childhood without ever entering a sandbox, but he visited the seashore every summer. On the other hand, Peggy was twenty before she saw the ocean.

Fellow New Englanders, Candace and Jack have their familiarity with the ocean in common, but very little else. He is certain she's the next best thing to a Boston Brahmin, a wealthy snob, and she can smell his disdain. There's friction, sure, but mostly there's friendly ribbing. "Why are you taking off your boots before you hug your visitor?" Candace asks, getting things started. "Didn't your momma teach you mann-ahs?"

"Manners? You know she didn't, Miss Candace," Jack replies. He is a little out of breath from the effort of wresting the boots from his feet, but he wants to hide this fact from their guest. "I'm from Brattleboro, not Boston."

"So I recall."

Jack smiles at his wife. "Smells good in here," he says. Then, "Bet it's been a while since you've had any good chile, eh Candace?"

As a rule, New Mexicans are chile snobs, something Candace knows well. "Definitely," she replies. Then she asks where he and Ian have been.

Jack glances at his wife, who has her back to him. She's busy tearing open a bag of tortilla chips and dumping them into a pottery bowl. "Peggy didn't tell you?"

"I'm sure she would have, eventually. We've been catching up, and there's a lot of it to do."

Peggy arrives at the table with two bowls, a large one for chips and a matching smaller one for salsa. Her expression is decidedly neutral. He can't tell whether she's been listening, so he tests her: "I've bought a house." Seeing the twitching of Peggy's eyebrows, he amends the statement. "*We've* bought a house. An investment, a handyman special, a fixer-upper. I'm doing the repairs and the remodeling. Getting a jump-start on retirement. Sundays I drag Ian along, teach him a little of this and that—how to wield a paintbrush, how to hammer a nail. Do we have any guacamole?" He's holding a chip in the air, and he uses it to make a dipping motion.

"Yes," Peggy replies. "Sophie made it. It's in the refrigerator."

"I'll get it, Peggy," Candace offers. She scoots away from the table and heads over to the refrigerator. After peeling away the Saran Wrap, she carries the bowl to the table, cradling it in two hands. The pottery is hand-thrown, distinctive both for its coloring—a mingling of tan, orange, and peach—and for the row of ridges along its belly. It's deep and squat and marred by a chip in its lip.

"This bowl is so familiar," Candace says, "and not just the look of it. The feel of it." She hefts it in her hands and gazes down at it.

"It was yours," Peggy tells her. "You left it behind after you and Beau got married. It was part of the Morningstar kitchen for as long as I lived there, and when I moved, I took it with me."

Candace smiles. "A souvenir?" she says.

It takes Peggy a second to comprehend the word because Candace doesn't pronounce the r. And does she say it with a little sneer? Peggy hopes not; she hopes she's imagining things. "Yes," she replies, "a souvenir."

Jack digs right into the guacamole. He might be listening, or he might not be. "Good stuff," he says, then, "Where is Sophie?"

Peggy has already explained to Jack that Candace will be staying in Sophie's room, but she is quick to repeat the explanation.

"I know, I know," Jack responds. "But she could be here for dinner, to meet Candace." He looks puzzled, and something more—guarded, perhaps? Peggy's heartbeat picks up. She can feel a flush coming over her face. "Belinda's ordering pizza. They've got homework to do. Let's just leave it be, shall we?"

"Whatever you say, Peggy," Jack replies.

She was thirty-five when she got pregnant with Sophie. By that time she'd been off birth control for several years. They'd begun discussing other ways of creating a family—adoption, mostly, but surrogates, too. The more Peggy couldn't get pregnant, the more she wanted to. Jack knew the problem was probably his because the pattern was the same in his parent's marriage: one child came after all hope was gone. In his parents' case, that child had been Jack. (His sister Gwen was a half sister, his mother's daughter from an earlier marriage.) In his own marriage, the one child was Ian. Not that they'd ever discussed it. If truth be told, Jack wasn't sure he wanted to know.

"I, for one, am disappointed," Candace says. Neither Jack nor Peggy replies. Even so, she decides to finish her thought. "I mean, I'm glad to meet Ian and all, but I was hoping to meet Sophie as well."

Ian's room is the smallest of the four bedrooms in the house. Strictly speaking it's not a bedroom at all, since it doesn't have a closet. At one time the whole upstairs was open space, large and airy, with a hardwood floor and a wall of westward-facing windows. The original owner cut a door into the east wall; he had plans to construct outdoor stairs. He wanted a game room and a separate entrance for his guests, which would allow them to bypass the scowling countenance of his wife. But then he got a divorce, his wife got the house, and the door was no longer necessary. The stairs, being an additional expense, never materialized.

Later, after the house was sold to its second owners, the upstairs floor was apportioned unequally. A wall was erected that divided one quarter of the space, creating a narrow rectangular room that served as a closet for Christmas decorations. When Peggy and Jack became the third owners, they'd joked that they would be a disappointment to their nearest neighbors, who would miss the annual appearance of a rooftop Santa and his reindeer. Jack was not one to string lights, so the small room remained empty.

During their first few years in the house, Jack and Peggy had only Sophie. Then Ian came along. That's the way they always spoke of his birth: *Ian came along*, as though a stranger stopped in and inexplicably, though not unhappily, took up residence. The Christmas closet made a pleasant-enough nursery. When Ian was a little older, Jack and Peggy took measures to ensure his safety. Together they shoved a heavy dresser against the blue door to nowhere, and Jack installed a sliding lock, one well above the reach of small children.

Now that Ian is twelve, he has seen fit to move the dresser to the middle of the room, the only space it can occupy without blocking the bed or the window. Sure, it's awkward, but this way he can open the outside door if he feels like it. At first he was simply invested in taking things— that is, the dresser and what it represented—into his own hands, but now that the door is unobstructed, he often finds reasons to throw it open. On summer evenings he and Sophie sometimes sit together, shoulder to shoulder, legs and feet dangling, gazing into the night sky.

When Candace appears in his doorway to call him to dinner, Ian is sitting on the floor in front of the open door.

"Hey," he says, glancing up from the printouts spread on the floor around him.

"Dinner's ready," she announces.

He's made his bed in honor of her visit. Not that he expected her to see it. Most often, company never makes it to his room. Long ago he accepted the fact that his efforts would be wasted—the run-of-the-mill grown-up doesn't find him particularly interesting—but his mother insists that he straighten up regardless.

Candace surprises him, then, when she edges around the dresser and takes a seat on his bed. "What are you looking at?"

He shrugs. He's researching teepees: costs, sizes, and availability. The pages spread out before him have been pulled from websites. Various teepees are depicted. Some are decorated with buffalo and horses, others with stars and stripes. Lodgepoles hold them upright, creating the iconic cylindrical shape. It's been years since Candace has laid eyes on one. Bostonians have no use, and no room, for them.

"Do you like teepees?" Candace inquires. The sight of a teepee makes her nostalgic, even downright wistful.

"I like the idea of them."

She leans over and squints at the images lined up across the bottom of one of the pages. "I used to have one," she tells him. "Or rather, my husband did."

Ian nods. "I know. I've seen pictures of it." He's seen only one photograph, the one hidden away in his father's underwear drawer. Ian supposes the photo is hidden because Peggy is topless in it, but the truth is both simpler and more complicated: Jack swiped the photo many years ago, long before Ian was born. "It was awesome."

"Really?" Candace reaches around the dresser to tousle his hair, raising a stale smell from his whitish mop. She's thinking aloud now. "I might still have it in storage."

"Really?" His loud response startles her into bumping her head on the dresser. He turns immediately solicitous: "You okay?"

Tears well up in her eyes. She wonders what's wrong with her. Is it the room? It's so confining. No wonder Ian dreams of a teepee, she thinks—it's something he can pack up and carry from place to place.

"I'll check when I get home," she promises, and before she can prepare for the embrace, he turns and throws his arms around her, knocking her sideways. She topples onto the bed. The pillowcase, too, she notes, reeks of his dirty hair. But she doesn't mind. She doesn't mind at all.

At dinner Candace asks Ian to be "a good little man" and pour her a glass of wine. The bottle is closest to Peggy, who holds it out and advises Ian to be careful. His mother expects him to make a mess of things, but Ian decides to ignore Peggy and focus entirely on her friend. He fills the glass a little less than half-full, the way they do in the movies. As he rights the bottle, he feels Candace's gaze on him. A warmth spreads through his body.

He's carrying the bottle away when she grabs his arm and pulls him back to her. "Don't you ever go outside?" she asks. "Look how pale you are! How is that possible, with the sun beating down the way it does here?"

"I don't brown," he says. "I just burn. I was outside all afternoon, but I had on sunscreen."

"Nordic genes," Candace replies. "I know just what you mean."

Jack finishes the food on his plate and the beer he poured to go with it. When he excuses himself, he explains that he needs to see to the bees. He doesn't, of course. The bees neither want nor need his tending. Still, it's a pleasant pretext.

"Want to come with me?" He directs the question to Ian, who replies with a tight little shake of his head.

Jack means well. He isn't trying to torture his son, though it certainly seems that way to Ian. Take earlier today, for instance. The morning began congenially, because Ian wore the new T-shirt his father had brought home from his visit to Vermont. For an hour or two after arriving at the casita, they were simpatico. Jack allowed Ian to use his best screwdriver. He put the boy to work in the larger of the two bedrooms, removing screws and disassembling the curtain rods over the three windows.

That was okay, but when Ian finished the task, Jack immediately assigned him another: now he was to pick up the rubbish on the left side of the casita. For some time, the space between the house and the ditch has served as a dumping ground for cardboard boxes, stray bricks, rusty pipes, and rolled and rusty chicken wire. Jack was explicit in his instructions: "Fill the wheelbarrow and transport the trash to the dumpster in the driveway. Wear these leather gloves. Sure, they're too big for you, but they'll protect your hands from rusty nails and cranky black widows. You're going to see some black widows, Ian. No doubt about it. And I want you to kill them, hear me son?"

Ian's skin crawled. He protested. He didn't want this particular job. Why couldn't his father find something else for him to do? But Jack's mind was made up. After a lengthy lecture on the importance of mastering your fears, Jack went indoors. Ian sighed and rolled the wheelbarrow to the side of the casita. Gingerly he picked up the largest piece of cardboard and peered underneath. This was the North Valley, so he knew he'd see snails and any number of pill bugs, but he was on the lookout for the telltale messy web of the black widow. The spider herself would be in hiding, her long legs curled around that plump black abdomen etched with a red hourglass.

He'd seen dozens of black widows, and he knew their habits. They'd be lurking close by but out of sight. He wouldn't get a chance to stomp on them as he might if, say, a wolf spider were to make an appearance. No, the black widow would be secreted inside a pipe or concealed in a crevice. He could picture it: he'd pick up a brick and the damn thing would scuttle into his oversized glove. The thought of it sent a shiver through him. Ian has an active imagination.

His plan was to calm the black widows. That's what his dad did with the bees: he smoked them to make them docile. What worked with bees would probably have the same effect on spiders—so Ian reasoned, anyway. His father kept a smoker in the back of the station wagon. Although Ian knew Jack generally burned horse manure, Ian didn't have any handy. Instead, he used newspaper. Jack had stowed the Sunday paper in the backseat of the car, and Ian pulled out some of the ads to use as kindling. He wadded them nicely, jammed the ads in the smoker, lit them with a match, and replaced the cone-shaped top with the hole in it. The smoke would be emitted from the hole when Ian squeezed the bellows.

He was just getting started when the neighbor who lives in front spotted the smoke and came running. She assumed all that rubbish had caught fire. Ian heard her at the front door wailing and banging; then his father came tearing around the corner. Jack grabbed the smoker and cussed up a storm. You'd have thought Ian had done the worst thing in the world! For the rest of the afternoon, they didn't speak. Even their lunch at Taco Bell was consumed silently as they sat in the fast-food chain's parking lot, the two of them chewing and staring through the dirty windshield at the street in front of them.

Recently a kindly teacher had taken the time to reassure Ian. "Some people have issues with insects. We don't choose our fears any more than we choose our vices. Our task in life is to tame them," she explained, then patted him on the back. "Don't worry about the taming part yet," she said, a relief, really, because he had already identified another of his vices, and he'd been giving it full rein.

Ian is a snoop. When his mother is out of the room, he is apt to go through her purse. He has rifled through his sister's backpack and his father's wallet. He reads the mail lying out on the kitchen table. He knows, for instance, the amount of water the family consumed last month, as well as the results of his mother's most recent mammogram. Occasionally he's picked up the extension and listened in on random phone calls. He needs to do these things. He doesn't ask himself why.

The door to nowhere comes in handy for eavesdropping. Having left it open earlier, Ian can't resist the temptation to listen in on his mother and Candace, who've finished cleaning up the dinner dishes and are relaxing on the porch. Their voices rise up to him, and so does the sweet reek of marijuana smoke. He's come across it a few times, in the restroom at school, for instance, or lingering in the backseat of Tam's car. But not at home. Jack must be asleep, Ian thinks. In fact, his father has slipped out to the fixer-upper.

"After Beau died," Candace is saying, "I thought I'd never sleep with another man, but only four months after we scattered his ashes, I woke up in some stranger's bed. Slunk home and tried to forget about it— what little I remembered in the first place."

"It's understandable," Peggy replies. Her voice is soft, but Ian is familiar with his mother's modulations and can make out the words. "I'm sure it was just a way of assuaging your grief."

"So I told myself," Candace says. "But here's the thing, Peggy: these days, a mistake like that can get you AIDS."

Peggy takes a minute to absorb the message. "Wow! You're right. I worry about Sophie, but I've never been concerned about myself. Been out of circulation too long, you know? Just think," she muses, "how AIDS would have changed the sixties."

"I don't know about you, but I wouldn't have been sleeping around. I did it to be agreeable. Because I felt sorry for someone or because I needed a place to sleep, but not because I was craving sex." Candace is thinking aloud. "We got screwed!" she says. "Old lady. *Old lady!* Remember that term of endearment?" She fakes a man's voice: "'Wanna be my old lady?'" Then resumes in hers, "We did that to ourselves, Peggy. Labeled ourselves as old ladies, allowed men to pass us around like—this doobie."

They lapse into silence. Then Peggy thinks aloud. "Kids are stupid. We were, but so are kids today. It comes with the territory." She goes quiet again. She clears her throat and says something that gets Ian's full attention: "Take Sophie, for instance."

He scoots forward an inch or two. Any more and he's apt to pitch face first into the darkness.

"What about Sophie?"

"She's pregnant."

Ian isn't all that surprised by the news, but Candace is stunned. "You're kidding me! In this day and age? It's so unnecessary."

"Agreed. Absolutely unnecessary. I'm sick about it."

Candace's tone turns soothing. "Of course you are." Then, again, "Of course. What does she want to do?"

Peggy hesitates, her thoughts returning to Candace's bad experience. But that was so long ago, before *Roe v. Wade* even. Ancient history, surely. "Planned Parenthood," Peggy replies. "She has an appointment for counseling next week."

"Thank goodness she has a choice."

Upstairs, Ian quietly closes his door. The lull of their voices makes him sleepy. When no one was looking, he had slipped a glass of wine. It's been a difficult day, as Sundays at the fixer-upper usually are. But it did end reasonably well. His mother's friend may still have her teepee, and what's more awesome, she actually offered it to him! He's dreaming of teepees even before his eyes are closed.

Downstairs, Peggy is talking. The wine and pot have loosened her tongue and she's telling Candace how close Sophie is to her father, how at first she wanted to get Jack's take on the pregnancy, but now she's done an about-face and she doesn't want him to know. "She's embarrassed. Sophie's such a daddy's girl. But I'm not sure how I'm going to find the money on the sly." And then, for good measure: "Not to mention that money's a little tight around here right now. . . . Jack and his fixer-upper. . . ."

Candace replies exactly as Peggy hoped she would. "Let me help out, Peggy. Really, I don't mind at all."

The relief Peggy feels comes in only slightly ahead of her resentment. Once again it's Candace to the rescue. Will the time never come when Peggy is the one in a position to give? She admonishes herself: Why does it matter? Sophie will keep her secret and have her procedure, and if Peggy feels a little humiliated in the process, so be it. She'll wrap up the chipped pottery bowl and mail it back to its owner. A souvenir indeed!

A few minutes later, just as they've both agreed that the air is feeling chilly, just as they've made up their minds to head inside and get ready for bed, the women hear the crunch of gravel. Seconds later, the headlights of a car appear down the lane. It approaches slowly, perhaps because it's Sophie behind the wheel. She's driving Tam's car illegally, since Tam—who is in the passenger seat—isn't twenty-one.

Whereas Peggy felt downright drunk a moment before, the realization that her daughter has arrived sobers her right up. Sophie parks on the other side of the house, and it takes another minute or two for the two girls to appear out of the darkness. Sophie yells, "Busted! Two old ladies smoking weed. I smelled it all the way down Guadalupe Trail."

Candace snorts and whispers an aside to Peggy: "Once an old lady, always an old lady." She reaches over, intending to punch her friend in the arm, but her aim is off. Her fist travels past Peggy's scrawny bicep and lands in the soft flesh of her breast. "Oh hell," she says. "I'm sorry."

Peggy doesn't notice. For the time being, she has stopped feeling.

"Busted!" Sophie shouts again.

"Hush, Sophie," Peggy hisses. "You'll wake the neighborhood."

Sophie spins in a circle. "What neighborhood?"

It's true. The Granger home is accessible only by a gravel road. The nearest houses are a third to a half a mile away. It would take a firecracker or a gunshot to make any impression.

The two young women are silhouettes, hardly visible in the gloom. Rather than gather on the porch with the "old ladies," they drop onto the steps with their backs to Peggy and Candace.

"Hello, Peggy," Tam says as she takes her seat. She's always well-mannered, and tonight is no exception. She goes on to introduce herself to Candace, a shadowy figure on the other side of the porch. "I'm Sophie's friend."

Peggy hopes it may still be possible to send them back into the night. "I thought you two were sleeping at Tam's," she says in a carefully modulated voice. "Remember? We agreed. Candace is sleeping in Sophie's room—"

Candace interrupts, "I don't want to cause—"

"We're on to Plan B," Sophie butts in. "Belinda freaked out. The worst thing in the world happened. Are you ready? Tam broke the vacuum cleaner! Ran over the cord and sent sparks flying all over the living room. Did Belinda worry about Tam's welfare? *No.* You'd think we destroyed the last vacuum cleaner on the planet." Sophie shakes her head. "Crazy-crazy," she concludes.

"Is not," Tam counters, taking Belinda's side as usual. "She was upset. And you made it worse by yelling at her."

Peggy groans. "You yelled at Belinda's mother?"

"Duh, *Tam's* mother," Sophie replies. "And just because I raised my voice doesn't mean I was yelling."

Tam gets up to go. "Sorry, everyone. I'm grounded. Got to get home. Mom said she'll call the cops if I'm not back in half an hour."

Sophie chuckles. "And we can't have police on the premises, given the pot smoking and all." She rises, too, and takes a moment to stretch her arms overhead. "I'm starving," she complains. "Any leftovers?"

Feeding the hungry comes naturally to Candace. "More than you can eat. Let me fix you a plate."

Peggy watches as her friend gets to her feet and follows Sophie through the front door and down the short hall to the kitchen. Instead of going after them, she leans back in her chair and closes her eyes. If she were to choose a card for this moment, she knows what it would be: the Tower. Walls come tumbling down.

Inside, Candace is rummaging through the contents of the refrigerator, unwrapping bowls and popping off plastic lids. Sophie grabs a plate from the cabinet and hands it to Candace, along with a spatula. Pretty soon the plate is loaded down with enchiladas. Sophie shoves it into the microwave, which she turns on. While the plate is bombarded—while the contents pop and sizzle and speckle the inside of the oven with bits of cheese and green chile—Sophie turns to Candace, who has collected her poncho and is wrapping herself in it.

"Looks like you two have been living it up. Where's Jack?"

Peggy enters the kitchen in time to say that Jack has gone to bed.

"No fun for Jack. That's not fair."

"He was tired. He and Ian worked all day at the—"

"Fixer-upper?" Sophie finishes the sentence. The microwave dings; she opens the door and sticks a finger in the middle of an enchilada. She likes her food hot, and it's not quite there yet, not in the middle anyway. She cranks up the microwave for another quick jolt.

Peggy heads over to the counter. "Guac-a-mole?" she stammers.

"Yes, please," Sophie replies.

"I feel like I'm seeing a ghost," Candace says.

Peggy turns from the refrigerator. Her hands cradle the bowl, that piece of their shared past. She hugs it to her chest and watches as Candace makes her way over to Sophie. Peggy knows what will happen next. Candace will reach out and insert a finger into the center of one of Sophie's corkscrew curls. Back at Morningstar, Peggy used to come across Candace and Beau talking, her with a finger lost in his hair. He hardly noticed. Neither does his daughter.

Sophie's plate is on the kitchen counter. She's eating standing up, something she learned from Jack. She puts down her fork and regards this strange woman whose cheeks are wet with tears. "Are you okay?" she asks.

Candace is intent on her own question: "What's your favorite color?"

Sophie replies that it's red, then asks whether she's being tested. Wanting to look away but not sure where to, Sophie glances down at the front of her blouse. Is it possible that she dropped food on it? But no, it looks okay. Wrinkled, but clean enough. The blouse is her mother's, a Mexican number, all cotton, with embroidered flowers and tasseled ties that hang seductively over the slopes of her breasts. When she filched it from Peggy's closet, when she slipped it on and admired her reflection in the bathroom mirror, Sophie thought it looked sexy, but now she feels like Heidi. Maybe she should yodel or something. Completely at a loss as to what to say or do, she picks up the fork and offers Candace a bite.

Obediently, Candace opens her mouth.

"Who are you, crazy woman?" Sophie asks.

Without so much as a "goodnight," Peggy slips away, down the long hallway to bed. She needs to sleep now, she tells herself. She needs to curl up next to Jack and rest. Tomorrow she will figure out what to do and what to say, or maybe, at least, what not to do, what not to say.

Early Monday morning, Sophie opens her eyes and sees the cowboy boots Candace kicked off before she toppled onto the mattress. It's love at first sight; the boots are so gorgeous that Sophie wonders if she's conjured them out of dreams. The uppers are white, heavily scalloped, and adorned with inlaid red roses in full bloom. In contrast, the pull straps feature tight red buds on long green stems. Sophie reaches out and strokes the right boot, the one within reach. The vamp and lower portion are made of red leather that's bumpy to the touch. Patsy Cline might have worn boots like these! Sophie can't wait to show them to Tam. Tam loves Patsy Cline. It's an affliction/affection she inherited from her mother, who can be counted on to play Patsy every time a man treats her wrong. And she plays Patsy on the record player, no less—she says nothing else does that voice justice.

The first time Sophie heard Patsy Cline, she would have been Ian's age and at a sleepover. It must have been a Friday, because Belinda had a date. She had actually hired a babysitter, a cross old woman who went to Tam's church. Sophie no longer remembers whether they were awake when Belinda got home, but she does recall the way they were awakened the next morning to a woeful rendering of "Crazy." Patsy was not the only one singing; so was Belinda, loudly, enthusiastically, and surprisingly on key.

Later Sophie will learn that the boots came from Lucchese's Vintage Collection. They cost nearly as much as Will's junker. Not that she concerns herself now with the value of the boots or their rightful owner. Right away she begins planning her day's outfit around them: a short, black velvet skirt, a tight red T-shirt. And the boots. They look to be about her size. If, by chance, they're too big, she'll stuff the toes, the way Tam does with her bras.

In the midst of reaching for the other boot, Sophie feels a tug on her hair. The woman is a pest. Off and on, all night long, she'd threaded a finger through one of Sophie's curls. Vaguely, Sophie recalls losing patience and slapping at the offending hand. She'd like to do it again, harder this time, but she tells herself to chill. If she offends this crazy woman, the woman's not likely to loan out her boots, now is she?

Sighing, Sophie rolls over. She is confronted by Candace's cross-eyed gaze of adoration. There's so much love in it that the girl is tempted to say something crazy. It's nearly out of her mouth, the question: *Are you my mother or something?* Which is whacked-out—Sophie knows perfectly well that her mother is downstairs. Peggy is likely moving about the kitchen, making coffee and sweet rolls. Whenever they have visitors—a relatively uncommon event—Peggy gets up early and does the whole bit: rolls out the dough, sprinkles it with cinnamon, douses it with sugar, cuts it into strips. They're beautiful, Peggy's sweet rolls. The best things she makes. Although the last few weeks have been a real downer, today is shaping up nicely.

"Do you want to go to Taos with me?" Candace asks.

"I have school," Sophie replies.

"Are you a good student?"

"What do you think?"

Candace shakes her head on the pillow. She covers her mouth, yawns, then says, "Smart but lazy. Am I right?"

"You got it. Lazy as in, I-have-a-calculus-test-today-and-haven't-studied-a-lick." Sophie laughs.

"I guess there are benefits to being middle-aged," Candace muses aloud. "I don't have a calculus test today."

Sophie rolls off the mattress and heads for the bathroom, hurrying down the stairs and through the kitchen, passing her mother at a run, the urgency of her bladder increasing with each step. She's afraid she won't make it, and the closer she gets, the more she dreads being confronted by a closed door. Here, at least, she's in luck. The room has just been vacated by Jack. The bathroom mirror is still fogged over, the air steamy and comfortably warm.

What a strange conversation, Sophie thinks as she perches on the toilet. The phrase "pillow talk" comes to mind; it just pops up, like a thought bubble in a cartoon. Something from an old movie, she supposes, or a book she's long since forgotten. When she was younger, Sophie was an avid reader. She went through the *Little House on the Prairie* books twice. She loved the *Borrower* series, *A Wrinkle in Time* by Madeleine L'Engle, and *The Outsiders* by S. E. Hinton. But in the last few years, she's gotten out of the habit. She reads whatever is required of her for school, but little more. Most recently she finished *To Kill a Mockingbird*. She lost patience with Scout, who struck her as too dense for her own good.

Firmly in possession of the bathroom, Sophie decides to take a shower. It can be rough in the mornings, with only one bathroom and everyone vying for it. You have to take your opportunities when they present themselves. The west wall of the room is lined with six hooks, and a different-colored towel hangs from each. Sophie's is red, of course; Ian's is green. Most often, Peggy's towel is lavender or white. Jack's is always blue. Guests use striped towels. Sophie notes that her mother has seen to that detail—a green-and-blue striped towel hangs neatly from the hook nearest the door. The bathroom walls are painted a bright buttery yellow, and the towels stand out in relief. Like the bee boxes outside, the line of towels is pleasing. Order soothes Sophie. Order is reassuring. But she doesn't value it enough to create it for herself, not yet anyway.

By the time Sophie has returned to her room, the red towel wrapped around her wet tresses, Candace has dozed off again. Sophie disappears into the dark recesses of her closet, a deep, narrow space lined with built-in shelves and one long rod for hangers. A few years back, Jack got a book on remodeling closets and set to work. For a while he enjoyed the challenge of making the most of small spaces. He began with Sophie's closet and worked his way through the house, adding shelves and hangers, hooks and wire-mesh drawers.

The organization is helpful, but Sophie has long since exceeded its limits. When the overhead light burned out a month or two ago, she resorted to a flashlight. What used to be merely messy is now a disaster. The wire drawers are a jumble of scarves, socks, panties, and bras, and the drawers are so full, each of them, that she's given up trying to slide them in and out on their runners. Instead, she's stacked them on the floor.

When she emerges, she's wearing the red T-shirt, but not the skirt. Inconveniently, she left her black skirt at Tam's. Jeans will have to do. Sophie heads over to her dresser for a pair and is opening a drawer when Candace speaks. "So, let me ask you something."

Sophie whirls around and crosses her arms, signaling her attention.

Candace sits up. She's hugging a pillow. "I came here to sell my land to a movie star—"

"What land?" Sophie interrupts.

"I thought you'd ask about the movie star."

Sophie shrugs and turns back to the drawer. She pulls out one of her oldest pairs of jeans. They're snug, and getting into them requires wriggling and dancing. (A day or two from now, Candace will reflect on Sophie struggling into the jeans. The image will return to her, and this time she'll remember the reason: Sophie is pregnant.) Just now the morning light slants across the scarred wooden floor, and Sophie's bare feet slide across the planks. As she bends her head to the task of buttoning her fly, as her mane of black curls cascades over her face, Candace sighs deeply.

"You okay?" Sophie asks.

Candace nods, but she appears sad and weary. Her face is puffy, her eyes circled with the remnants of mascara.

"You've got a bad case of raccoon eyes," Sophie says.

"Is that so? You remind me so much of someone."

Sophie doesn't know how to respond to this, but she does have an opinion on land ownership, and she offers it. "I don't believe individuals should own land," she states stiffly. "Maybe collectively, like at the pueblos." Slyly, as though she's just spotted them, Sophie edges over and picks up one of the boots. "These are way cool," she says.

"What size do you wear?"

"Eight."

"Try them on."

Sophie squeals and drops to the floor, rolling onto her back to pull them on. She can hardly believe her good luck. When the boots are on, she leaps to her feet and dances a little two-step.

"They look great on you. Go ahead, wear them to school."

Sophie is thrilled, obviously. She strides over and leans down, attempts a hug, then rushes out of the room and clatters down the stairs. She's anticipating cinnamon rolls—which will cap this as the perfect morning—and is only mildly disappointed to hear that Peggy has a hangover. She didn't feel up to baking. So Sophie makes do with a bowl of cereal.

By the time Candace dresses and finds her way downstairs, Sophie is gone.

"You're kidding," Candace exclaims when Peggy tells her that school starts at seven thirty.

Peggy agrees that it's preposterous to begin the school day that early. No wonder teenagers are so grouchy. They're all suffering from sleep deprivation. She explains that the day ends early, just after two, because a lot of kids in New Mexico have after-school jobs. "Sophie had a job for a while this summer," Peggy goes on, "but it didn't last long. She got fired. She's something of a handful."

"She's tired!" Candace asserts. "She's exhausted. Seven thirty isn't civilized; it isn't enlightened. Do you suppose," she wonders aloud, "school starts that early in Boston?"

Peggy shrugs. She could point out that over the summer, Sophie most often slept until noon; fatigue didn't cause her to lose her job. But what would be the point?

"You're going to love these apples," Peggy says. She's busy fixing toast and slicing apples from Dixon, New Mexico. "If you have room for apples in your carry-on, you should stop off at the Valdez Fruit Stand in Velarde. Do you remember where that is?" She doesn't wait for a response. "After you've passed through Española, after you've idled at the stoplights with all the lowriders, well, you'll be headed for the stretch of highway that winds through the gorge. Velarde is a little dip in the road. Watch for the signs."

Candace is entirely silent, and Peggy wonders whether she's addressing an empty room. Maybe Candace slipped off to the restroom? But when she turns around to check, her friend is sitting at the end of the table, gazing out the window. Her fine hair, always thin, barely covers her skull these days. She looks exhausted, and yet, when she speaks, she sounds positively exultant: "Life is flat-out crazy, isn't it? When we were young, we couldn't have imagined this particular turn of events, or how we would feel about it. But maybe I'm speaking for myself and not for you?"

Peggy smiles faintly in response. She was up all night, imagining all sorts of eventualities, none of them pleasant. But so far the morning has been uneventful, and she's managed to muster a little hope. Perhaps Candace is none the wiser. Perhaps Peggy was imagining things. Ian left first, then Sophie and Jack. Now, if Peggy can get Candace out the door, she may even be able to return to bed for an hour or two. It's a Monday, and the shop is closed.

"I'm sure the apples are wonderful," Candace continues, "but I may not be going to Taos." She glances at her feet and summons an excuse. "Sophie wore my boots to school, and now I'm barefoot!" It's true enough. She packed poorly and forgot a change of shoes. The cool brick floor feels good. If she were to stay in the house, she'd just go barefoot.

"Oh, for heaven's sake!" Peggy blurts out. "I saw those boots, but it just didn't register. I'll run up to the high school and snatch them off her feet. Believe me, I'll be happy to do it. She's a little thief now, too, is that it?"

97

Candace waves a hand in the air. "No, no, Peggy. She planned her whole outfit around those boots. How about I wear a pair of her shoes?"

"Sure," Peggy replies, clearly relieved. "Take whatever you like."

She serves a stack of buttered wheat toast on a yellow plate, enough for two or three people. With the plate, she offers a sticky ceramic honeypot. "From our bees," she says. "You have to try it."

Candace has her own hangover. "Maybe later," she says. "I'm skipping coffee, too." She picks up a slice of toast and begins nibbling around the edges. From experience, she knows not to look at the food; instead, she gazes out the long, narrow window beside the kitchen door. She sees the cholla standing guard just outside, its limbs stretched toward the window as though to tap at it.

"May I have a glass of water?" she asks. When Peggy has fulfilled the request, Candace takes a long drink, then continues, "Have I ever told you how I bought the land?"

Peggy is pecking away at her own piece of toast. "No," she replies. Rather than hover, she sits down across from Candace and watches as her friend drops the half-eaten slice to the plate and brushes the crumbs from her fingers.

"Well, I'd only been in Taos for a few days," Candace says, clearing her throat, "and a group of us went to an estate sale out in Arroyo Hondo. I rode in the back of a truck with several others. We were staying here and there, no place of our own, and for some reason, we thought we could fix our problems with a few dishes and a good frying pan. And a mattress. I seem to remember that we were looking for a mattress."

Peggy laughs. "Something to get you off the floor at night."

Candace nods. "Right. And someone said, 'Wouldn't it be a gas if we could just buy the place?' And I thought about it, and I knew I could do something in that direction. Land was cheap back then. I couldn't believe how cheap it was. I said to the woman standing next to me, 'I can buy this.' She thought I meant the pitcher I was holding in my hand. When I explained that I meant everything, the whole shooting match, she looked at me like I was crazy. 'So why are you sleeping on the floor?' she asked me. And I didn't really have an answer. I wanted to be part of the family. The rest of them were sleeping on the floor, so I wanted to do it, too. I ended up buying the land that adjoined that property."

"You always did refer to the motley crew at Morningstar as family."

Candace nodded. "So I did."

Just as Peggy has reached for the carton of orange juice, she hears Candace say something more. "You weren't going to tell me, were you?"

Peggy shakes the carton. "Do you want juice?"

"I'll stick to water." Then: "What I want is an answer, Peggy."

Peggy sighs. She sets the carton on the table. She tries to look directly at Candace, but she can't quite manage it. Instead, her gaze slips to Candace's hand, where Peggy takes note of the gold band on her ring finger. Was she wearing it yesterday? If so, Peggy didn't notice.

"What are you talking about?"

"Sophie is Beau's daughter," Candace says firmly. And, as though saying it aloud helps her understand the magnitude of the discovery, she restates it from her own perspective: "Beau has a child in this world!"

Peggy crosses her arms over her chest and leans back in the chair. "Sophie is Jack's daughter."

"In a manner of speaking, yes." Candace looks rumpled and dowdy in her pajamas. Her flattened hair has yet to see a comb. But as she gazes up at Peggy, a luminous smile crosses her face. She says it again. "I know now that Beau has a child in this world, and nothing you say will convince me otherwise. Sophie is his spitting image. She has his mannerisms, his wild enthusiasms, his corkscrew curls. Maybe you've been able to fool Jack all these years. Men see what they want to see, after all. But you certainly *are not going to fool me*." She bends her head to her plate, picks up her toast, and gingerly takes another bite.

"I could fall down in these things," Candace remarks as she steps through the doorway of Peggy's shop. Sophie's clogs are sloppily big on her. That much was obvious as she clomped over the uneven brick sidewalk.

Peggy asks if she should get the sneakers they left in the car. "Those seemed to fit you better."

But Candace has moved on to another topic. Now she is remarking on the peachy shade Peggy sponged on the walls. "It's nice, like being inside a pumpkin."

"My thought exactly!" Peggy is pleased, even charmed by her friend's gushing compliments. On the way to Old Town, Candace proposed buying a broomstick skirt to wear to Taos, something Southwestern *and* sexy. Peggy told Candace she didn't have to, to which Candace replied, "I want to!"

Evidently Peggy's fears were unfounded. Candace doesn't seem the least bit upset. Although she wants Peggy to verify her suspicions, she accepts Peggy's reticence and reluctance. Aside from the hangover, Candace appears buoyant, grateful even. Peggy guesses that her friend's reaction would be otherwise if Beau were alive and well, but his death has made Sophie's existence a gift of sorts, a happy surprise, and one that is all the more remarkable because it was entirely unexpected.

Candace stands before a rack of handmade skirts and fingers the fabric of first one, then another—of tiered velvet and pieced rayon—as Peggy goes about the business of opening the shop: switching on the lamps, turning on the old register, passing through the storeroom to the back door, checking outside for Donald. She was hoping Candace could meet him, "the ghost of hippies past," she'd called him, but there was no sign that he'd spent the night behind her shop. On Saturday she'd gone in early—she wanted to surprise him with a jacket that no longer fit Jack. Fall was upon them after all. Donald was awake when she arrived, sitting on an overturned crate and smoking a cigarette. He didn't want the jacket. His reaction was surprising and a little hurtful. "Don't be mothering me!" he'd said. She had injured his pride. She knew that at the time, but she was offended, and she lashed out. "*Someone* needs to take care of you!"

He snarled the words, "I take care of myself." Then he asked her to go inside and leave him alone, as though the alley were his space, and she the intruder. Ian is equally prickly. It's so easy to get on the wrong side of boys. And they hold grudges! Week after week, they nurse their wounds!

Peggy shouts to Candace from the back room. "He's not there. Shoot! I wanted you to meet him."

Candace calls back, "Another time. There'll be another time, Peggy."

She adds, "I'm ready for coffee now. How about you? Is there a coffee place nearby?" She's carrying an armful of skirts and wearing a smile on her face.

When Peggy offers to go get them a shot of caffeine, Candace says she'll treat. "Get the money out of my purse for me."

Peggy locates Candace's leather bucket bag on the glass counter, right next to the deck of tarot cards and a legal pad covered with Peggy's hen scratch. The silk scarf has slipped to the floor. Good thing the shop is dark, Peggy thinks. Candace might have insisted on a reading, and just now, Peggy couldn't handle another glimpse of the future. The one she's had is bracing enough. She scoops up the cards and grabs the pad, then scurries to the back room and stows them in a desk drawer.

She takes a twenty from Candace's wallet, which doesn't have any smaller bills. It must be nice not to have to worry about expenses all the time, not to be living on the edge, Peggy thinks as she leaves the store. Of course, Donald and others like him willingly dangle their feet into the abyss. Peggy has done it, too, but it's a young person's game. These days, she's not the least bit interested in a breeze from the canyon, though she remembers the Rio Grande Gorge in Taos and how thrilled she'd been to sit with Beau on its precipice.

The wait at the coffee shop is longer than usual, and by the time Peggy returns, Candace has found the bathroom. Peggy leaves her friend's latte on top of a box in the hallway. "Your coffee is waiting for you," she calls through the door. Candace says she'll be out in a few minutes.

So Peggy shelves her own coffee and slips through the narrow passageway to the dressing room, where she finds a mound of skirts—burgundy velvet, periwinkle silk, and a few others—pooled together on the brick floor. She is offended by the carelessness with which they've been treated. Candace must have stepped out of them and kicked them aside.

The sight brings to mind that long-ago wedding day. First Peggy conjures the colors: a cerulean sky and a grassy green hill. Candace's dress was an ivory satin edged with handmade lace. Someone back in Boston had slaved over it; that much was obvious.

Beau and Candace were married by a swami at a summer solstice celebration held outside of Santa Fe, in a place called Aspen Meadow.

The swami advocated group weddings, so several other couples stood up with them. Families were invited, and a few came and left rather quickly. But neither of Beau's parents attended, and Candace had only her aunt Agnes, who brought the beautiful dress.

After the couple left for their honeymoon—had they really taken one, or was that her imagination?—Peggy had discovered the dress on the floor of the room where Candace slept. Moby was stretched out across the train. Peggy left him there, but it made her sick inside, that sort of waste. Not that spoiled behavior was typical of Candace; it wasn't. In fact, Peggy couldn't recall another instance, and it occurs to her now that in this current situation, the skirts might simply have toppled off the bench.

Whatever the case, Peggy is in the process of returning them to their hangers when Candace appears in the doorway, looking flushed and feverish. She stands blocking Peggy's exit, tucks her hair behind her ears, and composes her face. It takes a second or two for Peggy to realize that Candace is scrutinizing herself in the dressing-room mirror.

"Did you find anything that worked?" Peggy asks.

"Not really," Candace replies. "I tried skirt after skirt and looked fat in every one of them. Do you suppose that could mean that I *am* fat?"

"Darling, you're not. I hear that all the time. These skirts aren't for everyone, that's for sure."

"I'm wondering . . ." Candace begins. She stops and starts again. "I have a question. A personal question."

"What?"

Candace reaches out and clutches a handful of the curtain, which has been pulled back to allow access to the dressing room. The satin is so gorgeous as to be garish—it's printed with enormous stargazer lilies, with pink-and-white petals peeled away to reveal orange stamens. "Where did you do it?" she asks. "You were married to Jack, right? Living in the same house you're living in now?"

"Where did we do it?"

"Fuck, Peggy. Where'd you and Beau fuck?"

Peggy's cheeks flush. She can't look at Candace, not for a minute anyway. She grabs one of the skirts in her lap, the burgundy velvet, and uses it to hide her face. Why is she embarrassed by something so heedless? Something so long ago in the past? She doesn't regret it, certainly not that day. How could she? To regret that day would be to regret Sophie, and she can't and won't do such a thing.

"Tell me," Candace insists. "I know you're thinking about him."

Peggy sighs and drops the skirt from her face. She doesn't want to cry on it, for heaven's sake. "I can think about him, can't I?" She sounds childish, even to herself.

Candace lets go of the curtain and gestures to the skirts in Peggy's lap.

"I bet you look good in those skirts. You look good in pretty much anything."

"Don't be absurd. I'm wrinkled and bony. I'm an old lady, and so are you. We weren't then, but we are now." Peggy is fifty-one and Candace is five years older, edging toward sixty—an eventuality that would have horrified their younger selves. "We were so foolish, weren't we?"

Candace hasn't moved; she doesn't look likely to move. "Tell me, Peggy," she says again.

Though Peggy knows better than to respond, it's too tempting, finally. She's never been able to share the secret. There is no one else she will ever tell, no one else she *can* ever tell.

"There," she says. "In the bathroom." She points past Candace. Her friend turns around and stares down the dark, narrow hallway. The bathroom light is on, the door ajar. "We broke the mirror."

For seventeen years she's been planning to replace it, a cheap piece of glass they knocked off in their urgency. It crashed into the sink, scaring both of them into nearly hysterical laughter. Over the years Peggy has dreamed of the mirror she wants, a rectangular one, tin-framed, with inlaid tiles depicting the various phases of the moon. (Beau was a Cancer, and as moody as any other.) Until she finds the one she has in mind, she makes do with the curling poster of Taos Pueblo.

Candace sounds a little out of breath, a little panicky. "That bathroom? The one I just left?"

Peggy nods and watches her friend turn and cast her gaze over the gloomy storeroom and its contents: boxes stacked on rickety shelves, a maimed wire mannequin, discarded clothes racks, a broken boom box, and, lined along the far wall, several ceramic flower pots. Recently the pots were moved inside. They still bear the remains of what was once summer color, zinnias, marigolds, and trailing ivy, reduced now to withered brown stalks and drying vines.

Evidently Candace is scanning the room for her handbag, because as soon as she spots it, she snatches it up and departs so quickly that Peggy hears the ringing bell of the front door before she can gather the skirts and get to her feet. Within a minute or two, Peggy has followed her friend out to the sidewalk. The buttery autumn light is blinding, and she has to wait for her eyes to adjust. No trace of Candace—not in the grassy park area across the street, not down the way, under the portico where Native jewelers spread their wares on blankets. Peggy proceeds down the sidewalk to the spot where Candace parked the car. Already, an SUV is maneuvering into the empty space. Candace is long gone.

Instead of regret, Peggy is surprised to feel relief. She wonders whether it is for the best, this rupture. By evening she will decide that yes, it is for the best. When Jack asks, she will tell him that it was lovely to see Candace, but the two of them have very little in common these days.

On Thursday the real estate agent calls Peggy's shop in search of Candace. She missed her Tuesday appointment, and she isn't answering her cell phone. Frankly, the agent tells her, he's getting a little frantic. He called Boston and left messages on her voicemail, although he had no particular reason to think she'd returned to the East Coast. He'd had no idea where she might be, but then he remembered that Candace had shared something of her plans, said she'd be staying with an old friend in Albuquerque, someone from the commune days. The agent is pleased to have tracked Peggy down, anyway.

"I asked around," he tells her. "Your name came up right away, but then I had to find someone who is still in touch with you. The silversmiths helped me out. They knew Beau, they knew Candace, and they knew you. One or two of them still do a little business with you, I hear."

Tears well up in her eyes. Surprising, bitter tears. Peggy doesn't have a response, and he doesn't seem to expect one. He moves on, explaining that the movie star is due in Taos by the weekend. "I think he's coming to see Julia," the agent confides. "I promised a contract all drawn up for him. Shouldn't have done that, I know, but I was all carried away."

He wants *her* to commiserate with *him*! As though they are friends or something! Peggy hates this sort of self-important talk, but she is drawn in anyway. She doesn't subscribe, but she isn't above thumbing through the pages of *People* while waiting in line at the grocery store. She knows, of course, that the "Julia" he is referencing is Julia Roberts, who owns land outside Arroyo Seco. She, her husband, and their twins live in the shadow of Taos Mountain, and Julia shops at the yarn store in Arroyo Seco. So says *People*, in any case. If only Peggy had opened a store in Arroyo Seco, Julia might have stopped in with her Hollywood friends. Retailers are always at the mercy of those who have money. Why not be at the mercy of those who have the most?

These are Peggy's thoughts as she moves to the end of the counter, where she has the best view through the front window. She doesn't know what she's looking for. "Honestly, I don't know what happened to Candace," she says. "She left here on Monday, just before noon."

"Do you know where she was planning to stay?"

Peggy tries to think. It's been a long time since she's spent much time in Taos. "Casa Benavides maybe, or Mabel's?" Casa Benavides is a bed-and-breakfast on Kit Carson Road, one of the more comfortable and well-situated places to stay. The owners serve up waffles and homemade granola for breakfast, and some of the rooms offer a splendid view of Taos Mountain. The living areas of the main house are worth a visit simply for the D. H. Lawrence memorabilia: photos of Lawrence and his wife Frieda; a painting of the ranch where they lived, capably rendered by Lawrence's acolyte Dorothy Brett. Taos is replete with history. It can be found in some of the least likely places.

But those with an interest in history or the arts almost always end up at the rambling Mabel Dodge Luhan House. During the decades she served as an art patroness, Mabel enticed some of the greatest minds of the twentieth century to travel to Taos and stay in her adobe retreat. Martha Graham, Carl Jung, D. H. Lawrence, Georgia O'Keeffe, Ansel Adams, and Willa Cather all made the trip to Taos when Mabel and her husband Tony were alive. Then, in 1970, Dennis Hopper bought the property, and a new wave of artists and rebels took up the trek: Bob

Dylan, Alan Watts, Joni Mitchell, Leonard Cohen, Jack Nicholson, Peter Fonda. When Hopper returned to Hollywood, he rented the house to a group of silversmiths.

After Beau left Morningstar, but before he married Candace, he lived at Mabel's. He and his friend Pepe moved in and made concho belts and bracelets.

"For nostalgic reasons, I'd bet on Mabel's," Peggy says.

But the agent has already called both places, and no one named Candace Cuzak is registered.

"The Fechin Inn?" Built behind the Nicolai Fechin House, the hotel is the upscale choice in Taos.

"Tried that, too."

Peggy's gaze turns unfocused and probing. Just the day before, she received a check in the mail, postmarked Taos. There'd been no note, no return address. Just a five-hundred-dollar check made out to Peggy Granger—Candace following through on her offer to help. Peggy peers through the window, across the sidewalk to the street, then on to the plaza and, beyond that, to the Old Town Basket & Rug Shop. Who could have imagined any of this? Back when they lived at Morningstar, did any of them ever wonder about the future? Did they have any sense at all of the people they would become when they "grew up"?

Peggy knows the answer. They didn't; they hadn't. They had lived from one day to the next, one moment to the next. They didn't worry about tomorrow because they didn't much believe in it. Theirs was a generation raised under the threat of annihilation, of duck and cover and mushroom clouds. Nearly every year she was in school, Peggy's class traveled to Dallas for the Texas State Fair. A few of those trips were memorable. She recalls one trip, made during middle school. Although they visited the midway and the agricultural displays, what she remembers from that particular excursion were the backyard bomb shelters and the salesmen who hawked them. Salvation could be bought and paid for, she realized. Such a thing had never occurred to her before—that they weren't all equally vulnerable.

The agent sighs deeply, calling Peggy back to the present. "Damned if this thing isn't falling apart," he complains.

That must be what Candace wants, Peggy thinks. But she doesn't say it. Instead, she tries to reassure the agent. "If I talk to her, I'll be sure to contact you." And dutifully, she takes down his name and number. The name sounds familiar. Later, driving home, she remembers him, a guy who lived at the New Buffalo commune in the summer of 1970. She thinks they might have slept together once or twice in the way of friendly acquaintances, which would explain his familiar tone.

Heedless pairing up had been a part of commune life. That's why, she told herself, it was okay to "ball" Beau, okay to fall in love with him, okay to betray the friend who had taken her in on that snowy night. Back then she would climb in bed with a man because everyone else had turned in for the night, or because she was away from home and didn't have another place to sleep. What was Stephen Stills's philosophy? Oh, yes: "Love the one you're with."

The call from the agent spurs Peggy to leave a couple of apologetic messages on Candace's machine in Boston. To protect herself, to protect her family, Peggy wishes she could let the friendship die, but that's not possible—not for someone with a conscience, and Peggy has one. All those years ago, Candace rescued Peggy, took her in out of a snowstorm, and befriended her. That first winter Peggy's backpack had been stolen, and she had nothing more to wear than the clothes on her back. What the thrift store didn't provide, Candace did: a sweater from Guatemala, a pair of Frye boots, not new but serviceable. Boots, Peggy thinks. Now Candace has given Sophie boots as well.

On Thursday the twenty-fifth, in the late afternoon, Candace calls the shop and checks in with Peggy. She is home in Boston, after having been laid up at Holy Cross Hospital for a few days. When Peggy asks what happened, she expects to hear that Candace had a heart attack. Now that Jack's heart has faltered, the whole world seems vulnerable. She is anxious for strangers, anxious for everyone, but she's especially anxious for herself and her family. Despite that wild launch into the world at seventeen, or maybe because of it, Peggy has given into her impulse to retreat from life.

Jack's heart attack was entirely unexpected, at least from her vantage point, though the cardiologist had labeled her naïve. "He's sixty, overweight, and under stress," the doctor had said. He pursed his nearly colorless lips and shook his head. He was perched on the edge of his desk, legs crossed in front of him. "He can't change his age, but he ought to do something about the other two factors. You need to help out here, Mrs. Granger. Put your husband on a diet and encourage him to get more exercise and relaxation."

Peggy assured the doctor that she was up to the task, but it turns out that she is no more of a disciplinarian with Jack than she is with Sophie or Ian. She can buy a roasted chicken at Costco with the best of them, and she can fill a bowl with fruit, but she can't very well snatch a pint of Häagen-Dazs out of Jack's grasp. She isn't that kind of woman, and he isn't that kind of man. He would be affronted, humiliated; she would be embarrassed. It is better to look the other way, to allow your spouse his or her failings. At least, so it seems to Peggy. Is this codependency then, she wonders, or merely a form of acceptance? Is it, she dares to ask herself, a form of love?

And does she love Candace, too? Is that why she exclaims so loudly and apologizes so profusely when Candace admits that she tripped on the boardwalk in Taos, toppled face first, and broke both her ankle and her nose?

"I had two black eyes," Candace says. "Now they're yellow. But here's the silver lining: I've lost weight because it's too hard to get up and hobble over to the refrigerator. My jeans are loose! It's such a relief. Really, a self-imposed diet. That's the way I think of it."

"Do you have anyone there helping you?"

"I'm okay, Peggy. Really. You don't need to worry about me."

"Somebody needs to," Peggy says, knowing full well how false this sentiment sounds.

Before she hangs up, Candace mentions that she talked to Sophie on the phone. "I tried you at home before I tried you at work," she explains.

Peggy struggles to keep her voice light. "I'm glad you gave me some advance notice," she says. She wraps her belted cardigan a little more tightly around her chest. It's chilly. She might need to plug in her space heater before the end of the day.

"What do you think? I'm going to broadcast your secret? Don't worry, Peggy. I'm not out to break up your family. I'm not into punishment at this stage of my life. Not ever. That's not who I am."

Peggy has been standing and clutching the receiver, but now she sinks onto a stool and closes her eyes. She takes one deep breath and then another. "How can I thank you?" she asks.

"Just be my friend," Candace replies. "Let me in a little bit. On the phone today, Ian called me Aunt Candace. I really liked the sound of that. And listen, good luck tomorrow."

Peggy has to think before she makes the connection: tomorrow is their appointment. "Did Sophie tell you we're going to Planned Parenthood?"

When Candace says yes, Peggy is taken aback. She can't imagine Sophie, her Sophie, being so forthcoming.

"How did she sound about it?"

"What?"

"The appointment at Planned Parenthood."

"Well, sad," Candace replies. "But you don't need to ask me. You're living with her. Anyway, she said it was just the exam and counseling."

Before they hang up, Candace has a question of her own. "Do you ever think about the day we met? We were her age, or you were, anyway. I was a little older, and I should have been a little wiser."

Peggy wants to excuse them both. She stares out into the dusk gathering around Old Town Plaza, and for just a second or two, she imagines the beginnings of a swirling snowstorm. "You weren't that much older. We were kids, both of us doing the best we could."

"And Sophie is doing the same, Peggy. Remember that: Sophie is doing the same. Don't you think the world must be just as confusing to her as it was to us?"

"I have no doubt of that," Peggy replies.

The Planned Parenthood office is a stone's throw from the University of New Mexico campus. It caters mostly to college students. The front window advertises a new service: PILLS NOW, PAY LATER. Most of the traffic seems to be walk-in, an irony since the building was originally a service station. Now, instead of fill-ups and lube jobs, the establishment provides treatment for sexually transmitted diseases; walk-in pregnancy testing; pregnancy options education; HIV testing; and, by appointment at another site, tubal ligation and abortions, with "both surgical and medical options available."

This morning, Sophie is driving. She insisted on it because she needs to log hours behind the wheel with a parent in tow. Mother and daughter argued; Peggy caved, but now she is giving Sophie the silent treatment. The morning traffic is intense, and as soon as they hit Central Avenue, Sophie's hands start to sweat. At lights, she wipes her palms in her lap, all the while sneaking peeks at her mother in the passenger seat. It's too much, really. The drive and the destination. She's about to learn more about herself and her condition than she feels prepared to know. Last week, and again yesterday, she sat down with a calendar and counted back weeks. She isn't sure when she last had a period. Well, she believes she had one in July, but as she told Candace, it could have been anytime during that month. She's never been the least bit regular.

Peggy spots the building at the last minute. She's been watching the addresses, but she isn't expecting a barely disguised service station. "There it is!" she calls out. Then, "Turn in, turn in!"

Sophie has mastered turning, and can do it with the best of them. She whips Peggy's Civic onto the empty cement island surrounding the small building, then comes to an abrupt stop before she bothers to puzzle aloud: "Am I allowed to park here? There aren't any lines."

The stopped car is angled toward the building. She looks to her mother for directions. She can back up, but she can't pull through. In the fifties and sixties, motorists maneuvered their cars beneath the overhang and waited for an attendant to rush out and fill the gas tank, wipe the windshield, and check the tire pressure. Now the space under the overhang has been transformed into a tiny, fortified park, complete with thorny rose bushes and a cement-block bench. Surrounding the space on three sides is a sturdy metal fence, which, like the building itself, is painted an off-shade of blue. It's not baby blue, but blue gray.

"No, I don't think so," Peggy says in a tight voice.

"Why not? There's plenty of space." Sophie clutches the wheel and frowns. When she speaks again, she sounds petulant. "Why not? I can't turn around. I don't have enough room to turn around." She is wearing lipstick, and in the last few minutes, she's smeared it by biting her lips. She does it again, carving little trench marks through the bright red. Peggy watches her. Something about this small gesture of worry is heartbreaking. It's all Peggy can do to keep from weeping.

"Here, why don't you let me take over," Peggy says. "I can drive now."

"No way!" Sophie protests. "We're here. I've done the hard part. Now I just need to park the car."

Peggy glances at the plate-glass windows, expecting to see an employee gesturing broadly. But it's early in the morning, just after eight, and no one is paying attention.

"Exactly. You drove here, and now I'll park. If we don't move the car soon, they'll come out and ask us to move it."

"What's the deal, Peggy?" Sophie asks. "What are you so worried about? I can just pull over beside the building and be out of the way."

Peggy shakes her head, sighs, then explains that Planned Parenthood is a target for attacks. "They've probably been threatened by car bombs. You know, like in Iraq."

Disbelieving, Sophie turns her gaze from her mother's face to the fortified front of the building. "Oh my gosh," she says. In that moment, she sounds like a little girl. She used to say much the same thing when Peggy told her it was bedtime. Anything she couldn't quite believe elicited an "oh my gosh."

In the end, Sophie is afraid to back into the street. The traffic is relentless, and she can't yet judge the speed of the cars as they approach. So she changes places with her mother, then watches as Peggy manages the feat and parallel parks on the street. Grudgingly, Sophie exits the car and starts across the street behind her mother. Her thumbs are tucked inside her fists. She walks stiffly, holding her dress against the tease of the wind. In her whole life she has never been so anxious. Until Peggy shared the little tidbit about car bombers, Sophie was coping with the situation. She'd told herself that it was simply a doctor's appointment, not unlike her yearly gynecological exam. Now she keeps her teeth from chattering by biting her lip.

What used to be the lobby of the service station is now the waiting area. Padded blue chairs line the walls, situated so those seated can gaze out the plate-glass windows. The building is at the intersection of Carlisle and Central, a busy area both day and night. The men's clothing store where Peggy once worked as an assistant manager is only a block or two away. Surprisingly, that poorly lit and overstocked shop is still in business. When she was working there, Peggy lived in a studio apartment just off Washington Street, which means she must have walked by this building hundreds of times. And yet she has no memory of it. Until now, it's never registered for her.

Sophie stands at the counter, waiting to check in. She has on a dress that Peggy has never seen before. It's a short purple affair. As they were crossing the street and hurrying toward the entrance, Sophie had to hold it down with two fists to keep the wind from whipping it up over her head. Underneath she is wearing black tights and black leather lace-ups. With her raven Shirley Temple curls, she resembles an overgrown girl, simultaneously darling and ridiculous.

The slight young man working the desk is ignoring Sophie. He's filling out a form on a clipboard, and it's not until he finishes the task that he looks up and asks if he can help. A shock of dark hair falls over his eyes; he reaches up and pushes it back as he asks her name. After Sophie tells him, he scans his printout, then hands her a clipboard of her own and points her in the direction of the waiting room.

She turns around and meets her mother's gaze. Peggy expects irony, a rolling of the eyes or some other dismissive gesture. But Sophie looks somber, and when she sits down, she reaches over and squeezes her mother's knee. "Thanks for coming with me," she whispers. "I'm kind of freaked."

"That's understandable," Peggy says, patting her daughter's hand. "You look very nice. But I don't remember that dress. Should I?"

Sophie takes her hand back and gives her mother a sly look. "You bought it for me," she says. Then, seeing her mother's confusion, she hurries to retract the glib response. "Fooling, just fooling. It's Tam's. I traded my black velvet skirt. It doesn't fit anymore."

"Ah," Peggy replies.

"I couldn't zip up my jeans this morning," Sophie admits. "That's why I took so long upstairs."

Because her daughter doesn't seem to expect a response, Peggy doesn't offer one. It's just as well. Her mind is blank. From the periphery of her vision she sees that Sophie is completing the form, filling in her name, address, and age; skipping the name of her doctor; then stopping to ponder the date of her last period. Peggy is intensely curious as to what Sophie will write down, but she sees that her daughter's hands are shaking. Simply to avoid making matters worse, she has to look away.

Suddenly she worries that Sophie hasn't been truthful with her. If she were only two months along, why would she be growing out of her clothes? As far as Peggy can tell, Sophie is subsisting on crackers, yogurt, and Progresso chicken noodle soup. She might as well be on a diet. In an effort to keep them both calm, Peggy stares straight ahead. Across the street is a flower shop, People's Flowers. Peggy wonders if the owners are her age, if they started the store in the spirit of the sixties. She supposes they did. Otherwise, why choose such a name? Power to the people, or if not power, then at least flowers. Flowers for the people! Let them eat flowers!

She tries to remember when she last received a bouquet. When the children were born, certainly. And Jack usually gives her roses on Valentine's Day. He began the tradition when they first married, and he likes to joke that it's not possible either to change the custom or to dispense with it. "Roses it is, roses it must be," he intones. "No candy for my Peggy." She remembers that first year they were dating. For Valentine's, he bought her a heart-shaped box of chocolates, which he ended up eating himself. She's never really cared for sweets, but she adores flowers.

The only other person waiting is a young black woman in a bulky, tan sweater, who hums under her breath and makes a game of crossing and uncrossing her feet. Peggy expects the woman to be the first called, but it doesn't happen that way. Instead, the fellow behind the counter says, "Sophie, they're ready for you back here."

Sophie bolts up and, clutching the clipboard to her chest, disappears through an open doorway. After she's gone, the waiting woman clears her throat and points to the floor in front of Sophie's chair. "I think she dropped something. She was holding it, and she dropped it in her lap when they called her name."

"Thanks," Peggy says. Leaning over, she closes her hand over a red glass heart.

It's a small, plump, stoplight-red object that fits easily into the palm of her hand. Both sides are decorated with tiny blue, yellow, and pink hearts; each is outlined in gold leaf. While Peggy examines it, the young woman rises from her chair and inches closer, her hand out.

"Can I see it?" she asks. She's wearing the saddest smile Peggy has ever seen. How can Peggy tell a sad smile from a happy one? Why, the eyes of course. Peggy nods and drops the heart into her outstretched palm.

Perhaps she observed Sophie doing it, Peggy thinks, or maybe it's just something she thinks to do. Whatever the reason, the young woman raises the heart to her ear and shakes it. "Sweet," she says, returning it to Peggy.

The heart makes the tiniest tinkling noise. If it weren't so still in the room, Peggy might not have heard it. She can't imagine what's inside, what's making the sound, and even after she's shaken it again and again, she still doesn't have the slightest idea. When the young woman's name, Lenore, is called, Peggy pockets the heart and gets up to move closer to the plate-glass window.

She needs something to divert her, and she gets her wish. Every once in a while, a bicyclist pedals past on the street; more often, pedestrians hurry down the sidewalk. It's the end of the workweek, and everyone is in a rush. So Peggy's attention is drawn to a figure on the other side of the street, someone pushing a bicycle slowly down the sidewalk, moving against the tide of timeliness. At first she takes the dreadlocks to be an unruly head of hair and assumes that the man is a woman, but the posture tells her otherwise. He pushes with his back, not with his arms.

I know him, she thinks, but it isn't until the wind catches several wadded lengths of dirty blonde hair and slaps them back against his face that she recognizes Donald. She hesitates, then heads out the door and calls after him. It's just as well that the roar of traffic drowns out her voice. Doesn't she have enough on her hands this morning?

After watching his figure retreat into the distance, she drops absently onto the concrete bench, and she's still there half an hour later when Sophie emerges from the building. Though her daughter looks worried, her face relaxes when she sees her mother. "I thought you'd gone off and left me."

"Since when have I ever done that?" Peggy asks. "Have a seat."

Sophie flops down, settles the purple dress around her knees, and rests a hand in her lap to keep the dress from billowing.

"What did the counselor say?" Peggy has to raise her voice to be heard over the traffic.

Sophie shrugs. "Not much of anything. She asked me questions and then she 'echoed back.'"

"Echoed back what?"

"My thoughts and feelings."

"And what are they?"

Sophie's curls are whipping around her face. "This is stupid!" she yells. "And I'm stupid. I should have made an appointment weeks ago."

Peggy scoots closer to her daughter, close enough so that she can take her daughter by the shoulders and speak to her in a normal voice. "No, *I* should have," Peggy corrects her. "I was in complete avoidance mode. But Sophie, you're not really that far along, are you?"

"I can't wear my pants!" Sophie wails.

When she tries to pull away, Peggy holds on. She grips her daughter's shoulders so tightly that she expects Sophie to cry out. "Maybe I dried them on high last time," Peggy offers. "That's perfectly possible—that I put in the pants after a load of towels and forgot to change the temperature."

Sophie wrenches away and stands up, gathering the material of her dress into one fist. "This is crazy! It's too windy to talk out here. Let's go."

As soon as Peggy pulls away from the former service station, Sophie clears her throat and says, "I'm more than three months, Peggy."

Peggy allows silence to fill the space between them.

"And I don't want to regret something my whole life, like Candace."

"What did you say?"

Sophie goes still and quiet. Her posture says it all. She doesn't want to repeat herself; she doesn't need to. Peggy heard her loud and clear.

"The little heart," Peggy hears herself say. "Did you get that from Candace?"

Sophie nods. "She bought it for me at a toy store in Taos."

A second or two later, Sophie begins digging in her bag. Peggy knows that she's looking for the heart, she's remembering having turned it over in her palm in the lobby, and she's realizing that she likely left it at Planned Parenthood. Sophie tells her mother that they need to turn around and go back. "I've lost it," she explains.

But Peggy has it in her pocket, and she tells Sophie so.

"Can you give it to me?"

Peggy doesn't answer right away. The light changes at the intersection of Central and Broadway, and she slows to a stop. An elderly man wearing an orange windbreaker and a backpack is venturing into the street. He is probably homeless. Peggy thinks briefly of Donald, wonders where he is and how he will spend his day.

Sophie asks again. Peggy reaches into her pocket and grasps the heart, which makes a tiny tinkling sound. She is tempted to roll down the window and toss it out, but she doesn't. Instead, she sighs and hands the heart over to Sophie, who immediately raises it to her ear and shakes it.

"How did you get it?" Peggy asks. "It didn't come in the mail. I would have seen it."

"She stopped by Valley. They called me to the office, and she was waiting for me. 'Aunt Candace,' she called herself. She was on crutches, and we went outside to the little rose garden and talked for a few minutes. When she left, she gave me the heart. It was in a black velvet bag, and she told me to wait and open it after she'd gone."

"What did she say?"

"Not much. She asked me not to mention her visit. Said you'd worry—maybe you'd have your feelings hurt because she didn't have time to see us both. Said you'd told her I was pregnant. . . ." Sophie pauses to let this news sink in. "Which wasn't, strictly speaking, actually necessary, now was it? *And* she said you were in favor of an abortion, which isn't, strictly speaking, something you've told me. I mean I could have guessed, but you told her and you didn't bother to tell me."

"Fair enough," Peggy says.

She is returning home via the surface streets rather than the highway. Her life feels so out of control at this moment that she isn't sure she would be able to avert an accident, should one come careening in her direction. At least on Central the collision would take place at a lower speed; they'd be more likely to survive it.

When the light changes and they enter downtown, Sophie is still talking, replaying the conversation seemingly word for word. "Candace said, 'If I were your mother, I might be urging you in that direction, too.' But she wanted me to think through the decision for myself, because it's one of the few choices in life that is ir-... ir—"

"Irrevocable?"

"Yes, irrevocable."

How dare she, Peggy thinks. *How dare she*. And then Peggy remembers their encounter in Everyday Satin, the way Candace ran out of the store. Is this about revenge, then? What the hell is she up to? Peggy takes a deep breath and tries to focus on her daughter. "This isn't Candace's business, Sophie, and she has no right to try and counsel you, particularly when she's doing it behind my back."

Sophie is silent. When she responds, she does so in a tight voice that Peggy hardly recognizes. "You're making this about *you* when it's supposed to be about *me*."

"If you have a baby, it's about all of us, damn it! We're all affected by that decision. While you may not understand that yet, I assure you that Candace does. Candace *certainly* does!"

Peggy drives quietly for several minutes. When they stop at Fifth and Central next to the Kimo Theater, she turns and addresses the back of her daughter's head. Sophie is pretending to study the tile work that distinguishes the Kimo from all the other buildings downtown. "It's your decision first, Sophie, but it isn't only your decision. What about Will?"

"What about him?" Sophie mumbles.

"If you're not going ahead with the abortion, you can't put off talking to him any longer. He should have some kind of say in all of this. Maybe not the determining say, but—"

"His mother is going to freak out," Sophie interrupts. "You have no idea." She looks over at Peggy, then sees that the light has turned green. "Get a move on, get a move on, Peggy," she says. "You're wasting time. I have to inform the whole world that I'm knocked up." She rolls down the window and makes a show of pretending to scream out the news.

The wind that blows in is cold around the edges. It will be winter before they know it, and, Peggy thinks, her daughter will be showing. She has to bite a lip to keep from groaning. "Oh, stop that!" she says. "Roll up the window. If you're going to be a mother, you're going to have to figure out how to impersonate an adult."

The remark surprises them both. They are too awed by the revelation to argue any more. Instead, both distract themselves with the hustle-bustle of downtown Central Avenue, the pedestrians at crosswalks, the policemen on bicycles, the occasional rumbling lowrider.

At the intersection of Central and Eleventh, they stop at a light alongside a *vato*. His car is one of those nondescript white sedans of the sort driven by undercover policemen, the windows so darkly tinted that the driver is scarcely visible. Only in this case, he rolls down the window, ostensibly to ash a cigarette. In the process, the driver glances over at Sophie and grins widely, showing off a front tooth enameled in gold. His eyes are small brown seeds pressed into the doughy expanse of his face. He flicks his tongue at her in an obscene gesture. Ordinarily Sophie would simply frown and turn away. She knows better than to engage a guy like this one. She goes to school with cholos like him.

But she is just distraught enough to do something brash. While he watches, she rolls down the window. "*Chingao!*" she cries out. "My eggo is preggo!"

He stares at her blankly, then, comprehending, offers a sly grin. He utters a response in Spanish that neither Sophie nor her mother understands. As soon as the light changes, Peggy puts her foot on the gas, roaring off in a way that might appear to be a provocation of its own. Peggy doesn't want to race. She just wants to get away. They're both relieved when the gangster speeds up and passes them. Peggy turns on Rio Grande and heads to Candelaria, where she will drop Sophie off at Valley High School just in time for fourth period.

For once Sophie heeds her mother's advice. She might have put off the unpleasantness of a talk with Will for weeks to come, but the idea that she is going to be a mother operates like an electric jolt. While she sits in French class, the room darkened to accommodate the film their teacher is showing, Sophie decides that she will simply blurt it out the very next time she lays eyes on Will. They don't have the same lunch period, but they often run into each other between sixth and seventh periods. Just spit it out, she tells herself. On screen, two girls enter a corner bakery. The class is asked to recite the word that flashes on the screen: "boulangerie."

Subtlety doesn't work with Will. Over the last month she has tried to hint at her condition. She has complained that she's nauseous, for instance. And she's shrugged off his offers to use condoms. "It's not really necessary," she's told him, but he doesn't ask any questions. Tam tells her she's being dense: "Duh! He thinks you're taking birth control pills."

The counselor at Planned Parenthood tried to make the same point, but it turns out that Sophie responds best to bald-faced truths, and in a moment of utter frustration, Peggy uttered one. "If you're going to be a mother, you're going to have to figure out how to impersonate an adult." She did not say, "You're going to have to grow up." Sophie has heard that piece of advice any number of times, and she has neither the inclination nor any idea of how to act on it. She simply ignores the suggestion. Growing up is not an act of will. Sophie knows this intuitively, just as she knows that not all adults are grown-ups.

The aftermath of Sophie's condition—the more or less inevitable conclusion—has yet to sink in. Until now, Sophie has only managed to absorb the fact of the pregnancy. Here, too, she was inclined to disbelieve the signs. Pregnancy tests and a queasy stomach weren't enough to convince her of her fate. It took the confirmation of a tarot card reading for her to take the matter seriously. Her disbelief is understandable, even rational. Over and over in her short life, Sophie has managed to escape the consequences. If she doesn't study, for instance, she may fail, but the repercussions of failure are a ways off, and they are only a possibility, not a certainty. Plenty of times, she has gambled and won, gotten an A when she deserved an F. She's a smart girl, and stealthy, too. In recent months she and Tam have swiped several pairs of lacy underwear from Dillard's, lip gloss from Walgreens, and hot cups of mocha cappuccino from an Allsup's convenience store. Each time they take a chance and get away with the theft, they are giddily excited, greedy for the next escapade.

But in the space of an afternoon, Sophie matures, noticeably so, even if only to herself. She does not want to address Will in the way she addressed the *vato*. She does not want to lose control and cry in the hallway, and they do not have the time to tuck themselves into some corner of the building for a private moment. Nor does she want to put off the inevitable, as the counselor put it. So Sophie tears out a piece of notebook paper and writes Will a short note:

Dear Will: I've been trying to tell you this for weeks and weeks!
I'm pregnant. We need to talk. Love, Sophie

The hardest part of writing the note is signing it, but the counselor at Planned Parenthood encouraged Sophie to listen to her inner voice, and Sophie is in the mood today to take advice. Later she will wonder if she came on too strong. Maybe LOL? But doesn't LOL say that it's a lark, this note? Though she will second-guess herself into the wee hours of the night, in the twilight of French class, while intoning the word "café," she folds the note and slips it into the pocket of her dress.

When the time comes, when she is swept up with the hundreds of others shouldering their way down the main hallway of Building A, Sophie sees Will approaching from the opposite side of the hallway. He has his head down, but even so he's taller than nearly everyone else in sight. The first thing she sees is the straight part down the middle of his head. She wants to tongue that part, to lick up and down the length of it. No sooner has the thought come and gone than he is beside her.

It's like a dance they do, she thinks later. She reaches out her hand and grabs his, directing it into her pocket. For the few seconds it takes to complete the transaction, they are stopped in the middle of the hallway, bodies sweeping past on all sides. Will grins at her and squeezes his lips together to make a kissing face. Then, before extracting the note and his hand, he gropes the inside of her thigh, creating a flash of heat that radiates all through her body. This is love, she thinks. This has got to be love. And for that moment, anyway, she doesn't regret any of it. Not a single damn thing.

Peggy waits nearly a week to call Candace. She doesn't want to be rash, and she's learned over the years that she can't curb her temper; she can only wait it out. She holds off until the store is closed, then turns out all the lights and sits quietly in the dark. It's Halloween in Old Town, and participating shops in the plaza are hosting a candy giveaway from five to eight. Peggy planned to take part. She was looking forward to seeing the children in their costumes, to smiling at the shy mothers pushing their toddlers in strollers. But she has been so preoccupied that she forgot the day, forgot the candy. So she is forced to close the shop and sit guiltily in the dark, watching the shadowy forms of children pass in front of the windows. She can just make out the outlines of their masks, see the sweeps of capes, hear their laughter and excited shouts of "trick or treat!"

Peggy holds the receiver in her lap and tries to summon confidence and certainty and control. It won't do to get angry and yell, though that may be her first impulse. She can't simply tell Candace to mind her own business. Clearly Candace believes that Sophie's decision *is* her business, and nothing Peggy can say to her will change that. She's known Candace for all these years. She's seen the way her friend can latch on and not let go, even when relinquishing would be wisest.

Peggy sighs and says a little prayer before dialing. *Let me say the right thing; let me keep my temper; let me get through to her.* She doesn't know to whom she's praying. Perhaps it's only to herself.

"Trick or treat!" Candace says when she answers the phone.

"Happy Halloween," Peggy replies, then, before Candace can say anything more, Peggy tells her about the children traipsing up and down the sidewalk in front of the shop. "They look like fairies out there in the dusky light."

"I wish I were there."

Peggy lets that sink in. "Look, Candace. I'm going to get straight to the point: I wish you'd bothered to check in with me when you returned to Albuquerque. Evidently you had time to visit with Sophie at Valley. . . ."

The line is silent. "Sophie told you, then?" Candace collects herself and continues, "I really was in an awful hurry. It took me longer to find the high school than I thought it would."

"And why did you need to find the high school, pray tell?"

"Honestly, Peggy. I was going to pick up my boots and give Sophie back her clogs."

"But Sophie had the boots on this morning—"

"Yes, I know. She didn't have them on the day I stopped in to see her. So, how did the appointment go?"

Peggy sighs, caught off guard by the reasonable response. Maybe this won't be as hard as she thought it would be. "All right, I guess. She's distraught, but at least she's awake now. She's promised to tell Will and—"

"How far along is she?"

"She doesn't know for sure," Peggy lies, "because it wasn't a complete exam."

"But she's finished the first trimester."

"That may be the case, but it doesn't really matter, Candace. There's still plenty of time for the procedure."

"The abortion, you mean. Call it by its name, Peggy. You of all people shouldn't be resorting to euphemisms."

"For god's sake, don't lecture me." Peggy kicks at a box under the counter, swings the toe of her boot, and clobbers it again and again. "Candace, you have to let Sophie get on with her life. You have to stay out of this!" She hears her voice rising. She takes a deep breath and wills herself to speak quietly. "It doesn't concern you. It doesn't concern you at all."

"How can you say that? *Nothing*, nothing in the world concerns me more right now."

Peggy closes her eyes. "Why?" she hears herself ask.

"A few days ago, I was telling a friend here the story—that I just found out Beau has a daughter. This is someone who knew and loved Beau, warts and all. We all knew he had a few warts, now didn't we? Anyway I told my friend that Beau's daughter is pregnant, and do you know what she said? She said, 'You have a grandchild in this world.' And, I do, *for now*. I have a grandchild whom I'd like to see grow up."

"What are you saying?"

"I'd like to adopt the baby, Peggy. You could make that happen, if you wanted to."

Peggy lowers herself off the three-legged stool and drops to the ground. She sits behind the counter. After releasing one breath, she takes another. "And extend the misery Sophie is going through right now? Make you happy at her expense?"

"I want to bring something good and valuable into the light, Peggy. Beau's death was a tragedy, and it's nearly killed me, living with it day after day. I don't want Sophie to be miserable, but an abortion isn't going to spare her. She's not the sort to have the thing done and forget about it. She's a girl with a conscience, and that's a credit to you. She wants to do the right thing, but she needs our guidance."

"*Our* guidance? This is not about you. Don't make this about you, Candace." Peggy hears herself, knows she's echoing her daughter. Tears spring to her eyes and evidently to Candace's, too, because she excuses herself. Peggy hears her fumbling with something, a box of Kleenex perhaps? She hears Candace blow her nose.

When Candace returns to the phone, she has new resolve. Her voice sounds downright steely. "You've been selfish your whole life, and most often you've gotten what you wanted."

Peggy would like to object, but she can't bring herself to do so. Ever since his heart attack, Jack has been telling her pretty much the same thing that Candace just said. Though there must be something to it, Peggy doesn't see it. To her way of thinking, it's Candace and Jack who have gotten what they wanted in life. *Perhaps we're all myopic*, she thinks. *Maybe it's not just me.*

"It's true that you didn't get Beau," Candace continues. "He married me. But evidently that didn't stop him from sneaking down to Albuquerque now and again to see you. And you weren't the only one, by the way. As far as I know, you *were* the only one who got pregnant. Just think of it: *you* could have had an abortion, but you didn't. *You could have had an abortion.* Beau would have paid for it if you'd asked him. Instead, you had the baby, and you kept her paternity a secret—by never telling Beau he had a daughter, or telling Jack he didn't. And then there's Sophie, who's been lied to her entire life."

Peggy is crying now. She sits cross-legged on the floor, weeping.

But Candace isn't finished. "I've stopped payment on the check, at least until I have a chance to talk to Sophie myself. It's not something I want to do, but it's something I feel I have to do. I promised to help in good faith, but that was before I knew the circumstances. You didn't tell me that I would be helping to destroy the life of my one and only grandchild. *Shame on you, Peggy!*"

"Candace," Peggy says. Then again, "Candace. Really, I need your understanding here."

But Candace won't be moved. "I really need *your* understanding. Once the pregnancy is over, I'll assume complete responsibility. Sophie can finish high school and go on to college. I'll be glad to help or stay entirely out of the picture. As you see fit."

"Sophie's going to make up her own mind, Candace," Peggy says. "I have never been very good at telling her what to do. She's promised to talk to Will, and I suppose if you're going to stop payment on the check—"

"I already have."

"Well, then we'll have to talk to Jack as well."

Candace is silent on the other end, silent for so long that Peggy thinks she may be privy to the words forming inside her friend's head. "If it's necessary," Candace says, "if it *becomes* necessary, I will talk to Jack myself."

"Good-bye, Candace," Peggy says. She hangs up quickly, before either one of them can make matters even worse.

When Peggy gets home, Sophie is putting the finishing touches on Ian's costume. He's dressing as a hippie, of all things, and attending a party at the middle school, both last-minute decisions. Sophie found a tie-dye T-shirt in Peggy's closet and a pair of Birkenstocks. Ian has his own pair of threadbare jeans, and Peggy provides love beads and a pair of rose-tinted spectacles. Sophie's final offering is an enormous doobie, which she rolls using a good half bottle of crumbled basil. It's the closest thing to marijuana they have on hand.

Jack objects when he sees it. "Looks like something out of a Cheech and Chong movie," he complains.

"That's the point," Sophie replies. She gestures for Ian to stop flashing the thing and stow it in a pocket.

Because it's chilly outside—the weatherman is predicting a frost overnight—Peggy goes through her closet and pulls out a suede fringe jacket. Sophie shrieks when she sees it. "I can't believe you're letting him wear that! You never let me!" Peggy makes a face and hushes Sophie.

The jacket is too big for Ian. The sleeves hang down over his hands. He looks a little clownish, but he's beaming, and none of them have the heart to tell him to take it off. "Besides," Sophie says when they've dropped him off at Taft, "he'd be cold without a coat."

"I'll say," Peggy replies. The car heater takes forever to warm up; she's shivering and looking ahead to a hot bath and her flannel pajamas.

When Sophie has pulled away from the school, Peggy asks, "What are you up to tonight, Sophie? You handled that well, by the way." Turning onto San Isidro, Sophie was suddenly confronted with a line of cars dropping off middle-schoolers, but she kept her cool and negotiated the traffic patiently, all the while holding her own with the clutch.

"Not sure," Sophie replies. "Will is supposed to have to work."

"What does that mean, 'supposed to have to?'"

"That's what he said: 'I think I have to work.'"

"Have you talked to him, Sophie?"

When Sophie makes her turn onto Fourth Street, Peggy repeats the question. "Have you talked to him?"

Sophie clears her throat. "I talk to him all the time," she says guardedly.

"You know what I mean, Sophie. Have you talked to him about the pregnancy?"

"No-o-o," she admits, "but I gave him a note after you dropped me off, in the hall during passing period."

The distress in her voice is enough to bring tears to Peggy's eyes. They haven't seen any trick-or-treaters, but just then children—three, maybe four of them—dart into the street in front of their car. At first the children are simply shapes in motion; then they turn their faces toward the headlights and wave happily. One of them is wearing a yellow mask of some kind, and another has on a pair of silvery wings. Thankfully they make it safely to the other side and disappear into the darkness.

Sophie reacts by gasping and braking abruptly and unnecessarily.

This learning-to-drive business is hard on everyone. "Are they going to run right out in front of me?" she cries.

"That's what makes driving tricky," Peggy answers. "Which is why you need the fifty hours with a parent."

Sophie grumbles that they seem like an eternity, those fifty hours, and Peggy agrees. They seem that way to her as well.

Once they are safely home again, once Sophie has taken the key out of the ignition and passed it across the console to her mother, Peggy reaches out and grabs her daughter's sleeve. "Just stay there, where you are, in the driver's seat for a minute. We need to talk."

Sophie nods. "You know, it's been a week since I gave him the note, and he hasn't said a word."

Her daughter is crying, but for the moment, Peggy is dry-eyed. To stay that way, she gazes through the windshield at the roughhewn side of the storage shed. She hears herself begin, "I talked to Candace this afternoon." Then she hears herself recounting the conversation, excising only the parts that relate to Beau. Candace has never had a child, Peggy tells Sophie, much as she has always wanted one. She's all alone in the world now, and more than anything, she'd like to adopt Sophie's baby. "That is, if you decide to go in that direction," Peggy concludes.

Sophie grips the steering wheel and ponders the situation. "Isn't she a little old to be adopting a newborn?"

"She is, yes, but not *too* old, at least I don't think so. What do you think?"

Sophie shrugs and opens the door. Chilly air rushes into the car. "I think it's fucking freezing!" she says, and they leave it at that.

Jack is in the living room watching television, or rather flipping through stations with the remote, looking for something to watch. Sophie retreats to her room upstairs as soon as she enters the house. Peggy hears her daughter's footfalls on the stairs. For a moment, she stands in the kitchen and collects herself. Before changing into her nightclothes, she decides to check on Jack.

The living room is lower than the rest of the house; it was added on in the seventies, when split-levels were popular with architects. Because it's a bit subterranean, the family refers to it as "the pool." Ian likes to joke that they could haul a hose inside and turn it into a giant wading pond in no time. Most often, the pool goes unused, except when they have guests, who retire to the sofa bed against the far wall. No one in the family is addicted to television. Sometimes a day or two will go by without its ever being turned on. Usually, though, when someone is watching, that someone is Jack.

"Everything okay?" he asks.

She nods and smiles. "What are you up to?"

"Waiting for the doorbell to ring," he says. They both know they won't have a single trick-or-treater. They never do, because their house is too far off the beaten path. "Vampire movie coming on in ten minutes. Better hurry up and put on your evening clothes."

When she returns dressed in pj's, a robe, and fuzzy slippers, she asks if he wants some popcorn. She knows the answer. In their whole married life, Jack has never turned down popcorn. Now that he's had his health scare, he does opt for a healthier brand—less fat, less sodium—but the concessions he's made in his diet are relatively few. She doesn't know why he's been scared off sex. Wouldn't the exercise be good for his heart? She wants to ask someone, but for the life of her, she can't think of anyone to confide in with such a question.

He calls after her, telling her to hurry up and punch the buttons on the microwave. "No one can say we didn't do our bit for Halloween if we watch a vampire flick. Should I go check with Sophie and see if she wants to join us?"

"Sure," Peggy calls over her shoulder, though here, too, she can predict the response.

She hears the squeak of the reclining chair as he raises it, then the shuffle of his slippers as he passes through the kitchen and mounts the stairs.

Standing in front of the microwave, watching the sack revolve, and waiting for that first reassuring pop, Peggy realizes that it's been weeks since she and Jack have had a whole evening together at home. Jack is either at CNM or he's over at the fixer-upper. The popcorn is making a racket now, so Peggy leaves it to finish up on its own and wanders over to the refrigerator to find a beverage. The kitchen is something of a mess, but she decides to ignore it. If she starts to clean, she'll miss the beginning of the movie. What to drink, what to drink? She knows Jack will want a beer. He doesn't drink much on weeknights, but this is a holiday, and he is evidently in a celebratory mood. Witness the vampire movie.

But when he comes downstairs, his joie de vivre is gone. "What's with her?" he asks Peggy. He stops at the other end of the kitchen, arms folded across his chest. He's wearing a gray sweat shirt and black sweat pants, the uniform of the males in the Granger household. Ian would wear his sweat pants to church if they went, which they don't.

The microwave dings to signal that the popcorn is done. Peggy takes down the plastic bowl they've assigned to popcorn and pretends to focus on the task of opening the bag and pouring out its steaming contents.

"Let's go into the living room," she says. "There's probably something we should talk about."

Jack closes his eyes. "She's pregnant, isn't she?"

Peggy looks up, astonished at his insight. "How did you know?"

He opens his eyes and steadies his gaze on Peggy. "That dress she's wearing today—it hides her shape. She runs around half-naked all the time, and suddenly she puts on a purple tent. Doesn't add up. And she's been walking around the house carrying handfuls of saltines. Moping. She's been wearing a sad-sack face morning, noon, and night."

Peggy had no idea her husband was so observant.

"How long have you known?" he asks. "And why have I been kept in the dark?"

"Sophie didn't want to worry you, and neither did I. In the beginning I thought we'd get it taken care of, then tell you about it afterward."

"I guess I wouldn't have minded that," he says.

Once they are in the living room, seated in front of the television, once the movie is underway, he mutes the sound. "We should have a family meeting, and get it all out in the open."

Over the years they've held Sunday-afternoon sessions—attendance required—during which the family can discuss matters of interest to all. While living at Morningstar, Peggy attended many such meetings. They didn't always settle differences, but they did dispel tension and promote understanding. Where the family is concerned, Peggy has often advocated for such meetings, but in this case she doesn't think it's a good idea. She says so.

Crossing his arms over his chest, peering at her pointedly, Jack asks for an explanation.

"It's personal, Jack. It's a private health matter."

"So was my heart attack," he fires back. "We sure as hell talked about that. This affects the rest of us, too. We deserve some say in the matter."

"The meeting you're referring to was about the fixer-upper," she counters. "And you'd already bought it, Jack. We were merely informing the kids and asking for their support. Don't you remember?"

Jack does recall, of course. And he knows Peggy is right. They did talk a little about the heart attack, but only as a means of introducing Jack's decision to begin shifting his priorities in order to regain his health. He had asked for the cooperation of the rest of the family because he knew it would be a stretch where finances were concerned. In the short term, he told them, he'd be busier, away from home even more than he had been. But he would be getting exercise and some quiet time, and he'd be taking one step toward realizing a dream.

He'd expected the kids to ask him about the dream, and he was disappointed when they didn't. Ian did agree to spend his Sundays at the fixer-upper, helping Jack with various tasks. And Sophie promised to get a job and put her earnings toward paying her car insurance. At the end of the meeting, they all felt a little better about things, a little closer to one another, a little more optimistic about their future. You couldn't ask for more than that. Of course, in the months since, nothing has gone according to plan, at least not where Sophie is concerned.

Peggy sighs and shakes her head. "I took her to the clinic last week, and afterward, she read me the riot act in the car. 'This is my fucking decision,' she said. She's finished the first trimester, Jack."

Jack closes his eyes and takes several deep breaths. "I'm going to resist yelling," he says quietly, "because I don't want to broadcast my anger to Sophie. But I am furious, Peg. This is entirely out of hand now." He sighs; one of his exhalations is worth two of Peggy's. "You've always been too easy on her. You've let her have her way for years, and now we are going to pay the price for it. We'll be spending our retirement raising a grandchild."

"No," she counters, "surely not."

Until the conversation with Candace, Peggy had worried about the same thing. Just last week, at the grocery store Smith's, she ended up in line behind a woman who appeared to be in her late fifties. It was late afternoon, and the woman was wearing an ill-fitting suit and high heels, which she teetered in. It appeared that she had just gotten off work and rushed to pick up her grandchild from day care. A toddler wearing a baseball cap rode in the woman's cart. He looked downcast, and after a minute or two, Peggy realized why: he had a cold. While Peggy looked on, the child sneezed violently, his head jerking forward with such force that the cap took to the air as though tossed. And the hat wasn't the only thing that went flying. Snot shot out of the boy's nose, thick greenish glop. Peggy had forgotten all about what Ian used to call "nose glue."

"Oh, dear god," the woman moaned. She bent over and fumbled in her bag.

"Do you need a Kleenex?" Peggy asked. She always carried the little cellophane packages. *You never know when you'll need a Kleenex*, her mother used to say.

The woman glanced up and, seeing the square of tissue Peggy was holding out, managed something of a smile. "Thanks so much," she said.

And that was it. The woman turned her back on Peggy and began the task of wiping the muck from her grandson's face. The cashier cleared her throat, prompting the harried grandmother to empty her cart onto the conveyor. She was buying a box of diapers. Of course she was. And a bottle of wine. The pairing made perfect sense to Peggy.

Jack might as well have read his wife's mind. "Take her back to Planned Parenthood. Ask them—no, beg them—to talk some sense into her."

Peggy wants to leave it there, but she knows she can't. She needs to finish what she's started. "Jack, the counselors at Planned Parenthood are not going to twist Sophie's arm when it comes to an abortion. They're not in the business of selling them, you know. If she doesn't want one, they're not going to reason with her. That's your job."

"How do you figure that?"

"Well, remember the Sunday when she went out to the hives with you? I don't know what all went on out there, but your killing the queen made such an impression on her. Don't you recall the discussion about sin at breakfast, her asking you—"

"If it was a sin to kill a bee?" Jack asks. "Well, it's not of course."

"But she was pregnant then. Don't you see?"

"Why didn't you tell me?" He's holding the bowl of popcorn in his lap. He has yet to eat a single kernel.

"I didn't know! I didn't have any idea. Maybe I should have wondered. I probably should have. Thinking back on it now, I can see that the questions about sin should have been a red flag."

"*DUH*," they both intone in unison.

Jack relents. "I'll talk to her. Not that I have the faintest idea of how to approach the subject, but I'll bumble through it as best I can."

To signal the end of the conversation, he reaches for the remote control and restores the sound. There's no dialogue; no scene is in progress. Night is falling on an old frame house on a hill. A plaintive violin wields its melody around them. Peggy leans back in her chair and closes her eyes. She knows better than to think she can fall asleep, but she certainly wishes she could. Instead, she does the next best thing: she turns her attention to the movie.

It's winding up when the phone rings. Jack is reclining in the La-Z-Boy and doesn't even attempt to get up. In spite of herself, Peggy has been beguiled by the movie. So many vampires, so little goodness in the world. The phone rings twice. Sophie gets it upstairs. Most often, they let her answer because they assume it's for her. And they're right. The call is from Ian, who was definitely hoping to reach his sister.

Ian is at the Century 14 downtown movie theater, miles from Taft Middle School. There will never be a satisfactory explanation for how he got there, though it will come to light that he borrowed the cell phone of a sympathetic adult to make the call. He wants to know if Sophie can sneak out of the house and come pick him up. He knows she isn't supposed to drive alone, and she knows that he knows, so she doesn't bother to tell him that it will necessitate sneaking out of the house and getting back quickly enough that neither parent notices. He knows he's asking a big favor, but it's one she's happy to grant.

As she slips down the stairs and heads for the kitchen door, she hears Jack saying, "Why don't you fix us another bag of corn?" And Sophie realizes she'll have to hightail it if she wants to get herself out of the house, and the car out of the drive, before Peggy reaches the kitchen. Her heart beats strongly as she grabs the car keys off the table and hurries out. But once she's outside she feels downright happy. She's been so good lately, she thinks to herself. It's not much fun being so good.

Her timing is excellent. The drone of the microwave drowns out the noise of the car as it starts up and pulls away.

Ian is at Century 14, and, as promised, he is waiting on the sidewalk. His arms are crossed over his narrow chest; his dyed hair stands out at odd angles. The jacket and bandana appear to have disappeared. So have the Birkenstocks. Ian is barefoot and shivering, and when he climbs into the passenger seat, Sophie notes that her brother is pressing the bandana against his nostrils. His cheek is smeared with blood, presumably from his nose.

"Is it broken?" Sophie asks.

Ian shakes his head. "I don't think so," he replies.

He won't tell her how it happened. He won't tell her anything more than he has to. "There's nothing you can do," he tells Sophie.

"Maybe there is!"

"What? Am I going to have my pregnant sister beat up the bullies?"

Sophie is paying attention to her driving, but when she stops at the light at Sixth and Central, she turns to Ian. "How did you know? I'm not showing, am I?"

He shakes his head. He knows enough to lie. "No, you look just the same."

"Does Jack know?" she asks.

Ian shrugs and gestures toward the windshield. The light has changed.

Sophie lurches to a start. She shushes Ian when he threatens to speak again. "I have to concentrate," she says. "If I have an accident, we're both screwed."

Ian mumbles something.

"What is it?" she barks.

"We're both screwed already," he says.

And as that observation settles into the air between them, the siblings decide independently that their parents will be beside themselves with worry by the time they pull into the drive, that Peggy and Jack will rush out and begin yelling before the two of them have even managed to get out of the car, that Sophie will lose her learner's permit, that Ian will be forced to name names—something he is loath to do.

But none of it happens. They get off scot-free with their parents. The movie is winding down when they creep through the kitchen door. Sophie gets Ian some ice cubes and wraps them in a kitchen towel. She carries the makeshift cold pack up to his room and holds it in place for him for a few minutes, as long as he will allow.

"What else do you know?" she asks. Then: "What else do you know about Aunt Candace?"

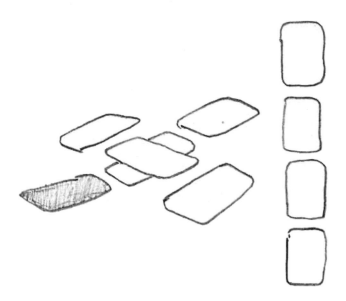

Position #3—"What Is Beneath Her"

Where did the problem begin? This card gives you insight into the origins of the situation. Be still; listen carefully. Voices from the past are attempting to speak.

~ Six of Cups ~

Children are capable of great love, and this pair, a boy and girl, reminds us of the sweetness of youth and times gone by. The boy has gathered more flowers than he has cups to hold them. He has so much love to give, and it's as free as the flowers. Or is it?

PEGGY ARRIVED IN Taos, New Mexico, on a darkly beautiful November afternoon in 1968, just ahead of the first big snowfall of the season. In those days the Greyhound bus stopped at the Conoco station on the edge of the village, where, most often, the driver gave his passengers a ten-minute break to use the facilities, get something to drink, and stretch their legs. On that Thursday the tall, thin fellow behind the wheel kept the engine running, and when the only departing passenger didn't make her way down the aisle quickly enough, he put the bus in park and went to offer his assistance. He had a storm at his back and Pueblo, Colorado, to make before nightfall.

Peggy was poky. She put away her colored pencils, then bundled her cards and stowed the lot in a fringed leather bag in her lap. At the urging of the driver, she climbed over her elderly seatmate and into the aisle, but then she changed her mind and returned to rummage beneath the seat. In the last few months she'd lost so much: the watch from her wrist, stolen as she slept in a hallway; a ten-dollar bill she'd curled into the toe of her shoe; and finally the shoes themselves, loaned to a runaway even more desperate than she.

Feeling around on the dark floor, Peggy kept up a steady stream of apologies to the driver in the aisle and to her white-haired seatmate, who registered his discomfort with the proceedings by clearing his throat and crossing and uncrossing his legs. Peggy swept her fingertips beneath her seat and thereabouts, grazing the rounded toes of the man's wingtips, a wadded candy wrapper, the bolted legs of the seat, and, as she was about to give up, two cards she otherwise would have lost forever: the III of Swords and the VII of Cups.

On the trip from San Francisco to New Mexico, she had occupied herself with making the cards her own. The tarot class she'd taken over the spring and summer had been held in the back room of a pawnshop, conducted around a rickety and crowded card table. The shop's owner was a sour little man who crossed his arms over his chest and gazed warily at his wife's students, clearly skeptical of the whole enterprise. His sweet wife didn't notice her husband's disapproval because the cards transported her elsewhere.

The tarot teacher advocated coloring the cards by hand as the best way to learn, and Peggy went about the task of transforming the black-and-white images using the instructions provided in her class. She wasn't an artist, and the jolting progress of the bus only added to the uncertainty of the enterprise, but she did her best. For weeks she had been working her way through the major arcana. With so many empty hours on the bus, she'd made considerable progress on the minor arcana as well—first the Cups and Swords, then the Wands. By the time she arrived in Taos, Peggy had only the Pentacles left to colorize.

The funds for both the class and the deck of cards had been raised by panhandling. As beggars go, Peggy was better than most because she was prettier than most. But she had no intention of panhandling in Taos. That's where the cards came in. Her friend Mary had come up with the idea after spotting a flyer in a bookstore window. "We can become fortune-tellers," she had said. "Wouldn't that be a fun way to earn a living?" At the time it had made perfect sense: take a class, then set up shop on a street corner.

Peggy had always been a dutiful student, and she found the weekly sessions and assignments enjoyable. In the months since running away from home, she'd missed the structure of school. Mary's reaction, on the other hand, was to reject the whole enterprise. She found the memorization and reading tiresome.

The driver hustled Peggy down the aisle, practically shooing her along in his haste. Then, at the very last second, he reached for the lever to open the doors—whoosh!—and escorted her off the bus. Peggy stumbled out into the cold just ahead of him. When she turned to face the road, the wind made a scarf of her waist-length brown hair, wrapping it tightly around her neck.

The thin denim of her bell-bottoms went stiff and cold against her ankles; the red cardigan she'd carefully buttoned against the winter weather was so thin that Peggy began shivering almost immediately. She had on a pair of Weejun penny loafers she'd picked up at the Diggers' Free Store in the Haight, but she was hatless, gloveless, and coatless.

Hastily the driver rummaged in the luggage compartment, grabbed the only backpack—a dense, cold bundle of green nylon, full of mostly summer clothes—and thrust it into her arms. Without so much as a *good-bye* or *good luck*, he scrambled back up the steps and pulled the doors closed behind him. Whoosh. Within seconds the bus was pulling away, leaving in its wake a blast of stinking exhaust that provided a mere second or two of welcome warmth.

And that's when it hit her: Peggy didn't know a soul in Taos, New Mexico. It was freezing, too cold to hunch in some doorway, as she'd done on the worst nights in the Haight. Here, she'd have to find shelter or risk freezing to death.

The first flakes began falling as Peggy trudged down Paseo del Pueblo Norte, the main through street in town. She didn't know it then, but the bus had let her off in Ranchos de Taos, so she had a long walk ahead of her. At first the snowflakes captured her attention; they were large enough to resemble bits of lace that landed and decorated the red sleeves of her sweater. In Waco, snow had been the next best thing to a miracle. What knowledge Peggy had of it was of the paper-and-scissors variety. She knew that snowflakes were fun to cut out and tape to the glass of her bedroom windows, an activity she'd undertaken nearly every holiday season since she had turned ten. Not this year, she thought. She didn't have windows. But she did have snowflakes, real ones, and Peggy opened her mouth and stuck out her tongue.

As minutes passed, then an hour, the beauty of the snow became less and less transporting. The slush by the roadside had seeped into her shoes. She was sniffling, from the cold and from her own misery. Seeing her reflection in the plate-glass front of a service station, she was reminded of a card she had yet to color, the V of Pentacles. It depicted a young girl and her lame brother trudging along in the snow, passing the stained-glass window of a church. Peggy had another reason for identifying with the card: her older brother walked with a limp, the result of a mild case of polio. The two had never been particularly close, but thinking of Todd now made Peggy ache inside.

At the sound of the next approaching car, she did what now came as second nature: she turned and stuck out her thumb. The first car didn't stop. Nor did the second, but the third vehicle to sputter past was a VW bus. A stooped young man peered at her through wire-rimmed glasses. "Hurry!" he said. "Get in! Throw your pack in back." In the winter weather, a car following too closely might rear-end him. He dropped her off at the plaza and gifted her with a purple wool cap, left behind by another passenger.

Peggy's first glimpse of the plaza was through a curtain of falling snow. She was reminded of her father's favorite Westerns. The buildings were squat, one-story, constructed of adobe and connected by a boardwalk. Before arriving in New Mexico, Peggy had never seen a flat roof, and she found the boxy shape of many of the buildings odd and disconcerting. Her gaze was drawn to the buildings with pitched roofs. Frosted with a layer of snow and outlined in Christmas lights, they reminded her of gingerbread houses. She was famished; everything she saw made her think of food. During two days on the road, she had eaten only two real meals, and the cold exacerbated her empty stomach and light head.

Like thousands of other young people that year, Peggy had arrived at the mountain village more or less by chance. Back in San Francisco, a guy named Danny Blue Eyes had talked nonstop about getting back to the land. Then someone she met in the Free Store had waxed eloquent on the beauty of Taos, the closest thing to paradise he'd ever seen. She was tripping at the time, which may be why she remembered the name of the place but not the person who'd uttered it. In three days, three different people had murmured the words "Taos, New Mexico." And in the same breath: "We have to get back to the land." What did it mean to get back to the land? She had only the vaguest idea.

By that time, Peggy had been gone from home for eight months. She'd left on a lark, setting out from Dallas with Mary. The two of them had been part of a group excursion—their senior class had been transported on buses to the state fair in Dallas. When it came time to go home, Mary suggested they give the chaperones the slip: "We'll never get another chance, you know?" It wasn't difficult; after they were accounted for, they'd stolen off and away, to a concert at the State Fair Music Hall. The date of the excursion was March 10, 1968. It wasn't until after their arrival at the music hall that the girls learned that Eric Burdon and the Animals would be performing that night.

Mary and Peggy just had to hear "We Gotta Get Out of this Place" and Burdon's rendition of "The House of the Rising Sun." And so they did. With the same ease with which they'd slipped off the bus, Mary and Peggy made their way into the concert, bypassing the ticket takers and snagging a pair of empty seats in the balcony.

Later that night, in the backseat of someone's broken-down Chevy, they'd belted out their own rendition: "We're gonna get out of Waco, if it's the last thing we ever do!" They had made running away look easy. For days, they laughed at their own exploits. But it would not be so easy to *stay* away. A few months after her arrival in Taos, Peggy heard through the grapevine that Mary had returned home to Waco, that she was back in school and working Saturdays at the local Dairy Queen.

When Peggy wandered past, Candace was sitting in her truck, contemplating the chances of making the birthday call. The young woman was obviously a newcomer, and she'd arrived at the worst possible time. The first big winter storm of the season was approaching. Candace had driven to town determined to complete a few necessary tasks: make a birthday call to her aunt Agnes, get a pregnancy test, and buy a fifty-pound bag of brown rice.

First Candace had headed to the phone booth in the square, but the line stretched down the sidewalk to the street. Every freak in town had a call to make. They all looked cold standing there, wrapped in ponchos and serapes or wearing fringed suede jackets that were mighty groovy but didn't really cut the cold wind. Most appeared resigned, even resolute, as they stamped their feet and hugged their arms tightly to their chests. She didn't see anyone who owed her a favor. So many people did. Why couldn't one of them be waiting to use the phone?

Candace considered offering Peggy a ride. Of course she knew where Peggy was headed. She was going there herself. La Clínica was in the space next to the general store. But in the swirling snow, she lost sight of the girl, and she quickly moved on to other matters. She couldn't afford to waste time. In a few short months she'd gone from being a pampered niece in Boston who never raised a finger to feed or care for herself, to provider for all manner of luckless and clueless freaks. Crazy thing was, in her whole life, she'd never been so happy or felt so competent. At long last, someone needed her; someone missed her when she was gone; someone would be watching out the window to remark on her return.

Back at Morningstar they needed brown rice and flour. They needed pinto beans, too, but Candace wasn't sure she had the money for all that. The end of the month came for her as well. But she'd buy as much as she could, especially because they might be snowed in for a few days.

She pulled away from her parking place along the plaza and headed for the storefront that housed both the general store and La Clínica. A wide, wooden sidewalk traversed the length of the building, and in good weather, hippies congregated—some with business to transact, others hoping for a place to sleep or someone to sleep with, and still others just to hang out and enjoy the day. Usually, unkempt kids ran up and down the boardwalk, chasing balls or dogs. Someone would be crouched over a guitar, fingering frets and glancing up at passersby, hoping for a donation. If the musician was proficient, a small crowd might gather. That was one of the great things about those warm-weather days. No one was ever in a hurry.

Only, on this particular winter afternoon Candace *was* in a bit of a rush. The tires on the truck were all but bald, and she knew she needed to get back on the highway toward Arroyo Seco before the snow began building up on the streets in town. She'd lived her whole life in a snowy climate, so she was wary of winter weather. Off to the north, the whole of Taos Mountain was already socked in. Sighing heavily, she took the key from the ignition and pressed her weight against the door. Slowly, the door swung open—groaning, creaking, making every sort of objection—and Candace hopped out.

La Clínica was one of the first free clinics in the country, and Candace was proud to be one of its supporters. Yet on this occasion she would have preferred anonymity. She knew the student interns working inside, both men, one from El Paso and the other from Massachusetts. Holy Cross Hospital refused to treat hippies, so this was the place to come regardless of the complaint. The system was, of course, first come, first served, and the plate-glass windows allowed passersby to assess the state of the wait inside. The glass was foggy; even so, Candace could see enough to determine that the wait would be at least an hour.

Just as she hadn't managed to make the birthday call, neither would she end up getting the pregnancy test. Six people were ahead of her, and nearly all of them were familiar. *Why are you here?* they would ask. Nobody had a secret. Nobody wanted one. But Candace had her pride, and she had her reasons as well. She went in and talked to one of the interns—just a friendly visit, she explained. Then she left. She told herself there wasn't any particular hurry. Once the storm had blown through, once the roads were passable again, she'd take the truck into Santa Fe. She would get her test and decide what to do.

The snowflakes were large and feathery, beautiful cutouts, every one entirely different. Like people, Candace thought. She pulled the red wool scarf over her head, knotted the ends under her chin, and, for a minute or two, simply stood and watched the flakes fall. If she had known for sure whose baby was growing in her belly, she might have been more willing to carry it. If, for instance, she'd known it was Beau's. She loved him. Of that she was certain. But his affections for her were hard to gauge. And he wasn't ready to settle down, not with her, not with anyone. He'd made that point clear.

Later they would make much of the coincidence, the way Candace took note of Peggy in the plaza, then, entering the store, encountered her again. Peggy noticed Candace as well, particularly when she ducked through the door of the store. The snow had blown in with her, and for a second or two, the air around the tall young woman glinted and glittered. Candace stomped her boots on the mat longer and harder than was necessary. Peggy observed that as well.

Peggy had situated herself against an inside wall for warmth and was using her backpack as a tabletop. A small but colorful sign advertised TAROT CARD READINGS. Candace stopped to admire the neat lettering in rainbow-colored inks. Later she would tell Peggy that she had tried her hand at calligraphy back in Boston, but she'd found it difficult to master. Candace would confide that she admired people who did the small things well. It gave her confidence in their ability to handle the larger things.

Of course she wanted a reading, but she was not inclined to squat down in the midst of the bulk foods, passersby stealing glimpses, their wet boots clomping past. Then gossiping later. Call it what you would, but Candace had her pride.

While she hesitated, another young woman dropped onto the dusty wooden floor across from Peggy, and the two of them immediately got down to business. Peggy passed the deck of cards across the backpack to the young woman, then leaned in to whisper instructions. Candace moved away.

The store was out of brown rice, so Candace bought oatmeal instead. She got everything left in the bin. And she bought a fifty-pound bag of pinto beans. She dragged it to the counter, aware that Peggy was stealing glances.

"Stocking up for the snowstorm?" the man behind the counter asked. Candace nodded curtly.

By the time she had finished her transaction, Peggy was waiting at the door with her backpack. "Let me help you carry some of that," Peggy offered. Together the two of them lugged the bag of beans out into the snow and tossed it in the back of the truck.

"I'd like a reading, but not here," Candace admitted. "And it looks to me like you need a place to stay."

Peggy nodded. Climbing into the truck, she thanked her lucky stars for the flyer and for Mary, whose idea it had been to take the class. Now, at least, Peggy had something to offer to strangers, something besides sex. More than once in the Haight she'd been reduced to spreading her legs in return for a place to sleep. Not that she'd allowed herself to think about it in those terms; instead, she'd simply pretended to have an attraction that she didn't really feel.

Candace felt lucky, too. Or rather, Candace felt guided. It would seem to her later that she was meant to pick up Peggy. In the cab of the truck on that first afternoon, as she leaned into the steering wheel and struggled to see the road, Candace poured out her worries to her new best friend. "I don't want to have a baby," she explained. "Good lord, I don't even know whose it is for sure. I mean there are only a couple of possibilities, but still. . . . My family just wouldn't understand. Some things you can keep to yourself; others you can't. A baby is something you have to share, something you *want* to share."

Peggy simply listened. It was the easiest thing in the world to do, to slouch down in the seat, to wrap her numb hands in the scarlet scarf Candace had tossed into her lap, and to gaze out at the wondrous world of white. The mountains were entirely hidden by clouds. At that moment Peggy didn't have a clue that Taos was nestled in a valley. Even so, she'd already wondered aloud at the beauty of the place. She felt like Alice in Wonderland.

"No wonder everyone is coming here," she said when Candace finally stopped talking. "Did you know I was raised in Waco, Texas? I can't believe all of those people live *there* when they could be living *here*."

Startled, Candace looked Peggy's way. "Don't tell them. Thousands showed up last summer. Most needed food and a place to stay."

"Like me," Peggy replied.

"No, no, that's not what I meant. You have something to offer. I'm not just coming to your rescue. You're coming to mine as well."

On her third morning at Morningstar, Peggy ventured outside with a few of the others. The clouds had lifted such that the majestic mountain reappeared. It stood out against the blue sky, its edges filigreed by snow. Peggy was shaken by the sight of it.

The locals call it El Monte Sagrado, the sacred mountain, in part because it is a holy place for the Taos Pueblo Indians who have lived in its shadow for a thousand years. Just over the shoulder of Taos Mountain stands Wheeler Peak, an outcropping of rock that scrapes up against the sky at over thirteen thousand feet. It is the highest point in New Mexico. The word "majestic" comes to mind; so do the words "magical" and "monumental."

For Peggy, the only words that served to measure her astonishment were "far out." The others gathered around were in agreement. "Far out," they murmured among themselves.

Candace stayed inside. Born and raised in Boston, she was more or less immune to the beauty of snow. But before Beau braved the cold, she insisted that he wear her striped wool cap. She pulled it over his dark, unruly curls herself. "There," she said when he was wearing both the hat and a navy pea coat. "Now you won't freeze."

He thrust his hands into the pockets of the coat and grinned wickedly. "Thanks, Momma," he quipped.

Standing in the knee-deep snow, Beau warbled the refrain to a Donovan song: "First there is a mountain, then there is no mountain, then there is." He had an uncanny way with accents. Mimicking the Scottish rock star was no more difficult for him than aping Candace's Boston brogue or imitating Elvis.

Until that moment, the lyrics had never made any sense to Peggy. But now they did. She began to sing as well. Though neither knew all the words, they belted out the chorus several times, until a crow swept over their heads and, cawing, pleaded with them to stop.

When he noticed that Peggy was shivering, Beau sidled over and pulled her close. He was half a head taller than she, and he draped his arms around her shoulders and pressed his chin into her hair. Beau was Candace's old man; that much was obvious. But Peggy was more than willing to share. She didn't ask herself whether Candace felt the same way. Later she would admit that she had been rendered stupid by love.

She didn't know that then. She wouldn't have the first idea for years and years to come.

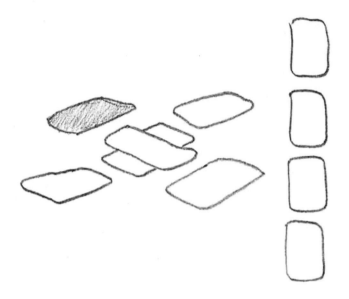

Position #4—"What Is Behind Her"

Here, the focus is on the recent past—and perhaps on someone who is playing an important role in the proceedings.

~ The Moon ~

THE MOON.

When the moon is full and we venture out into the night world, we can see more and farther, but what we see appears mysterious and unfamiliar. Transfixed by the moon, the dog and the wolf don't notice the crayfish inching up out of the waters of the subconscious. Look back on a time of upheaval and change, insomnia and strange dreams.

WILL WAS ALREADY in the kitchen getting breakfast. Laurel heard him opening cabinets and whistling as he poured himself the first of three bowls of Frosted Cheerios. Will's senior year at Valley High School began that day, and both mother and son were running behind. They had yet to establish a morning routine. He'd dressed in a hurry and, for the first time in maybe a month, left his bed unmade.

Laurel was on her way down the hall when she glimpsed the brown stains on the bedsheets. Her first thought was menstrual blood. Will had the occasional nosebleed, sure, but these stains were not on the pillowcase. They were dead center on the fitted sheet, three spots like a Rorschach inkblot.

For a minute or two, she stood befuddled in the doorway, her bare toes clutching at the grimy carpet. Don't go ballistic, she told herself. Stay calm. Try to make sense of things. In this case, the blood was all she had to go on. It had been smudged before it dried, undoubtedly by Will's body and/or his girlfriend's, and the splotches against the white background called up a succession of images: butterflies coupling; a squadron of jet fighters; and, when Laurel shifted her perspective, moving from the doorway to the bedside, storm clouds accompanied by one wavy bolt of lightning.

Even before she could fix on one image and relinquish the others, tears began sliding down her cheeks. She wasn't sure why she was crying. If she had been asked, she'd have said it was her son's lost boyhood she was weeping over—that and the indignity of discovering it. But she was grieving over the stain, too, a blotch on the sheets her mother had given her as a wedding gift. The marriage was over, her mother was dead, and now the sheets had been ruined by the blood of this obnoxious girl.

No wonder Will had been making his bed, she thought as she stripped it, revealing the discolored mattress. Yes, the blood had seeped through the pad and down into the mattress itself, creating a smaller version of the original stain.

Lately it was all she could do to keep milk in the refrigerator, toilet paper next to the commode, and a clear path from the front door to the kitchen. She wanted to be a good mother, she really did, but on a day-to-day basis, the choices weren't easy to make. Laurel told herself that it was more important to buy groceries, more important to buy Will a new pair of shoes and school supplies. The sheets and the vacuuming and the dusting could wait, she told herself. Only in this case, they couldn't.

She hustled to the bathroom for a washcloth, grabbed the last clean one, and doused it with cold water. Her mother had taught her that the first remedy for blood was to blot it with cold water, but that was when it was fresh. Laurel hadn't changed Will's sheets in a month, maybe longer. When blotting had no effect, she began to scrub, stubbornly ignoring what she already knew: the stain had set.

Once or twice she glanced over at Will's bedside table, cluttered with glasses of water, crumpled Kleenex, and a small basket of the Easter variety crammed with stubs and receipts and matchbooks. Her son is sentimental. So is she. In the back of her closet, she keeps a box of school papers, every A he's ever made and, once he hit high school, every B.

Lately, even Bs are getting scarce. She wondered what his senior year would hold in store for the two of them. Would things get better or would they get worse?

Bundling the sheets in her arms, Laurel was careful to wad the spots inward. She was in the doorway of the laundry room before she bent her head to the cotton. Yes, she could smell it there: the faintest trace of patchouli, Sophie's signature scent. Laurel dropped the sheets on top of the washing machine. The least Will could do was wash them himself, and she would tell him so.

As she dressed for work, Laurel recalled a dinner conversation with Sophie. The three of them had had an impromptu meal together at Dion's Pizza. It was Laurel's idea, Laurel's treat. Sophie and Will sat together on one side of the booth, and Laurel sat alone on the other side. Sophie said her mother had turned her on to patchouli. "They all wore it in Haight-Ashbury," she explained, waving her hand grandly so that the silver bracelets on her wrists tinkled and twirled.

"So your mother was a hippie?" Laurel asked. They were waiting for a pepperoni-and-mushroom pizza. Laurel had ordered a salad, and that had already arrived. Every minute or so, she snatched up yet another crouton. She was starving, but she was also on a diet.

Sophie explained that her mother had actually hitchhiked to San Francisco. "Pretty cool, huh?"

Will nodded. "Cool," he said, then craned his neck to see whether the pizza was on its way.

Freeloaders who believed in free love: that's the way Laurel would have defined the word "hippie." But she didn't say so. "Your mother must have been very brave, getting in cars with strangers."

Sophie nodded repeatedly, all that dark curly hair rising and falling, the one lock of bleached blonde settling over her shoulder. "She hitchhiked to Woodstock, too," Sophie continued. "Have you ever seen the movie? My mom's in it."

"Awesome," Will said. He beamed at the waiter who slid their pizza onto the table. The sweet smell of tomato sauce drifted over to Laurel's side of the table. She sighed deeply.

"I never saw that movie," Laurel replied. But the moment had passed. Both young people were busy loading up their paper plates.

"Would you like a piece?" Sophie asked Laurel.

"I don't mind if I do."

Laurel did give Sophie grudging credit for her table manners—she ate her pizza with a knife and fork, she shook out a paper napkin and pressed it into her lap—but she resented the girl's dazzling smile and the way it just kept shining, shining, shining on her son.

Will was still eating breakfast when Laurel slipped into the kitchen, a rectangular space separated from the dining room by a low bar. These days he wore his dark wavy hair so long that it brushed his collar. He parted it down the middle, and with his dark skin and Roman nose, he looked positively biblical—like one of Jesus's apostles, a fisherman. Back when she'd been pregnant, Laurel had imagined her son's childhood stretching into her old age. To care endlessly for a kid had seemed an ordeal, something she might not survive. Eighteen years. At the time she was seventeen, and getting there had been a lifelong endeavor. Yet here she was, seventeen years later, still struggling to fit into size-ten jeans, still parting her hair down the middle, still in love with Will's father, Carlos, who had never been in love with her. Nothing had changed except Will, who was now this man-child she hardly recognized.

Caked dinner dishes and smudged glasses filled the sink. A quick look told her that Will had had guests for dinner, and that he'd fixed fried eggs, bacon, and toast. If he could have his way—and most often he does—Will would eat breakfast all day long. Not so for Laurel. She rarely takes the time for breakfast, though she does need at least one cup of coffee; if she is in a hurry she can make do with instant.

While waiting for the microwave to boil her water, she ran water over the dirty plates. Will had his back to her, and he didn't turn around, but he thought it best to acknowledge the mess. "Hey, Ma. I'll do those."

Doing the dishes is one of Will's chores. Laurel is the assistant manager of Movies West, which means she works nights. Back when Will was younger, it was a good job because it gave her flexibility. Now it gives her grief. In the last five years the duties haven't changed and neither has the salary, though her expenses are higher. To make ends meet, she cleans houses two days a week. The other three mornings, she takes classes at the university. Next year she'll be awarded a BS in psychology. What awaits her after graduation is still unclear, but Laurel expects to make a new life for herself. She has to. She wants this cereal-eating machine to go to college, too, so it's necessary to prove to him that college is worth the effort.

"If you were going to do them, you should have done them last night." Laurel used her huffy, offended-mother tone, the one she'd learned from *her* mother, who'd learned it from *hers*. Whereas Laurel's grandmother had sounded wounded and her mother had come off as peevish, Laurel exuded hostility. Not that she heard her own rancor; she didn't.

"It's not the dishes I want to talk to you about," she continued. She turned off the faucet and reached for the first plate. Automatically she began filing the plates into the slots in the dishwasher. She had done this chore so many times that she didn't have to look at what she was doing. "I've just stripped your sheets. It's been a while, and I couldn't help but notice—"

Will groaned. "Don't say it, okay? It's the first day of school. Let's just chill." Then he was up and out of his seat. He collected his bowl and spoon and tucked the cereal box under his arm. After pitching the box into the cupboard, he moved on to the sink, coming so close that she got a whiff of his deodorant. It smelled of talcum with a dash of lime.

She yearned to reach out and grab him, to pull him in close until he gave himself up to her embrace. She also itched to slap him across the jaw, so hard that the palm of her hand would sting. She'd done both in the past—sometimes the first and then the second, sometimes the second and then the first. She'd done the wrong thing so many times. Above all, she wanted to do the right thing now.

"We'll talk later," she said, "but we should have talked sooner. I just didn't realize. . . . It was stupid of me, but I didn't realize. . . ." She saw it coming over his face, the shadow of something larger than either of them. "Why didn't you wash the sheets?" she blurted out. "Why'd you leave that mess for me?"

His mouth went hard, a straight slit across the bottom of his face. "You're really a bitch," he snarled, his milk breath washing over her. "I swear I hate you sometimes."

"Hate me or not, those sheets better be clean by the time I get home tonight."

The stains were set, but let him find that out himself, she thought.

Sophie didn't work on Tuesday nights, which was just as well for both of them. Laurel needed a little more space, a little more time to chill, as Will had said. The theater was quiet, though across the way, Target was packed with back-to-school shoppers. Going about her work, Laurel reminded herself of Sophie's good traits. As an employee, she was dependable and prompt. Back in April, when Sophie first started, Laurel had been so charmed by the girl that she'd told Will about her, eventually introducing the two of them. "You go to the same school, after all!" she'd said. "You should know each other!" By then it was nearly the end of the school year, but Will had managed to ask Sophie to a dance. The next time Sophie worked a shift at Movies West, he was waiting when she got off. It had been that way all summer. Laurel knew she had no one to blame but herself.

It was after midnight when she left the theater. Driving home, she watched lightning lick at the periphery of the city. The horizon was black, but occasionally the surrounding desert was lit up by multiple bolts of lightning, jagged streaks like stick figures dancing in the sky. Usually the lightning displays occurred earlier in the evening, while Laurel was busy overseeing the running of the theater, but this was a late-night storm. All over the city sleepers tossed in their beds, vaguely disturbed by the rumble of thunder and the flash of light. Laurel felt lucky to be awake.

When she got into the house, she found lights on in the living room and kitchen. The counter was clear, the dishwasher loaded and ready to be turned on. Briefly, Laurel stepped into the laundry room. The sheets had disappeared. They weren't inside the dryer; nor were they in the washer, which is where Laurel expected them to be. Will is pretty good about putting detergent in the washer and turning it on, but he rarely remembers the clothes once the load is done. Sometimes she doesn't think to check the machine for a few days, by which time the clothes have mildewed and the machine needs to be run again.

Laurel discovered her son asleep in the middle of his bare mattress. He was wearing boxer shorts but no shirt, and his feet dangled off the end of the bed. Next to his head was an open textbook. It was too dark to see what he'd been studying, but whatever it was, she was pleased.

The narrow bedroom window was wide open. Outside a shower was in progress. The pat-a-pat sound of raindrops on gravel soothed her. Laurel moved to the window, though there was nothing to see but the neighbor's wooden fence. The rain would pass quickly. Tomorrow yellow brittlebush, purple sage, and orange globe mallow would blossom along the roadsides and in the open spaces around Albuquerque. Things happen so quickly in the desert; what appears dead and gone can be resurrected overnight. The blessing of a little rain is all it takes.

Cooled by the moist breeze, Laurel stood at the window for quite a while. When she turned away, she saw that Will was chilly. In his sleep, he'd curled in on himself, so that he looked smaller and more vulnerable. He *is* vulnerable, she thought, every bit as vulnerable as he was when he was ten. Only he didn't believe it, and he wouldn't for some time to come. She took a breath and, holding it, leaned down and kissed his cheek and the corner of his lips. She inhaled as he exhaled, trying to be one with her son, until the phone rang and she had to run to catch it.

She grabbed the receiver on the third ring. "Yes, Ralph?" Ralph Avery lives in a house Laurel cleans every other Thursday morning.

"Can I come over?"

She knew exactly where he was at that moment: in the kitchen, hunched over the counter with the phone in one hand, staring at a bulldog cookie jar. Several times, Laurel has picked up the jar, planning to clean under it, only to have the dog's head come off in her hand. His head detaches neatly, just above his wide red collar. Whenever Laurel thinks of Ralph and his marriage, the cookie jar comes to mind. Things can look intact, when in reality they are coming to pieces.

Why Ralph was awake at this hour was a mystery. He claimed he didn't sleep well. When he was a child, he walked in his sleep. Now, once or twice a week, he drives in his sleep, making his way to Laurel's house, where he sidles in through the garage door. Will is a sound sleeper, and Ralph never stays long—a couple of hours at most.

"No, no," Laurel said. "I don't think it's a good idea."

Silence on the other end. Ralph knows that for Laurel, silence is more convincing than any entreaty. Laurel hates silence; she gives in to silence.

Now that he had figured that out, he was making good use of the knowledge. The first time they made love was an accident. He'd been sick in bed, but Laurel didn't know that. She had breezed into the kitchen and turned on the radio. While she cleans, Laurel listens to country. The lyrics remind her that others are just as lonely and low-down as she is, though the music is often upbeat. She can swing her hips while she sweeps. So there she'd been, straightening up the kitchen and singing along with Garth Brooks, when Ralph stumbled in, wearing white Jockey underwear and red socks. In his left hand, he brandished a pistol.

Laurel dropped a jar of raspberry jelly and screamed bloody murder. The jar didn't break, but when it hit the linoleum, the lid rolled off and jelly spurted in an arc across the floor. The gun hit the floor, too. Ralph tossed it—"Just wanted to get rid of it," he explained later—and it spun across the slick linoleum, sliding through the jelly and spreading it like a knife. What a mess, Laurel thought. She went right on screaming. It was exhilarating, really. It felt great to yell her head off in the presence of a perfect stranger. He was absolutely captivated by her scream, and so was she.

Then Ralph did the strangest thing. He reached for her, pulled her into his arms, and held her tight. Somehow they ended up in bed to-gether. Actually, now Laurel understands how it happened, though she didn't at the time. She's learned this much in her psychology classes: arousal is arousal. Whether it comes from fear or sexual excitement, it feels pretty much the same.

In any case, the sex has never been as good as it was that first time. That first time was something fantastic, almost otherworldly. Despite his headache and nausea. Despite her messy ponytail and old jeans, so tight he had to peel them off. Despite the light of day shining in on them, revealing them as so clearly imperfect, so clearly total strangers. Despite it all, that afternoon in bed will be one of the best times either of them ever has.

"All right then, Ralph, but hurry please."

She was dozing until he entered the room. "Wake up, Sleeping Beauty," he whispered. He undressed and slid onto the bed next to her.

She pretended to sleep while his hand brushed her shoulder, while his fingertips flicked away her hair so that he could kiss her bare skin. While he peeled back the sheet and ran his fingers up her thigh and across her rib cage, back and forth, rippling over the bones as though he were playing a harp. Not until his fingers closed around her left breast did Laurel shiver and open her eyes.

In the moments before she'd dropped off, Laurel had been thinking of Sophie. Not all girls are holdouts, not all girls are afraid to spread their legs. Some girls want it even before they know what they want. They feel an absence, a tingling around the absence, an urge to rub it against whatever is nearest: waxed stair railings, overstuffed chair arms, the wide patient backs of horses. They're looking for relief, and when they're fifteen or so, they find it in the arms of boys who are only too happy to fill them up and up. These are the girls who get pregnant, not only because they're the first to open their legs and hearts but also because they yearn to be filled. They love what fills them: the boy and then the baby. She was such a girl. So is Sophie. She needs to warn her son, but she has no idea how to.

Laurel hadn't intended to make a sound, but as soon as Ralph entered her, she filled the room with a moaning sound, a kind of keening. It came out of her and out of her. Ralph hovered over her in the darkness. "Laurel?" he whispered. He almost always addressed her in a whisper. "Are you all right?"

The next morning, Laurel slept in a half hour later than usual, and by the time she'd dressed, Will was already finishing his second bowl of cereal.

"What happened to the sheets?" she asked.

"I threw 'em away," Will replied. His voice carried a challenge, but she wasn't going to rise to it.

"Why'd you throw them away?" She didn't believe him, but she could pretend, too. "They're my sheets, Will, a gift from my mother."

That sort of sentiment meant very little to him. Because he didn't know how to address it, he ignored it altogether. "The stain wouldn't come out," he said.

"Did you try to get it out?"

His temper flared. "No. No, as a matter of fact I didn't. Now will you quit bugging me?"

"I can't. Not yet. You're having sex with Sophie and I'm worried. Is it safe sex at least? Are you using a condom?"

Will didn't answer. He was ready for his third bowl. He grabbed the box and tipped it over the bowl, pouring out white Os in a rush, filling the bowl and more. Cereal spilled onto the plastic place mat. "Uh-oh," he said. It was something he used to say as a toddler. Every mess was an "uh-oh."

His inadvertent slip into the past gave Laurel the gift of memory, and she was able to ignore the cereal and try again. "Are you going to answer me?" she managed to ask, and in a calm voice, too. It was admirable, this restraint. Her dead mother smiled down on her.

"Relax, Mom. Sophie's on the pill. It's cool."

Laurel ached inside. "How do you know? How do you know she's on the pill?"

Will was incredulous now. "I think she told me."

Laurel had her answer ready. "What if she told you she's runner-up for Miss America? Would you believe that, too?"

As he was pouring the milk, he turned his head and gave her that withering expression he saved for those who were stupid beyond words. The milk overflowed, too, wetting the cereal on the place mat. All of it would have to be thrown away. Four dollars a box. *Four dollars a box*, she wanted to say.

"Why would she lie?" he asked. Ignoring the mess he'd made, he bent over the bowl and began shoveling cereal.

Laurel watched him eat for a minute, then said, "Maybe the same reason I did."

Not until he'd washed down the last bite of cereal with a slug of orange juice did Will bother to reply, and by then his mother was busying herself at the sink, her face flushed with embarrassment. What if Will asked her why she got pregnant on purpose? What answer could she give that would make even a little bit of sense? *I was seventeen and stupid.* That's it. End of story.

But he wasn't interested in pursuing his mother's adolescent angst. He was still indignant on his girlfriend's behalf. "It's none of your business really, but until last month, Sophie was a virgin," he said. "The blood on the sheets, what do you think that was?"

Laurel crossed her arms over her chest and stared down at him. "Her period," she replied flatly. She would have bet her life on it. "But it's not just pregnancy I'm worried about, Will. There are diseases, too. All kinds of diseases."

Will stood and picked up his bowl, sloshing leftover milk across the linoleum floor. "Were you worrying about a disease last night? You tell that asshole you're on the pill?" He strode past and dropped his bowl into the sink, hard enough to break it. The spoon was still clattering against the porcelain when he turned to face her. "Who'd you think you were fooling?"

Laurel couldn't say anything. She blinked her eyes; it was a code. She was asking him to relent, to touch her. But he didn't read codes, this young man. He was out the door before she could manage to call his name.

Milk was the worst, she decided as she sank to her hands and knees to mop up her son's mess. First she'd clean here, then she'd clean her Wednesday house, the Murphys'. Slobs that they were, they didn't even bother to throw away their pizza boxes. Instead, they just left them stacked on the stovetop for her to deal with.

As she was rinsing out the sponge in the sink and shaking away the Os that stuck to her palms, it occurred to her to wonder what had become of the sheets. She returned to his room and opened each of Will's four dresser drawers in turn. There was no rhyme or reason to the contents. Underwear was kept in the top drawer—and in the bottom second one, depending on space. He'd found room for the sheets in his bottom drawer, by his shorts. Laurel pulled them out and, for the second day in a row, carried them down the hall to the laundry room. Before she left for work, she taped a note to the refrigerator door: WASH THE DAMN SHEETS, WILL!

That Saturday, Sophie was scheduled to work concessions from five to ten, but at five thirty she still hadn't arrived. Sophie was a punctual employee. She never called in sick, and most often she arrived a full twenty minutes early. She was quick behind the counter and polite to customers, and Laurel had never once caught her sneaking friends through the back door. Once or twice Sophie's red eyes and runaway giggle had aroused suspicion, but for all Laurel knew, the girl had allergies. Until Sophie had begun dating Will, Laurel was certainly willing to give her the benefit of the doubt. More puzzled than peeved, Laurel checked the message board, which was only as accurate as the message-taker. Then she tried the bathroom where Sophie holed up in the moments before her shift started.

Though others arrived dressed in uniform, Sophie prepared for work in public. She changed into her white blouse; clipped on the purple vinyl bow tie; plaited her unruly hair into a messy French braid; and, finally, painted on a thick coat of purple lipstick. The shade matched the awful bow tie and the carpeting in the lobby. Until Sophie went out and found lipstick to match the décor, Laurel was pretty good at ignoring her garish surroundings. Now she was reminded of them anew each time Sophie worked a shift.

The bathroom was empty, so Laurel returned to the office and looked up Sophie's number. Her father answered, and Laurel introduced herself. "I'm just checking to see if she's coming to work. Her shift started at five, and she's never been late."

Her father seemed puzzled. He said he'd dropped her off at least a half hour before. "She said she wanted to stop in at Target for something. She must have gotten hung up."

But at this point, Laurel stopped listening because Sophie burst in the door, out of breath and flushed from running. "Sorry, sorry, sorry!" she repeated.

"Oh good, she's there," her father said. "I hear her voice." And he quickly hung up.

Sophie ran off to the bathroom to get dressed, and stayed gone so long that Laurel went in after her. "You in here, Sophie?" The girl was ensconced in the first stall. She promised to be right out, and she was.

All night they spilled things. First Laurel dropped a cup of popcorn kernels. Just as she lifted the container to feed the machine, it tilted and tipped. Seeds scattered across the tile floor like hundreds of BBs, and before Sophie could sweep them up, a pudgy ticket taker named Stephanie stepped behind the counter and fell flat on her back. Stephanie swore she was okay, but Laurel heard the thud of her body as it hit the tiles, a dull, definitive noise.

"Are you sure you didn't hit your head?" Laurel asked. Stephanie's face was red, though it might have been from embarrassment, all those people staring down at her, customers leaning across the counter to get a good look. Laurel didn't want to take a chance. She sent Stephanie home to rest, which meant someone else had to man the ticket booth. Near the end of the seven o'clock rush, Sophie spilled a large Coke, bumping the cup with her elbow so that it spun across the counter and sprayed its contents over the three people standing at the head of the line. Anyone could have done it—so many of them squeezed behind the counter, rushing to fill orders—but Sophie was the culprit. The man in the middle was doused. After gasping, he broke into abrupt and noisy laughter. His large mouth opened like a cavern to reveal long rows of silver fillings. "Whew," he cried, "was that ever refreshing!"

Hearing this, Sophie began to giggle, and pretty soon she was laughing so hard that she was helpless to do anything else. Tears ran down her face; she clutched at her stomach. While she mopped up the mess, Laurel glanced over at the girl. Her abundant hair hid her face, but her shoulders were shaking, and, intermittently, a gasping sound erupted from behind the curtain of hair.

"Sophie, pull it together!" Laurel said sharply. Sophie would do no such thing. She went right on laughing. Laurel considered shaking her, but the customers needed her attention. The line was getting long and restless, and the women who received Coke baths were awaiting apologies and assistance. One wore a crisp white blouse, splotched now with brown. A large stain outlined her left breast, and beads of brown syrup slid down her cheek. As Laurel began to speak, the woman reached up to wipe at the Coke running down her face. She did this gingerly, so as not to disturb her makeup. Unlike the man, she didn't look the least bit refreshed. She looked furious. The other woman was calmer. She dabbed at the front of her green T-shirt with a wad of napkins. When Laurel caught her eye, the woman shrugged and pursed her lips.

"I'm so sorry," Laurel offered. "Why don't you step over to the restroom, where you can wash up? If you tell us what you'd like to eat and drink, I'll have it ready for you when you get back. Free, of course."

Immediately the woman in the green T-shirt ordered a large popcorn and a small Sprite, then slipped out of line and disappeared into the hallway. But the woman in white stayed put. She glared at Sophie, who, though still snickering, had returned to work at the register.

"I'd like to see the manager," the woman said between tightly pressed lips. If she had opened her mouth, she might have spit at them. The happy man edged over and draped an arm across the woman's shoulders. They were two sides of a coin: the calmer he was, the angrier she got. He was so agreeable, and she so obviously unreasonable. Laurel couldn't help but feel just the tiniest bit sorry for her.

"Why don't we put this behind us?" the man suggested.

"You put it behind you," the woman replied. "I want to see the manager."

"I'm the manager," Laurel said brightly. "Perhaps you'd like to talk in my office." She set the bucket of popcorn on the counter. "This is for the woman in the green T-shirt," she instructed Sophie, who managed to nod though she was still not in control. A small snort escaped from her nose; she clapped a hand over her mouth. She's stoned, Laurel thought. She has to be.

"You're the assistant manager," the woman corrected. She'd read

Laurel's name tag. Those behind her began grumbling, but the woman held her ground. "I want to talk to the manager."

Laurel explained that the manager didn't work on Saturdays, and that she was in charge.

"You may think you are, but you're not," the woman shot back. "If you were, that little bitch wouldn't be snickering right now." The woman's eyebrows were pale blonde. Viewed from a distance, she looked hairless and permanently startled.

Laurel turned to Sophie, who still had a hand clapped over her mouth. All the laughter the girl had ever tried to hold back was erupting to the surface. Suddenly Laurel was certain that they—the prim, Coke-stained woman; her jovial husband; Laurel; even lovesick Will—were the butt of some ugly joke. "Sophie, this isn't funny!" Laurel said sharply.

The words literally brought Sophie to her knees. She sank slowly behind the register, her face red and distorted. The hilarity was painful. Sophie was bent over double, her shoulders heaving. To a stranger it looked like grief, terrible, unmitigated grief. The woman in white leaned over the counter.

"She's out of control, completely out of control. Aren't you going to do something?" she asked Laurel.

Whereupon Laurel did the only thing she could think to do. She grabbed a large drink from the counter and heaved the liquid at Sophie. The girl gasped, then went still, so still that Laurel worried. The movie *Carrie* flashed through her mind. She considered the possibility of teenage girl retribution.

But eventually Sophie turned her head and gazed up at Laurel. "I quit," she said flatly. She rose calmly to her feet and shouldered her way out from behind the counter.

"Well, that's not what I would have done," the woman remarked loudly, but Laurel ignored her. Automatically she began taking the orders of those nearest in line. Mrs. Angry and Mr. Calm accepted buckets of popcorn, large Mr. Pibbs, and two packages of Reese's Peanut Butter Cups. They were talking amiably as they walked away.

Laurel filled in for Sophie. She willed herself to work quickly and not to think, and in this way she passed her entire shift. At the end of that very long night, she went in to clean the bathroom and discovered the discarded box for a pregnancy test. Was it Sophie's? Laurel worried that it might be, but she put the thought out of her mind. She had a way of doing that, of just forgetting the things she didn't want to remember.

The night sky was brilliant with stars. As she crossed the parking lot, Laurel stopped and looked up for a moment, taking solace in the black bowl above her. Albuquerque is known for its enormous sky. "Vast" is the word that comes to mind.

The wind picked up. A paper cup scudded across her foot and a plastic bag from Target drifted by overhead. She reached out to catch the bag, but it got caught in an updraft and floated just above her head.

Driving home, Laurel tried to think of somewhere else to go. She yearned for a friend to visit, someone to share a cup of decaf with—another single mother of a teenager, maybe—but no one came to mind. Working two jobs and going to school, Laurel had no time for friends; the ones she used to see had gone by the wayside. Evidently Ralph was her only friend. For a moment, Laurel contemplated driving to Ralph's house and using the key she had for cleaning to unlock the door. She pictured herself crossing the tile floors in her bare feet, climbing into bed between Ralph and his wife, Cynthia. Their bed was huge. They wouldn't notice her there until morning.

Instead, she followed the usual path, driving down Paseo del Norte, taking the Second Street exit to her little house—a "bungalow," the real estate agent had called it. Actually the house is a stucco box, made livable by a small covered patio in back and a large cottonwood growing in the side yard. It gets enough shade in the summer that Laurel's bedroom is almost always cool. "An oasis," Ralph calls it.

Will's rusty old junker was parked in front of the house. The front door was unlocked, and stepping inside, Laurel called out, "Hello!" in what she hoped was a cheerful voice.

The living room was dark, and so was the kitchen. Laurel flipped on the kitchen light and was surprised to find the sink empty, the stainless steel shining. The counters, too, were clean, so polished they glowed. She doused the light and stood in the dark, trying to decide what to do next. She assumed that Sophie had called Will by now, and that her son would be furious. Much as she regretted the ending of the confrontation, she still had no idea what else she could have done. Just thinking about how Will might respond made Laurel feel defensive and put upon. And then she heard the chug of the washing machine.

The light was on in the laundry room. As Laurel moved down the hallway, she took note of the fact that Will's bedroom door was closed, and that, beyond the door, the room was quiet. She hesitated, then continued on to the tiny laundry room, barely big enough for the washer and dryer. The cycle had just begun. Will must have turned on the machine only moments before Laurel pulled up in front of the house.

When she opened the lid—something she did cautiously, as if some huge rubber snake might pop out at her—she was relieved to see sheets swirling in the soapy water. For a long moment, she stared down at the whirling, swirling mass. Then, just as she was feeling hypnotized by the motion, she noted the faded pink flowers on the white background. *Her* sheets, she realized. Will was washing *her* sheets instead of his. Dropping the lid, Laurel hurried back down the hallway to her bedroom.

Her bed had been hastily stripped, the blanket and bedspread heaped on the floor. The mattress cover had been removed, too, laying bare all the stains she had never been able to get out. When Will was a baby, he had slept in her bed, and sometimes in the early mornings, he let loose with a flood of urine, wetting his bedclothes and her nightgown and staining the mattress in the process. She washed the mattress, of course; she'd scrubbed it with soap and water and Lysol. But what she hadn't realized—not for a while anyway—was that water leaves its own stain. Uneven, wavy rings marked the spots where she had cleaned. And as if that wasn't bad enough, there was her blood, too, several small splotches in the middle of the mattress and a small, circular one in the far right corner. She knew how that small one got there, but she hated to think about it.

Only, Sophie wouldn't let her forget. As Laurel bent to pick up the blanket and pull it over her mattress, she heard a peal of familiar laughter echoing down the hall. Part of her wanted to order the girl out of her house and out of her life once and for all. But she couldn't do that. Experience had taught her that some things, you couldn't get rid of; others, you couldn't get back.

The small stain in the corner was Will's blood, and though hardly more than a drop, it remains exactly what it was: the spilled blood of a three-year-old boy. Fourteen years ago, Will had perched on the corner of her bed, a little boy who was supposed to be potty-trained but wasn't, at least not for the middle of the night. She had been a mother who was supposed to know better than to slap her own child, to make his nose bleed, to lock herself in the bathroom while he cried his little heart out.

Laurel bundled the blanket in her arms and carried it down the hall. Will's door was closed, but she knew it wasn't locked. She knocked once before turning the knob and letting the door swing open. Sophie and Will sat cross-legged in the middle of the bed, playing cards. Between them was a discard pile. Laurel didn't need to look at Sophie's hand to know that she was winning. And she didn't need to look at Will's face to know that he didn't care.

The bed was neatly made, covered by an Indian-print spread of red and blue. Laurel didn't recognize the spread, but she guessed that it must have belonged to Peggy, who probably saved it as a souvenir of her years in Haight-Ashbury. Laurel wondered whether it helped to believe in free love. Did the belief itself make love easier to find and keep? She had always considered love to be precious, the sort of thing others were apt to steal from her. And so it took real effort to find her voice and say the only thing she could think of: "Thanks for doing the laundry."

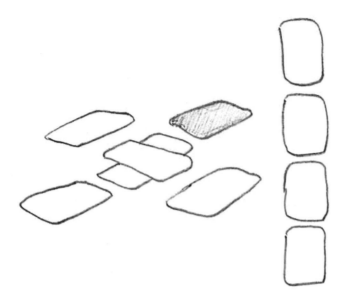

Position #5—"What Crowns Her"

This card represents your highest and wisest self or, alternatively, the possible outcome of the matter. Given that the outcome will be influenced by the values and beliefs you rely on to make your decision, the two meanings are intertwined.

~ Two of Swords ~

What an arresting picture! The young woman is in a precarious situation, likely one of her own making. Afraid of being hurt, she holds the pose and balances the swords. A stalled situation is preferable to a wrong move—which could be disastrous. But she can't sit there forever!

THE SHOP IS long and narrow. A tinkling bell over the door alerts Peggy to the fact that she has a customer. She's unpacking a box of sweaters, and rather than leave the task, she calls out a welcome to the shadowy figure up front. "Let me know if I there's anything I can do to help you."

Peggy continues to sort the sweaters by color—red, purple, and black—and by size. She stacks them neatly into piles, and as she does so, she takes pleasure in the boxy shapes and open weaves, which will complement the broomstick skirts she sells. As the woman approaches, Peggy shakes out a red one and holds it up in front of her. "Cute, don't you think?"

"Very cute," the woman replies. "How much is it?"

When Peggy tells her that the sweater is sixty dollars, the woman whistles through her teeth. "Out of *my* price range," she says. "Are you Peggy Granger, by any chance?"

"I am." Peggy drapes the sweater over her arm and regards the small, plain woman standing before her. "Do we know each other?"

"Not really," the stranger replies.

Not really? She doesn't look the least bit familiar, with her odd little brush of a ponytail and bright red lipstick.

"Our children know each other, though," she adds, "and I decided it was time we should meet."

Peggy tries to smile. Past time, she thinks. November 6, to be exact. "You must be Will's mom," she says. "Thanks for stopping in." Sophie swears Laurel is a witch, but Peggy notes that she doesn't look like one. The woman before her appears overworked and utterly ordinary, an older-than-average college student, wearing too-tight jeans and a wrinkled white blouse. As they talk, she tugs at the cuffs with her fingertips.

She introduces herself as Laurel Cassidy, then, seeing the confusion on Peggy's face, explains that Will uses his father's last name. "Carlos lives in Lubbock, rarely sees or calls his son. But you know, Will won't hear a bad word about the man."

Peggy nods. "It's understandable."

"Not to me," Laurel shoots back.

"Well, *that's* understandable, too," Peggy offers. "But I guess I know why you're here."

"You probably do, but let's get this much out of the way: Will still doesn't have a clue."

"What do you mean?"

"I mean that I got the note, but Will didn't, or hasn't. My son has a tendency to shove things in his pockets and forget about them. I find them when I get ready to do a load of laundry. And sometimes that takes a while. Don't know how long ago she gave it to him."

"Sophie wrote a note?"

"Yes! Do you want to see it?"

Laurel is shouldering a heavier-than-average bag, which she now hoists onto the counter. That it contains a little bit of everything becomes apparent as soon as she begins digging through it. Peggy sees a canister of pepper spray; a travel-size deodorant; numerous pens, most missing their covers; multiple tubes of lipstick; and a grungy-looking hairbrush.

"Oh," Laurel says to herself. "I must have put it in the inside pocket."

Sure enough, she extracts a note, still neatly folded, and passes it over the counter to Peggy, who can't help but sigh mightily. This is all going horribly wrong. From the moment she got the news, from the moment she saw the cards that announced it plain as day, she has been completely flummoxed. She wants to do the right thing. "I want to do the right thing," she tells Laurel as she holds the unopened note in her hand.

"You're not going to read it?" Laurel asks. She is restuffing her big black bag. "Are you one of those parents who respects her child's privacy? No wonder we're in this mess."

"No!" Peggy replies. "Did I say that?" Just to prove otherwise, she unfolds the half sheet of notebook paper. And there it is, her daughter's handwriting.

Dear Will: I've been trying to tell you this for weeks and weeks! I'm pregnant. We need to talk. Love, Sophie

Evidently Laurel is rereading it upside down, because her next question is taken directly from the message. "How many 'weeks and weeks' are we talking about, if you don't mind my asking?"

"I'm not sure," Peggy replies, though that isn't really true.

"How long have you known?"

Peggy thinks about it. "Six weeks, maybe seven."

"So she must be further along than a couple of months." Laurel stops and thinks. "In fact, I know when she took the test. In the bathroom at Movies West, her last day on the job."

Instead of responding, Peggy returns her attention to the pile of sweaters on the counter. She pats the stacks, then straightens what she's patted. She feels tears welling in the corners of her eyes, and she realizes how entirely unprepared she is for any of the many encounters that are yet to come. "Yes-s-s," she replies haltingly. "You are probably right about that."

"So when Sophie told you, what did she say?"

Peggy could lie, but she doesn't. "She didn't tell me exactly. Sophie has her own way with things."

"So I've noticed."

This is the woman who fired my daughter, who threw a drink in her face, Peggy thinks. *We are adversaries, and yet we must put aside our differences and act on behalf of our children. You don't have to like a person to sell him a car, Jack likes to say.*

"She asked me to read her cards."

"What?"

"I read the pregnancy in the cards."

"Are you a fortune-teller?"

Peggy shakes her head. "But I know a thing or two about tarot cards."

"I see," Laurel says slowly. "So, has Sophie been to the doctor?" She tucks a stray lock of lank hair behind her ear.

"I got her to Planned Parenthood, but she didn't get any further than counseling. She doesn't want an abortion."

Laurel shakes her head. "Of course not. No one wants an abortion. That's not the point. But I'm here to tell her that she doesn't want to be a single mother. And she will be. . . . My son is not even remotely ready to be a father."

Peggy tries to interrupt, but Laurel has something she needs to express. She wants to share a story about Will. "Just last year he tried to take in a stray cat, but within days, he'd forgotten to feed it. He *never* changed the litter. Not once. I finally took the cat to the shelter, and when he asked, I told him it ran away. I hated to lie, but it's the kind of thing you're forced into when you have no help whatsoever."

"I understand."

"No, I don't think you do." Laurel looks around. "Is this what you do, then? Is this your shop?"

Peggy nods slowly and resumes her task. "I'm the owner."

"You make a living?" Laurel asks.

Peggy shrugs. She wants to say that it's a personal question, that it's absolutely none of Laurel's business, but she is too taken aback to speak.

Laurel offers a tight-lipped smile, then launches in: "I'm begging you. Talk some sense into your daughter. Surely you have some influence."

"Honestly, I don't know if I do. Your son is the one with the influence, and he told Sophie that he doesn't believe in abortion."

Laurel shakes her head. "Why would he tell her that? Will does *not* know Sophie is pregnant. Believe me, he doesn't have a clue. He was *humming* when he left for school this morning. Happy as a clam." She lets this last sink in, then adds, "Peggy, please. Are we on the same page or not?"

"I think we're on the same page." Peggy glances down and sees that she's clutching one of the sweaters. She forces herself to let it go, to back up a step or two and take a deep breath. "We just need to stay calm."

"No," Laurel replies. "Calmness is not what is called for here. How about Sophie's father? I spoke to him on the phone once, and he sounded like he might have a backbone." She hears herself and retracks. "Not that you don't."

Peggy shrugs. "I'm not sure anymore."

"But does he know? Have you told him? Surely he's heartsick over it."

Peggy sighs. "Yes, he knows, and he wants Sophie to have an abortion."

"And has he told her so?"

"They had a talk. I know they did, but I haven't heard much about it."

"This is very frustrating," Laurel says. She begins rummaging around in her purse again. "I thought I had some gum in here," she explains. "My dentist suggested that I chew gum when I feel like gritting my teeth. Honestly, Peggy, I feel like I'm not getting through to you."

Peggy responds stiffly, saying the first thing that comes to mind. "So, what are you going to do? Pick up a drink and throw it in my face?"

Laurel doesn't answer right away. She collects her purse and slings it over her shoulder. "If I had a drink right now, I might well do that," she says. "Maybe it would wake you up. Maybe you'd turn on the lights and see what's right in front of your face!"

She backs away and begins to make her way out, but when she reaches the door, she turns back. "Haven't you noticed that it's too damn dark in here? I can't see the clothes, but I know I can't afford them. And it's just as well, because nothing in here would look good on a woman like me." She raises her voice to be sure she's heard. "Most of the women who come through this door look more like me than you! How many skinny bitches do you see roaming the sidewalks of Old Town?"

Laurel slams the door behind her, and the bell rings and rings and rings. Even after it has finally stopped, Peggy still hears it. No doubt Laurel will talk to Will soon, and if her encounter with Peggy is any indication, she's going to scare the living daylights out of him. Peggy can't imagine how the situation will be resolved, whose needs will be met and whose won't be. Is she in the dark then, as Laurel contended? Peggy does feel oddly removed from the struggle. She can no longer fix the game so that Sophie will win, and in fact, Peggy isn't sure what winning would mean in this instance.

The note is still on the counter. Peggy picks it up, refolds it, and slips it into her pocket. She will return it to Sophie as soon as she gets home.

It's the end of the second six-week reporting period, and Will is sweating his grade in each and every class. When the last bell rings on Wednesday, he finds his girlfriend in the hall and gives her the key to his car.

"It may take me a while to finish the makeup test," he tells her. "You can do homework or take a little nap."

Sophie gives him a long look. "Have you studied?"

He shakes his head. "I lost the book." He explains that he can't get another one until he has paid for the one he lost. And his mother has insisted that he foot the bill. "In case you haven't noticed, she's all about teaching people lessons."

"I've noticed all right," Sophie replies. She wishes him luck, then strides for the nearest exit. The buildings are stuffy and never more so than in the late fall. Will's car is parked in the middle of the student lot, and as she makes her way there, Sophie yawns once and then again.

The afternoon air is cool but not cold, and the sunshine coming through the windshield warms the vinyl seat covers. Sophie manages to doze off for a few minutes. When she awakens, a group of pigeons has fanned out across the parking lot. One of them—white with large brown spots, the kind Ian calls a "pinto pigeon"—is perched on the front of Will's car, surveying the scene, looking like a feathery hood ornament.

Until recently Sophie had never noticed the trash-strewn parking lot or the pigeons attracted by teenage trash. Until recently she didn't listen to the announcements at the beginning of first period. They didn't pertain to her, or so she thought. Until recently she was so concerned with her own appearance, her own feelings, and her own problems that she barely registered the rest of the world. But now she is all ears: she tunes in to the announcements, she listens to the homework assignments and writes them down in her agenda. Her grades are actually improving now that she's knocked up. She hasn't told Will that she is going to make the honor roll this semester. If she did, he would certainly be resentful.

When he opens the door and slides into the driver's seat, he seems relieved. "That test wasn't half as hard as I thought it would be. I think I passed it!" He's feeling cocky, having pulled one over on his elders. Then he notices the pigeon perched on his hood. "What the fuck," he mutters.

"Start the car," Sophie says. "The bird will get the idea."

Why didn't that occur to him? It's the obvious solution, but now that Sophie's suggested it in that sarcastic, smarter-than-thou voice, he can't consider doing it. He's worried that she'll laugh at him, something she's done once or twice lately. Because he doesn't see that he has any choice, Will opens the door and climbs out, taking a step or two in the pigeon's direction until, wearily, the bird rises into the air, leaving behind the last word: an offering the color and consistency of wet mortar.

"You didn't listen to the announcements this morning, did you?"

He shrugs. "I missed first period."

"'Over the weekend the school premises will be closed to allow exterminators to deal with the *pigeon problem*.'" She is quoting the principal's measured speech, and her inflection is spot-on. "They're killing the pigeons, Will. Doesn't that bother you?"

He doesn't look familiar to her from this angle. The fringe of hair at the nape of his neck appears raggedy, as though his mother trimmed it, which is in fact the case. His profile is all nose and fleshy lips, and the cheek that's closest to her is marred by a sudden flush of acne.

"They carry diseases, Sophie."

"So do people," Sophie says grimly. "Maybe we should *get rid* of them, too. Anything that causes us a problem, let's just kill it."

And like that, his happy mood is sucked out the window, a red balloon snatched away in a sudden breeze. It's there and then it's gone. Slowly, dramatically, he grips the wheel with both hands, then lowers his head until his crown is pressed against the padded middle.

He has struck this pose before, with his mother when she was teaching him to drive. At the end of one of his lessons, Will hopped a curb and nearly lost control of the car. His mother went berserk. For half an hour she moaned about insurance and how it would take just one accident, even a fender-bender, for their payments to skyrocket out of control. "Neither one of us will be able to drive, Will! Both of us will be taking the bus!" His posture spoke for his frame of mind, which said, I'm screwed. I'm totally screwed, and I give up trying to pretend otherwise. He was at the mercy of his mother then; now he's at the mercy of his girlfriend.

At lunchtime he had tried to share with Sophie something that his mother had impressed upon him: "The best decision is the one that honors your future." Laurel wanted Will to understand that the fetus was the size of a fingernail. "No bigger than that!" she'd exclaimed. But when Will told Sophie, she said, "The queen bee was about that big as well."

He knows now that Jack killed a queen bee and then ordered a new one, which arrived in the mail. (He was surprised to hear that you can order insects and have them delivered by USPS.) But what he doesn't get is why the death of the bee has any bearing on their current situation, and he is afraid to ask for fear of looking stupid. Off and on for months, he's noticed that Sophie knows more than he does, and that she makes better use of what she knows. This dawning realization—that his girlfriend is smarter than he is—does not endear her to him.

Back inside the car, Will refuses to look in Sophie's direction.

Instead, he thrusts the stick shift into reverse and backs out of the space, though there's no real need to do so. The parking lot is open in almost every direction. As they rumble down Candelaria toward Fourth Street, Sophie advises Will to drive smoothly. "I'm feeling a little nauseous." She waits until he stops the car at the light before asking, "So, do you want me to get an abortion then?"

It's the counterpoint to the question he asked her at lunchtime: "So, what are you saying? Do you want to get married or something?"

She didn't answer that question, so he doesn't answer this one. But he does want her to get an abortion; he wants it more with each passing day. He drops his right foot on the accelerator, even as he holds his left foot on the brake. The car makes a squealing noise, and when the light changes and he releases the brake, it lurches forward.

Beside him, Sophie wails.

He doesn't turn to look, but he knows that she is hunched over, fumbling in her backpack, and he hears the rustle of a plastic sack followed by the sickening sound of his girlfriend retching what she'd managed to choke down at lunch: a pile of saltines and a small banana. At Second Street he takes a wide left-hand turn into an Allsup's. Before Sophie can inquire as to their whereabouts, he parks and runs into the convenience store. He buys her a 7 Up, a Sprite, and a Dr Pepper, then carries all three out in a plastic bag just like the one she has vomited into.

She selects the Dr Pepper, sighs, and leans her head back. The acidy smell of vomit is just starting to dissipate.

"Do you need me to toss the puke?" he asks.

She shakes her head, all those dark curls shifting about her face and neck. "I did it while you were in line," she replies.

"Are you feeling any better?"

She raises her head long enough to take a sip, stows the plastic bottle between her thighs, then reclines again. "If we just sit here for a few minutes, I'm sure my stomach will settle."

"I'm not in any rush," Will says.

Strictly speaking, that isn't true. He has only an hour and a half or so before he's due for a shift at Garduños. He has to go home and change clothes, and before he can do that, he has to drop off Sophie at her house. He hates having so much to do. Or rather, he hates having a schedule. He's a loafer at heart; he chafes at having to watch the clock. But for the moment, he'll pretend that he has all the time in the world. He unscrews the cap from the Sprite and takes a long swig, then another. He's thirsty, he realizes. He drinks again, luxuriating in the sweet fizz of carbonation, the mild burning that accompanies the liquid coursing down his throat.

The car is parked in front of the store's double glass doors, and for a few minutes, he simply observes the parade of people pushing their way in and out. Some of them are empty-handed; he assumes they purchased cigarettes or lottery tickets or both. It's diverting to take note of the way people enter the store. Some shoulder their way in. Others use the handle, and one wiry Asian-looking fellow actually turns his back to the door and pushes it open with his butt. He's got a cell phone pressed to his ear, which might explain the unthinking way he moves through the world.

Sophie's voice is low, and with her head reclined against the seat back, she speaks to the ceiling. Still, Will hears her clearly. "I'm sorry I puked."

He shrugs. "Used to be, I would have been grossed out, but you'd be surprised by the kind of crap you have to clean up bussing tables, and from perfect strangers, too." He starts to tell her about the dirty diaper he found recently, left behind in the seat of a high chair. But he thinks better of it. Babies are not a good subject.

Sophie is silent. Every once in a while she raises her head and takes a sip of Dr Pepper. Finally, she sighs and says she's feeling better. Then she asks Will if he could just tell her the truth.

"You know that stuff you told me at lunch about the fingernail?" She holds up her own little finger and regards it carefully. "Is that something you really believe, or is it just what your mother brainwashed you into saying? Because really, Will, your mother is full of crap. I looked online, and at twelve weeks the fetus is the size of a lime." She regards her little finger from several different angles and waits for his response. But he doesn't have one, so she continues: "I mean, she should at least be accurate, don't you think? Do you suppose that when she was pregnant with you, her mom was telling her you were the size of a fingernail, when you were really as big as a lime? Good thing for you she didn't listen!"

Before he realizes he's done it, Will squeezes the Sprite bottle, sending liquid up and out and dousing a leg of his jeans. He shouts, "Shit!"

which startles Sophie. The next thing he knows, she is crying. She doesn't make a sound, but tears race down her cheeks. The tears undo him. He leans across the space between them and kisses her wet, salty skin. He kisses her eyelids and her snotty nose. Then he kisses her on the mouth, too, just to let her know that he's not afraid of the taste of a little lingering vomit. When they are finished, he puts his hands on her shoulders and looks into her red-rimmed eyes.

"You're killing me, Sophie. All this talk of fingernails and limes: what difference does it make? You're not thinking straight."

Yesterday Peggy had suggested that Sophie invite Will and his mother over for Thanksgiving dinner. At the time it seemed like a lame thing to do, but Peggy was pretty adamant about it. "If you have your way, they're going to be family," she said.

Sophie clears her throat. "Do you and your mom have plans for Thanksgiving?" she asks.

"Didn't you just say my mom is full of crap?"

"She is, but what does that have to do with anything? Peggy says, 'We have to get beyond our differences.'"

He shrugs. "I usually go over to my grandma Sylvia's, *mi abuela*. She makes tamale stuffing for the turkey." Just thinking of it makes him hungry. Will and Carlos toss the football in the backyard, and they all eat until they're sick. It's a tradition, really, and it's one of the few times when Will gets to see his father. The more he thinks about it, the less inclined he is to miss it. But when he glances over in Sophie's direction, he sees that she is distressed.

"I'll stop by," he promises, "but I'm going to spend most of the day at *mi abuela*'s." There, he's said it.

He starts the car and pretends to concentrate completely on backing out of a tight space. He knows she's expecting an invitation; he knows she'd like to accompany him. But he's not going to offer. Neither is he going to tell her that Carlos will be there. His father is his own business. Will doesn't share Carlos, not with his mother, not even with Sophie. He has very little of Carlos, and what he has he keeps to himself.

Sophie's first doctor's appointment is on November 12. Peggy picks up her daughter at Valley High School, then cedes the driver's seat to Sophie, who announces her intention to take the slowest route. "Let's just tool up Montgomery," Sophie says as she pulls out of the school parking lot and takes a left onto Candelaria. Peggy suggests they take Interstate 25, but Sophie doesn't want to get on the expressway.

"We'll be late," Peggy counters, but she isn't going to insist. Because Sophie knows that, she doesn't even bother to reply.

Most often, Sophie gets her way. As a child she was something of a handful. She took crayons to the walls and scissors to the heads of dolls, and her mother stood by and let her. Occasionally Jack suggested teaching Sophie some manners—curbing her enthusiasm, so to speak—but Peggy wouldn't hear of it. "You don't tame what's wild and beautiful," she insisted. "You stand back and admire it." Initially Jack had his doubts about Peggy's methods, but he subscribed to the "mother knows best" theory of child-rearing, which meant giving his wife her way. Now he holds Peggy accountable for their daughter's excesses.

It turns out that the obstetrician's office is in the Lovelace Women's Hospital, something neither Peggy nor Sophie anticipated. Twice they drive by the massive building. On the third pass, Peggy spots the address posted on the decorative wall out front. Sophie whips into the lot—she prides herself on her quick turns—but instead of finding a spot close to the building, she pulls alongside the wall and idles.

"I'm not sure about this. Are you?" she asks Peggy.

"What do you mean?"

"How did you hear of this guy? Why is his office in the hospital?"

Peggy shakes her head. She doesn't know. He was recommended by Laurel. He is Laurel's gynecologist, but Peggy doesn't want to say so. She's afraid this information will further spook Sophie. "It's just an examination. You don't have to see this doctor again if you don't like him."

Sophie is wearing sunglasses, and she slides them down and peers closely at her mother, revealing green eyes swollen from crying. When was Sophie weeping, and where? In the bathroom at Valley? "If I go see this guy, does that mean I won't be able to go back to Planned Parenthood?"

Peggy's chest aches. "Not at all," she says. She reaches out a hand for the car keys. "Come on, let's go. We're already ten minutes late."

The doctor is an old man with pale blue eyes who likes to say, "Don't get your hopes up." It's an all-purpose response, tailored by tone to convey any number of messages, be they cautionary or ironic. He's painfully unobservant, this man, or so it seems to Sophie. In fact, he misses very little of what goes on around him, which is why he rarely allows his own hopes to rise any higher than the low ceiling of his examining room.

He notices Sophie's tears, but he also sees that she's relieved he is pretending otherwise. Once her heels are firmly planted in the metal stirrups, Sophie allows herself to weep silently, tears sliding off the slopes of her cheeks and dropping onto the paper.

"Are you okay?" the nurse asks.

"No," Sophie replies.

The doctor halts in his preparations, closes his eyes, the better to listen. His wife has been dying these past months, and he finds it hard to concentrate on anything other than her features, which fade and change faster than he can memorize them. He hears a small, strangled sound, and then Sophie clears her throat to speak. "It's nothing. I'm just scared."

The doctor opens his eyes and tries, in his own wry way, to be reassuring. "There's nothing and everything to be scared about." Then he gives his usual warning. "This is going to be cold, Sophie." He squeezes a big dollop of jelly from a tube and spreads it across her belly in big, messy circles.

"I'm too young to be a mother, don't you think?" Sophie asks as the doctor wipes his gloved hands.

"Doesn't matter what I think. What do you think?"

Sophie shakes her head. She has already said as much as she can manage.

He stations his stethoscope, moving it slowly until he finds the baby's heartbeat, which fills the room with a swooshing noise that might be coming from outer space. She's never heard anything so otherworldly in her life.

"Sounds like the heartbeat of an alien," she remarks.

"Don't get your hopes up," the doctor says mildly. "They're most often babies." He closes his eyes again, counts the beats in a minute, and makes his pronouncement. "This one sounds like a boy."

"A boy?" Sophie asks. She's told herself not to feel anything, but she can't help it. "Why do you say that?"

"Has to do with the number of beats per minute. But sometimes I'm wrong. Just so you don't start painting the walls blue."

"He listened for the heartbeat," Sophie says when they are back in the car.

"Did you hear it?" Peggy asks.

"I still hear it," Sophie replies, bobbing her head as though to dislodge water from her ears. It's like the Taos hum, she thinks, that low-level sound some people hear in the mountains of northern New Mexico. Hippy-dippy bullshit, she's always thought, low-level craziness. Now she's not so sure.

On the way home, they stop by Smith's for milk. Suddenly ravenous, Sophie seizes on the idea of cooking dinner. She decides to fix meatloaf, corn on the cob, and biscuits.

"Just as a novelty, of course," she explains in the produce aisle. "I'm not trying to set a precedent or anything."

"Very funny," Peggy replies. She doesn't look up from the task of selecting a bunch of bananas. She can get stuck in acts of this sort, like picking up and putting down perfectly acceptable produce. She is looking for something without blemishes, nothing small or withered or so large that it looks to have grown with the help of hormones. She seems persnickety in these moments, and a little addled.

After a moment or two, Sophie can't bear to watch her mother's tortured selection. She wanders over to the artichokes, dark green monstrosities that appeal to her because they can be held by their stems and pointed menacingly at the small children who ride by in their mothers' carts. She amuses herself in this way for a few minutes, until it occurs to her that by May, she will have her own brat to push around. The prospect is dizzying. Sophie tightens her grip on the stem of an artichoke and, slipping behind her mother, begins running the thorny edges of the leaves over the nape of Peggy's neck.

"What is that, Sophie?" Peggy asks.

"How'd you know it was me?"

Peggy turns around, bunches of bananas held up in either hand. "Who else would it be? Been a while since a man tried to pick me up in the produce aisle."

"I'm scared, Peggy," Sophie says. Using the artichoke as a makeshift torch, she strikes a pose that resembles the Statue of Liberty. It's a mixed message: I'm funny or I'm frightened. Take your pick. Sophie does this sort of thing to test those she loves, and Peggy never fails the tests. Never.

"You'd be crazy if you weren't scared. I'm scared, too, Sophie. How far along are you?"

"Fifteen weeks? I don't know, but getting rid of something with a heartbeat—that's wrong, don't you think?"

Peggy looks around. For the moment they have the produce aisle to themselves. It's not the place for a conversation like this one, but Peggy knows she needs to take the opening. Sophie may clam up on her again at any moment. "What do you mean by 'wrong'?"

"Immoral." She is holding the artichoke heart by its stem, and she stares down at it rather than meet her mother's watery hazel eyes. "As in, a mortal sin." She uses the artichoke to point at her head. "That whoosh, whoosh, whoosh. It's up here now." She presses the vegetable to her heart. "And here, too, for all I know."

When they get home, Peggy excuses herself and goes into the bedroom. She has promised to call Laurel. She has the number on the back of a receipt in her billfold, which she ferrets out. After punching in the first three numbers, she hangs up and returns the receiver to its cradle. She needs to cry a little, a few tears. Then she'll call. But she doesn't. She gets sidetracked because the nursing home in Vermont is calling. They need to speak to Jack right away.

Peggy gives them Jack's work number, then asks if everything is all right. The young woman on the phone sounds flustered. She's not sure she can reveal patient information to strangers.

"But I'm not a stranger," Peggy argues. "I'm Jack's wife; I'm Vernie's daughter-in-law." Her dander is up. First she had to stay in the waiting room while Sophie met with the doctor, and now she's being told she's a stranger, when she is certainly a member of the family.

The young woman is not convinced. "I'll just say this," she tells

Peggy. "Mrs. Granger is okay for now. But we're worried about her. She keeps sneaking out of the center. 'I'm going out for a walk,' she tells us. That is, when we catch her in the act. But we don't always catch her."

"I'll tell Jack to give you a call," Peggy promises. As soon as she hangs up, the phone rings again. This time it's Laurel.

Laurel wants to know all about the visit to the doctor, and she's disappointed when Peggy admits that she didn't go into the examining room with Sophie. "But you did talk to the doctor?" Peggy has to confess that she did not talk to the doctor, that Sophie insisted on her privacy, and that Peggy wasn't going to upset the apple cart by overruling her daughter's wishes. Laurel is silent on the other end of the line before conceding that Peggy was probably wise. *Probably wise.*

When she hears that Sophie is more than nine weeks pregnant, but probably not more than fourteen or fifteen weeks, Laurel is relieved. While it may be too late to take the pill that will bring on bleeding, it is still early in the second trimester. "We just need to steer her back in the direction of Planned Parenthood! Will agrees, but he's worried, Peggy. He thinks Sophie may resist doing the reasonable thing out of some romantic belief that she's saving a life."

"Romantic impulses appeal to teenage girls," Peggy replies quietly.

"What do you mean?"

"I agree with you. It's *not* too late, but Sophie isn't listening to me, and she isn't listening to her father, and she isn't listening to Will. I'm not sure how to get through to her."

Laurel is undeterred. "We need to work together," she says, "you and me, as mothers and as enlightened and educated women."

Peggy recalls that Laurel is eking out her degree one painful semester after another. She takes a deep breath and responds in kind: "We *will* work together. But I'm going to have to pawn a few things to come up with the cash. Can you help at all in that capacity?"

Laurel thinks a minute. She can help, she says. If that's what it takes, she can find a hundred dollars, maybe two.

"Two would be better than one," Peggy replies.

They agree to speak again in a few days, after Peggy has talked to Sophie about returning to Planned Parenthood. They also agree that Thanksgiving at the Grangers is a good idea, that Sophie and Will should be pressed into washing the dishes after dinner and imagining what Thanksgiving will be like in the years to come, with a baby and all the attendant responsibilities.

"If I could borrow a baby, I would," Laurel says. "The kids need to be force-fed a big dose of reality while there's still time to change course. It's the best thing for everyone."

Not for everyone, Peggy thinks as she hangs up. Candace has left two messages at Everyday Satin, one yesterday and another this morning. "I need to talk to you," she said both times. "Don't do something stupid and break both our hearts, Peggy. Sophie wants to do the right thing; you just need to support her in the decision."

On Friday, the sixteenth, a FedEx truck barrels down the gravel drive and stops on a dime. The driver emerges briskly in a cloud of dust, carrying a letter-sized mailer. Ian signs for it. He's reminded of the last time he signed for a package—the one with the queen bee—but this one is flat and bears no special-handling labels. When he hands it over, he gives Sophie all the information he's been able to glean: "It's from Aunt Candace. She mailed it overnight. From Boston, of course." Ian is hoping that at least some part of the message is meant for him, so he's frustrated when Sophie carries the important-looking envelope to her room and closes the door.

The mailer contains a note and several photographs of exquisite antique furniture. "I couldn't help noticing that your room was a little barren. Perhaps you like it that way, but if not, please consider taking these pieces off my hands. They come from a French country house! The dresser is at least three hundred years old! *Très belle, n'est-ce pas?*" Has Sophie mentioned her French class to Candace?

"Call me and I'll have them shipped," the note continues. Candace has provided two phone numbers, a cell and a home number.

Sophie calls the cell. She can't wait to say yes. "*Oui, oui!*" she squeals when Candace answers. Then she adds one of the first French phrases she learned: "*Je m'appelle* Sophie!"

"*Bonjour*, Sophie!"

"*Merci pour le cadeau! Je suis très . . .*" She can't remember the words for "happy" or "excited." Not for a moment anyway. Then it occurs to her: *heureux*. But Sophie is not the least bit confident in her pronunciation.

"*Parlez-vous Français*, Sophie?"

"*Mais oui!*" Sophie replies. "*Un peu.*"

"*Bon. Comment ça va*, Sophie?"

"*Ça va bien*, Candace."

"*Es-tu sûr?*"

Sophie notices that Candace has shifted to the familiar, and something about the gesture moves her. She suspects Candace is at least proficient in French, and she is both impressed and a little intimidated. "Did you ask me if I'm sure?"

"*Mais oui!*" Candace replies.

Sophie hesitates before deciding to try to communicate her true feelings: "*Ça va mal*," she tries.

"*Je suis désolé. Qu'est-ce qui ne va pas?*"

"I give up, Aunt Candace. I think we have to switch to English."

"But you were handling it beautifully, Sophie!"

"*Mais non*," Sophie says miserably. "I'm not really handling anything beautifully."

"What's wrong, darling girl? Forgive me. I'm still in French mode, which is a little gushy."

"It's okay," Sophie replies. "But I'm so confused. Did Peggy tell you I've been to the doctor?"

Candace hesitates, then says no.

Sophie describes hearing the heartbeat. "It was just so awesome!"

"*Formidable!*"

"*Oui, formidable!*"

"Nothing is quite so miraculous," Candace says. She goes silent.

"What is it?" Sophie asks.

She is standing and looking out the bank of windows in her room. As she watches, her eyes worry the line of bee boxes in the field. Autumn is a quiet time for bees, a time of preparation, a time to regroup. She recalls her stunt, which was only a couple of months ago but seems as though it had been performed by some other girl. Why would she do something so foolish? To get her father's attention. To put herself back in his good graces. She could entice a hundred bees to cover her mouth and cheeks, but she couldn't tell her father what was in her mind and heart. What a silly girl.

"I don't want to have an abortion," Sophie hears herself say.

On the other end of the line, Candace is suddenly weeping.

"Are you okay?" Sophie asks.

"*Je suis heureux!*" Candace replies, and because once is not enough, "*Je suis heureux*, Sophie."

Sophie listens to and repeats the pronunciation. Candace stops crying long enough to laugh. "You better watch out, girlie. You'll end up speaking French with a Boston brogue. And that will definitely confuse your teacher." Candace goes on to explain that it will take time to get the furniture shipped, maybe as much as a month or two. "But I'll start the process today, as soon as we hang up."

When the call is finished, Sophie stands for a moment and listens to a siren out on Fourth Street, and beyond that, the hum of traffic. Although it has changed since her girlhood, the North Valley still retains something of its rural agrarian heritage. Neighbors coddle chickens; in a nearby pasture a dozen or so sheep graze. Those willing to walk a few blocks can entertain a young child with a veritable barnyard of animals: goats, ducks, roosters, horses—lots of horses—and, for the jaded young one, an alpaca and a llama or two.

The area is crisscrossed with ditches that carry water away from the Rio Grande and are still used periodically to flood the land that was once tilled and farmed. Now, for the most part, the sandy paths along the ditches are lined with mature cottonwoods. They serve mostly as shady byways for dog walkers. The water sluicing through the ditches irrigates the lawns of the well-to-do in Los Ranchos de Albuquerque. Vineyards and fields of lavender border a few of the stucco mansions, but the land is now so valuable that only the rich can afford to cultivate it.

Ian is milling about in the hallway, so Sophie invites him in and shares the photos of the furniture. "Can you believe it?"

"Did she say anything about the teepee?"

Sophie shakes her head.

"Do you think you could ask her? Next time she calls?"

Sophie promises. She feels a little guilty, both because she is the one getting a gift and because she had completely forgotten her brother. She realizes he was standing outside the door the whole time she was on the phone.

"Why am I so important to her?" Sophie wonders aloud.

Ian shrugs. "You could ask her."

"I did."

"What did she say?"

"She said I'm the closest thing she has to family. Then she started talking about the commune, and how she's missed that sort of friendship. I mean, it just sounds like she's lonely."

"But why pick you?"

Sophie regards him carefully. "What do you think?"

Ian has been considering the question, and he has at least part of the answer: "It has something to do with the past, Sophie."

In Albuquerque, the sun shines 76 percent of the time, making it one of the sunnier cities in the United States. Most of the rainfall comes on late summer afternoons in July and August, during what is referred to by locals as the "monsoon season." So when a day dawns to drizzle and gray skies, locals are apt to turn peevish—particularly if that day is Thanksgiving.

But not Sophie. When she wakes to the pitter-patter of rain on the tin roof, she smiles broadly and rolls out of bed. After dressing quickly in a purple sweat shirt and black yoga pants, she hurries downstairs to help her mother cook.

"It's sure as hell not touch-football weather," she announces loudly. "It's been raining off and on since midnight!"

Peggy is standing over the stove, close enough to monitor the progress of a skillet of frying bacon, but not close enough to get splattered. In response to the pronouncement, she turns around, a spatula in one hand, a cup of coffee in the other. "Thank you, Willard Scott," she says. "I know you're pleased, but keep in mind that Will is bound to be disappointed."

Peggy is still wearing her chenille robe, which is nearly the same shade of purple as Sophie's sweat shirt. She probably won't dress until she has the stuffing mixed and the turkey prepared. Shuffling around in her fuzzy house slippers is a Thanksgiving tradition. She's happy with the overcast sky, too, because it means the weather will be cool and fall-like, which is both the natural order of things and Peggy's preference.

"What's your point?" Sophie asks.

"My point is that your boyfriend's happiness should be a consideration in your own."

Sophie sighs. "Is that your way of calling me selfish?"

"Maybe."

Sophie sidles around the table to the counter next to the stove, where a dozen crispy strips of bacon are draining on a bed of paper towels. She snatches two pieces, eats one in two bites, and grabs another. Lucy is nearby of course, having been lured from Ian's bed by the salty-sweet smell of pork. Seeing that Sophie has bacon, the dog scoots forward on her haunches until she's close enough to snatch a piece from the girl's outstretched hand. The bacon is there one instant and gone the next. "Lucy!" Sophie cries. "You don't need to swallow it whole."

Peggy sighs and asks Sophie to stop feeding Lucy bacon. The dog is too heavy by at least ten pounds.

"Okay, but can I make myself a BLT for breakfast?" Sophie asks. The nausea has lifted, at least for the time being, and Sophie is starving.

"I suppose," Peggy replies. "But I'd appreciate some help with the apple salad after you eat."

"Okay, but don't go and make the green bean casserole while my back is turned. That's Will's favorite."

"So you've told me."

Sophie is feeding bread to the toaster, and she doesn't respond until she's pressed the lever down. "And I want to be able to say that I made it."

Peggy nods and returns her attention to the frying pan. "No more than three strips of bacon on that sandwich," she says, "or I won't have enough for the stuffing."

Dinner is scheduled for three, yet the house is all but empty when the hour arrives. Jack and Ian are still at the fixer-upper installing kitchen cabinets, and Jack doesn't answer the phone when Peggy calls to give her husband a nudge. Sophie offers to drive over and check on them, but

Peggy opts to give them another half hour. "They probably don't want to stop in the middle of hanging a cabinet," she says.

Laurel calls at three fifteen to apologize. She's waiting for Will to return home from his grandmother's house. They agreed to come together, but now he isn't answering the phone either. "What good are cell phones," Sophie complains, "if people don't answer them?" Finally, at about four, Laurel arrives alone.

Five minutes later, Jack and Ian show up. It seems they were busy most of the afternoon locating leaks in the roof. "I'd never been over there when it was raining," Jack tells Peggy. The fixer-upper has a flat roof, and everyone knows that the older ones are prone to leaking.

What used to be hot—the turkey and the mashed potatoes—is cold, and what used to be cold—the cranberry sauce and the apple salad—is tepid. "Let's serve," Laurel finally insists. "If he's going to show up at all, he'll make an appearance just as soon as we begin passing around the food." Sophie offers everyone a Dr Pepper as they take their seats. The water glasses have been filled, and the adults all have wine glasses as well. But one by one, each accepts a red soda can. Laurel sits down and lines up beverages in front of her plate. She is anxious and a little defensive on her son's account. He's at his grandmother Sylvia's, Laurel has explained, and it's always a madhouse over there.

"But they can't be playing touch football in this weather," Sophie says. She has opened her own can of DP and is taking quick swigs to settle her suddenly touchy stomach.

"They can *watch* football, though," Laurel counters.

Jack is carrying the turkey to the table, and as he sets it down, he agrees with Laurel. "Game starting at five that I want to watch," he says.

Laurel knows her son. Sophie has just picked up a shallow pottery bowl full of apple salad and handed it off to Laurel when Will ducks in through the kitchen door. He doesn't knock; nor does he call out a greeting. Like someone who is late to a play, he slips into his seat, and when offered a Dr Pepper, he heartily accepts. Sophie is so moved by his arrival that she feels tears brimming in her eyes, and she has to use the corner of her napkin to wipe them away. Only Laurel notices the girl's show of emotion. She wishes she hadn't seen it. It confuses her to identify with Sophie, yet that's what she's beginning to do.

After the meal is over, Sophie and Will offer to clean up while Jack takes Peggy and Laurel over to see the kitchen cabinets. Ian is invited along, but he declines. "We're supposed to play Scrabble," he says by way of explanation.

Jack is flummoxed. On the way out to the car, he complains to Laurel and Peggy, "*Supposed* to play Scrabble? What the hell does that mean?"

Laurel offers an explanation. "He wants to hang out with the teenagers," she says.

Peggy says, "And he doesn't want to hang out with us. You know what he wants for Christmas, right?"

Jack shakes his head.

"A teepee," Peggy says.

"You're kidding." Jack replies.

Laurel laughs. "When Will was younger, he spent most of one summer sleeping in a tent he pitched in the backyard."

The word "teepee" is in the air, and as Ian happens to know, it has several acceptable spellings, which make it a natural in a game of Scrabble. "Teepee," "tipi," and "tepee": all three iterations are in the dictionary. Once the dishes are washed, dried, and put away, Ian retrieves the Scrabble game from the top shelf of the hall closet. Lucy follows him down the hallway to the closet and then back again, wagging her tail in anticipation of a good time. The three "young people"—as Laurel referred to them during dinner—are alone in the house.

The top of the Scrabble box is dusty, and Ian makes a swipe at cleaning it with the back of his sleeve. Once he's deposited the game on the table, Lucy skulks between the chairs and collapses on the cold brick floor. It's a concession she makes to being near family. Not that she is being entirely unselfish. The playing of games is often accompanied by the popping of corn, and she loves the salty, oily goodness of those white kernels and the way they pop between her teeth.

Will is in the bathroom and Sophie is in the living room, returning a small crystal bowl to its place in the china hutch. When she returns, she sings out, "Scrabble time!" and waves the kitchen towel she has in one hand. She's wearing a purple chenille sweater and jeans that no longer button up all the way. As she waves the towel, the bottom of the sweater rides up and displays this fact. Ian smiles and pretends not to notice.

When Will ambles back into the room, he is carrying a bottle of Tecate. Seeing that Sophie is helping to unpack the game, he frowns. He was planning his escape. He wants to get back to his dad and uncles, who will all be gathered around the television set. Will isn't crazy about football, but he likes it better than he does word games, and anyway that's not the point, really. The point is Carlos. The point is sitting on the floor near Carlos's chair, breathing in the presence of his father. It's really just that simple. Sophie and her goofy brother are available anytime.

"What's this?" he asks.

"Scrabble," Sophie says flatly. "We always play on Thanksgiving. It's a tradition."

"I don't play . . . Scrabble."

Sophie snorts. "Of course you do. Everyone plays Scrabble."

Ian is at the microwave, manning the making of popcorn. The kernels begin to explode against the inside of the bag, and the air fills with the delectable aroma. Under the table Lucy raises her head and takes a long, satisfying sniff. "It's easy!" Ian says. "We'll show you."

Will looks down at his shoes and sighs. "I'm not really good at this sort of thing. But I'll play for half an hour." He raises his head and meets Sophie's gaze. "Then I'm going to head over to *mi abuela*'s. I told my dad I'd be back."

Sophie was hoping he'd ask her along, but she can tell that he doesn't intend to extend an invitation. Her disappointment is palpable. She feels it settle over her like the vest the dental assistant drapes over her chest when she takes x-rays. It's something Sophie will have to wear the rest of the evening. Meanwhile, Ian is retrieving the popcorn bag and pouring the contents in a bowl. He runs off to his room to find the dictionary. Since it's Will's first time to play, they have agreed that he can make unlimited use of the dictionary.

By the time the game gets underway, by the time Ian locates a pad of paper and a pencil to keep score, it's after seven. Sophie starts them out with CUPID. As she leans forward to place the D tile, she belches loudly.

Dropping back into her seat, she covers her mouth and flushes red at her cheeks and neck. Ordinarily she wouldn't care, but she's become increasingly aware of the way her body is surprising her, and not in the pleasurable ways of the past. Other girls her age don't really care for sex—like Tam, for instance. Tam's had it a few times, but now she's vowed not to have it again until she's married. She took a pledge at church, and it didn't bother her because she didn't like sex in the first place.

But Sophie took to sex the way other girls her age take to swimming. She dove in and felt suddenly in her element. Her body knew just what to do, just where to take her. On discovering the ecstasy of physical climax, she was elated. She wanted to hug herself. She *did* hug herself. Stupid, she thinks now, stupid, stupid, stupid. If she'd had an S and a T instead of a C she'd have spelled it out on the Scrabble board. As it is, she mutters to herself, says something she doesn't mean to say. "*Stupid.*"

"Your turn," she tells Will.

He doesn't like to be reminded of things. He reacts with antagonism and disappointment, something she knows perfectly well. In this case, he simply frowns and studies his tiles. She can see each and every one of them because he's sitting next to her, and she wants to show him that he can make the word REPLAY. Before she thinks, she reaches over to rearrange his vowels; he slaps her hand away. "I'm not stupid!" he says sharply. She flushes again, dismayed. *Did he think I was referring to him?*

Before she can stop herself, tears brim at the corners of her eyes. She cries now at odd moments and without provocation. And for reasons she does not understand, she cries more often in Will's presence than she does at other times. Just last night they went to see *In the Valley of Elah*, and Sophie wept through the last half of the film. Something about the weary, worried face of the Tommy Lee Jones character broke her heart. She's scared these days, and seeing the vulnerability of others further unnerves her. It's not just her own future she's worried about. It's her baby's future as well. Where are they all going? Where will they end up?

For someone in a hurry to finish the game, Will takes his time. Each time it's his turn, he ignores the tiny hourglass that measures out two minutes. Time and again, Ian reaches out and silently, surreptitiously, turns it over. He's keeping track of time, but he doesn't make Will answerable for its passing. Sophie watches as her brother nonchalantly flips the hourglass, never looking in Will's direction. It's remarkable the way Ian has intuited Will's insecurity, the way he is both holding him accountable *and* letting him off the hook at the same time.

Ian doesn't look enlightened. His hair resembles a cheap wig, whitish blonde and the consistency of straw. Throughout the day he runs his fingers through it, and by early evening, some of the strands are standing straight up. Left to his own devices, Ian would thrive. He'd be like the kid in the movie *Home Alone*, who manages his own affairs with an ingenuity and energy most others couldn't muster. Sophie has to look away from him to keep from weeping. Even her little brother breaks her heart.

By the time Will places his word—REPLY—using Sophie's P, the hourglass has been turned over six times. Not that they're counting. In spite of her best intentions, Sophie is yawning as Will records his score. She positions a hand over her mouth and pretends to concentrate as Ian congratulates Will, who is clearly quite pleased with himself. As she sits quietly, she is surprised by the fluttering sensation she's noticed once or twice in the past week. She has looked up the term, and if she could, she would put it down on the board right now: QUICKEN. She's reminded of moths that are drawn to outdoor lamps. On occasion she's watched the way their wings brush the glass surface of a globe in their quest for warmth and light. And now she has a moth inside her, quivering in the darkness, tossing itself against the walls of her womb. She likes that word, WOMB; she would make it, too, if she could.

It's Ian's turn, and he has a word waiting. He plays it immediately: READ. Sophie's turn again. She doesn't have any of the letters for WOMB, but she does take immediate advantage of a triple-word-score square and puts down GREY, using the Y in Ian's word PLAY. That takes them back to Will. In spite of his best intentions, Ian sighs, revealing the dread he feels for another twelve-minute wait. Will doesn't bristle as Sophie expects him to. Nor does he take as long to place his word. He settles on ROT, then, with a flourish, adds an S.

Ian sees his chance, and he can't help himself. He pounds the table with his fist, making the tiles jitter and displacing several words. "Will you contain yourself?" Sophie complains as she neatens the board. Ian is waiting for her to finish, waiting for Will to record his score, officially making it his turn.

"TIPI!" he crows as he sets it down.

"What's the big deal?" Will asks.

Sophie rolls her eyes. "He's obsessed," she offers by way of explanation.

Will is frowning. "That doesn't look right," he says. "Are you sure that's the way you spell it?"

"Dude! I happen to know that 'teepee' has three accepted spellings: T-E-E-P-E-E, T-I-P-I, and T-E-P-E-E."

Sophie shakes her head and puts up a hand. "Don't challenge him, Will. Let's just move on."

But Will seems not to hear. He's still studying the tiles. "It just doesn't look right to me."

At which point Ian leaps up and runs out of the room, pounding up the stairs and calling out as he goes: "Hold on! Hold on! I'll be right back."

Sophie shrugs and busies herself with clearing the table of empties, fetching another beer for her boyfriend and grabbing her third Dr Pepper of the day. She's ashamed to ply Will with liquor. But she doesn't want him to leave. She knows that once he's gone, she'll be bereft.

"Don't you want a beer?" he asks her when she sits back down.

She tells him no, and is about to remind him that responsible pregnant women don't drink, but she isn't so anxious to have him think of her as any of the three: responsible, pregnant, a woman. For as long as possible, she wants to impersonate the zany, carefree Sophie, that girl she used to be. "I'm not crazy about beer," she says. "But I wish like hell we had some Captain Morgan and Coke."

Sophie is zapping another bag of microwave popcorn when Ian returns to the table, waving a handful of papers. They're printouts from websites that sell teepees, one of which features the alternative spellings. Standing behind Will's chair, Ian thrusts the piece of paper in front of Will, who grabs it and reads aloud: "'Since our tipis (teepees, tepees) are as authentic as possible in our contemporary world, they bring to the twenty-first century a living artifact.'" The printout features an interior photo of a deluxe teepee, with wraparound seating and a fire pit at its center.

"Pretty cool," Will says amiably, returning the handout.

"I'm getting one for Christmas," Ian tells him. He's breathing heavily, as though he's been running in place. He's so excited that he's practically hyperventilating. Watching him, Sophie can see why he gets picked on at school. His appearance is only part of the problem. If he acts like this very often—doofus deluxe—he's bound to get beaten up as a matter of course.

"Earth to Ian," Sophie says. "You're setting yourself up for massive disappointment, *dude*. Peggy and Jack can't afford to buy you a teepee." She snatches up several of the printouts and scans the information for prices. "A thousand dollars will barely get you through the door."

"They're not buying it. Aunt Candace is getting it out of storage!" He's explained the situation to Sophie more than once. All he can think is that she's stopped listening to him. "She's giving me the one in the photo."

"What photo?" The question comes from Will, who is still studying the printouts.

Once again, Ian says he'll be right back. This time he charges off down the hallway, in the direction of the bathroom and his parents' room.

Jack has secreted the photo in a manila envelope with his birth certificate and social security card—the records of his life. Yet the photo was taken long before Jack and Peggy met. In it, Peggy is posed in the doorway of a teepee, wearing a ruffled skirt and nothing else—no shirt or shoes. Her long, wiry hair is braided in a plait down her back. In the minutes before the photo was taken, she had been sitting inside the cool, shaded space of the teepee and braiding her hair; when she emerged, the first thing she did was raise one hand and shield her face. The photographer caught her in that instant.

The viewer who doesn't know Peggy might assume that she was watching for someone's arrival, but Ian knows better: his mother adopts this stance almost every time she goes outdoors. If she can't survey the skyline, Peggy gets claustrophobic. As a consequence, she finds Muir Woods and New York City equally disconcerting. But she loves the Grand Canyon. Ian has never seen her as happy as she was the afternoon they spent peering over the edge of the North Rim. "Don't get so close to the edge," Jack kept admonishing her. Ian has noticed that his father is afraid of heights.

Peggy isn't the only person in the photograph, though the young man sitting outside the teepee was of no interest to Ian in the beginning. He's shirtless, too, and, like Peggy, he appears posed for the shot. He sits in lotus position, his spine straight, his shoulders thrust back. Whether his goal is to look like a yogi or a Cherokee, Ian has no idea. The young man's distinguishing feature is an abundant head of hair, black and wildly curly.

The photo has been tucked away in Jack's underwear drawer for safekeeping for longer than Sophie has been alive. Jack has all but forgotten it, but Ian has been keeping it alive. The boy is thorough in his excavations of family life, and as soon as he found the photo, he recognized its importance as a family document. Although some children might be, Ian isn't troubled by the fact that his mother appears topless. After all, he's been confronted by her naked form on any number of occasions. They have only one bathroom, so they are bound to barge in on one another.

Of late, he's been fascinated by the teepee. According to Candace, that same teepee appeared in the movie of Woodstock. It traveled some distance to make its film appearance. The lodgepoles and white canvas were transported in the hold of a 747 from Albuquerque to Kennedy Airport in New York, then back again. The organizers of the world's biggest rock concert had sent the plane to transport a group of hippies from a commune in northern New Mexico, called the Hog Farm. The hippies, Wavy Gravy and his compadres, had signed on as the concert's security force, but they ended up as cooks and caretakers. The teepee they brought with them served as a trip tent for those weathering bad acid trips.

A year or so later, that same teepee was pitched for the wedding in Aspen Meadows. Candace sat in its shady interior and contemplated the consequences of marrying a man who didn't love her best. But then, no one had ever loved her best, certainly not her mother or father. She'd learned as a little girl that some people have to make do with second place. And once you got used to it, second place really wasn't so bad.

Sophie collects the bag of popcorn—which has long since finished popping—and dumps it in the bowl on the table. Then she walks behind Will's chair, bends over, and rests her head on his shoulder. "Sorry," she whispers. She nibbles his neck. "My brother is a bit of a geek."

He reaches up and tousles her hair. "He's a kid, that's all. When I was his age, I'd have been just as excited as he is. A teepee! My ass! It's the closest a twelve-year-old can come to having his own apartment."

Sophie straightens when she hears Ian returning up the hall. He enters the kitchen waving the photo. "Got it!" He slaps the picture down in front of Will, jostling the bottle of beer in the process. Sophie reaches out and steadies the bottle, barking out a warning to her brother that he ignores entirely. Now Ian has moved around behind Will's chair, where he can continue looking at the photo even as Will checks it out.

"Aunt Candace thinks she may still have the teepee in storage. She's promised to look for it."

Will shakes his head. He has suffered more than his own share of disappointment at the hands of adults, and he feels sorry for the kid, who is bound to have his heart broken. "Pretty cool," he says. "I hope she comes through for you."

Sophie reaches for the photo, but Will isn't ready to relinquish it. He holds it away from her and continues his conversation with Ian. "So, who's the hottie?" he asks.

Sophie peers over his shoulder. "That's my mother!" she exclaims.

"Where'd you get this photo?" Will asks. Ian explains that his dad keeps it in his underwear drawer.

"Naturally," Will replies, and Ian snickers.

Sophie feels the need to explain. "Those were the Woodstock days. It was cool to go topless."

"It's still cool," Will quips. Ian laughs loudly.

Sophie reaches around and tries to steal the photo, but Will doesn't want to give it up. "Who's the dude?" he asks. All evening he and Ian have been using that word—"dude," "dude," "dude." She's good and sick of it by now. "No, wait. Don't tell me," Will continues. "That's your *dad*, Sophie! He looks just like you."

For a second, Sophie is confused. She hasn't really gotten a good look at the picture, but she knows Jack is a relative newcomer to her mother's life. He wasn't part of the commune crowd; he's never been a hippie.

But Ian is explaining. As usual, Ian can explain everything. "That's Beau. He used to be married to Aunt Candace."

Abruptly, Sophie reaches over Will's shoulder and snatches the photo. She's determined to lay her hands on it, and good thing Will lets go, because otherwise the picture would be ripped in half. She holds it up to the light and peers at the man who sits to one side of the teepee. He's in lotus position, with his hands draped over his knees. He looks intently toward the camera as the wind lifts the curls around his face. While she continues studying the image, Sophie reaches up and tugs at a curl of her own.

Meanwhile, Ian is filling Will in on the story. Beau is dead. He might have taken his own life; no one can say for sure. Beau lost control of his sports car and wrapped it around a tree. Ian asks Will if he's ever read the play *Death of a Salesman*. Ian's English class studied it at the beginning of the year, and that's what happens at the end of the play: Willy Loman gives up on life and drives himself off the road.

Sophie's had enough of it. "Would you just shut up, Ian! Here, put this away and let's finish the game."

As she returns the photo, as it passes from her hands to his, she flashes on Candace sitting up on Sophie's mattress, her face droopy and sad. "You remind me of someone," she'd said. The thought is there, palpable as the photo, as pressing as the life growing inside her. But it's fleeting. It disappears in the time it takes Sophie to watch her brother carry the evidence out of the room.

She escapes to the bathroom for a few minutes. When she returns, they end up scrapping the game. Will says he has to go, and Sophie doesn't protest. She gives him a kiss on the cheek, and he's out of the house before Ian returns to the kitchen. "What the hell?" he says when he hears that Will is gone. "Aren't we going to finish the game?"

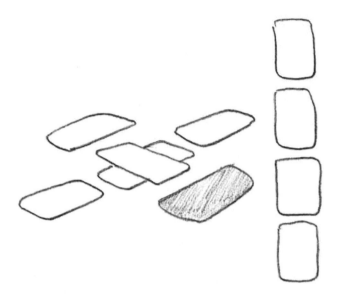

Position #6—"What She Must Face"

Some things we can influence or alter; others we must simply accept. This card provides guidance on what will be—on that which cannot be changed.

~ Knight of Swords ~

KNIGHT of SWORDS.

He's known as the Knight of Winds and Breezes because when he rides through your life, he arrives just ahead of a storm. The Knight is on a quest and is so sure of his own perspective that he may seem arrogant and unfeeling. Notice how he is looking off into the distance as he charges forward? Stay out of his way or you may get hurt.

BECAUSE IT'S THE holiday season and people are eating out, Will has been picking up extra shifts. For weeks now, Sophie has seen very little of him. Either he's in school or he's working. Not surprisingly, she's looking forward to Christmas vacation, when she expects to have him all to herself. She knows better than to be clingy, but she can't help holding on for just a second when she sees him in the hallway during passing period on Friday afternoon, the last day of classes before the holiday break. She grabs him by the sleeve as he's about to pull away, and kisses him smack on the lips. "Dude, I miss you so much," she whispers in his ear.

His response is to squeeze first her hand and then her tit, a quick grope that she still feels as she drops into her seat in French class. At the front of the room, Ms. Hernandez, dressed festively in a red-and-green plaid jumper, is preparing for the holiday show-and-tell. She arranges seasonal items on a table up front: a Santa Claus figurine, a bowl of peppermint sticks, a tabletop Christmas tree decorated with tinsel, a Nativity scene, and a plush toy reindeer. Catching Sophie's eye, Ms. Hernandez raises the wrapped gift in her hand and waits for a response.

Sophie pipes up happily. Here's one she knows: "*Un cadeau!*"

"*Très bon!*" Ms. Hernandez glances about the room. Although the bell will ring in only another minute or two, most of the desks have yet to fill. Because it's the last day before break, students are still loitering and laughing in the halls. No one is in any rush to get started—including Ms. Hernandez. After adding the boxed gift to the collection, she heads down the aisle toward Sophie, a goofy smile on her face. She looks tipsy, Sophie thinks, though later she will realize that Ms. Hernandez is simply happy.

Because she insists on holding all of her conversations in French, Ms. Hernandez augments her dialogue with sign language. Sophie has learned to watch her teacher's hands, so she sees Ms. Hernandez make a clasping motion at her plaid belly. A whole string of French words accompanies the gesture, but Sophie needs to know only one of them to get the gist of the message. That word is "*bébé.*"

"You're having a baby?" Sophie has no idea how to say this in French.

Ms. Hernandez nods happily, then brings a finger to her lips. "*Un secret! Entre toi et moi. Avez-vous vu le film* Juno?"

Sophie shakes her head, a little mystified. Ms. Hernandez glances up and sees that the class is convening. Reluctantly, she turns on her heel and begins back up the aisle to take roll, then turns back. "*Sophie, n'oubliez pas:* Juno! *C'est un must!*"

"*Oui!*" Sophie replies. "*Merci, Madame Hernandez.*"

Classes will be over for the day, Sophie will be standing at her locker and struggling to zip up her jacket, when it will dawn on her why Ms. Hernandez confided in her and not one of the other girls. *I look pregnant.* She knows. They all know. Reading a review of *Juno* in a back issue of the *Albuquerque Journal* confirms her suspicions. "Mouthy teenage girl gets knocked up and lives to tell about it." That's the way Sophie describes it to Tam, who says she'd be glad to see it, though it might have to wait until she and her mother get back from their Christmas visit to Minneapolis.

"Maybe you should go with Will," Tam suggests. "It might be a conversation starter, if you know what I mean."

Sophie admits that it's a good idea, and it turns out that the next day provides a golden opportunity. Will calls just after dinner on Friday. He's at work. Sophie can hear the telltale noises of the restaurant kitchen behind her boyfriend's voice. She wouldn't have believed she'd be the sort to sweat the whereabouts of a guy. But then, she wouldn't have pictured herself knocked up and stupid either.

"Wanna go Christmas shopping tomorrow?" Will asks.

Sophie says, "Definitely," and adds something about the movie. "Everyone is telling me to be sure to see it."

Will is amenable. The plan is to have lunch at the food court, buy a few gifts, and go see *Juno*. Sophie has checked the listings; it's showing at the Starport Theater at two fifteen.

"Ms. Hernandez says I need to see it," she tells Will. He knows Ms. Hernandez because she was his homeroom teacher last year. Evidently she speaks French in homeroom as well. Not all the time, but often enough to get on everyone's nerves. "*Très* pain in the butt," Will has told Sophie. Sophie asked him why he didn't respond in Spanish. She'd have gotten the point. To which Will shook his head. "I go along to get along. You're the hell-raiser, Sophie."

When he picks her up on Saturday, Sophie is dressed in her denim skirt, a black velvet blouse—untucked—and the red rose cowboy boots. The waistline of the skirt fits like a vise around the middle, and it's all she can do not to huff loudly when she gets in the car. She reminds herself to eat lightly for the rest of the day. In the middle of the night, she had woken up starving and, zombie-like, found her way downstairs to the refrigerator. She'd devoured a pint of chocolate ice cream and half a box of graham crackers slathered with peanut butter. Thinking about everything she ate, Sophie feels a little nauseous. One thing she's realized about herself lately: she has no self-control.

The wheels of Will's car spin on the gravel before catching hold. He's

pissed. Sophie can tell, but she has no idea why until he makes his announcement. "No way am I going to that movie." His mom told him he
needed to see it, and that's the kiss of death as far as he's concerned.
"You couldn't pay me to see it. It's about teen pregnancy," he tells
Sophie stiffly. He's gazing out the windshield as he says it, but when
they stop at the light at Fourth and Guadalupe Trail, he turns and meets
her eyes briefly.

She is the one who looks away. "It's fine, Will," she says. "If you
don't want to see it—"

"I don't. It's a chick flick! Go with Tam, or your mom, or *my* mom
for that matter."

Sophie considers a number of smart-alecky replies, but manages not
to utter any of them. Instead, she simply says, "Gotcha." The day is
gloomy, the blue sky masked by clouds. The weatherman has predicted
a light snow. "So, do you want to eat lunch before we shop?"

Will says he does, and in another minute or two he has recovered his
usual good humor. Before she knows it, they are circling the lot in
search of a parking place. All around them, in every direction, are uninterrupted lines of cars.

He needs Sophie's help in picking out a present for Laurel. "Do you
have any ideas?" he asks.

Sophie gives herself a few minutes to consider the options. She is relieved that he's asked for her help. She can do this. She is good at buying
gifts.

"Peggy likes a warm robe in the winter. If the house is cold, she puts
it on over her clothes. What about a robe?"

"How would I know what size to get?"

Here, too, Sophie has a ready answer. "I can try it on. If it's a little
too big for me, then it will fit your mom."

"Perfect," Will replies. He whips his car into the only open parking
space either of them is likely to see. Although Sophie doesn't know
whether he's responding to her suggestion or the miracle parking place,
either way, she is satisfied. She feels that she has things more or less in
hand.

Sophie likes crowds—the more the merrier. Once she's escaped the
overcast sky, her spirits lift. The mall decorations, gaudy purple and

gold ornaments, please her; the sea of people gives her the opportunity to stand out. She is up to the task of selecting a robe for Laurel. Right away, she suggests they head down the escalators to Victoria's Secret.

"She's my mother, not my girlfriend," Will quips. "I was thinking J. C. Penney's." He recommends they eat first, since the food concourse is already buzzing and will only get more crowded in the next hour. "Are you hungry?" he asks.

In fact, she's starving. She could eat an entire pizza—any of them, even the one with the artichokes, bell peppers, and black olives—and not even burp. The nausea that has dogged her for months has finally lifted for good. But she is self-conscious about the weight she's gained, and determined not to stuff her face in front of Will. So she tells him that she had a late breakfast and probably won't eat much.

He suggests they order three slices, two for him and one for her, and says he'll eat whatever she doesn't. Once they're in line, they agree to share a drink as well. "We can get a large," Will says. He turns and grins widely at Sophie. He looks downright jolly. She's ready to believe that his happiness has everything to do with her presence. Evidently he's been missing her every bit as much as she's missed him.

"Maybe I'll have a salad, too," Sophie says, "and one of those bread-sticks." She picks up two fat packets of Italian dressing and tosses them onto the scarred plastic tray. Will takes no notice of this change of order, but the little guy in the paper hat behind the heat lamps hears. He hops to attention when she points to the fattest of the braided bread-sticks on the greasy cookie sheet. By the time they reach the cashier, Sophie is actually salivating. If Will weren't carrying the tray, she'd have picked off a piece of pepperoni and stuffed it into her mouth.

As it is, she follows as closely as she dares. They have to thread their way through a number of occupied tables. Sophie is expecting to see one or more familiar faces. She's ready to wave and smile, just like a beauty queen. Being with Will has that effect on her. It's a bit of a disappointment that they get all the way to the table without seeing anyone they even recognize.

"Who are all these people?" she asks Will, and as soon they get seated, she pounces, reaching over and ripping a piece of pepperoni from first one slice and then another.

"Hey!" he calls out. "Knock it off."

She sighs and slouches down in her seat. How embarrassing. Now she's relieved that she doesn't see anyone she knows.

They eat in silence during the time it takes Will to consume both slices. In the same interval, Sophie devours the salad and breadstick. She sees that he's eying her piece, and before he can get any bright ideas, she slides the paper plate in front of her.

"Are you still sharing yours?" he asks. "You don't have to."

"I'm going to cut it in half," she informs him.

Will would prefer to pass the slice back and forth, but Sophie knows that he takes larger bites than she does, so she pushes his hand away when he reaches for the slice and insists on using a plastic knife to divide it lengthwise. He watches as she saws away, her curly locks hiding her face from view.

"Can you keep a secret?" he asks.

"Of course." In fact, she has never kept a secret in her whole life.

Will has big news: he is going to Lubbock for Christmas. "For the first time in ten years," he tells her, "I get to spend Christmas with my dad." He plans to leave on Sunday morning. He's going in to work early that night, in hopes that he'll be allowed to clock out at ten and head home for a good night's sleep. He will set his alarm, something he never does on Sunday mornings. From Albuquerque, the drive to Lubbock takes six hours, and he wants to arrive well before dark.

"Tomorrow?"

He nods and holds out a hand for his share of the food.

Sophie pushes the plate back into the middle of the table. The two halves have been neatly separated, but she forgets hers for the moment. "What if it snows? Will you stay here if it snows?"

He shakes his head. "I borrowed chains from a guy at work. They're in the trunk of the car. I haven't been to Lubbock since I was a little kid—since I was eight years old. I remember getting a football, and we took it outside into the street and threw it back and forth for the longest time. My dad would ask me a simple question: 'What's your favorite subject in school?' That kind of thing. And I couldn't answer, Sophie. I was so scared I'd say the wrong thing. It was like being in a play and forgetting your lines." He reaches over idly for his half of the slice. "The next Christmas, I assumed I must have said something dumb, because he didn't ask me back. I tried to remember everything I'd said and everything he'd said." He takes a bite and chews. "Pretty lame, huh?"

Sophie takes a deep breath. She remembers her mother's remark at Thanksgiving, remembers it verbatim: *Your boyfriend's happiness should be a consideration in your own.* "I'm happy for you, Will," she stutters, "but . . ." She isn't sure how to go on, so she reaches for her half and begins to eat. One or two bites into it, she chokes, then has to endure the indignity of Will banging on her back. No way can she hold back the tears. They drip down her cheeks, and in between coughs, she sniffles.

When it's clear that she's going to live, he sighs, a small, bitter exhalation. "I should have known you wouldn't be happy for me."

Sophie hears herself say that she *is* happy for Will, but she's unhappy for herself. "These tears are selfish." She grabs a napkin and makes a show of wiping them away. "But damn, you've got to understand, dude. I'm knocked up and getting bigger every day. What do you expect from me?"

When he answers, his voice is loud enough to make those sitting nearby shift in their uncomfortable chairs. "What do you expect from *me*?" He waves a hand in her direction. "I can't believe you're having a kid. I really can't wrap my brain around it, Sophie!"

"Believe it!" she hisses, then reaches over and snatches the crust he's left on the plate. "I'm starving, dude! I need my nourishment."

"Why didn't you just say so? I hate it when women play games. My mom does that, which is why I'm not telling her up front. I'm leaving her a note and a gift. You, I thought I could trust. You, I thought, would be happy for me."

Now Sophie must rise to the occasion. She can't be pissed like Laurel. To be like Laurel in any way, shape, or form, well, that's the last thing she'd want. "It's just that I'm really going to miss you," she tells him.

"And I'm going to miss you, too," he replies.

And it's true. Sure it is. Will loves the way her butt sways when she walks away from him, the way she sticks out her tongue in exasperation and whispers directions to herself when she drives. He loves her scrambled eggs, cooked with so many chiles that they're more green than yellow. He loves it that Sophie knows what she wants, though lately she can't make up her mind. Only a few minutes ago, he had asked her what she wanted for Christmas, and she'd said, "I want my life back," then immediately added, "or at least some sexy lingerie."

Once they've tossed their trash, they walk toward the escalator. She gets on first, and he brings up the rear, draping his arm around her shoulder and whispering in her ear, "I love you, Sophie."

His words rush through her, and she literally stumbles when the stairs disappear on the ground floor. Will's arms steady her. "I love you, too," she whispers back. Sophie wishes she could break away from him for just a minute, just long enough to make a quick call to Tam to broadcast the news: *All's well because Will says he loves me.*

She wants to love him back, and it won't do simply to say the words. She's ready to venture into J. C. Penney's to select a robe for his mother, but he steers her instead into the deep, dark cave of Victoria's Secret. He has it in mind to check off both of the women on his list. While Sophie selects a robe for Laurel, something lovely and silky but not too sexy, Will fingers the red bras and panties.

He gets all the help he needs from one of the sales associates, a young woman whose name tag reads Amelia and who is more than happy to help Will pick out the sexiest lingerie in the store. Will is really very attractive, especially when he ducks his chin and gazes into her eyes.

"Have you ever seen anything half this hot?" she asks, holding up a red lacy bra.

"Sure I have," he replies, smiling shyly. "But it's just what I'm looking for."

"What size do you think she'd wear?" Will asks Amelia. The salesgirl is considerably shorter than he is, and to be discreet, he moves in closer. "I'm picking out her Christmas present," he whispers, pointing to Sophie in the next room.

"I see," says Amelia. Reluctantly, she leaves Will's side and sidles over to Sophie. "Can I help you?" Amelia asks. She's hoping to get a better look at Sophie's bust, but it's hidden from view by the robes she has draped over her left arm.

Sophie shakes her head firmly. She doesn't believe in sales help. Then she reconsiders and hands over her load. "As a matter of fact," she says, "I do need a changing room."

"Certainly," Amelia says. The robes are cumbersome for someone so small. Even though she hoists them over one shoulder, the hems still trail the floor. But no matter. She has two reasons to be accommodating: Will has deep, dark eyes to die for, and Amelia works on commission. So she unlocks the door to one of the half dozen changing rooms and carefully hangs and arranges the robes on a long, shining rod.

The wall-sized mirror is framed in black, which Sophie finds alluring. It's a far cry from the changing room she's most familiar with: the one in her mother's shop. That's a little makeshift affair without even a modicum of privacy—its door is a heavy piece of drapery that has to be coaxed across a jerry-rigged curtain rod. Inevitably, there are gaps that allow anyone passing by to get an eyeful. Not so at Victoria's Secret. The heavy black doors close firmly and lock tightly.

Amelia is quite clear about the changing-room policy: no males allowed. To Will, she points out a burgundy upholstered chair near the three-way mirror. "Make yourself comfortable. Once your girlfriend has a robe on, she can come out and model it for you." Will takes a seat, a frothy, lacy pile of red lingerie heaped in his lap.

When Sophie emerges from the changing room, she is wearing a red-and-white-striped satin robe. She is barefoot, and her curly black locks spill over one shoulder. A spotlight illuminates the area beneath the three-way mirror, and when Sophie steps into it, she smiles at Will and even, a little devilishly, sticks out her tongue.

"What do you think?"

She looks gorgeous, and he tells her so.

"Thanks," she replies in a breathy voice. "What have you got there in your lap?"

She crosses the parquet floor and leans over, affording him an eyeful. Her luscious, swollen breasts are right under his nose. She's naked under the robe, and just as he's made this discovery, she plunges her hand through the pile of panties and squeezes his crotch. She knows how firmly to grab and how long to hold on. It's all Will can do to suppress a loud moan.

"You're a little slut," he whispers in her ear.

She laughs loudly, then whispers in his: "Wanna come see me in my little room, big boy?" She grabs his hand, and he is up and out of the burgundy chair. Within seconds, Sophie has secreted him into her changing room and closed the door with a click. She puts a finger to his lips and warns him to be quiet. "Don't make a sound," she hisses, then drops the robe around her feet.

Because Amelia is busy waiting on someone else, she takes longer than she should to circle back around to the waiting area. Even from across the room, she can see that the chair is empty, and when she gets closer, she notes the strewn panties and bras, tossed about the chair like outsize rose petals. Without thinking, she bends to collect them, irked at Will's thoughtlessness. Her head is down, blood rushing to her face, when the situation dawns on her. The online training she finished only last week warns of changing room trysts; the company believes in propriety, and so does Amelia.

However, she is not one to take matters into her own hands. Instead, Amelia scuttles over to the bank of cash registers, where the manager is finishing up a transaction. As soon as the manager hears the low groans and giggles coming from the changing room, she decides to turn the awkward situation over to mall security, who in turn call the police.

It is Saturday evening before Sophie and Will are released, separately, into the custody of their parents. As relieved as Sophie is not to have to face Laurel, she is heartbroken at not being able to say good-bye to Will. Their tryst in the dressing room is the closest Sophie has ever come to bliss. She hopes Will feels the same, though when she doesn't hear from him on Christmas Eve or Christmas Day, she begins to worry. She remembers the way he avoided her gaze in the police station, the way he refused even to meet her eyes in the reflection of a mirror. She thought he was embarrassed, but now she's afraid he was angry.

Ian doesn't get what he wants for Christmas either. He gets a cheap-ass telescope and a note of apology from Candace. She couldn't "put her hands on the teepee." She calls and offers an additional explanation: "It isn't where I thought it would be, in storage with some of my aunt's furniture. It could be that we got rid of it some time ago, and I just don't remember."

As she talks, Ian does his best not to blubber into the receiver. He stares at Lucy, splayed out on the brick floor. She looks cold and uncomfortable, so, still holding the remote receiver, he walks over to the coatrack and removes his mother's black dress coat. He's angry, and he needs to act on his feelings right away so that he doesn't convey them to Aunt Candace. He spreads the coat out on the floor and wordlessly coaxes the dog to curl up on top of it. He's never understood why they don't get Lucy a bed.

"Don't worry about it, Aunt Candace," he says. "You tried. You made the effort. I really appreciate it."

Christmas joy eludes his parents as well. Despite beaucoup icicle lights and promises of free Southwestern designer wrapping—brown paper printed with jolly red and green peppers—Peggy's shop will not get out of the red for Christmas. Consequently, Jack has to put off ordering the Saltillo tiles for the fixer-upper. He hoped to get the work done over the Christmas break—he was looking forward to it—but instead he keeps himself busy with the roof repairs. He and Peggy don't argue; neither do they speak. Peggy knows he holds her responsible for Sophie's stunt at Victoria's Secret. Sophie knows it, too. Jack is giving both of them the silent treatment.

In the late afternoon on New Year's Day, Sophie breaks down and calls Will's house. She calls from her parents' bedroom. Peggy is in the midst of rustling up a traditional New Year's Day meal: black-eyed peas and greens for good luck in the new year, ham, and mashed potatoes. Every year of her short life, Sophie has started the new year with a mushy mouthful of black-eyed peas, and what does she have to show for it?

Ordinarily Jack spends New Year's Day watching football. His absence is all too noticeable when she goes down to the kitchen and is greeted by nothing more than her mother's forced hum and the bubbling of boiling peas.

Though she sucks at apologizing, she knows she has to try. The fiasco at Victoria's Secret is her fault, all hers. She's ready to promise just about anything, if only he'll forgive her. During the last nine days, she's had considerable time to think about her situation. She's even working on a list of New Year's resolutions. So far she has one: it's called "WWTD?" or "What Would Tam Do?" It was suggested by Tam herself, who couldn't hide her incredulity when Sophie related the details of her arrest: "You did what? You hooked up at Victoria's Secret? Are you kidding me? Are you kidding me? It was your idea?"

Laurel answers the phone, sounding sick. "Hello?" she croaks. For a second or two, Sophie wonders whether she has dialed the wrong number. Laurel is congested, and the effort of talking leads to a coughing fit.

"Happy New Year, Laurel," Sophie says. "You sound awful."

"Sophie, is that you?" Laurel asks.

"It's me. Is Will there?"

"No, he's not. He's not here and he's not going to be here." Another coughing fit ensues.

Sophie steels herself to be patient, though she is anything but. "What do you mean?" she finally asks.

"What I said: he's not coming home, Sophie. He's staying in Lubbock."

"Why?"

In spite of her irritation, in spite of her grief, Laurel feels some measure of Sophie's pain. She's been there. So she blows her nose and continues in a calmer voice. "What can I say? It's the genes. Just when you need them to be men, they run off to Lubbock and become firefighters."

"What are you talking about?" Sophie is feeling panicky. With her free hand, she reaches out for one of her mother's decorative pillows and squeezes it tightly to her chest.

"His father is a firefighter. Carlos is a firefighter."

"So?" Sophie says. "So what?"

Laurel sighs. "Like father, like son."

"What about school? School starts tomorrow."

"He's going to transfer. He'll finish high school in Lubbock."

"Is that what he told you?"

"That's what his father told me."

Sophie is silent for a moment; then despair takes over. "Is this because we got arrested? I'm really so, so sorry about that, Laurel."

"I'm sure you are, Sophie. People tend to be sorry for things when they get caught." She is silent for a moment. "And I can't help noticing that you don't seem to get away with much, Sophie, especially when it comes to sex. Me, I'm the same way."

On the other end, Sophie is weeping silently. If she tries to speak, she'll blubber, so she keeps her mouth closed.

"Will isn't ready to be a father. That's what this is about. He's still a kid. You're still a kid, too." She waits for Sophie to disagree, but Sophie is pointedly silent. Laurel has an idea: "Have you seen *Juno?*"

Sophie has forgotten all about the movie. She manages to say no, and Laurel tells her that she really must see it.

"If ever a movie was relevant . . ." Though Laurel doesn't finish the thought, Sophie catches the drift. "It's playing at Movies West."

Sophie thanks Laurel, then hangs up without a good-bye. A single insistent sob threatens to strangle her. She'd like to see the movie, but no way is she showing her face at Movies West. Not in this lifetime.

Recently the multiplex at Cottonwood Mall has renovated its theaters, installing stadium seating and high-backed, plush seats. The seats in every other row are rockers, and when Tam and Sophie arrive, Sophie insists on trying them out. She wants to rock; Tam wants to sit in the middle of the row. Because the girls have arrived early, both preferences are easy to satisfy. While they wait for the coming attractions to begin, the girls raise their feet off the sticky concrete and rock gently. Tam enjoys the sensation, but Sophie loves it. She leans into the headrest and gazes off into the darkness. She hasn't felt this relaxed in weeks. No one can see her; she can't see anyone. For the moment, the theater is silent. She and Tam have it nearly all to themselves.

The two of them split the cost of a tub of popcorn. Because it's the biggie, they're entitled to a refill. They can eat as greedily as they like, spilling kernels into their laps, and neither worries because they have another tub in their future. This time, Tam is the keeper of the popcorn. Ordinarily Sophie has the honors, but her lap is disappearing. Neither of them remarks on it. They simply make the wordless accommodation of true friends.

Once the movie begins, however, Tam has the popcorn to herself. For a good hour, Sophie forgets to eat. She is transfixed, so engaged by Juno and her nearly identical dilemma to Sophie's own that she loses herself in the story. When Juno and her best friend read the *PennySaver* classifieds to find prospective adoptive parents, Sophie punches Tam in the shoulder, prompting Tam to pelt her best friend with popcorn.

For the last hour of the film, Sophie weeps quietly, a steady stream of tears rolling down her cheeks. A few years from now, she will explain to Candace how she made her decision. "After I saw *Juno*, adoption just seemed like a good idea. It worked for her, you know?" That the movie was released in December of 2007, just as Sophie was finishing her second trimester, seemed fated. She needed counsel; she needed distraction; she needed hope for the future. The movie offered all of those and more.

"Juno's pretty cool," Sophie remarks afterward, "but she wasn't my favorite character."

They've just gotten into the car. Tam has turned on the ignition and is waiting for the engine to warm up. "Mine either," she replies, rubbing her hands together. It was so cold in Minneapolis that she wore gloves to bed. Now that she is home in Albuquerque, it seems she shouldn't need them. She left them in the pockets of her other coat, and she regrets that now. "You know who my favorite character was?" Tam asks.

She is about to answer her own question, but Sophie breaks in. "The dad," she says.

Tam is surprised. "How'd you know?"

In the darkness of the car, Sophie gives way to a little smirking smile. If there can be such a thing, it's a sympathetic smirk. She loves Tam like a sister. "Well, it wasn't going to be that doofus of a boyfriend, now was it?"

"God!" Tam wails. "Who could love that momma's boy?"

Sophie wonders whether Ian will grow up to be a towheaded version of Paulie Bleeker. She certainly hopes not, but Ian does appear to be similarly self-absorbed and nerdy. He has Paulie's long, angular face and heart-shaped mouth. He hides away in his room—except when the rest of them are gone, in which case he slips out and snoops around. Sophie is irritated with Ian. Once or twice lately, she's sat at the breakfast table and considered the consequences of tripping him as he passes. She likes to imagine him toppling over headfirst. Of course, he'll catch himself before his head cracks on the bricks. She wouldn't want to kill him. She just wants to teach him a lesson; she wants to tell him that he shouldn't be such a damn snoop.

Once they're on the road, Sophie clears her throat. "So, I've always wondered something."

"What?" Tam asks. She peers through the windshield at the car lights in front of them. Tam is a cautious driver, but only when it comes to those ahead of her. What's in front she can control. What's coming up, in the side mirrors or rearview mirror, well, that's all out of her control. She doesn't see any reason to stress herself out by keeping an eye on those coming up from behind. Tam's policy is to stay in her lane and hope for the best.

"Do you know your dad? Do you know who he is?"

Tam leans into the steering wheel, as though to press her nose against the glass. She can't see well enough at night, she thinks. Maybe she needs glasses, though vanity would preclude wearing them. She's never lied to Sophie, but she does so now. She tells Sophie that she does know her father, that she's met him a time or two.

"Really?" Sophie is warming to her subject, a fact revealed by the fogging up of first the passenger-side window and then the passenger-side windshield.

Tam waits for the test. She's expecting Sophie to ask questions, to try to trip her up, in which case Tam will have to pull to the side of the road and sob. She doesn't know a damn thing about her father, and that's because Belinda is a stone wall when it comes to the question of who knocked her up. At the light at Coors and Irving, Tam reaches under her seat and grabs a small white hand towel, which she tosses into Sophie's lap. She has it in mind that Sophie will wipe the windshield, although she doesn't voice the request. Should she have to? After all, her friend knows good and well that, like the air conditioner, the defroster in the car doesn't work.

"Do you realize how clueless fathers are when it comes to a little thing like paternity? They don't actually have any real idea whether the child they shelter and care for actually belongs to them."

"Or the child they *don't* shelter and care for," grumbles Tam.

But Sophie is not going to be diverted. "Take Juno, for instance," she goes on. "Her dad is a sweet loser who takes it on faith that Juno is truly his. And maybe she is, but he and his first wife parted ways. Juno's mom isn't even in Juno's life these days, much less the father's."

By the time Sophie pauses to take a breath, all the glass inside the car is blanketed in fog—front and back, driver and passenger side. The two friends are enveloped in a moving cocoon. The green light asserts itself in streaks across the glass. Hesitantly, Tam puts her foot to the gas. "I can't see a fucking thing," she says under her breath. She leans into the steering wheel and uses the back of her left sleeve to reveal a little swatch of clarity.

Sophie is twisting the white towel in her hands, wringing it urgently. She doesn't appear to have heard. "Jack's never home anymore. He seems to be living at the fixer-upper." Suddenly Sophie is sobbing into the white towel. Her whole face is pressed into the cotton surface. Tam wants to tell her friend that the towel may not be clean. She doesn't know where it's been.

Instead, she pulls into an Allsup's parking lot and puts the car in park. "I'm sorry about your dad, Sophie, and I'm sorry about Will, too. The ways of men are a mystery to me." She is wearing a black wool cap pulled down over her ears and forehead, and the rest of her face appears moonlike. Sophie thinks, What would Tam do?

"I haven't wanted to tell you this," Tam continues, "but maybe we should just empty 'all the trash,' as Mom likes to say. I have some bad news. American Airlines is downsizing at the Sunport. Either we have to relocate to Dallas or my mom has to find another job."

Sophie renews her weeping. "This sucks!" she yells, and the two of them proceed to cry their hearts out.

"Why did I ever want to know the future?" Tam wails. "The future sucks!"

On Friday, January 18, FedEx delivers a fat envelope of paperwork from an adoption agency in Boston. Peggy is home with a fever, so she signs for the package. The weather is as wintery as it gets in Albuquerque—it's windy and bone-chillingly cold. The FedEx deliveryman is wearing a cap with earflaps and leather gloves. "Stay warm!" he calls as he jumps back into his truck.

Peggy shivers and closes the door against the cold. For maybe a minute, she stands with her back to the door, hugging the fat envelope to her chest. It gets heavier as she ponders the possibilities. How much has Candace shared with Sophie? When have the two talked, and for how long? Peggy considers calling Candace to find out, but she's not up to knowing the truth just now. Chills run from her torso to her arms and legs. Her teeth begin to chatter as she carries the package down the hall to the dining table. She leaves it there for Sophie to find.

As she climbs back into bed and pulls a pile of blankets over her shaking frame, Peggy tries to imagine a conversation with her daughter, something constructive and comforting, but she gets no further than a question: *Is this what you want, darling?* How silly is that? Of course she doesn't want a package of forms from an adoption agency in Boston. But neither does she want the alternatives. None of them do. Peggy wants to weep. She'd feel better if she could cry. Instead, she falls into a restless, sweaty sleep.

Ian has already examined the outside of the package by the time Sophie gets home. He is sitting at the table drinking chocolate milk when she arrives, and although he has a textbook propped up in front of him, Sophie isn't fooled.

"What's in the envelope?" she asks in a challenging tone.

He gives her a blank look over the top of his book. "It's addressed to you."

"That's never stopped you."

She drops into a nearby chair and eyes his chocolate milk. Ian pushes the glass in her direction, then gets up to make more. By the time he's mixed a new glass of Hershey's and milk and carried it back to the table, she has torn open the envelope and begun examining the contents.

The first form Sophie encounters is called the "Statement of Understanding." The directions ask the birth mother to answer yes or no to a number of questions. Sophie scans the page and stops at the statement, "I understand that the birth father has parental rights and that I must be honest about him and his whereabouts in order to properly terminate his rights."

She takes a quick slug of chocolate milk, then shuffles through the other forms: Common Questions Asked by Birth Parents, Authorizations and Confidentiality, Birth Mother Disclosure Form, Birth Father Disclosure Form, Birth Mother Intake Form and Questionnaire, Birth Parents' Legal Rights, Medical Information Release, Birth Family Service Agreement. The intake form alone is seven pages long. Sophie picks up the glass of chocolate milk, drinks the last of it, and leans back in her chair.

"Holy shit, Ian. I'm in way over my head."

He nods and holds out a hand for the glass. "More chocolate milk?"

Sophie is afraid to call Laurel, and she puts off the task for nearly a week. In the meantime she works her way through the intake form, discovering a number of questions about the paternal family that either Will or Laurel will have to answer. Finally, one evening when she is working on the forms rather than her homework, Sophie manages to dial Laurel's number. Without preliminaries, she launches into the reason for her call.

"I've decided to give the baby up for adoption," Sophie tells Laurel. She is sitting on the top stair of the dark stairwell. It's her favorite place in the house these days. She feels enclosed but not entrapped.

"That's going to be hard," Laurel replies, "but I think it's a good decision."

"Yeah, well, I have to get Will to give up his rights. Do you think he'll do that?"

Laurel is silent for a moment. "He'll do it," she says. "So you need to send him something in the mail, then?"

"Yep."

Laurel puts down the phone and goes off for what seems like an eternity. She's sniffling when she returns. She reads the address slowly so that Sophie can write it down.

"Maybe I can ask you some questions about Will's health history?" Sophie asks. "I'd rather not send him any more forms than are necessary."

"Sure, Sophie," Laurel says. "What do you need to know?"

By the end of the month, Sophie has put the form in the mail, along with a letter.

Dear Will:

Are you having a good ole time in Lubbock? I hear it's ugly and the weather sucks. For reasons I won't go into but that can be summed up in five words—I'M TOO YOUNG AND STUPID— I've decided on adoption. If you want to know the truth, it really pisses me off that I have to ask your permission. Most of the time I'd like to forget you exist, but there's this baby I'm carrying that's part yours. So says the state of New Mexico. I'm not going to cry. . . . I'm not going to cry. . . . I'm not going to fucking cry. Please sign the form enclosed, which relinquishes all your rights, and return it. Unless of course you want me to show up on your doorstep.

I don't love you anymore—Sophie

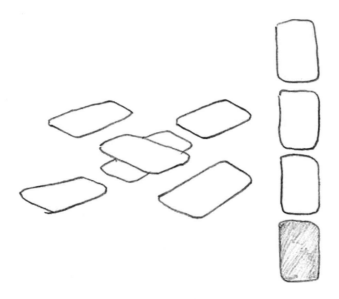

Position #7—"What She Feels"

Whatever the card, there you are. This position is about your thoughts and how they make you feel. Sometimes the position is labeled "The Self," but aren't we most ourselves in our reactions to the world?

～ Three of Swords ～

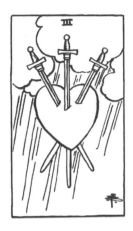

The meaning is apparent. The heart has been pierced through not once but three times. And to deepen the heartache, a driving rain falls from dark, massed clouds. The three is indicative of the family unit: 1 + 2 = 3. Those who give us the most happiness are also capable of inflicting the most pain.

WHEN IAN PULLS the kitchen door closed behind him, he is shocked by the bitter cold. In Albuquerque, late January mornings require coats, but middle-schoolers often rush off without them. The sweat shirt he's wearing does little to stave off the cold. Later, rushing from his last class to catch the bus home, he may push up his sleeves and sweat at the collar, but right now he begins shivering almost immediately. In late winter, Albuquerque temperatures swing from frosty to mild and back again. The following month will bring the first signs of spring—crocuses will push their heads through the cold, dry ground by the end of February—but this particular January morning holds no hints of spring.

Ian has bolted down his bowl of Rice Krispies, and either the sudden cold or a bad case of nerves—he dreads the impending ordeal—unsettles his stomach. Suddenly he has to burp and burp again, painful eruptions that nearly gag him. He stands on the porch for a moment, trying to collect himself before trudging across the pea-sized gravel to join Sophie at the edge of the field. His sister is wearing a navy-blue hoodie that he suspects belongs to Jack. It's so big on her that her hands don't emerge from the sleeves, yet he can see the swelling of her belly when she stands in profile.

She has a challenge for him, she says. She wants him to get to know the bees, and to come to terms with his fear of them. As Ian stands in the drive shivering, Sophie explains her reasoning: bravery isn't a trait you're born with. It's something you cultivate, something you acquire. To deter the run-of-the-mill bully, a person needs self-confidence, and Sophie has devised a task to get Ian started down the road.

In the time it takes Sophie to give her pep talk, the light strengthens, revealing their surroundings: their home, the low-slung adobe off to the east, with its wide porch and shining tin roof; the gnarled trunk of an elderly cottonwood to the north of them; and, to the west, the acre of land that is home to five bee colonies. The boxes are protected by a slight rise. Between the boy and the bees stretches a sandy lot dotted with sage, chamisa, and bundles of tumbleweed.

"The bees are clustering now, Ian," Sophie tells him, nodding toward the hives. "That means they're staying inside, where it's nice and warm. You probably won't even see one. Not from this distance, and not so early in the day."

Ian nods. He continues to shiver, then burp, then shiver again.

"So here's the deal," Sophie explains. "You come out here every morning, before you go meet the bus, and every morning you take another step into the field. You think about how you're getting braver, and about how most of the things that scare you aren't really worth getting worked up about—"

"What happens when I reach the hives?" Ian interrupts, aware of the trembling in his voice.

"Nothing. That's the beauty of it, *manito*. The bees will still be clustering, but you'll be stronger and braver."

"Are you sure?" He's carrying his backpack, which is loaded with textbooks; the weight of it pulls at the muscles in his arms and shoulders. He adjusts his grasp and considers what he can see of Sophie's face. She's pulled up her hood, but he can still make out her eyes. Ian is good at reading the expressions of others. If Sophie were lying to him, he would see it.

"I'm positive."

Ian takes his sister at her word. While she might be mistaken in her prediction that he'll be stronger and braver by the time he reaches the hive, Sophie is certain to be right about the bees. That's good enough for him.

On the first Saturday after beginning the task, Ian enters the field at about ten o'clock in the morning, and in the full light of day he observes something that strikes him as miraculous: a worker bee is removing the bodies of the dead from the hive. He isn't sure what's going on until the worker emerges and, with tremendous effort but no ceremony, carries a body a short distance, before dropping it and circling back to the entrance hole. It might be the same worker or a different one who lugs out a second body and then a third. Ian forgets all about his fear and watches, transfixed.

Later in the day, when Candace calls, Ian is the only one at home. He tells her about the bees, and she is silent, listening. She doesn't have a question or even a comment—not where the bees are concerned, anyway. Instead, she asks whether Sophie is home yet. "She had a doctor's appointment this morning, didn't she?"

In spite of himself, Ian is impressed. For a woman who lives thousands of miles away, Candace manages to stay pretty current on the comings and goings of the Grangers. You'd think they were on a reality show, and she was tuning in every week. Ian admits that he overheard a phone conversation between the doctor's receptionist and his mother.

"Sometimes when I answer and then Mom picks up, I listen for a minute or two."

Candace is reassuring: "Of course you do! So much going on at your house! I have to call and get caught up, you see, because there's never anything going on here in Boston." She adds that it *is* snowing in Boston, at least. It's been snowing steadily for several hours. "Snow is happening," she says, "but that's about it."

She is calling, she goes on, because she wants to let Sophie know that, at long last, the furniture is on its way. So many things conspired to slow down the delivery, she says. She proceeds to detail them, but Ian zones out. When Candace called, he was about to fix himself lunch. He's hungry. Starving, in fact. He carries the receiver over to the refrigerator, but instead of opening the door as he intends, he simply stands and studies what's posted in front of him. It's the usual family collage. A magnetized clip holds the bell schedules for Taft and Valley. Plastic magnetic cacti secure a selection of photographs: last year's school photos and a picture of the fixer-upper, taken from the real-estate flyer.

Also affixed to the fridge is a purple Post-it note that Ian has just added to the collection. It's a message for his dad from Alice at the River View Manor, along with a phone number. Alice sounded so young on the phone—more like the daughter of a caregiver than a caregiver herself—and she sounded breathless, too, as if she'd just run for the phone. Why run for the phone when you're in Vermont and the person you are calling is in New Mexico? What can speed have to do with it?

Candace is still talking. She is back to the subject of snow; she's saying that the snow lifts her spirits.

"It's snowing in Brattleboro, too," Ian breaks in.

Candace is caught off guard. She falls silent.

"How far is it from Boston to Brattleboro?" he asks.

Candace doesn't ask why he wants to know. She isn't teacherly or parent-like. She doesn't assume the worst or rush to judgment. Nor does she correct or lecture him. She'll stop her own train of thought on a dime and attend to his. "Well, let's see. Maybe two hundred miles or so."

"That's not so far, is it?"

"Three or four hours. The New England states are smaller than the western states, and they've been populated for so much longer. Everything is closer together."

"A little while ago someone phoned from the River View Manor in Brattleboro, where my grandmother lives."

"Is she okay?"

"She's lost."

"What do you mean?"

"She's like our dog, Lucy," Ian explains. "She gets out and wanders off." He looks around the kitchen for the golden retriever. Lucy has a tendency to slip out the back door and traipse around the neighborhood, which might not be so bad if she were car savvy, but she's not. He's seen farm dogs that look both ways before crossing a two-lane highway, but Lucy doesn't comprehend anything larger and faster than she is.

"Oh, dear. Does your dad know?"

"No, not yet. He knows she's been wandering off, but he doesn't know that she's on the loose again. He went over to the fixer-upper early this morning, and he forgot to take his cell phone."

"What about your mom? Does she know?"

Frankly, it hasn't occurred to Ian to call his mom. What can she do about it? "No, she's at the shop. Do you think I should call her?"

But Candace is on the same page as Ian. She doesn't see the point of worrying Peggy. Instead, she asks Ian to read off the information on the note: the name of the nursing home and the phone number. "I'll go check on your grandmother. How's that? Does your dad come home for lunch?"

Ian says that he doesn't, but he offers to ride his bike over to the fixer-upper.

"Tell him I'll call this evening, after I've had a chance to check in at the center. It's just what I need, a little road trip. I'll pack an overnight bag and be on my way in an hour or so. Now, the snow may slow me down a bit, but I assume they've been out there plowing."

Ian will hold up his end of the bargain—he'll set out for the fixer-upper as soon as he finishes a peanut butter sandwich and three sweet pickles. His bicycle is stowed in the shed where Jack stores his beekeeping paraphernalia, or whatever he doesn't end up carrying around in his car. The shed smells sweet.

Ian has heard that honey never spoils, not ever. And he wonders how that could be. Bees live only a few short weeks, start to finish, and the flowers from which they collect nectar are even more fleeting. And yet the union of the two can last indefinitely, long after all traces of both bug and bloom are gone. Ian is beginning to understand his dad's fascination with bees.

What might have been an easy three-hour trip takes Candace nearly five. The delay is caused mostly by her tendency to drive slowly. The roads are clear, or nearly so, and New Englanders are used to driving in the snow. Or rather, those who drive regularly are used to it. Candace herself rarely drives. She's thought of selling her car—it seems a waste to keep one in a garage, to pay for the space it occupies and the insurance premiums. But when she does need to drive, the necessity comes up quickly, and she's relieved that she can simply hop in and go. There's no ticket to buy or schedule to consult.

Once on the road, though, she has trouble maintaining a consistent speed. Whenever her attention is diverted, either by something outside the car or by a thought that pops into her head, she lets up on the accelerator. Her foot goes slack and the speed at which she's traveling falls off, until the honking of another driver's horn reminds her of the primary task and she reasserts pressure.

This is the way life is, she tells herself. You forget what's most important. You get sidelined over and over again. As she drives west on Interstate 90, she finds herself remembering a childhood outing with Aunt Agnes, a drive to Worcester to see someone the older woman described only as a friend. The trip must have occurred shortly after Candace went to live with Agnes, because Candace can date it by the car her aunt drove: a gold Mustang with a loud tail pipe. For a little while, the car led Candace to make an error in judgment where Agnes was concerned. It seemed to her that Agnes had escaped the fate of Candace's mother—that Agnes was her own woman, independent, even fearless. In fact, she was anything but.

The fellow must have been her lover, Candace thinks now. She wishes she could remember his name. But she recalls very little about the trip, except that the man's hands shook as he speared his wedge of iceberg lettuce and sliced off a mouthful. Because no one was saying anything as he went about the task, they all merely beheld his knife sliding across the pool of Thousand Island dressing. Candace watched the man mop up the mess and push the plate aside, abandoning the salad altogether. It had disappointed him. In much the same way, he must have given up on Agnes, Candace realizes as she watches for the sign that will lead her north to Interstate 91. He must have made a mess of things between them, then shoved her away.

Of course, Agnes probably played a role. Back then, the indiscreet referred to Agnes as an "old maid." Sometimes she called herself a "spinster," but only to provoke irritation or sympathy in others. She had scoliosis and a weakness for brandy. Under the influence, she'd turn weepy and vindictive. On the other hand, she was also loyal, to the point of lunacy. She'd taken in poor Candace, after all. And where the man friend was concerned, Agnes had made the effort, at least on that one occasion. She'd driven the distance with her niece in tow.

For Candace, Agnes wanted something better, so she encouraged the girl to get out and meet as many people as possible. Agnes need not have worried. Candace had no intention of emulating her aunt; she did not want to be single, nor did she want to be childless. But neither did she want her children to be accidents of fate. She didn't want a baby by just anyone, and she didn't want to raise a child by herself.

For all of those reasons, in the spring of 1969, Candace had a second-trimester abortion in Mexico City. The procedure was still illegal in the United States. It would be another three years before any woman could have a legal abortion in this country. By then Candace had recovered from the complications caused by unsterilized surgical tools. She would feel just fine, but she wasn't *actually* fine. Some choices are simply much more lasting than others. The result of this desperate interlude was life-long childlessness.

Although she wasn't mature enough to embrace motherhood as a twenty-year-old, by the time Candace turned thirty, she was married, back in Boston, and aching for a baby. She and Beau had spent a small fortune—hers, of course—trying to trick her body into conceiving, but nothing worked. Some things money can't buy; some things money can't undo. Many women are lucky when it comes to in vitro fertilization.

Others are not. Beau got sick of it. She knew he did. But Candace lost all sense of perspective.

One day she gave in to every wrong impulse, every unrequited longing. She spotted a pregnant woman on the streets and followed her home. The mother-to-be looked so satisfied, so comfortable, so *full*, that Candace couldn't help herself. When the young woman disappeared into a brownstone apartment building, Candace followed her inside. On the landing of the third floor, the woman turned around and demanded to know just who Candace was and what she was doing.

It's been years since Candace has allowed herself to remember the embarrassing encounter. Now, as Worcester vanishes in her rearview mirror and she pushes on toward Springfield, where she will turn off onto I-91, she gives herself permission to replay what hasn't been forcibly forgotten. Somehow or another, the woman had invited Candace into her apartment, which struck Candace as barren. Perhaps the woman had just moved into a new place, a larger place that would accommodate a baby. Candace recalls sitting on the couch, which was covered in plastic sheeting so that it made odd aching sounds each time she shifted her weight. Usually Candace listened to the plight of others, but this time she spilled her own story, including the abortion in Mexico City. She wasn't expecting any particular reaction, yet the one she got from the smug young woman surprised and hurt her.

"You're being punished, of course," the young woman concluded. "You're being punished for your sins."

Stunned, Candace fled the apartment and, upon reaching the street, felt immediately bereft. She cried for hours afterward. Much as she disagreed with the sentiment, she took the young woman's verdict to heart. Although she wasn't sure that she believed in God, Candace definitely believed in punishment. Doesn't everyone? The baby dreams dried up. For years they'd been a feature of her nighttime life, but no more. The encounter with the pregnant woman banished them. Once she gave up hoping, the fantasies fled, too.

Entering Vermont, Candace is forced to give her whole attention to the road. What was a light snow has turned heavy, swirling over and around the car, a bright white in the darkness. As she leans closer to the windshield and slows down to navigate safely, Candace feels the spirit of her husband draw near. He stays with her for the rest of the drive.

By the time Candace has found her way to River View Manor, Vernie has been safely delivered to the facility. She is in bed, sleeping off her adventure. Because it was a bitterly cold day, the police chief had called in all of his officers, many of whom enlisted relatives and friends.

"Pretty much the whole town turned out," Candace tells Jack. She doesn't know who found Vernie, but she does know that the elderly woman was discovered in the early evening, wandering the wooded area that borders the river's edge.

"She was wearing house shoes with wool slacks and her best pink sweater," Candace continues. "Fortunately, she was wearing a coat and gloves as well. Thank god for that." Candace is stretched out on a sofa in River View's dayroom; it's the same one Jack sat on when he visited back in October. Most of the residents have already turned in, but a few are sitting in armchairs around the television. One elderly gentleman in a wheelchair pores over his Bible in the hallway, where the fluorescent lights are bright.

"Pink is Mom's favorite color," Jack offers.

According to the nurse on duty, Vernie has ruined her only pair of shoes. Candace wonders what could have become of the other pairs. Jack doesn't know. He admits that he might have neglected to pack his mother's shoes when he moved her into the nursing home, but Candace offers another alternative. The nurse has disclosed that the floor staff sometimes helps themselves to a tempting this or that. "If they don't see a resident making use of something," she clarified. "The job doesn't pay much, and it's hard work—it's hard on the body and even harder on the psyche. Some feel entitled to the possessions of those they care for."

Candace relays all of this to Jack. Then she offers to stay on for a day or two, shop for a few pairs of shoes, make sure that Vernie isn't going to end up with some exposure-related illness. "They think I'm your mother's niece," Candace explains. "I had to tell them that I'm a member of the family, you see. I hope you don't mind."

Jack assures her that he doesn't mind, that he is grateful. He is even more so when Candace calls a day or two later to say that she will stay on in Brattleboro long enough to help move Vernie to a room on the other side of the building. The reasoning is that Vernie will be less tempted to wander away if her window looks out onto the street rather than toward the wooded river's edge. "For some reason, she wants to get to the water." Candace wonders whether Jack has any sort of insight into his mother's sudden interest in the Connecticut River, but he hasn't the slightest idea.

When Candace rings again two days later to report that the move was successful, Jack solves a new mystery. Candace starts off by remarking on Vernie's beauty: "All my life, I've heard people exclaim about skin like parchment. That's your mother's skin. It's gorgeous, really." Candace has grown fond of Vernie, and the reverse seems true as well. "I told her my name is Candace, but she insists on calling me Gwen."

Jack's quick intake of breath is audible, and Candace stops and waits for his explanation. "Gwendolyn was my sister," he tells her.

"I didn't know you had a sister."

"I don't. Not anymore. She died when she was ten, hit by a drunk driver. She was a fair-skinned blonde, which is probably why Mom made the connection."

Touched, Candace is quick to reassure Jack. "Don't worry about us. We'll be fine. I'll stay for another day or two. I've scoped out all the antiques in Brattleboro, but now I've heard of a place I want to visit in Putney."

"We owe you, Candace," Jack says. "*I* owe you."

"Nonsense."

"No, seriously. This is one of the nicest things anyone has ever done for me."

"You know, Jack, I just want to be part of the family. That's all."

"So Sophie told me." They'd had a talk a few days after Christmas. He was taking Lucy out for a walk along the ditch, and he asked Sophie to tag along. She was reluctant, but he persisted, even going upstairs to grab her jean jacket and sneakers.

Candace hesitates. "So you're in the loop now! Great. I know Peggy was trying to spare you the stress, and that's understandable. . . ."

Jack is remembering the walk, in the gathering dark, during which he tried to explain to Sophie the concept of the greater good as it applies to both bees and humans. "Are you going to take matters into your own hands, or are you going to allow fate to have its way with you?" he had asked her. Sophie refused to see things through the lens he offered. Instead, she told him that she had a plan in place, surely an impossibility for a sixteen-year-old girl. How could that be? But then he remembered the way she'd strolled out to the hives with a glop of honey on her tongue. She was fearless, his daughter. She thought she could handle almost anything.

Candace is talking about the heart attack; Jack protests that he's really not all that fragile. "It's Sophie I'm worried about." He takes a deep breath, then jumps off the deep end. "A few weeks ago, she told me you want to adopt the baby."

"Yes, I do! With all my heart I do. It makes perfect sense, don't you think?"

"That's just what Sophie said. 'It makes perfect sense.' But it doesn't make any sense to me. Why does this matter concern you, Candace? You are a good person. I'm convinced of that. But you and Peggy aren't really that close. You were friends back in the day, but you aren't friends now. Friends keep in touch, and correct me if I'm wrong, but isn't this the first time you've met our children?"

"You're right about that. It's the first time I've met them."

He isn't finished. "You live on the other side of the country. And forgive me if I'm not especially tactful. You're old enough to be this baby's grandmother. . . ."

Candace sighs. She gathers herself, then says it: "You really have been kept in the dark, Jack. I'm sorry. Truly, I am. But, as it turns out, I *am* this baby's grandmother."

He feels like such a fool. The idea that Candace knows something he doesn't—something so personal, so vital to him and to every member of his family—strikes him as a double betrayal. He can't believe that Peggy would allow him to be blindsided this way, or that she would put him in a position where he could be humiliated, where he could be told his business by someone he hardly knows. He has his pride. It shocks him, frankly, that his wife managed to tell Candace what she has never had the conviction to tell him. Not that he didn't suspect. He did, and has, off and on throughout the years, but he's never been inclined to seek either a confirmation or a denial. Maybe if Peggy were the sort to carry on affairs, or in other ways betray his trust. But she isn't, at least not that he knows of. Perhaps he's just too gullible for his own good.

Quickly, before he can say something stupid or begin to blubber, Jack concludes the call. "We'll talk again," he tells Candace as he hangs up.

That night in bed, he and Peggy have an exchange that further infuriates him. It's a frigid night, necessitating measures to keep the pipes from bursting. Jack goes out after dinner and covers the outdoor faucets, first at the Granger home and then at the fixer-upper. Peggy offers to go over to Old Town to set the bathroom faucet to a slow drip, but Jack doesn't want her there alone at night. He says it's just as easy for him to stop by the shop—he'll already be out, after all.

He doesn't return home until nearly eleven, by which time he's dead tired. When he slips in under the covers with a groan, Peggy quips that his feet are like ice cubes. He responds with his usual rejoinder: "And your toenails are sharp as a cat's incisors."

The bed is warm and inviting because Peggy has been in it for nearly an hour, reading and rereading the same passage from the Dalai Lama's book *The Art of Happiness*. It's not a book she reads cover to cover, but rather it's one she dips into for perspective and solace. She keeps it handy on her bedside table. "If the situation or problem is such that it can be remedied, then there is no need to worry about it. Alternatively, if there is no way out, no solution, no possibility of resolution, then there is also no point in being worried about it, because you can't do anything about it anyway." So says the Dalai Lama.

"Long day," Peggy says as she reaches over to switch off the light.

It's easier to tell the truth in the dark, Jack thinks, and so he says what's in his heart: "It's been one of the longest days of my life." He can feel Peggy shifting next to him, reaching out to grasp his hand, but he moves it away with a warning. "Don't touch me, Peggy."

Their arguments are always modulated, carried on in low voices regardless of the situation. It's something they agreed on years back, when the children were still small. They both had parents who'd broadcasted their disagreements to the world. Peggy referred to her parents' fights as "the knock-down drag-outs," which sounded worse than his parents' shouting matches. One thing they agreed on: they would not subject their own children to anything similar. They promised themselves and each other that, at least in this way, they would be better parents to Sophie and Ian than their own parents had been to them.

"What is it?" she whispers. "What have I done now?"

"You've been doing this for more than sixteen years. Maybe *you* can tell *me* what it is."

He hears her sigh, but she doesn't speak. Neither does he. He knows her habits and has already determined that he will wait her out, make her ask him the questions rather than the other way around.

But she doesn't need to ask. She knows full well how he learned her secret. "Candace had no business telling you, Jack. She's damned and determined to get her hands on Sophie's baby, and she doesn't seem to care who she hurts in the process."

"Well, I'm glad *somebody* told me. You would have carried the truth to your grave."

"What difference does it make? What difference, Jack?" Peggy is surprised at herself. She knows full well that she ought to be begging her husband's forgiveness, but, unaccountably, she is more irate than contrite. It occurs to her that this situation is exactly the sort of thing the Dalai Lama was talking about—it involves something that can't be changed, something she wouldn't change even if she could. "What would have been the point in telling you? I've asked myself that question hundreds of times. Would it help? I couldn't see that it *would* help. It seemed to me that it could only hurt."

"So why did you tell *Candace*?" Just after he utters the words, he realizes that he's gone and asked her a question.

"I didn't tell her. One look at Sophie and she knew. I was afraid it would be like that. Which is why I sent Sophie over to Tam's in the first place."

"I see," Jack replies. "I knew she didn't look like me," he grumbles. "That seemed like a good thing. What man in his right mind wants his daughter to favor him? But she doesn't look like you either, does she?" Evidently Sophie favors Beau.

"Did you do it on purpose then?" The words are difficult to say. "Let him get you pregnant?" He has to wonder, of course, because Peggy wasn't having any luck getting pregnant by him.

If Peggy is shocked, she gets over it rather quickly. "No, it was an accident. A fluke, really. He was in town, and it happened. Just once—that's all, Jack."

"So, he didn't have any trouble knocking you up," Jack notes bitterly.

"Would you rather not have Sophie?" she asks.

Clearly she's had years to think about it, and has found a way to live with herself.

He's careful to look at the ceiling and not at her. If he doesn't turn his gaze on Peggy's face, he believes he can keep the exchange civilized—he can avert his tears and his temper. Over the years he has learned to regulate, or at least modulate, his emotions. Handling bees has taught him to slow his reactions and stay calm in the midst of a crisis. "How can you even ask me such a question?"

"Well, if you erase my relationship with Beau, Sophie goes with it. She no longer exists."

"So you're saying the end justifies the means?"

Peggy is quiet for a minute. "In this case, I think it does. It doesn't excuse *me*, certainly. Am I a shit? Definitely. But am I sorry? How could I be?"

Staring at the ceiling isn't giving him sufficient distance. "You know there's a term for this, Peggy. It's called "cuckolding." Ever heard of it?"

"Yes, yes, of course."

She shifts her body. For a second he thinks she's about to move closer to him, but instead she slides out of the bed. He can hear the shuffling of her feet as she feels about in the dark for her slippers.

"There are cuckolding bees, you know," he goes on. "Instead of making nests of their own, they deposit their eggs in the cells of other hives. What do you think of that?"

"Not much," she says. She is somewhere else in the room now, perhaps looking for her robe.

"You never have shown an interest in bees—or in me, for that matter. But the point is that we humans are supposed to behave better than bees. At the very least, we're supposed to have a little common decency. We're supposed to avoid making fools of those who love us."

"You've been a wonderful father." Peggy is crying now, making little gasping sounds that slow down the speech she seems determined to make. "Beau wouldn't have been half so good. Maybe that's why the bees deposit their eggs elsewhere, because they know they're selfish or immature or some damn thing. They're smart enough to know their limitations. God knows Beau had his."

"Did he know he had a daughter?"

Peggy is silent. She is terrible about answering questions, always has been. But he stays silent and forces her to speak.

"I didn't tell anyone. I didn't admit it to myself most of the time. It was easy to ignore the resemblance. Most often, I just didn't take notice of it. I knew, but I didn't know. I *wanted* her to be yours, and to my way of thinking, she is in all the important ways—"

"Except one." Nothing she says is making him feel better. If anything, he feels worse.

"I love you, Jack." She's blowing her nose, and he realizes that it was the Kleenex box she was hunting for. Now that she's found it, she'll be returning to bed.

"Saying 'I love you' just doesn't mean much in a situation like this one."

She's so slight that the mattress barely shifts as she climbs back into bed. She takes a long time to settle herself beneath the covers. Then she speaks again: "I'm sorry from the bottom of my heart, Jack, but I'm afraid that's not going to make a damned bit of difference to you."

"It can't. Would it have made a difference fifteen years ago? Yes, I think it might have. You should have screwed up your courage and admitted your mistake when I was younger and more forgiving. But then, maybe somewhere deep inside I knew this moment was coming. Maybe that's why I bought the fixer-upper, why I was so damned determined to have it. So I'd have someplace to go."

She gasps and then, to stifle the sound of weeping, pulls the covers over her head. Minutes pass before she speaks again. "Please, Jack. Don't move out *now*, not in the middle of the pregnancy. Sophie needs you here."

"I'll be here, but I won't be here," he says. "What I mean is, I'll be here for the kids, but I probably won't sleep here. Not for now, anyway."

Maybe an hour later, Peggy asks if he's still awake. When he says that he is, she asks whether they should tell Sophie.

"No!" Jack replies. "Don't you dare. I'm her father. I'm all she knows and all she can ever know. He's dead, and I won't have her pining over him. One more person I love who loves him better."

"She'd never love him better, Jack." Peggy doesn't trust herself to say more. To apologize again would be wrong. To gloss over would be wrong. To justify or pretend it was just an accident would be wrong. And so she says nothing at all. She turns on her side and pretends to sleep, and eventually so does he.

In the morning they will go about their business as usual. The kids won't notice that breakfast is prepared and consumed in near silence, or that Jack leaves without kissing Peggy good-bye. Peggy will notice, of course. She hopes he will forgive her in time, but she knows that Jack is the sort to nurse a grudge. "Don't get on my wrong side," he used to tease her. The warning had seemed like a joke, funny because it wasn't possible. The future would teach them otherwise.

When the doctor asked Sophie how she was feeling at her twenty-six-week checkup, Sophie opened her mouth to speak, but nothing came out. He had just helped her back to a sitting position, and he stood back and crossed his arms over his chest. (He is used to waiting for answers. His wife is in hospice care now, and slow to speak.) He didn't react when Sophie took her time to shape an answer. Unlike most doctors, he seldom shows impatience; he seldom feels it.

"I'm lost," she finally managed. "I don't know who I am. I don't know this body," she explained, sweeping a hand over her distended breasts and belly. "I don't know this mind." She tapped her head.

"When I look in the mirror, I think: Who is this person? Where is Sophie?"

The doctor nodded thoughtfully. "It makes sense," he said. "I'd be lying if I said you look like the same girl. You don't. You'll never look like that girl again." He smiled at her as tears dripped down her face. "You know why?"

She shook her head.

"Because you've left girlhood behind. It's all right, though. You were a girl for a good long time."

Not nearly long enough, Sophie thought, but she didn't argue. She wanted to punch someone, but not her sweet, sad gynecologist. She had Will in mind, or his mother Laurel, or Peggy or Jack. But she didn't punch any of them. Instead, it would be her creative writing teacher. Less than two days later, she was to hit her creative writing teacher, Ms. Sherman, over a Valentine's Day assignment.

Write a poem about love: that's the assignment. Sophie stays up half the night composing hers, not that she can sleep much anyway. The pizza they had for dinner, with green chile and sausage, gave her a wicked case of heartburn. Around midnight she collects all the throw pillows in the house and props herself up in a sitting position with a legal pad in her lap. Her poem is to Will, of course, and the plan is to mail it to him as soon as Ms. Sherman returns it with a grade, an A of course, if not an A+. The grade will make Will jealous, and the poem will make him ashamed. That's the plan, anyway.

But Ms. Sherman doesn't like the poem. She selects several to share with the class, and Sophie's isn't one of them. Instead, she requests that Sophie stay after class and explain why she used the word "fuck" as a rhyming word. Sophie's poem is a villanelle, and the repeated line is: "The ugliest word in the world is 'fuck.'"

At the bottom of the page, Ms. Sherman has scrawled a one-line comment: "I agree, so why repeat it again and again?" But no grade. After class Ms. Sherman explains that Sophie's poem isn't about love, and it therefore doesn't meet the assignment. "Try again," she tells Sophie. "Something more fitting for Valentine's Day."

Until now, Sophie has perceived Ms. Sherman to be divorced and bitter, a likely sympathizer. "I thought you, of all people, would understand," Sophie says.

Ms. Sherman shakes her head firmly. "I'm not a fan of foul language, or of unwed mothers."

To which Sophie replies, "Go fuck yourself!"

Ms. Sherman responds by slapping Sophie across her cheek. The action is more surprising than it is painful. Of course, Sophie slaps her back, which, to Sophie's way of thinking, makes them even. But Ms. Sherman doesn't see it that way. In the middle of Sophie's calculus class, the hall monitor slips a note to the teacher. Sophie is summoned to the principal's office.

By the time she gets home, Sophie is both irate and bereft. Nothing is going right in her life, absolutely nothing. She doesn't bother to knock on her mother's door. She just swings it open and stands in the doorway. "Petulant" is the word that comes to Peggy's mind—Sophie is petulantly pissed, as well as quite apparently pregnant. She's wearing a pair of maternity jeans and a black turtleneck that hugs her protruding belly. Her hair is pulled up in a messy ponytail. She is sniffling and raccoon-eyed.

Peggy looks up from the fabric catalogue she's been studying and squints at Sophie over the tops of her wire-rimmed reading glasses. She's perched on the bed, propped up against pillows, and decked out in a purple sweat suit and warm socks. She's been sleeping off and on all afternoon, waking in a sweat. She has a doctor's appointment on Thursday, and she's dreading it.

"You're home from school already?" she asks. "Seems like you just left."

"I've been suspended for three days," Sophie announces.

Caught off guard, Peggy asks her daughter to repeat what she just said. Sophie obliges.

"Oh, good lord!" Peggy peers closely at her daughter. "You've got to be kidding me. How? Why?"

"I wrote a poem with the word 'fuck' in it."

"That's it? Are you kidding me?" Peggy replies, though she can see from Sophie's face that none of this is a joke.

Peggy turns her gaze on the mobile that hangs over the bed, a gift from Jack. Stained glass shapes—circles, triangles, squares, rectangles—spin in the air, catching light from the lamp and casting it onto the far wall. When Jack gave her the mobile, he'd told her he made it, and she had believed him. It wasn't until a visitor commented on it, and Peggy had begun to brag about him, that Jack chuckled to himself and admitted the truth. "You're so damn gullible," he said, as though the problem were hers. How to discern the truth? She's never been the least bit good at it.

"They tried to call you to pick me up, but you weren't in the shop."

"The shop is closed on Mondays. You know that."

"Well, maybe I knew it once upon a time, but I didn't remember it today. So I had to sit in the office all afternoon. You'll have to go over to Valley and talk to the authorities. But tell you what: I'll stand behind the counter in Old Town while you're gone. It's the least I can do."

Sighing, Peggy drops the catalogue into her lap and takes up her mug of green tea. She sips with a vengeance. It tastes terrible. Recently she's given up honey—screw Jack and his bees—but without the sweetness, the tea is weak and bitter on her tongue, like she's brewed up blades of grass snatched from the side yard. Nothing is what it used to be.

"All things must pass," she mutters. "All things *will* pass." She's speaking to herself as much as to Sophie.

"It's bullshit, you know."

"What's bullshit?"

"'All things will pass.' They won't. They don't."

"Wait until you're fifty, and see whether you still feel the same."

Peggy assumes Sophie will have some smart reply, but she doesn't say anything. Instead, the girl wanders around the periphery of the room, picking up first a hairbrush and then a tube of hand lotion, which she decides to use on her hands and face. When Peggy looks away, Sophie is pushing up her sleeves, preparing to slather lotion on her arms. The winter is so dry in New Mexico, and pregnancy plays havoc on the skin. Sophie has been complaining that her belly itches. Likely she will pull up the hem of her turtleneck next.

Peggy doesn't want to watch, so she returns her attention to the catalogue. Perhaps because they're on the cusp of Valentine's Day, every spring print Peggy has circled relies on some shade of red: cabernet, burgundy, ruby, or rust. This time around, her favorite print is an off-white cotton scattered with the petals of red, red roses. What a gorgeous skirt it will make! She can see it now: some willowy young woman will slip it over her head and twirl before the mirror, enchantment in her eyes.

"Look, Sophie," Peggy says, holding out the page. "Isn't this lovely?"

Sophie comes around to the other side of the bed and climbs up next to her mother. "Very pretty," she says. She hasn't bothered to remove her shoes, but they don't look dirty, so Peggy holds her tongue. She shoves the open catalogue across the comforter, until it lands right under her daughter's nose.

"You didn't look." She takes up her tea again.

Sophie's slaps at the catalogue, which slips off the end of the bed and onto the floor. "This is all your fault," she complains.

The jostling leaves Peggy with a wet chest and lap. The tea is warm, and as it runs down her crotch she feels the flare of a response that has nowhere to go. "How dare you, Sophie?" she cries out. "Stop taking your misery out on everyone else!"

Her daughter lies in a heap recovering her senses, but in another minute or two she'll storm out. Lately people flee when Peggy opens her mouth. She's always been such a private person, but just yesterday, she blurted out to a complete stranger—a customer, no less—that she hasn't had sex in nearly a year, which isn't even true, not technically. Though that wasn't even the worst part. The poor woman, who was about to make a sizable purchase, seemed to feel that she had to confide in kind. Her broad, wrinkled face flushed with embarrassment as she whispered her own confession: "No man's touched me in *ten years*." Then she rushed out without buying a damn thing. Peggy folded the clothes and wrapped them in tissue, leaving them in a tidy bundle on the counter for the rest of the afternoon. They're still there. She hasn't had the heart yet to return them to stock.

Before Sophie leaves, Peggy clears her throat and asks about the adoption paperwork. "Have you heard anything from Will yet?" Candace has been calling. Peggy isn't picking up, but she's heard the messages. There have been two at work and another at home.

Sophie hasn't heard from Will. Not a word. It's been over two weeks, and she's begun to wonder whether she should have sent a self-addressed, stamped envelope with the consent form. She can practically see it in her mind's eye, the folded piece of paper. It's probably inside a textbook or stashed in his underwear drawer or, worse yet, collecting dust under his bed.

"I've been working on the rest of the forms, but I haven't heard back from Will."

"Well, you'd better give him a call. Can you do that sometime tomorrow? Just go ahead and dial him from the shop. You have his number, don't you?"

Sophie nods and backs out of the room. "The poem was for Will," she says, though not loud enough for her mother to hear.

The receptionist at Valley is sweet but homely. Her wide, brown cheeks are pitted with acne scars, and her upper body is as shapeless as an old feather pillow. And yet she has not one, but two bouquets on her desk. She peeks through a gap in the flowers at Peggy, who is waiting in one of four straight chairs lined up against the wall, an unfortunate who—so far—has received neither flowers nor candy nor a single card on Valentine's Day. It's still early in the day, just after ten, but she doesn't hold out much hope. Why would Jack buy her flowers? Why would anyone?

"It'll just be a minute," the receptionist reassures her, a lank lock of hair and one brown eye all that are visible from behind an enormous stargazer lily. Its velvety white petals are streaked with red; it's so lovely that Peggy could weep.

She closes her eyes against the dingy office and the magnificent flowers. She doesn't want to look at them. Nor does she have the energy to be jealous of the high school receptionist. It seems such a petty place to end up. Peggy has always been a sucker for flowers and sappy valentines. For her, Valentine's Day has been a barometer of sorts. Does *he* love me? Does *someone* love me? For most of her life, someone has, Jack has, but this year she knows better than to hope. These past few weeks, they've exchanged only a few words and not one single smile.

When Peggy reopens her eyes, the lilies are as they should be: achingly lovely. They will be so for another few days. All things must pass, Peggy tells herself. Looking away to the other side of the room, she surveys the doorway of the assistant principals' offices, three to a room, narrow rectangles graced with two windows. One faces into the courtyard, providing light, and the other faces the outer office. She is waiting for Ms. Holcomb, whose door is closed. Peggy stares at the door, willing it to open. She needs to get this over with. She has a doctor's appointment in just over an hour.

To divert herself, she speaks to the receptionist. "I love lilies, don't you? I can smell the perfume from here."

The homely woman turns and offers a distracted smile. "It'll just be a minute," she says.

Does the woman know the lily from the rose? Can she love and appreciate what she can't name? Such thoughts are uncharitable; Peggy knows that. But they persist. She wants to ask the receptionist who sent her such amazing bouquets, though it's really none of her business. Fortunately, Ms. Holcomb chooses this moment to open her door. Evidently she's been in there all along, sitting alone with only a desk lamp for comfort and company.

"You didn't bring Sophie with you?" Ms. Holcomb asks, twisting her mouth to signal disapproval or disappointment. She's a young woman, late twenties maybe, dressed in a burgundy suit and black heels, her long blonde hair pulled back in one of those calculatedly careless ponytails. She isn't especially attractive, but she dresses as though she believes she is. Her clothes are expensive and corporate, which must mean that she's married to a man who makes more money than she does. She's wearing a wedding ring. Suddenly Peggy feels far too tired to get to her feet.

"I didn't realize I was supposed to bring her," Peggy says from her seat. Perhaps she'd just as soon camp out here in the outer office, where she can admire the receptionist's flowers. "She's watching my shop, but I suppose—"

Ms. Holcomb cuts in. "No, no, it's fine." She gestures for Peggy to join her, then disappears again into the shadowy recesses of her office.

More flowers, Peggy thinks as she seats herself in an uncomfortable chair across the desk from the assistant principal. So the husband must love this sulky woman enough to send her a dozen dark-red rosebuds, beautifully accented with greenery and clouds of baby's breath.

Ms. Holcomb consults her file, frowning. "So did Sophie tell you what happened?"

Peggy nods and shifts in her seat. "She said she wrote a poem with the word 'fuck' in it."

"That's all?"

"There's more to the story?"

"Well, yeah." Ms. Holcomb purses her lips and glances over at the flowers, which are actually the sweet gesture of a faithful father. "When Ms. Sherman asked Sophie to write another, more appropriate poem, Sophie told her, 'Go fuck yourself'—and then slapped her."

"Sophie slapped her teacher? Surely not."

"She didn't tell you that part?"

Peggy shakes her head. She doesn't know what to say. "I apologize for my daughter's behavior. She's never had problems of this sort before, but the stress of her situation . . ."

Ms. Holcomb folds her hands together on her desk. "Some of us think Sophie might be happier at New Futures." She scans Peggy's face for name recognition, then explains: "It's a high school for expectant and teen mothers." She pushes an informational flyer in Peggy's direction. In the darkness of the room, Peggy can't make much out except the mascot, a regal-looking lioness surrounded by three cubs.

"Why don't you talk this over with Sophie?"

Peggy tries to sit tall. She registers an ache in her lower back. She has to come to Sophie's defense, although she feels inadequate to the task. "Seems like you're segregating the girls who . . . who . . . get themselves in trouble." Immediately she regrets the wording, which reaches back to her own adolescence.

Ms. Holcomb smiles. "Not at all," she replies smoothly. "The days of one-room schools are over. We've accepted that we can't be all things to all young people."

"So the policy is to send the troubled ones to a school of their own?" Now she's labeled her own daughter as "troubled." She isn't sure why she's arguing. In theory, she agrees with the policy. It makes sense; it's even humane and progressive. Only in this particular instance, it's Sophie they're talking about.

Ms. Holcomb leans across the desk. The wayward ponytail flops over one shoulder and brushes a blotter as she speaks. "I'm not the enemy," she says. "Believe me, I understand full well what you're feeling."

"Do you?"

Later Peggy will wonder whether she did this intentionally, whether she purposefully engaged Ms. Holcomb in conversation when she should have been on her way to the doctor's office. Did she care about the assistant principal's sister, who had the bad luck to get pregnant on the very night she lost her virginity? She sits slumped in her chair and commiserates with Ms. Holcomb, whose sister gave up a beautiful little girl for adoption and went on to regret it for the rest of her life. They could easily continue on this way for some time, and Peggy might miss her appointment altogether, but Ms. Holcomb waves her arms to indicate all the sadness in the world and, in so doing, topples the vase of roses. That brings them back. A dozen long-stemmed roses lie strewn across the desktop, water everywhere. No real damage has been done, except to Sophie's file, of course.

Peggy helps sop up the water with paper towels from the girls' restroom. She replaces the last of the roses, and in the process, she takes the opportunity to raise a bud to her nose. But it's too tightly furled to have a scent. The fragrance will come later, when the petals are fully opened, when the rose is past its prime, fading, even.

Peggy sits shivering on the edge of the examination table, dressed only in a paper gown, a paper sheet spread across her lap. As the doctor continues his exam, her hands clutch at the sheet's scratchy, insubstantial surface. It's a scanty thing; she could rip it to shreds.

"Just to be safe, I think we should do some blood work," the doctor says as he raises Peggy's arm to examine her lymph nodes. He's a short, squat man with a bristly white mustache and fleshy lips.

His fingers press, then palpate, then press again.

"Remember the paper dresses from the sixties?" Peggy asks. He should remember them. He's got to be her age at least.

The doctor smiles absently, but doesn't reply. Instead, he shuffles a bit, the better to situate himself in front of her. "Are you cold?" he asks, his hand straying from beneath her arm and coming to rest on her shoulder.

She nods.

"This shouldn't take too long," he says. "How long since you've had a period?"

Peggy considers the question. She hasn't had a real period in some time, maybe a year or more, but she occasionally spots her underwear or her sheets.

"Hot flashes?" he asks.

She nods. "I think so. How do you tell the difference between night sweats and hot flashes?"

He smiles. "It sucks, doesn't it?"

She nods wearily. "I'm so tired," she says. "Sometimes I can't move. One night recently, I slept on the couch, just because I couldn't bring myself to walk down the hall to the bedroom."

He frowns. "Anything going on? Unusual stresses?"

She laughs ruefully and ticks them off: financial woes, marital woes, and parental woes. "I've just come from a meeting with an assistant principal at Valley High School. Would you believe that my daughter, Sophie is a pregnant rabble-rouser, and they think it's better if she transfers to New Futures, which is—"

"I know about New Futures," he interrupts, nodding solemnly.

"Do you ever look back at your life and just wonder, 'What the hell was I thinking?'"

"Sure I do."

"Every day?"

He shakes his head. "No. That would be debilitating."

"It is," she says, and she hears it, the flat affect. She doesn't sound like herself. When did she stop sounding like herself?

He crosses his arms over his chest and presses his lips together. His bushy mustache flexes like a furry caterpillar.

Peggy frowns. Tears leak from the corners of her eyes. She doesn't realize she's crying until he hands her a Kleenex.

"Why don't you get dressed and go upstairs to the lab? They'll take a little blood, and we'll see what's what." And he does it again. He pats her shoulder. "You look depressed, Peggy," he says gently before leaving the room. "Have you ever thought of giving Zoloft a whirl?"

The day had begun as most do in Albuquerque, with a burst of sunshine and pink-tinted clouds that stretched like a spider's web over the mountain ranges to the east of the city. Nothing out of the ordinary. So when Peggy emerges from the clinic, she is surprised to see flakes of snow floating in the air. She'd heard it on the news, but she didn't much believe it. The parched and dusty land is always thirsty; so are the people who reside on it. Given a 10 percent chance of rain, the local weatherman will do a little tap dance.

Peggy is wearing a sweater from Peru, of alpaca wool dyed at least six different shades of green. It was a Christmas gift from Candace. Wrapping it around herself, Peggy shivers in the cold air but makes no move for the car. For the moment, the beauty of the scene fills her with awe, pushing away the dread she feels almost all the time these days. Large, tender snowflakes swirl in the air and whiten the windshields of the cars in the parking lot. In the last hour, heavy clouds have completely obscured the two mountain ranges to the east.

Near the summits of the Sandia Mountains, a dense snow blankets the shoulders and heads of jubilant skiers and weights the limbs of ponderosa pines, junipers, and bushy piñons. Truckers hurtling in from Texas are startled to attention as they begin the long slide into Albuquerque. Thoughts of those they love flicker like faraway headlights as they lean into their windshields and strain to see through miles of blowing snow. Letting up on the gas, they hope for the best, though the grade is steeper than they remembered or had any reason to expect.

Sophie is surprised by how quiet it is at Everyday Satin. She doesn't remember the store being this way. When she was a toddler she spent every day there, and it seemed there were always people—mostly women—to peek at from under the clothes racks where she played house, who would ask her name and age. Sophie never tired of the attention. She enjoyed the wide smiles and silly questions. She loved performing, offering customers sips of pretend tea from her tiny china service while holding up three fingers. All manner of happy memories reside here.

Late winter finds Old Town all but deserted, but come June the pavilion will host a succession of weddings and receptions. Though most of the ceremonies are conducted in the church, a number are held outdoors, in the hexagonal space of the pavilion itself. Even as the ceremony proceeds, tourists will stroll along the sidewalks and take shortcuts across the grass, stopping to admire the bride's dress or the toddling ring bearer. Everyone is more or less welcome. Lowriders, some decorated with crepe-paper streamers and window dressing, motor slowly around and around the square, horns blaring. Now and again, clouds of confetti drift from open windows.

Sophie loves Old Town, and she can become indignant when tourists complain that it's rundown and kitschy, too quaint for its own good. "The plaza in Santa Fe is only an hour away," they'll say, "and it's a good deal more sophisticated"—to which Sophie is quick to add, "and twice as expensive." Newcomers often feel oppressed by the prevalence of earth colors, in Old Town and elsewhere in Albuquerque. Because Sophie has lived in New Mexico all her life, she takes the color scheme for granted. The background of brown, brown, and more brown begs for a foreground of bold colors. So, for instance, the purple, red, and yellow of her mother's signs draw the eye. What might be labeled garish elsewhere appears merely cheerful in New Mexico.

After nearly an hour has passed between customers, Sophie screws up her courage and digs the slip of paper up from her pocket. Sitting in the silence of the shop, she holds her breath, dials, then listens as the phone rings in Lubbock. She exhales slowly. One ringy-dingy, as her mother would say, then two and three. She's in the process of composing a voicemail message when a breathless Will picks up.

"Hello?" His voice is hesitant and wary. "Who is it?"

"It's me, Will." Perched on the wooden stool, she feels suddenly unsteady, so much so that she reaches out with her free hand for the stability of the counter.

"Sophie?" He sounds relieved. He explains that the caller ID on his father's landline read EVERYDAY SATAN. "Shit, Sophie," he breathes.

"That gave me pause. Everyone is so religious here. Who knows? Maybe Satan solicits."

"And what? There's everyday Satan and Sunday Satan?"

"Something like that." He pauses. "It's good to hear your voice."

"I miss you," she says. She could just kick herself. She's mad at him; he's let her down. Hell, he's run away and left her with the big belly and all the difficult decisions.

But she caves when he admits that he misses her, too. "We were both a little crazy there at Christmastime," he says. "It wasn't *all* your fault."

"Are you talking about Victoria's Secret?"

"Yeah. What'd you think?" Another pause. "Oh, the pregnancy? My mom likes to remind me that it takes two to tango."

"Your mom should know," Sophie quips. She's pleased to hear that familiar snort of approval on the other end of the line.

"So, you've decided on adoption," he goes on. "That makes sense, Sophie. I mean it, but it must be really hard."

Sophie is quick to volunteer a few relevant facts. Candace is practically part of the family, she tells him, though she leaves it at that. It will be an open adoption, which will make the loss a little bit easier to bear. When Will inquires as to the meaning of "open," Sophie explains that she will be able to see the child occasionally, get updates and photographs.

"Don't you think that will make it harder?" Will asks.

"I hope not, but how can I know for sure?"

"I don't want any updates, Sophie," he tells her.

She sighs, realizing that she was hoping he would. But before she can say something she might regret, a mother and child enter the store. Sophie asks Will to hold on a minute.

"Can I help you?" she calls out to the pair.

The little girl is dancing about in the small open space in front of an antique chifforobe. She conveys her discomfort prettily, with the air of a sprite or a tiny whirling dervish. The pink-and-white swirl of energy whips past the rack of velvet broomstick skirts without a second glance, while her mother stops and lingers, fingering a red velvet, six-tiered skirt, perfect for Valentine's Day.

"Why are they so expensive?" the woman calls out to Sophie. The one she's handling, with its elegant drape and antique black lace accents, is nearly $200.

"Those skirts are handmade by Naomi Begay of the Navajo Nation," Sophie explains. "They're the real thing."

"I can see the workmanship," the young woman replies.

On the other end of the line, Will tells Sophie to go ahead and wait on the customer. "You can call me back."

Sophie replies, "It'll just take a minute. Can you stay on the line?" She waits until she hears his assent before putting down the receiver and coming out from behind the counter.

"That would look good on you," Sophie prompts. She sees the opportunity for a sale, something substantial she can point to when she asks her mother to pay her just a little for her time.

It isn't just bullshit, either. Sophie doesn't lie to people. The young woman has the perfect figure for a broomstick skirt. Not everyone does. Most women can get into them, since the waists are elastic and the skirts bell-shaped. But the broad-hipped might as well be wearing lampshades, and short women tend to get lost in all the material. Already a plan is forming: when the time comes, Sophie will tell the woman that broomstick skirts don't really look their best without a concho belt. Everyday Satin sells those, too, but they're pricey, which is why they are displayed on the wall behind the register. Interested customers have to ask to try them on.

"I know the woman who made that skirt," Sophie says. Used to be, she enjoyed tagging along to Shiprock in the Navajo Nation with her mom. Peggy could be counted on to act just kooky enough to keep things interesting. For instance, on one trip they did a rain dance. They'd been driving for nearly two hours, and they were both hot and tired. Sophie was spread out across the backseat reading, having long since grown weary of watching the desert scenery whip by. Quite unexpectedly, their Toyota passed under a storm cloud, one small, dark bundle of rain hovering over the highway. Fat drops splattered the windshield for all of thirty seconds. Then the shower was gone, so quickly that Sophie didn't really register it, although her mother did. Peggy decided to turn the car around, to whiz back to that precise place—that particular patch on the planet—to stop the car on the side of the highway and offer up a small dance of gratitude. Peggy hates missed opportunities, and if she's taught Sophie anything, it's to rue the things that could be done but aren't. "Don't be scared," she'd soothed Sophie on that day. Dance beside the highway? It seemed crazy, but it turned out to be fun!

The young mother strikes Sophie as the same sort of free spirit. "I'd like to try on the skirt," she says, "but my daughter needs to pee."

Sophie regards the dancing girl. She's given up whirling for tap dancing; her pink sneakers make a frenzied thumping sound on the wooden floor. She chants a single word: "potty," "potty," "potty."

"Sophie? Sophie?" The receiver chants, too, but Sophie doesn't hear it.

"We don't have a public restroom," Sophie begins. She's heard her mother make this speech a hundred times. Everyday Satan, as she thinks of it now, is located on the northwest corner of the plaza, just a few short steps from the mission church San Felipe de Neri. *Head just past the church there, then on behind the Basket Shop. You'll see a white building, well-marked. It's hard to miss.*

But the child will never make it that far. Not a chance. And Sophie takes pity on her. "The plumbing is ancient," Sophie warns. "You can't put anything in the toilet, okay?" The little girl bobs her head in agreement.

"You're expecting!" the mother chirps. "Congratulations!" She follows her daughter and Sophie behind the counter, the red velvet skirt draped over one arm.

Sophie glances down at the growing mound of her belly, dismayed that her condition is now evident to strangers. "We're not exactly celebrating," she says. She leads the way to the storage room.

When Sophie was a little girl, she occasionally played dress-up in the makeshift dressing room. Peggy provided scarves and tiaras and a cigar box of rhinestone jewelry. Sophie would pretend that she was a princess weighted down by jewels, a threadbare loveseat pressed into service as her throne.

"Are we almost there?" The little girl grasps the fingers of Sophie's left hand and squeezes, leaving behind a trace of something sticky.

They are. The tiny bathroom is housed in what was once a closet, and the facilities are rickety at best. Most often, they make do with flushing once a day. At the tail end of her second trimester, Sophie pees more often than seems possible. She would swear that she's expelling more liquid than she takes in. Thus the water in the bowl is yellow, markedly so, though Sophie has dutifully deposited the toilet paper in the trash can.

The little girl stops her dancing. Her urgency seems to have vanished. She stands contemplating the contents of the toilet. Her nose is wrinkled.

"Come on," Sophie grouses. "If you need to go, you need to go. It's just a little piss. Look around. This is the desert. We need to save water."

Suddenly the little girl snaps back to life. "Please close the door?"

Sophie salutes and pulls the turquoise door shut. She stands just outside for a moment, leaning against a stack of boxes. In the silence between the store's ancient adobe walls, the hiss of urine sounds louder than it would elsewhere. The child pees and pees and pees some more. Just listening gives Sophie the urge to go. "Oh, for heaven's sake," she groans. She has to go do something else to distract herself; otherwise she's liable to wet her pants.

Because it's already getting dark, she takes this moment to move around the shop and up the wattage on the Tiffany-style lamps. One is on the counter; another is a pole lamp next to the two-drawer mahogany dresser, which is filled now with cashmere and beaded cotton sweaters. By the time Sophie returns to the receiver, Will has hung up. She dials him again. Her mood has changed, and so has his.

"I don't know when she did it," Sophie tells Will. "That damned bitch cleaned out the cash register, and I didn't notice because she bought the skirt with a credit card."

"I bet the credit card was stolen or something."

Sophie knows Will is right, but she can't say it. Her face flushes. She begins straightening the counter with her free hand. She squirts Windex on the glass and wipes it with an old dish towel. Beneath the counter, on a surface draped in scarlet satin, is a collection of quirky beaded earrings. The earrings are silly-looking, but she likes a necklace she sees, a silver wishbone strung on a leather cord. She reaches under the counter and watches as her hand grasps the necklace and pulls it out. "I have to get a plumber over here."

"Well, then let's talk later. Hang up and call the plumber."

"I've already called. Now I'm waiting for a call back. It's starting to snow. Do you think it's going to stick?" Flakes are flying past the windows. Sophie sighs and wishes for a snow day.

Will is silent on the other end. "I'm in Lubbock, Sophie. The sun is shining here."

"You don't have to rub it in. I know you're in Lubbock. I know you're having the time of your life, and I'm dealing with all manner of crap." She asks if he got the form she sent.

"I did," he says. "I filled in most of the blanks and signed it."

"And? Did you mail it?"

As she suspected, he got hung up by the envelope and stamp. He doesn't have either. Sophie can't help responding sarcastically. She tells him that's what post offices are for. "They have those in Lubbock, don't they?"

"You're such a bitch, Sophie. My dad is right. You're just like my mom. I didn't believe him when he told me I needed to wise up."

"Wise up about what?" She feels her throat closing up. She isn't sure she'll be able to speak.

"So, tell me something. Be real, okay? Did you get pregnant on purpose?"

"What? Why would I do that?"

"To make me marry you. It's what my mother did."

"No, Will." She squeezes out the words. "Is that the story your dad tells?"

"He says women do it all the time. Here's the thing, Sophie. I'm not ready to be a father. I may never be ready to be one."

Silence gathers around her as she stands before the empty cash register. She can hear everything there is to hear: the rustling of a mouse in the back room and, after another minute or two, the gonging of the grandfather clock next door. Suddenly she hears herself speaking, saying exactly the right thing: "Oh, you'll be one all right. Even if you never lay eyes on this baby, you'll *still* be the father."

When she hangs up, she sees that it's four o'clock, an hour earlier than she thought it was. How did that happen? Maybe she was on Lubbock time there for a few minutes, and now she's back in Albuquerque. She notices that bright-red ridges mark the inside of her palm, and when she holds the wishbone up to the light, she can see that she's bent the two sides closer together.

"You've ruined it," she whispers to herself. She is trying to bend it back into place when the phone startles her by ringing.

"Hi, it's Kevin, with Davis the Plumber." This is the call she's been waiting for. He sounds jolly and energetic. "I'm over here in the Northeast Heights," he tells her. "Is it snowing over there?"

"Just enough to be pretty."

"Coming down like crazy over this way," he says.

That would make sense. The part of the city closest to the mountains is at a higher elevation. It's always a little colder there, and generally, it gets more snow than other parts of Albuquerque.

"I think I can make it over there before you close at five," Kevin tells Sophie. "That is, if you're going to stay."

"Sure, I'll stay," she says. She has to wait for her mother to get here. Peggy's doctor's appointment wasn't until three o'clock. She was going there right after she finished talking to the assistant principal at Valley.

Fortunately, the silver wishbone is malleable. Sophie is able to straighten the two prongs. While she's waiting for Kevin to arrive, she digs in her purse and finds just enough money to buy it. She rings the purchase into the otherwise empty cash register and slips the leather cord over her head.

On the last Saturday in February, while Peggy is in the shower allowing the hot spray to soothe her sore neck, a truck carrying Sophie's furniture arrives. Hearing the doorbell, Peggy turns off the water and waits for Ian's footfall on the stairs and down the hall. "The movers are here, Sophie!" she hears him yell.

Peggy hurriedly dries off and slips into a robe. She ventures out of the foggy bathroom and into the hall. A young man stands at the front door, and out in the drive, a full-size moving van is parked.

"What's going on?" she asks Sophie, who has followed her brother down the stairs and is now headed for the front door. Sophie is wearing overalls and a lavender turtleneck sweater. Peggy thinks the overalls used to be Jack's, but she isn't sure.

"Ian says the movers are here!" Sophie calls over her shoulder.

Peggy's fears shape her response. "What movers?" she shouts back. So Jack's moving out, then? How has he decided what to take, and why didn't he discuss it with her in advance? She presses a fist to her mouth to avoid crying. The front door stands open; a gust of cold air leaves her shivering. Whatever relief she managed to find in the shower is quickly swept away. It is all she can do to stay upright. The grief and regret she feels are sickening. Why did she think it was all right, what she'd been doing all these years?

Jack has been as good as his word. He comes home for dinner, then leaves again as soon as the kids are in their rooms. Once or twice Sophie or Ian has asked where he's going, but they seem to take his absence for granted these days. Jack did tell Peggy that he picked up a comfortable sleeper sofa at an estate sale. No need to worry about him, he's said more than once. She couldn't tell whether he was being sarcastic. She never has been able to read him.

Peggy is lost in thought when Sophie ducks back in, arms crossed tightly over her chest. "I need my coat," she says. "My furniture's here!"

But that doesn't explain a single thing, at least not to Peggy. She pads out to the porch and snags Ian. There are three movers, and one is a whistler who seems overly fond of "Yankee Doodle Dandy." He's the driver, evidently, because he calls directions to the other two.

Ian stands on the porch, hands on his hips. Peggy calls him to her side. "What's this about?"

"Aunt Candace sent Sophie furniture from France!" In fact, the furniture has been shipped from Boston, but it *is* French furniture. Distracted, he turns to watch as the first piece is unloaded. "My teepee may be in there, too."

"She did what?" Peggy asks, but Ian and Sophie have wandered back out to the truck, where the movers are calling directions to one another.

Wrapped in blankets and shrink-wrapped in plastic, the furniture is unrecognizable. The first piece is tall and wide, so big that the third mover steps in to assist the two who are wheeling it down the gangplank.

"What do you suppose it is?" Ian asks.

Peggy knows what it has to be, given the size. "An armoire," she replies.

Ian wrinkles his nose. He's never heard that word.

Before they carry it up the stairs, the whistler measures the height of Sophie's bedroom ceiling. "No need to struggle up those stairs only to find we can't stand it up," he explains to Sophie, who has her hands clasped at her chest. She looks dazed and delighted. She'd forgotten all about the furniture. In her whole life, nothing so unexpected has ever happened.

The armoire is over eight feet tall, but the ceiling is ten feet high, so the movers are obligated to lug the enormous package up the narrow flight of stairs. For a while it looks as though the doorway might need to be widened, but they unwrap one side and manage to slip the armoire through. As they struggle with the load, it occurs to Peggy that, should they need to move the piece again—and of course they will—it will probably be necessary to complete the set of stairs outside Ian's bedroom.

"This baby's come a long way," the driver comments to the room at large. "Circa 1750," he says, with a little whistle of appreciation. "I've got her papers for you." He turns to smile at Sophie, then at Peggy, then at Sophie again.

"It's hers," Peggy says, so the driver presses an envelope into Sophie's hands. For once, Sophie is speechless. She accepts the paperwork with a small "thank you," then stands admiring the massive antique.

The oak doors are heavily carved with raised panels. A graceful scalloped top frames a basket of carved flowers above and between the two doors. It turns out that the whistler is fairly knowledgeable about this piece of furniture. He explains that it's a wedding armoire, from a French tradition in the eighteenth century. The father of the future bride would carve the piece by hand and decorate it with symbols of prosperity. When the girl was still quite young, she would begin to fill it with her trousseau. After opening one of the doors, the whistler runs a hand across the top shelf.

"Can't you just imagine it?" he asks, which raises a snicker from one of the other movers.

The rosewood bed frame is for a double bed, and Sophie's mattress is a queen, so they don't assemble the pieces right away. Instead, they leave them crated in one corner of the large room. The driver makes a point of telling Peggy that the frame can be altered to fit a queen bed. Peggy smiles and nods. It dawns on her that she will need to tip these men. When she has a chance, she excuses herself and rushes downstairs to check on the state of her wallet.

The third piece is a dressing mirror. Sophie isn't sure she's ever seen one, and she gasps when the deliverymen uncrate it. Her first view of herself in the mirror is of a silly sixteen-year-old with a hand clapped over her mouth. Even to herself, she looks foolish, but the youngest of the movers is immediately smitten. He sidles up behind her, locks eyes with her reflection, and smiles shyly.

"That's one lucky mirror," he says. Sophie wheels around and dazzles him with her widest grin.

"Why, thank you!" she gushes. The driver snickers under his breath, but later in the truck, he concedes the point—the girl is lovely, though she looks to be pregnant. Regardless, it was a clever-enough come-on.

"You two don't understand romance," the young man says expansively. He sits behind the other two, crammed in a bench space. "It's all about taking advantage of the moment."

"But you'll never see that girl again." Now the driver's assistant weighs in.

"It doesn't matter." The young man is leaning over the seat. "Suppose I run into her someday. She'll remember me. She'll flash on that moment we just had, the two of us looking at one another in the mirror. And if we never see each other again, well, we will still have it, that one nice moment." The young man grasps the assistant's shoulder and squeezes. "I've got it, and what have you got?"

"A headache, maybe?"

But the driver is nodding slowly. "Better listen up," he advises his friend. "You could learn a thing or two."

Dinner is quieter than usual. They have pizza delivered by Jack. It's their usual Saturday evening meal: pizza and a bowl of salad. If they finish the pizza—and they typically do—they are duty-bound to finish the salad. Sophie and Ian keep up the conversation, most of which has to do with the delivery and the furniture. Jack listens quietly, but when dinner is over, he begs off going upstairs to see it. Instead, he says he wants to see the news. "I'll go up a little later," he tells Sophie, giving her a pat on the shoulder.

Though it's chilly, Ian throws open the door to nowhere. He sits cross-legged and regards the eastern view. Sophie looks for him after she's finished cleaning up the kitchen. They haven't had a chance to talk privately in the last few hours, and she knows he must be disappointed. He'd been hoping Candace would surprise him. When they talked, she had said only that she hadn't found the teepee. In the months since, he thought, maybe it had turned up and she'd sent it along. Evidently not.

Sophie stares off into the distance, puzzling. In only a few moments, she's shivering, but she's not about to complain of the cold. The early evening sky is tinged purple by the streetlights and neon signs. She can hear the distant hum of traffic.

Sophie waits for Ian to say something, but he remains silent, so she clears her throat and says what she's thinking: "It sucks that you didn't get your teepee, Ian." She wants to commiserate, but she can't. She has a roomful of French furniture.

He nods. "Yep." Then he turns to look at her. "Don't you want to get to the bottom of this? Don't you want the truth?" Later he will lie awake and wonder whether he should have kept his mouth shut. Was he being mean, then? Or jealous? Or mean *and* jealous?

Her heartbeat picks up—the idea of *the truth* scares her—and the fear she feels is transferred nearly immediately to the baby. He or she stirs, then kicks. "Whoa!" she says, moving a hand down to cover the spot.

"What is it?"

"The baby is kicking!" She has felt stirrings on a daily basis for some weeks now, but this was a jolt, something so surprising that she forgets everything else for a moment or two. "Oh my god," she mutters. "This is so damned unreal."

She turns and regards her brother in the half light. He's a little squirrely-looking, and his towhead is the least of it, really. His ears are too big, his neck's too long, and there's something a little amiss about his teeth. When her English class read *To Kill a Mockingbird*, Sophie took a particular interest in Dill, who reminded her of Ian. Until she read about Dill, she'd never come across anyone like her brother—someone strange and a little aloof, the sort of child who draws attention to himself merely by being different. Or maybe it was simply that she hasn't noticed the outliers, those relegated to the shadowy corners of the room. She's always been situated smack-dab in the middle of the room.

It has occurred to her that Ian doesn't look anything like her, and she has wondered on occasion if one of them might be adopted, not just because of the physical difference but because the rooms seem to harbor secrets. Her parents' arguments take place in whispers, for heaven's sake! No wonder Ian is always snooping. He must feel it, too: the empty space at the center of their household. Since Thanksgiving Day, Sophie has been putting the pieces together, and as painful as it may be, she is relieved to have some sense of the whys in the equation: why Peggy sent Sophie away when Candace came to visit; why Candace was so fascinated first with Sophie and then with her baby; why Candace wants the baby so desperately; and why Jack has more or less moved out.

"So you think Jack knows?"

Ian nods. "Pretty sure." He is more than pretty sure. He is certain, because he was privy to the phone conversation between Candace and Jack. And it hasn't escaped his notice that Jack is spending his nights away from home, or that he bought a sleeper sofa for the fixer-upper. As of a day or two ago, a rickety table has occupied the space in the breakfast area. There are no chairs yet, but they can't be far behind.

Ian says fiercely: "You're still my sister."

"I'm always your sister, dope!"

"Don't call me dope."

"Don't act like a dope, then."

Both fight back tears. The last light leaves the sky as they go on sitting in the open doorway, shoulder to shoulder, shivering and wiping their faces with their sleeves. Eventually they hear the ignition of Jack's car, and in another second or two, the station wagon sputters to life. The twin beams of the car's headlights swing out over the gravel road; son and daughter watch until the taillights disappear around the curve.

"If someone has to leave, I wish it wasn't him," Ian says with a sigh.

Sophie was thinking precisely the same thing, but she wouldn't have said the words sadly. She would have said them vehemently; she would have spit them out like bits of gristle. That's yet another difference between brother and sister. Whereas her brother gets sad, Sophie gets angry, not that she shows it right away or is even all that aware of it. In recent weeks, she's been quieter than usual. Sometimes she has a hard time accessing her thoughts. Even as her organs become increasingly crowded for space, even as her ankles swell and her face gets puffy, her head and heart feel vacant.

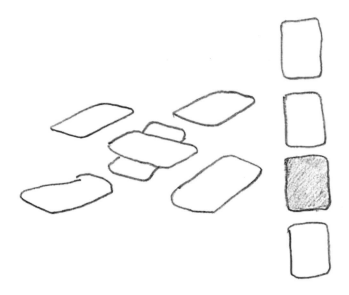

Position #8—"Her House"

Traditionally, this position is designated as "That Which Surrounds You"; for most of us, that's a house and those who live in it. This card is about the feelings of our nearest and dearest.

~ Eight of Swords ~

Although the young woman appears helpless and alone, the situation may not be as bad as it looks. There's a castle in the distance, and her feet are free to take her there. The swords are only an obstacle, not an enclosure. She is not as powerless as she may feel. To make the most of her life, she has only to take off the blinder and look around.

IT FALLS TO Jack to enroll Sophie at New Futures, because Peggy is in bed with the flu. He picks up Sophie at just a little after seven, and neither one says anything about the fact that he is apparently sleeping elsewhere. Sophie is waiting on the front porch for him, though it's chilly and she isn't dressed to be outdoors. Her coat no longer closes in the front; the black leggings she wears don't cut the wind.

Sophie is shivering when she gets in the car and slams the door. Jack trains the air vents in her direction. She's relieved that the car is warm. Once they're on the road, Jack asks Sophie how long her mother has been sick.

"I'm a little worried about her," he admits.

Sophie thinks of saying something smart: *If you're so worried, why don't you come home and take care of her?* But she only shrugs. "She's getting better. She didn't want to take the chance of infecting anyone at New Futures."

"And that's another thing," Jack says as he whizzes down Rio Grande toward I-40. "*You're* staying away from her, aren't you?"

Sophie nods wearily, then realizes that her father is concentrating on driving, that he can't read her gestures. "Yeah, absolutely. The woman insists on wearing a mask anytime she gets within ten feet of me."

Jack is relieved. He worries that his family is suffering in his absence. Peggy would have him believe they are. Her defenses are down, surely, but he wonders, too, whether her illness is an unconscious bid for attention. She's been doted on for a couple of decades; he has always been an attentive husband. Perhaps Peggy is simply not accustomed to taking care of herself. He suspects that she's also depressed. He's sad on occasion, but not nearly as often as he might have predicted. "You roll with the punches," Vernie always told him. Even from the time he was learning to walk, Jack was always resilient. Taking a topple, he was as apt to laugh as he was to cry.

Father and daughter are silent on their way across town, or mostly so. About halfway there, Jack thinks to ask whether Sophie needs something in the way of school supplies. Sophie kicks the backpack on the floorboard near her feet.

"Got everything I need," she says. She sneaks a look at Jack, who is wearing a plaid wool cap she's never seen before. The jaunty cap gives him the look of a golfer or an Irish innkeeper.

"Where'd you get the cap?"

As he stops at the light at Indian School Road, Jack reaches up and grabs the hat by its bill. "Do you like it?"

"Hard to say."

"Keeps my head warm," he says. "Candace sent it to me for Christmas." Lost in thought, he misses the San Mateo exit off I-40 and has to get off at Louisiana and double back. He apologizes to Sophie.

"Come on, Jack. Do you actually think I'm anxious to get there?" She has taken to chewing her fingernails, a satisfying, relatively harmless diversion, except that her fingernails don't grow quickly enough, so she ends up nibbling at her cuticles and the tender skin around the nails.

(Teachers at New Futures will come to recognize Sophie's homework assignments by the smudges of blood that often mark the margins.)

Jack glances over at her, catching her in the act. His smile is rueful. "Of course not." And then: "I'm sorry your life has gotten so rough around the edges."

"Not just around the edges. And it's my own fault," she says. She is thinking of the poem and the ugly confrontation with Ms. Sherman. If not for that piece of nastiness, she would still be at Valley, where at least everything was more or less familiar.

He pulls over into the left-hand lane and surprises Sophie by turning into a Sonic Drive-In. "Don't know about you," he says when they are parked next to a menu board and speaker, "but I didn't take the time to eat breakfast."

Sophie shrugs. "I don't generally eat when I first wake up."

"I should have thought of that," he says quickly. He is about to turn the key in the ignition when Sophie reaches over and grabs his hand.

"Don't go, Jack. I've been up for at least an hour. What do you recommend?"

"How hungry are you?"

Sophie smiles. "Hungrier than you are, I bet. A bottomless pit, that's what I am."

Jack rolls down the window and orders burritos and tater tots. "Coffee?" he asks Sophie.

She makes a face. These days, coffee disgusts her. "Dr Pepper," she says.

New Futures is located in the middle of an older residential neighborhood in central Albuquerque. The school itself is newer than the surrounding houses, all of which are smallish stucco boxes built in the late fifties and early sixties, when both the houses and the people who lived in them tended to be smaller. Now the neighborhood is dated but still respectable, though the presence of New Futures and the nearby Freedom High must be a nuisance to residents.

Twice each day, a dozen or more school buses screech to a halt in front of the flesh-toned stucco building, and a small army of young women come stumbling off, lugging all manner of baggage: backpacks, diaper bags, and baby seats. Pink and blue blankets ruffle in the breeze. In their haste, the girls lose track of the smaller objects, including pacifiers, keys, stuffed animals, and cell phones. One of the teachers is stationed outside to assist in pickup. Here and there a baby wails, but the scene is quieter than most onlookers would expect, considering that these are teenage girls and babies, two noisy populations.

The blue-gray front doors open onto a multipurpose space that houses the cafeteria, the receptionist's desk, and a waiting area complete with a long bench and expanses of linoleum—ideal for toddlers intent on practicing their locomotion skills. When Jack and Sophie push through the doors, the spacious room is crowded with girls and their children. Some girls are finishing their homework, while others eat breakfast. Babies in high chairs pummel banana slices with their clumsy little fists or chase Cheerios around their plastic trays. In the cafeteria kitchen, someone has burned a batch of toast, and the scorched smell drifts across the room to the newcomers.

For a moment, father and daughter stop stock-still in the entryway and survey the scene. It's both cheery and chaotic. The room is full of natural light—the walls on two sides are made of plate glass. As schools go, New Futures is a good deal more pleasant than Valley, and a good deal more recent as well. The building that houses New Futures was constructed the year after Laurel gave birth to Will, though the program actually began in the late 1960s in the basement of a YWCA.

The first school of its kind in the United States—one entirely dedicated to the education of pregnant teens and teen moms—the Albuquerque alternative school has served as both a model and an inspiration for others that have sprung up around the country. Would that the building had been funded a few years earlier, in time to assist teenage Laurel and her infant son. Thank goodness, Sophie will come to think, that it existed for herself when she got in such a bad way in the spring of 2007. "I don't know what I would have done without them," she'll say later, laughing ruefully.

"I'm pretty sure I'm the only man on the premises," Jack remarks. "Do you think they have any male teachers?"

"I doubt it," Sophie replies. She feels suddenly shy and, for the first time in several months, ordinary. Other girls pushing past are equally or more pregnant, and those who aren't expecting are toting babies or toddlers.

Before first period, Sophie ducks into the restroom nearest the front of the building. It's full of pregnant girls, and Sophie can't help but laugh aloud at the utter absurdity of the situation. Suddenly she's surrounded by her own kind. She has to wait for a stall to open up. While she does, she finds herself talking to the girl standing next to her. The girl is slightly built, with a bulbous belly only half-covered by red-and-black plaid flannel pajama bottoms. Pajama pants are a fashion staple at New Futures, worn by students and teachers alike.

"Do you know what you're having?" the girl asks Sophie.

Sophie shakes her head. "Not really."

A black girl stationed at the sink whirls around. "You're too far gone not to know! I've had three ultrasounds."

Sophie feels a little stung. Each time the doctor has suggested an ultrasound, she's refused. "I don't want to know," she admits.

Both girls demand an explanation, and though Sophie would have imagined being affronted by such aggressive curiosity, instead she feels relief. "I'm not really ready to know. Sometimes I wake up in the middle of the night and I don't quite believe that I'm pregnant."

Pajama Pants reaches out and slaps a hand on Sophie's belly. "You knocked up all right."

"For sure," someone else says from inside a stall. "Otherwise you wouldn't be at New Futures."

"But I just got here," Sophie says. "Give me a little time to adjust. I'll get with the program."

The black girl nods at Sophie in the mirror. "Sure," she says. "I'm down with that."

It doesn't take long for Sophie to be glad she ended up at New Futures. One of the best parts, she tells Tam, is her counselor, Juanita Jimenez.

"Call me Nita," the counselor had said at their first meeting. "At New Futures, everyone is on a first-name basis." She fished in her purse for a compact and handed it to Sophie. "You've got something green between your teeth."

Sophie laughed nervously and checked in the mirror. Sure enough.

After Sophie removed the offending bit of broccoli and returned the compact, Nita explained herself: "You might have gone to the bathroom right after our meeting, seen yourself in the mirror, and wondered why I didn't say anything. We'd have gotten off to a bumpy start that way. Now you know I'm in your corner."

"So, what does this Nita look like?" Tam asks.

It's one of their last days together. Tam is going to finish out the school year, or what's left of it, at her new school in Dallas. Belinda has convinced Tam that it's for the best, this abrupt transition, because this way Tam will be familiar with the school come September. Now that Tam is leaving, Sophie is all the more grateful for New Futures. It would be too sad to be alone at Valley without Tam or Will.

The two friends are standing in Tam's empty living room, gazing out the picture window. The view is of a struggling group of desert plants—Joshua tree, spindly red yucca, and a trio of battered prickly pear cacti—surrounded by a sea of gray pea gravel. Locals refer to this sort of yard as "xeriscaped." Someone unrolls a length of black plastic, backs up a truck, and dumps a small mountain of gravel on top of it.

This house, Tam's house, is FOR RENT, as evidenced by a sign near the driveway.

Sophie has been thinking about how to describe Nita. "A fat Frida Kahlo," she replies. Tam is playing with her hair, wrapping a length of it around her finger. She continues to regard the window, as does Sophie. Only, Sophie is looking through it, and Tam isn't. Just now they find it easier not to focus on one another.

"Who's Frida Kahlo?" Tam asks.

Sophie is aghast. They saw the movie together, for Christ's sake, and it wasn't all that long ago. "The Mexican artist with the unibrow. Salma Hayek. Remember?"

Tam nods thoughtfully and, letting go of her hair, reaches out a finger to trace the outline of a lily on the dusty window. "Oh yeah," she says as she adds a stamen to her stylized and toothy flower. "She was married to that horrible, ugly womanizer. What was his name?"

"Diego Rivera," Sophie replies. She read the biography, or most of it anyway, and she recalls some mitigating circumstances. Diego Rivera wasn't entirely bad, or Frida wasn't entirely good. But that isn't really the point. "I was telling you about Nita Jimenez. And she says that the people you love are bound to disappoint you. You're bound to disappoint the people you love. It's to be expected, really."

"There's disappointment and then there's disappointment," Tam says, referencing the marriage of Frida and Diego. "If someone is going to be ugly, they damn sure better be faithful."

They are both silent a moment. Then Tam speaks again: "Is she married? Miss Jimenez, I mean."

The question surprises Sophie. She watches while Tam busies herself with adding another flower to her window garden. This one looks like a cross between a daisy and a rose. "How would I know?"

Tam turns to Sophie. She holds up her left hand and wiggles the fingers. "Wedding ring? Most married people wear rings."

Sophie shrugs. She doesn't remember ever looking at Nita's hands.

"Let's hope not," Tam continues. "I'm *never* getting married. Everything bad that's ever happened to me has had something to do with one of my mother's marriages."

"But I thought you wanted to fall in love."

"I do, but marriage ruins love, Sophie. You're smart to have a baby without getting married. That's what Jodie Foster did. And Rosie O'Donnell."

"Rosie O'Donnell is a special case."

"True, but tell me this: Wouldn't Frida Kahlo have been better off without Diego Rivera?"

"I don't know." Suddenly Sophie is exhausted. She hasn't told Tam that she's promised her baby to her mother's friend Candace. She wants to tell her, but she's afraid of being judged. Aside from Peggy, Jack, and Ian, aside from Will and Laurel and Candace herself, the only person who knows is Nita Jimenez. Nita suggested that Sophie keep the news to herself for the time being. "Quite honestly," she said, "it's no one else's business." Sophie was relieved that her counselor didn't insist on her sharing, or on her being bold and brave and all that crap. The decision feels fragile, as though it might not survive the weight of the world's indignation.

Take Tam for instance, who loves babies the same way she loves puppies and Disney cartoon characters. Sophie has rarely ever kept a secret from Tam, although she suspects that Tam has kept a number of secrets from her. Once Peggy described Tam as "self-possessed." Sophie didn't have the slightest idea of what her mother meant. Now the term makes sense. Tam is in charge of herself. She doesn't blurt out secrets or have unprotected sex. She just doesn't. She might moon over a baby, but it wouldn't be hers. Not unless she's thirty and married and has some money in the bank. Tam might seem like a ditz, but she knows how to protect herself.

Sophie looks for a chair to flop onto or a sofa to throw her exhausted self across, but the room is all but empty. Along the back wall, boxes are stacked one on top of another, neat new boxes sealed with lengths of shiny brown packing tape, the work of a team of professional movers. When Sophie learned that American Airlines would be paying to transport the contents of Belinda and Tam's house to Dallas, she was surprised they were bothering with a garage sale. "Why not just take everything?" she asked Belinda, who had a ready reply: "We don't need everything, Sophie." Belinda offered a forced smile. "We're getting rid of the things we no longer want in our lives."

Right then, Sophie suspected that *she* was one of those things—a knocked-up teenager going nowhere. When all was said and done, Belinda was relieved they were moving. "A blessing in disguise," Belinda called their move. Sophie hasn't shared her suspicion with Tam. Her pride won't allow it. But at least Belinda has seen to the pizza. She's left enough money for the girls to order lunch. When Tam leaves the room to make the call to Domino's, Sophie takes the liberty of adding a bee to Tam's window garden, a fat worker bee set to alight on the daisy-rose. What are flowers without bees, after all?

On March 13, her seventeenth birthday, Sophie attends school but leaves at lunchtime for a doctor's appointment. She doesn't tell anyone at school that it's her birthday. She isn't celebrating, she informed her mother; she is simply enduring. In her thirty-fourth week, Sophie is off-kilter and unbalanced, so large in the belly that she finds walking awkward and uncomfortable. Sophie worries that she may be waddling, and that the other girls will tease her. Just this past week, she awoke in the middle of the night with a burning sensation in her belly button. In the morning she noticed that her belly button had popped out, like a turkey timer. Sophie has taken to covering it with a Band-Aid.

This year's birthday is as quiet as last year's was loud. For her sixteenth, Peggy and Tam had conspired to throw a surprise party. The bulk of the party was supposed to be outside, but the weather didn't cooperate, so instead of making s'mores in the fire pit, they used a fire in the fireplace, built by Jack. All night the girls squealed and shrieked, while the boys crowded around the television and watched basketball. When Sophie inquired as to what was up, Jack replied, "March Madness."

As per usual on her birthday, winter has made something of a return. Skittering leaves rush into the lobby as Sophie opens the plate-glass door. The sky is overcast, a gloomy day for a gloomy birthday girl. Peggy is waiting in the parking lot in her little Toyota, windows rolled up and heater blasting. Trudging across the lot toward her mother's car, Sophie hears laughter and the beginning of song: a dozen or so voices launch into "Happy Birthday to You." The adults carry the tune for the children, who contribute only to the ends of the lines—"to you, to you." For a second Sophie assumes they are singing for her, these children and their caregivers, but in the time it takes her to smile, she realizes that someone in the toddler nursery shares her birthday. The song is for a child, and Sophie has left childhood behind.

"Do you hear them singing?" Sophie asks when she opens the car door.

Peggy smiles and shakes her head. She's wearing a red wool skullcap that someone left in the shop, and whoever owned it previously had a larger head. Peggy has used the extra space to hide her hair, which she didn't bother to wash or style. She looks gnome-like in the red cap and a black turtleneck.

They're late to Sophie's appointment. As soon as Sophie gets herself situated—it takes time these days—Peggy pulls out of the parking lot.

"Do you have someone watching the shop?" Sophie asks her mother at a stoplight.

Peggy shakes her head vigorously, which displaces a lock or two of hair and softens the look. Sophie reaches over and teases out a strand on the other side of her mother's face. "There," she says, then, "I'm sorry you had to close up."

Her mother answers that it doesn't matter; it doesn't matter at all. "I hate that the weather is so cold and clammy," Peggy adds just as the light changes and traffic resumes. "Nothing is going the way I planned. The universe isn't cooperating."

Sophie can't help herself. "All things will pass," she replies, bringing a smile to her mother's face.

As though to prove the point, a week later, spring will arrive in earnest. The warmth of the sun will tease the daffodils into bloom; a dozen or more will open every day for at least a week. Sophie and Peggy will sit companionably in the front-porch rockers and admire the bulb garden. Sophie will think of Tam tracing the heads of daffodils on the dusty glass. She misses Tam terribly, enough to coax tears into her eyes. Sophie will allow them to fall, and will be relieved that her mother is on the other side of the porch and nearsighted.

On the last Saturday in March, Ian has the house to himself. As usual, Jack is at the fixer-upper; Ian has an assignment for school and has managed to haggle a day off from helping his father. Peggy has accompanied Sophie to Lamaze class. A half hour earlier, they had trooped out the door, pillows tucked under their arms, both of them grumbling, though not at each other.

Because he has a deadline—the teacher who sponsors the middle-school newspaper awaits his e-mail—Ian can't settle down. He wanders from one side of the house to the other, eventually ending up in front of the bank of windows in Sophie's room. The view is the best in the house. Outside, a glorious spring day is in progress. Whipped cream clouds float on the surface of an immense blue heaven. In the North Valley of Albuquerque, the air is cool and fresh. The wind has yet to pick up, as it will later in the afternoon.

From this vantage point Ian can see all the way to the five inert volcanoes on the horizon, the Sleeping Sisters. He could write a newspaper article on the volcanoes, but where's the currency in that story? Then his gaze falls on the hives, red, yellow, and two shades of bright blue. Until recently the boxes held something precious, something rich and golden, but now three of the five are empty.

Jack discovered the extent of his loss just last Sunday. Ian tagged along when his father went to check on things, staying a few steps behind—not out of fear this time but out of concern. He was standing nearby when Jack opened the fourth and fifth hives, prying off the lids with a hive tool. "Mighty quiet, isn't it, Ian?"

Ian didn't say anything. He was waiting for Jack to look inside.

"I'll be darned," his father said. "They're gone."

The bees in the blue and yellow boxes had vanished. Ian and Jack searched the area for bodies, but found nothing at all that would explain the disappearance. The hive Jack had requeened was healthy enough, as was the one next to it. But the three boxes on the end were simply empty. Peering inside, studying the abandoned comb, Ian said, "Looks like they evacuated."

Jack stood and scratched his head. "It's a good thing you're standing out here with me, son," he said. "Otherwise I think I might break down and cry."

Ian spots a spiral notebook and a pencil on Sophie's dresser. She won't care if he borrows them. He doesn't want to go downstairs to the table. It's better to stay where he can get a glimpse of the boxes, in case he needs inspiration. And so he drops down onto the floor next to the window and leans his back against the wall. Right away, he begins taking notes the way his journalism teacher has taught. Eventually, after doing a little more research, he composes an article for the school paper.

ARE CELL PHONES KILLING BEES?

By Ian Granger

Honeybees are disappearing and no one knows why. According to the Apiary Inspectors of America and the Department of Agriculture, approximately 38 percent of beekeepers are reporting the deaths of entire colonies. Some commercial beekeepers have lost 70 percent of their hives. Scientists call it "Colony Collapse Disorder," or CCD.

For as long as I can remember, my dad has kept bees. In the vacant field across from our house, you'll see five bee boxes. These are not white but bright colors, like yellow and blue. Over this past winter,

I learned to like the bees, and even to watch them in the morning before going to school. They have habits and routines, and I got to be familiar with them and their habits and I observed things like undertaker bees, which rid the hives of carcasses.

Because I watch them every day, I noticed when the activity around the boxes stopped. One day one of the hives was quiet, no buzzing about, no bees entering or exiting. It was like an airport without planes. Then a week later, two more hives went empty. I told my dad, and he checked and sure enough, the bees were gone. He couldn't believe it, and neither could I.

No one knows what is happening to the bees or what has caused whole hives to just up and disappear. Some people blame cell phone towers for confusing the bees. Scientists say the problem may be pesticides or genetically altered crops. Only one thing is for sure: human beings need bees to pollinate crops. As Albert Einstein said, "If the bees disappeared off the globe, then man would have only four years of life left. No more bees, no more pollination, no more plants, no animals, no more man."

I don't know about you, but I'm kind of freaked out about it.

Once he gets started, the article writes itself. He feels good about it. He has conquered two fears, and in the process he has discovered confidence and conviction. He can't wait to share the article with his sister. He knows she will be excited for him. By the time Sophie returns from Lamaze class, he's printed a copy, which he slips to her as she sits at the dining table eating a ham sandwich. "Lamaze class makes me hungry," she grumbles as he sits down beside her. "Everything makes me hungry."

But Sophie is glowing when she finishes reading his article. "Dude, I'm so proud of you!" she says loudly. Both of them half-expect Peggy to emerge from the hallway and ask what's going on, but these days everything makes her tired, and she's returned to bed.

Sophie's baby is due on Friday, April 28. Candace makes arrangements to fly into the Albuquerque Sunport on the sixteenth, just to be safe. Her flight is due at six at night, and the plan is to pick her up and then go out to dinner. Sophie insists on driving to the airport, though the traffic is terrible. I-25 is backed up for at least a mile; rush hour is complicated by a lane closure. For at least ten or fifteen minutes they travel at a snail's pace, inching forward, or so it seems to both Sophie and Peggy. Sophie grips the wheel intently and squints through the windshield.

"Would you like some sunglasses?" Peggy asks. "I have an extra pair in the glove compartment."

Sophie shakes her head. Peggy knows what her daughter is thinking and voices it for her: "You don't believe in sunglasses?"

"Exactly," Sophie says grimly.

"Okay, then."

Just now Sophie is merging into traffic, getting on I-25 behind a red VW Bug that slows, sputters, then picks up speed again. Following too closely, Sophie is forced to brake, and she does so abruptly, eliciting a sharp exhalation from Peggy.

"Sor-ry," Sophie snaps. She's absurdly pregnant at this point, so much so that her belly is pressed right up against the steering wheel, which looks perilous to Peggy. She wishes she'd insisted on driving.

"Are you ready?" Peggy asks. It's not the question she meant to ask; she didn't mean to ask a question at all. She meant to say *okay* again, or maybe, *Are you okay?* In her own inept way, she is checking in. She's a little late maybe, a little foolhardy in her timing. Yes, all those things and more. Still . . .

"No," Sophie cries. "No, no, no!"

Do they think she's giving birth to a football, then? Sophie wonders. Do they believe she can hand it off to Candace, who will run up the field in the direction of Boston, carrying the football/baby safely into the future? And will Sophie simply slip back to the sidelines to resume the oblivious life of an American teen, à la Juno, who took up with her goofy boyfriend again as though the pregnancy had never happened? Who wants life to go backward? Sophie wonders as she maneuvers the car into the middle lane. Isn't life all about the future—looking forward to it, planning for it?

Yet Sophie can't, or won't, think beyond today. The traffic snarl doesn't trouble her. She isn't in any hurry to arrive at the airport. And she dreads labor and delivery. She thinks of labor and delivery as the beginning of the end. Ms. Jimenez told her to concentrate on getting her life back, but Sophie doesn't remember the life she had before the pregnancy, so it must not have been much. The life that's growing inside her is all Sophie can think about right now. Nothing else seems to matter.

If she is honest, she has to admit that the last few months have taught her things she would just as soon not know—about others and about herself—and if she *could* go back in time, she would definitely make different choices. She would not get pregnant in the first place. She would be a hell of a lot more careful. Sophie recognizes the looks people give her at the grocery store; they're pitying, baffled, and even belligerent. She swears that some people—her former creative writing teacher, for instance—actively dislike her. *In this day and age*, Ms. Sherman would say. Birth control pills, diaphragms, not to mention rubbers: all the various means of contraception are available, and yet willful girls like Sophie still manage to get themselves knocked up.

"Going on welfare?" a familiar-looking man inquired of her while she was waiting to fill a prescription at Walgreens. He was in front of Sophie in line, and he made a point of sidling around to insult her before turning back to the counter again. "Go to hell!" Sophie replied, then added under her breath, "straight to *fucking* hell." He smirked—she could see him in the round mirror behind the counter—and then the smirk melted into something like a leer. He was about to say something obscene. Sophie could tell he was. But the pharmacist reappeared, and within a minute or two, the man had his medication. He shouldered past her on his way out, a hand brushing her belly even as he ducked his head so that she couldn't meet his eyes.

As soon as she's able to pick up speed again, it occurs to Sophie that she could end it all right now, the pain of this moment. She could swerve the car into the concrete barrier. That would do it. After all, it's the path her father took—her biological father, Beau, Beau-What's-His-Face. She doesn't even know his last name, she realizes. Evidently no one knows whether he lost control of the car or chose suicide by tree trunk. For an instant or two, Sophie considers the option of taking after him. But she doesn't. She won't. She holds the wheel steady. She tells herself that her mother is in the car; her *child* is in the car.

"What was so great about him?" Sophie asks as they approach the exit for the Sunport.

"Who?"

"You know, Beau." Is this the first time she's uttered his name? It may be. "I'm just wondering. I mean, you were both in love with him, right?"

Peggy is startled and then quickly relieved. Over the past couple of months, Sophie has gone silent on her. She's been angry and indignant, but until now she has not been curious.

"He was a little crazy," Peggy replies haltingly. "But in a good way. And beautiful." For the first time in years, she can see him in her mind's eye, a slow smile transforming his angular face as he reaches up and brushes away those black corkscrew curls. He had eyes the color of sage, a dusty gray-green. In summers he went shirtless, and his back was gorgeous—long and lean, shiny with sweat, bronzed by the sun. And there was that lovely indentation down the center of his back, which disappeared into his worn and baggy jeans. Peggy keeps these memories to herself.

Rather than take the turnoff for first-floor, short-term parking, Sophie drives up the access ramp to the second floor and then higher, to the third. Once she has steered the car into an empty space between two nearly identical white trucks, she persists: "Crazy how?" She turns off the ignition and hands her mother the keys. "Tell me," she presses.

"Let's talk about this later." Peggy already has the door open and one foot out.

"No, now!"

So Peggy closes the door again. "He was very good at making others feel loved," she says. "You remind me of him in that way. He had a three-legged border collie named Moby, and he would have done anything to protect that dog. There was this one time . . ." Her voice dies away, and she gazes through the windshield and into the past.

"Go on," Sophie urges.

Peggy tells the story of the time some locals ganged up on Beau. "They didn't much like hippies," she explains.

The fight happened outside the hardware store during the first summer Peggy lived in Taos. Somebody called Beau a faggot or a fairy, and he would have shrugged it off except that one of the four or five men began to throw rocks at Moby, who yelped and ran blindly about, eliciting laughs from the other assholes. And that was it. Beau ended up in the hospital with a broken nose and bruised ribs. Before they took off, the locals sheared his hair, chopped it off with grass clippers, or so Peggy remembers it. Beau himself never spoke of it. For weeks he was bruised, scratched, and scraped up. After the wounds healed, he still had the mess of his hair, which he insisted on wearing as they'd left it. A raggedy-ass burr was the way Peggy thought of it. Months would pass before he looked like himself again.

Peggy remembers the aftermath, too, but she doesn't share that part of the story. After that encounter Beau would get all worked up every time he had to go into Taos. He required a little pot to mellow himself out, and Candace was always the one to make sure he had one joint to toke in the truck. No more than that. She didn't want to get him busted. They all looked after him, Candace first of all, but the rest of them, too. Even Jimbo and Denise, who were pretty much focused on each other— even they would run after Beau with a coat if they thought he needed one, or they'd save him a boiled egg or a chocolate chip cookie. Denise always had an empty pocket handy.

"Can we go in?" Peggy asks when she's finished her story. Her eyes are shiny with tears. She is wide awake, though, and for the first time in months, she's fully aware of what Candace has known all along: this baby is Beau's grandchild.

So what if they are a few minutes late? Sophie doesn't see what the big deal is, but Peggy insists on rushing up three escalators, climbing the escalator stairs rather than standing and waiting to be taken to the top. They push past all manner of people with suitcases and bags and children in tow. "Excuse me, excuse me," they say again and again. Of course, it's easy enough for skinny Peggy to sidle past, but it's another matter altogether for ponderous Sophie.

By the time they've reached the revolving doors that mark the boundaries for those meeting passengers, Sophie is flushed, and her smallish T-shirt has worked its way up over her swollen belly. She needs to reach into the sides of her overalls to wrestle it down again, but she doesn't want to adjust her clothes in public. "I'm going to the bathroom," she says.

Peggy nods and offers an absent smile. She's checking the large board that updates arrivals and departures. "Wouldn't you know it?" she says. "Candace's plane is delayed a few minutes."

"So plowing down all those innocents wasn't exactly necessary."

Peggy waves a hand to dismiss her grouchy daughter.

The Sunport's bathrooms are shaped like long hallways, with a row of stalls on one side and a wall-length mirror and counter on the other. Ordinarily they are quiet, virtually unoccupied, unlike the labyrinthine restrooms at other airports. Sophie feels better as soon as she rounds the corner and finds herself entirely alone. She stands before the sink and a plate-glass mirror and unfastens the bib of her overalls. As the bib drops, the bulbous expanse of her belly appears. Almost overnight, it seems, her skin has reached its limits and sent out long pink rivulets. Her hand goes to her mouth, and she stares in dismay. In the bright fluorescent light of the bathroom, her stretch marks shine. They're ugly, but at least she knows that other women are similarly marked. At New Futures some girls have revealed their own stretch marks, which lace their bellies and hips and stripe their breasts. She hates Will for doing this to her, and she hates herself for caring. Quickly, before anyone else can see, she jerks the pink T-shirt down over the dome of her belly and refastens her bib.

Then, just as she's closed herself inside a stall, the melody of "Clair de Lune" rings out from her pocket. It's Tam. Seeing the name flash across the screen of her cell phone, Sophie's heart lifts. Having to trudge through the last trimester of pregnancy without Tam at her side has been almost unbearable.

"I can twirl now!" Tam says excitedly. She's talking about ice-skating, of all things. Ordinarily Sophie would scoff. Ordinarily she'd be scornful. But she needs Tam. She misses Tam.

Tam is shopping. She shops by herself these days, or rather, she shops with Sophie. She calls Sophie as she walks into the first store, then wanders about, commenting idly as she examines whatever she sees displayed. Today she is in a Gap Kids. She wants to buy a present for Sophie's baby.

"Are you going to get pissed if I buy your baby a pair of overalls? They're so cute."

Sophie laughs ruefully. "Guess what? I'm actually pissing, Tam. Right now, in the upper-level airport bathroom. I have it all to myself."

She's camped out in the handicapped stall at the end of the row; it's three times larger than any of the other stalls. As she quickly runs out of space inside her body, Sophie is looking for breathing room in the outside world.

"So, what's up?" Tam asks. "Why are you at the airport? I wish you'd come see me."

"I can't," Sophie says flatly. "I'm about to give birth."

Tam inhales. "Right now?"

"No. I told you yesterday, Tam. Candace is flying in from Boston."

Tam doesn't listen all that closely to Sophie's reports. The act of shopping takes the edge off Sophie's commentary, which can be pretty gloomy these days. It also distracts Tam from the particulars. Just now she is admiring a diminutive pair of embroidered overalls.

"Don't you just love overalls on babies?" she asks.

Sophie glances down at the pooled pair around her feet. "I love them on everyone. That's all I wear these days, Tam."

"How cool!" Tam replies happily. "It's like I'm reading your mind. Which size should I get? The sizes are confusing."

Sophie sighs. "It's a sweet thought, Tam, but—"

"But what size? Newborn looks so small. It doesn't appear that you're going to have a teeny-tiny little one."

"Fuck, Tam. Do you ever listen to anything I say to you?"

The adoption is something they've gone over on the phone at least a couple of times, but Tam can't wrap her head around it. She keeps forgetting the central fact of Sophie's life right now. Sophie unwinds a length of toilet paper and dabs beneath her eyes. If she's not peeing, she's crying, and sometimes she does both at once, as in this moment.

"I've promised to relinquish the kid. That's why Aunt Candace is here, to take my baby home with her. If you send a pair of overalls, I'll be relinquishing those, too. Up to you. Just thought I'd remind you of the circumstances."

On that note, Candace and Peggy enter Sophie's sanctuary. "I know she came in here," Peggy says. "Sophie! Sophie, are you in here?"

Instead of responding, Sophie lifts her feet from the floor and whispers "shush" into the receiver.

"She came in here a few minutes ago," Peggy says again. Her voice echoes in the long, silent space. Sophie ceases to breathe. Suddenly her mother's presence is dreaded; Candace's is even more so.

"She's probably finished her business and is in one of the gift shops now," Candace offers.

"You think she's shopping?" Peggy asks. Given Sophie's sour mood, it seems unlikely.

"Well, she's not in here," Candace says. And the two of them wander back out.

As soon as they're gone, Sophie drops her feet to the floor and registers a pull in one of her groin muscles. She groans with pain.

For the first time maybe, it occurs to her that choices take us somewhere, and evidently this is where hers have led: straight to a bathroom stall in the Albuquerque airport. Any day now, she could give birth to a child she's neither prepared to care for nor resolved to give up. Until now, Sophie's never had anything but disdain for the regrets and disappointments of adults. Bunch of fuckups is the way she's thought of them. Take Will's mother Laurel, for instance. From the relative safety and distance of adolescence, it's easy to pass judgment, to laugh at a woman who's struggling to hold onto a crappy job and a married man, to finish a college degree at the ripe old age of thirty-five.

Or her mother: she loves this guy Beau, who marries Candace, evidently for her money. Peggy marries, too, a very decent type who isn't her type. She's still secretly pining for Beau, who knocks her up. And then what does she do? Peggy pretends to the world that the child belongs to one man, when she actually belongs to another.

Sophie's begun to see that the really big screw-ups, the mistakes that steer you wrong for the rest of your life, are all about love and sex. Shouldn't someone have warned her?

"What am I going to do?" Sophie asks. She stands up in the stall, tries to stretch, and once again aggravates a groin muscle. It seems that every ligament is stretched to its limits, and her skin, my god, her skin. It's so itchy and tight.

"Is there someone you can trust?" Tam asks.

"You," Sophie replies. She goes still as she hears someone entering. Have Peggy and Candace come back again? She feels her heartbeat pick up and then, nearly instantaneously, registers the baby's agitation. She presses her hands to her belly and closes her eyes, trying to send this new life some reassuring, calm thoughts. *I love you*, she thinks. *I love you*. This is new, and she takes note of it. She's never thought such a thing. Is it that she's never allowed herself to, or that she's never really felt it until now?

"Besides me," Tam is saying. "Someone who knows something. Someone who will tell you the truth."

The empty lobby of Movies West is lined with rows of deserted video games that beep and chatter incessantly. The worn but still garish carpet is sprinkled with popcorn—all the work of one little boy who gets a bag and then, in a delirium of happiness, circles the wide-open space, leaving a trail of oily white kernels in his wake. His mother tries to catch him, but really, that only encourages his caprice. He thinks it's a game, and he shrieks with laughter as he hurtles around the empty space. He can really run, that little boy.

Watching the boy dart past his mother for the third or fourth time, Laurel can't help yearning for Will, who ran circles around her in just the same way. For a while after he left for Lubbock, Laurel consoled herself with the thought that Will needed a father to get him through the tumultuous teen years, someone to take a stronger hand. In this way she managed to reconcile herself with the loss, in a motherly sacrifice of sorts. But last week she got an email from her son. Will said that he was sorry to disappoint her, but he wouldn't be graduating with the rest of his class at Lubbock High. He's flunking a couple of his classes, but he'll make them up in summer school. He and Carlos got a little hooked on playing *Grand Theft Auto*, though he's sworn off video games for now, he told her, or at least until he has his high school diploma. So much for the stronger hand.

Tonight Laurel is holding down the fort alone. On weekdays they no longer pay someone to sit behind the ticket window. She and her boss Roger discussed it and decided that it's just not cost effective. Instead, they've posted hand-lettered signs out front, taped to the ticket window and at eye-level on the glass doors: TICKETS AVAILABLE AT THE SNACK BAR. She is half-expecting Movies West to close, and since she can't afford to be surprised—she has no rainy-day funds to draw on— she's started looking for another job. She knows she could probably find one at one of the new multiplexes, but she doesn't have the heart to in- quire. Laurel has a streak of loyalty that gets in the way of personal advancement.

But then, it's also true that she's tired of sweeping up popcorn and hauling big bags of scarcely used pasteboard out to the dumpster. It all feels so frivolous and wasteful to her. She imagines landfills full of trash from just this one theater, with grease-stained popcorn buckets and liter-sized coke containers still half-full of dark, sugary liquid.

The seven o'clock features are already beginning. But just as there are early arrivers—those who show up a good half hour before the feature begins—so, too, are there stragglers. And though you'd expect them to be, these folks aren't in a hurry when they arrive. Laurel marvels at the way they'll actually waste time debating what size of popcorn to order, then take a leisurely trip to the restroom before ambling into the theater, disturbing the punctual customers with their search for seats in an al- ready darkened space.

So Laurel doesn't think much about this girl coming in late. She doesn't really look up until she hears the greeting.

"Hi, Laurel," the girl says. "Where is everyone?" Even without the new multiplex luring away customers, business would be slow on a weekday evening.

"It's just me," Laurel says, shrugging and smiling.

"You don't recognize me, do you?"

The smile fades slowly as Laurel stares and stares at the girl across the counter. "No, I recognize you, Sophie," she says. "How are you?"

It's a stupid question. Laurel can see how she is: immensely pregnant and pretty miserable. She takes in the girl's features, both familiar and strange. For one thing, Sophie's face is rounder and marred by angry breakouts around her nose and chin. And Laurel is used to the wild storm of hair framing Sophie's features. She doesn't know that she's ever seen Sophie's hair pulled back. But none of that is really the point. None of that is really the difference.

Sophie shrugs and backs off a few feet from the counter, in order to afford Laurel a complete view. "Pretty pregnant," she says.

"Oh god," Laurel replies. "Your due date's around the corner. Have you heard from Will?"

Sophie shakes her head. "He sent the paperwork, but other than that, nada."

Laurel makes her way out from behind the counter and hurries to Sophie's side. Here she's been feeling that Will deserted *her*, but now she's reminded of how Sophie must feel. Laurel knows the disappointment, the anxiety, the loss of self-esteem.

Awkwardly, the two embrace, and when they pull away, Sophie tugs at the T-shirt inside her overalls, pulling it down over several inches of exposed skin. She wears a rueful grimace. "For months my mom has been after me to buy more maternity clothes, but I just feel stupid when I think of going to one of those places at the mall."

"Motherhood Maternity?"

"Yeah, right. That's it. I haven't been to a mall since Christmas." Sophie grimaces. "Imagine that."

"The overalls work," Laurel says. "The overalls look good, actually." She continues, "Will said they dropped the charges."

"Thank goodness. My punishment is that I'm supposed to stay out of Victoria's Secret. 'Don't darken our doorway,' they said. No pushup bras for Sophie."

"Doesn't look like you're in need of a pushup."

"I'm due next week."

Sophie insists on helping with the stocking and cleaning, the sweeping and trash removal. She knows the routine, and in under an hour the work is done. Though they consider having their talk in the office, the chairs are uncomfortable and Sophie wants to put up her feet. "Let's pretend we're watching a movie," she suggests, casting a glance toward the boxes of peanut M&Ms.

Laurel laughs and tosses her a box of candy, then fixes both of them something to drink. They make their way down the purple-carpeted hallway and into one of the empty theaters. As they pass through the doorway, Laurel flips the switch that illuminates the center aisle. It's just enough light to offer a dim view of the rows of seats. They're both tired, and as they settle into the back row, they sigh in tandem.

"So, what can I do to help?" Laurel asks.

Sophie is staring at the empty white screen. She doesn't answer right away. Laurel is about to repeat her question when Sophie clears her throat and sighs deeply, directing the exhalation through her lips and making the blowing sound she's learned in her Lamaze class. "Let's see. Where should I start?" She positions her hands on the dome of her belly, fingers splayed, facing one another. A smile plays across her face.

"Is the baby kicking?" Laurel asks.

Sophie nods.

"May I feel?"

"Yeah, sure. Why should you be any different than every stranger on the street?"

This is more like it, Laurel thinks. The old insouciant Sophie. But the past is gone the instant Laurel presses her hand to Sophie's flesh, then allows Sophie to reposition her hand to a spot much closer to the girl's groin.

Even though she knows what she's going to feel, Laurel is still awed. Who wouldn't be? And as Sophie is quick to point out, "That's your grandchild throwing punches."

They are both silent for a moment, lost in what they feel going on beneath their hands.

"I'm sorry this is so fucked up, Laurel," Sophie says. "In your own crazed way you tried to bring us to our senses, but it just didn't seem real, not to me and probably not to Will either." She smiles to herself. "Sure as hell feels real to me now."

Laurel is ashamed. Here she's been through it, this same ordeal, and yet she's ignored Sophie's plight. Dramatic word, "plight," but it's the one that comes to mind. "What can I do to help you?"

"I need a place to stay."

"How is that? You can't go home?"

Sophie shrugs. She doesn't want to mention Candace just yet. "I need to get away and figure things out. I don't know what to do. I keep changing my mind."

"Oh, Sophie," Laurel moans. "This is *so* hard. I remember how hard this is."

"You were around my age, weren't you? When you had Will, I mean?"

Laurel nods. "Yes, as a matter of fact."

"And what did they say to you? Your parents, I mean."

"They were ashamed and embarrassed, and they begged me to get married."

Sophie is silent. "And you did."

"And I did, but it was a disaster. The only upside was this: marriage made it possible for me to keep Will. Otherwise I don't think I could have . . ."

Sophie has given up on the blank screen and is sitting slouched, belly aloft, face to the ceiling. Tears are running down the sides of her cheeks. She's biting her lip. "And I guess there's no way Will would consider marrying me?"

"That's not necessary, is it?"

"It might be," Sophie replies, then thinks better of it. "I'm joking. You know I'm not that pathetic. Not that *you* were pathetic," she adds.

"I know what you mean. Times have changed."

It's after midnight when they pull into Laurel's driveway. Before they go inside, Laurel insists that Sophie turn on her cell phone and call home. Sophie moans and tries to beg off—"They'll be asleep"—but Laurel points out that they won't sleep until they've heard from her, until they know she's safe. And Laurel is right, of course. Peggy answers on the first ring, and immediately thanks Sophie for calling.

"I know it wasn't easy, baby girl," she says.

Sophie replies crossly, "I'm not a baby girl. I'm about to be a baby's mother." Then she bursts into tears. Laurel pries the phone out of her hands and finishes the conversation. She volunteers to take Sophie to New Futures on Thursday and Friday; then on Saturday, they'll all get together and talk it through.

When she hands the phone back to Sophie, she says, "There, now everyone will be able to sleep peacefully, including me."

Sophie is so tired that she considers going to bed without even washing her face. But she hates the zits. The zits are killing her. So she goes into the one and only bathroom and tries to turn on the hot water, forgetting that the knob is stuck. Still. It's been this way for how long? Ever since Sophie has known Laurel.

This time last year, she had stood before this same sink and regarded her reflection in the mirror. She'd looked pretty good, except for the big-ass catsup stain on the front of a cotton blouse she'd borrowed from Peggy. "Shit, shit, shit," she'd chanted as she wiped at the spot with a washcloth that smelled of mold. "What's wrong with the hot water?" she called down the hall to Will.

"It doesn't work!" he yelled back. She was incredulous. Whose bathroom sink doesn't have hot water?

It seems so long ago, that moment. Now she hardly remembers what Will looks like. She can no longer picture him in her mind's eye. She goes to the tub and, after steadying herself with a hand on the wall, sits down gingerly on the ledge. She turns on the tap, adjusting the temperature of the water and leaning over as best she can to splash her face.

The door is open. Laurel stops in to apologize. "I've been meaning to date a plumber, Sophie."

Sophie looks up, surprised. "Do you date?" she asks, then rushes to apologize. "I don't mean—"

"No offense taken."

Laurel is waiting for Sophie to finish in the bathroom so she can brush her teeth. She's wearing a pink chenille robe, which makes Sophie think of the fiasco at Victoria's Secret. She wonders what Will ended up getting his mother for Christmas. Perhaps he got a robe after all—this robe, even—but not at Victoria's Secret. She would ask, but she doesn't want to bring up a sore subject.

Laurel concedes that it's true she doesn't do much dating.

"Why not?"

"No time. No energy. No takers. When Will was younger, I didn't have the money for a sitter. These days I hardly ever meet anyone. I'm not the sort to strike up a conversation in the grocery store. I have a friend who cruises the aisles of Home Depot, but I have my pride." She leans against the doorway and shakes her head slowly. "So I make do with a married lover. Two nights a week he tiptoes in around midnight. We whisper to one another in the dark. He skulks here, he skulks home again." She stops and considers the day of the week. "Today's Wednesday, right?"

Sophie nods. She pretends the lover is news to her, though he isn't.

"Well, Ralph won't be over tonight." She sighs. "Just as well cuz I'm really tired."

She disappears and then returns, bringing Sophie a washcloth. "I've put clean sheets on Will's bed." A strange smile comes over her face. "Think you'll sleep okay?"

Sophie shrugs. She's too tired to see the irony in any of this, and too young.

On Thursday morning, Laurel jostles Sophie awake just after six. By the time the girl has showered and raided Will's closet for a clean T-shirt to wear under her overalls, it's after six forty and time to leave. School starts at seven thirty. She doesn't have her backpack, which means she doesn't have her books. But it's not the end of the world, she tells Laurel as she sits down to a quick bowl of cereal in the kitchen. Her first class of the day is creative writing, and her teacher is a sweet and forgiving woman named Nancy. "She never gets mad," Sophie says. "She's so encouraging, too."

"You call your teachers by their first names?"

Sophie nods. "A lot of the girls wear those flannel pajama pants to school, and Nancy wears them, too."

Laurel is eating oatmeal. She pauses, the spoon halfway to her mouth, to observe that the school sounds like a multigenerational slumber party.

Sophie nods happily. "Cool," she says. "A slumber party with tests and grades." After pouring another half bowl of Cheerios, she goes on to describe the school's two day-care centers—one for the babies, another for the toddlers. "And you can nurse during class!" Sophie exclaims, a fine spray of milk coming out with her words. "They page you from the nursery when your baby is hungry."

Laurel is amazed. "God, I wish they'd had a place like that when *I* was pregnant. It would have made all the difference."

Sophie nods repeatedly, though she seems not to have processed Laurel's realization. "I like it there because I'm just like everyone else," she concludes.

For two trimesters, Laurel had managed to hide her pregnancy with baggy clothes. But in her seventh month, realizing the futility of the effort, she broke the news to her mother, who in turn informed Laurel's father. Such a disappointment Laurel was! Thanks to Title IX, the 1972 educational act, Laurel didn't have to worry about being kicked out of school—as had happened to Carlos's mother, Sylvia—but federal legislation couldn't mitigate a father's disappointment. He didn't speak to her; he didn't look at her. For all intents and purposes, she ceased to exist.

As a consequence, Will never developed a bond with his maternal grandparents. Although he did meet his grandmother, the meetings were uncomfortable for both of them. His grandmother would hug him too tightly, kiss him too fervently. Then he got to be six or so, and he couldn't be coaxed into sitting in her lap any longer. Laurel would arrange to meet at the park, where Will's grandmother would sit on a bench, hands folded in her lap, and watch as he made a show of playing on the equipment. He wore himself out at the task of having fun. Knowing he was being observed, Will couldn't relax.

This state of affairs continued until the death of Laurel's mother. At the funeral, Laurel finally had the opportunity to introduce her son to his grandfather, who wept openly at the sight of the boy. Compounding the loss, even today Will sees little enough of his paternal grandparents, though they live only a few miles away. Poor boy. He's starving for family. Often, those who've suffered continue the cycle. So it was with Carlos's mother, who labeled Laurel "*la cusca* Laurel." But being called a slut wasn't nearly as upsetting as being forced to sit out in the car whenever Carlos took baby Will to visit his grandmother. Laurel's heart was broken.

To her credit, she manages to break the cycle. She will not give as good as she got in the weeks to come. She will, in fact, give something better: compassion.

In the car on the way across town, Sophie asks Laurel how she made her decision, how she decided what to do about the pregnancy. Laurel has anticipated the question and thought about her answer.

"Well, I suppose I could have had an abortion, but not without some assistance, and Carlos's parents are devout Catholics. My mother was equally religious in her own way. Not that I asked her advice. I certainly didn't. To the best of my ability, I hid my condition. I remember swiping a girdle out of my mom's drawer. I wore it through my sixth month, if you can believe that."

Sophie can't really fathom it. "That doesn't sound healthy."

Laurel turns to look at Sophie directly. "I'm sure it wasn't ideal, but he was just fine—not a big boy, but not small either."

The light changes, and someone behind their car honks impatiently. Startled, Laurel lets off the clutch and lurches into the intersection. Sophie gasps at the jerking motion and the seatbelt tightening against her belly. This close to her due date, she thinks anything might induce labor, even something inconsequential. "I'm not ready!" she blurts out.

"What?" Seeing Sophie's face, Laurel allows herself a little smirk. "Don't worry. It's not that easy to induce labor, especially the first time around. You'll probably hold onto that baby for at least another week or so."

Sophie hopes so. She wouldn't have imagined this moment even a few weeks ago: riding in a car with Laurel, just the two of them, and hoping to stay pregnant forever.

Saturday dawns. It's a gloriously calm and brilliant weekend morning. Laurel has agreed to take Sophie home in the morning, in time for a family meeting scheduled for nine. It all sounds so civilized to Laurel, and as the two are leaving the house, she shares this observation with Sophie.

"Maybe," Sophie replies. "I've never thought about it. We always have them. Like after my dad's heart attack. That way, everyone can voice an opinion . . . and immediately get shot down for it by the rest of the family."

"That's what I mean," Laurel says, smiling warmly and locking the door behind her. "Civilized!"

Laurel has all sorts of smiles. Most people convey emotions through their eyes, but Laurel's eyes are small and widely spaced. She relies, then, on her mouth—which is certainly her best facial feature. Her lips are fleshy, her teeth white and evenly spaced. She draws attention to her mouth with red lipstick, which she carries at all times and reapplies frequently.

On the way across town, Sophie shares everything she knows about the commune meetings. Laurel is surprised to learn that the tradition of Granger family meetings grew out of Peggy's experience at the commune. At Morningstar the meetings were generally weekly, and they were mandatory. Miss three meetings and you were out on your ass. Somebody put up a sign, and they all abided by it. Otherwise, though, the meetings tended to be unruly and unproductive. Unlike the Granger meetings, during which Jack imposes Robert's Rules of Order, the commune meetings were free-for-alls.

The morning people were pitted against the evening people. That was the situation in a nutshell. Two groups of people tended to be drawn to communal living; Peggy called them the "morning people" and the "evening people." The morning people believed in structure—they tended to get up early, meditate or practice yoga, work in the garden. They smoked pot if they needed to unwind, and they communed with nature and each other. The evening people were the partiers. They crawled out of their sleeping bags around noon, and from then on they were gearing up for some sort of celebration. They rode motorcycles and horses; they hunted; and at night they built bonfires, drummed loudly, and got drunk.

"The morning people sound like adults, and the evening people sound like children," Laurel comments.

Sophie nods. "I guess that's true," she says.

For the rest of the ride, they are silent. Neither feels the need for small talk. Laurel hums as she waits for the light to change at Osuna and Fourth Street. Last night she slept better than she has of late, perhaps because someone else was in the house. She hasn't often been alone in the last seventeen years, and in the last few months, she's discovered that she doesn't much care for solitude.

The gravel approach to the house is only wide enough for one car at a time, but it's a straight shot, so drivers have advance notice. The accepted protocol is that the outbound vehicle has the right-of-way. Sophie spots a red sedan headed out and directs Laurel to pull off the road. "Never seen that car," she says, then quickly realizes that it's Candace's rental and that Ian is in the passenger seat.

When the sedan slows and then stops alongside Laurel's car, Sophie rolls down her window. Ian's is already down. His hair is combed, still damp from the shower, and he's wearing a bright-green Celtics T-shirt, apparently a gift from Candace. Sophie is about to ask if they're on their way to Dunkin' Donuts. But before she can even inquire, Ian provides the answer.

"We're going to get my teepee!" His face is flushed. To prove his point, he waves a fistful of printouts from the web.

From behind the wheel, Candace calls out, "Good morning! We're sorry to miss the meeting, but Ian has been waiting for his teepee long enough. I hope I'll have another chance to meet you, Laurel," she adds, crouching to make eye contact.

"Certainly!" Laurel replies. "Maybe you'll be back before I leave."

"We're going to Taos!" Ian interrupts.

"Are you sure?" Sophie asks. She feels tears welling up, along with a fear she can't really account for. Ian shrinks back in the seat and allows Candace to lean closer to the window.

"You need some space, Sophie. You and Peggy and Jack sit down with Laurel and talk it through. I'll find a way to be okay with whatever decision you make. *Really*, I promise you."

And then, before Sophie can muster an answer, Candace offers a short wave and the car pulls away.

"Gosh," Sophie says. And then again, "Gosh."

"Are you disappointed?" Laurel asks when they've pulled around the corner of the house and parked.

"No, I mean, it's great for Ian. You have no idea how much he wants a teepee. But I was just imagining that she would be sitting across the table from me, telling me all the reasons why my baby would be better off with her."

Laurel shrugs. "Guess she surprised you, huh?"

"No kidding!" Sophie replies. When she can't hold back the tears, she simply bends over, headfirst, and weeps onto her belly.

Laurel sits for a few minutes and rubs Sophie's back. She focuses on the red T-shirt Sophie is wearing, recalling exactly the circumstances under which she gave it to her son. She'd just enrolled in classes at the University of New Mexico, and in addition to buying an armful of used textbooks, she'd picked up a shirt for Will. The front is emblazoned with the fierce face of a wolf—the UNM Lobo—but the bib of Sophie's overalls hides the mascot.

For a few seconds, Laurel's thoughts drift away from the moment at hand. She wonders why he chose to leave the shirt behind. Was it because she gave it to him? That's ridiculous, she tells herself. He's probably outgrown it. But the thought circles back and presents itself again: *because I gave it to him.* Before she starts weeping herself, out of self-pity, out of pure self-pity, Laurel reapplies her lipstick, then opens the door and climbs out of the car. She thinks about telling Sophie to take her time, but that seems gratuitous. Sophie is home, after all. Laurel is the visitor.

Jack is out in the field behind the house. He turns when the car door slams, and gestures for Laurel to join him. He's wearing bee overalls and a long-sleeved white T-shirt, but no veil.

"Me?" she shouts, pointing to herself. She can't imagine what he would want with her out there, though she doesn't mind making the short trek to the hives. She'd just as soon visit the bees—she'd just as soon get stung by one or two of them as sit down at the kitchen table with Sophie and Peggy. Slowly, Laurel weaves her way around the bushy sage and chamisa, picking her route carefully in order to safeguard her white cloth sneakers, her favorite spring and summer shoes—a ridiculously impractical choice for the sandy, dusty environment in which she finds herself. But it could be worse, she thinks. She could be wearing slingbacks or high heels, or something equally silly. She doesn't worry too much about getting the sneakers dirty. She throws them in the washing machine with a little bleach, and when they wear out, she heads to Target for another pair.

Before she's reached the hive boxes, she stops short, more out of deference than fear. She assumes Jack wouldn't have invited her out here if there were any real danger, but she'll stand back and wait for him to give her further directions.

"Hold on just a minute," he says.

Once a week or so, he's made a habit of checking on the hives he still has left, just to assure himself that all is well. He hasn't yet decided whether to invest in three new packages of bees. He wants to wait and see how the rest of his bees fare this summer. All over the country, all over the world, bees are vanishing; it's a mystery that's been much in the news. Jack has taken to meeting for coffee with three or four local bee-keepers. None of the others have lost bees yet, but they are following the news just as closely as Jack is.

The morning air is a little chilly. Laurel pulls her jean jacket closed and folds her arms under her breasts. She watches as Jack removes the outside cover from the red box and then, with the help of a tool that resembles a beer opener, pries away the inner cover. Nearby, on the ground, his smoker stands ready. To Laurel, anyway, it resembles the disembodied head of the Tin Man in *The Wizard of Oz*.

Practiced and comfortable, Jack reaches down for the smoker, and as he raises and directs it, he presses the bellow smartly between his arm and belly, dousing the bees with smoke. He wears a wide grin when he turns to her, and it occurs to Laurel that he's showing off. In fact, he's relieved, even a little giddy, because all is well with the other hives. The colony is making honey. He can see that the bees are going about their business, heading out the entrance in a steady stream. They are bound for the banks of the Rio Grande, where the salt cedar is in bloom. The pink, frothy flowers resemble cotton candy, and for the bees at least, they're just as sweet.

Still holding the smoker, Jack strolls over to Laurel. "Do you like bees?" he asks. He squints in the bright sun, which gives his broad, weathered face a tentative expression.

"I don't know any bees," she replies.

He laughs appreciatively.

Laurel asks the obvious question: "Why the smoke?"

Again he grins. "Simple. The smoke makes them act like their hives are on fire. Which predisposes them to fill their bellies with honey."

"In preparation for abandoning the hive?"

"Exactly. When their bellies are full, they have trouble assuming the stinging posture." With his free hand, he crooks a finger to show her how it looks. "That's the rationale, but you know, I think they're just happier when their little tummies are full."

"Is that why you buy donuts for the family meetings?"

"Did Sophie tell you? She probably thinks I forgot, but I just left the box in the backseat of my car for safekeeping."

"She'll be delighted. I fed her breakfast, but I think she was looking forward to the sweets."

Jack shrugs. "We are all looking forward to the sweets. No different than the bees, I suppose."

He waits until they're standing beside his dusty station wagon to tell her that Peggy is closing Everyday Satin. "Best if you don't mention the place to my wife. She's taking it pretty hard."

Laurel has a mental picture of Peggy standing behind the counter in that shadowy little shop. "Hi there," she'd called when Laurel came through the door. No doubt Peggy's identity is bound up in being the proprietor, something Laurel intuited on the day she visited. That explains why Laurel lashed out as she did, making fun of Peggy's merchandise and not the woman herself. Now Laurel regrets her words. At the time she blamed Peggy for their situation, but that was shortsighted and unfair.

"Such a shame," Laurel says.

Jack shrugs. "It was time, you know. No, hell, it was way, *way* past time." He leans against the car door and sighs deeply. "We should have pulled the plug on that place five or ten years ago. Maybe it would have been easier on Peg if we'd done it back then. I know this much: it certainly would have saved us a hell of a lot of money." He shakes his head and sighs deeply. For another few seconds, he goes on leaning against the car, then, exhaling loudly, he pushes himself to a standing position.

Once he's collected the box of donuts from the backseat, he clears his throat and offers Laurel a smile. The back door is still standing open. She can see that he's not the neatest man. The floorboards are littered with Taco Bell trash.

"I assume you feel as I do," he says, "that we should be looking out for the baby's best interests?"

Laurel nods repeatedly. "Absolutely."

"I'm not a sentimental man," he says, his eyes searching her face. "I don't want to do the sentimental thing. I've gone to New Futures with Sophie, and I've seen those girls hauling their babies and their backpacks and their diaper bags, shoulders hunched to the load. It's a brave thing they're doing, and maybe it's the best thing in their particular situations. I'm not making judgments here, you understand. But I don't think Sophie is ready for motherhood. You have your own vote, of course, but I hope you'll consider following my lead."

Laurel is a little perplexed. "Do we vote?" she asks.

He laughs and hands the box of donuts over to her. "No, we don't vote. But we speak our minds. Excuse me a minute," he says, "while I rid myself of this infernal bee suit."

He drops onto the edge of the backseat and begins to peel off the white overalls. In spite of her intention to do otherwise, Laurel watches the process. When he's finished, when the bee suit is rolled up and stowed in the storage space behind the seat, Laurel addresses him.

"I've spoken my mind already. Sophie's asked me what it's like to be a single mother, and I've tried to give her an unvarnished, accurate picture. It's not hard to sound bitter and disappointed."

He pats her on the shoulder. "She came to you in her hour of need, as we say. And you didn't let her down."

She grins broadly. "If I weren't holding this box of donuts, I'd be tempted to give you a hug."

"Don't you endanger those donuts, young lady! We won't get through this meeting without them, I can guarantee that."

Position #9—"Her Hopes And Fears"

To be self-aware is to know your hopes and fears and look beyond them. This card shows you the way.

⁓ The Fool (Reversed) ⁓

In the upright position, we are all foolish when we are young. The Fool is an innocent. Approaching a cliff, he gazes raptly into the future. The white rose he clutches symbolizes purity, and his canine companion represents animal instincts. The Fool's belongings are tied up in the satchel. He is ready to take a leap of faith.

In the reversed position, the Fool's journey may be longer and harder, but the destination is still within reach. It's in your power to change your thoughts and feelings, and thus the energy surrounding the situation.

LATER SOPHIE WILL wish she hadn't waited, that she'd forced herself to get up and trudge downstairs to pee. But these days she's like a camel, always holding onto a little water. So what's a little more? When she awakens in the midst of a dream, she is too deep in her misery to be practical. For the first time, Sophie has dreamed of Anna Marie, Will's Lubbock girlfriend and Sophie's rival. Tam has told her about this kind of Texas girl—grown only in the Lone Star State—and in the weeks since, Sophie has brooded on the particulars. Anna Marie wears her blonde hair in a ponytail and is Southern Baptist through and through.

She has signed an abstinence agreement at her church, and she torments Will by offering him sexy kisses and no follow-through, or at least none that will break her hymen. This is the kind of girl he'll marry, Sophie thinks. *I'm the kind of girl he knocked up.* And then she has a surprising revelation: Laurel was the kind of girl Carlos knocked up.

For a few minutes, she drops back into a deep sleep, arms and hands curled around her belly. When she wakes again, her bladder is achingly full. The baby is pressing down harder than she can remember. Sophie rolls onto her back and stretches her legs, pointing her toes and releasing them. The exercise is something she saw one of the other girls doing in her Lamaze class, but for Sophie, the stretching precipitates a charley horse, an odd, wrenching pain that fades slowly. Groaning, she rolls off the mattress and pushes up onto all fours, then rises to her feet.

It's early morning, and the house is still. New light coming through Sophie's windows rounds off the surfaces of things; her bedroom resembles a photograph rather than real life. In the days to come, she won't be able to say what happened or why. She thinks maybe the charley horse returned, or she might have tripped. Any number of small calamities might be blamed for the fall, a short tumble in the stairwell that she announces with a loud scream.

Ian arrives first. He hustles down the stairs and bends over her, and when he can't think of what else to do, he crouches close and kisses her cheek.

"Are you okay?" he asks again and again, not sure at first why it is so wet around her. He's been reading Sophie's pregnancy book, the one she was issued at New Futures, so he knows about the bag of water that can break before labor begins. But the smell is familiar. Sophie has wet herself, and a puddle of urine seeps into the spaces between the bricks, pooling around her. She is crying, so loudly and so long that Peggy comes running, too.

Candace is holed up in Taos and Jack is in Vermont with his mother. That leaves Peggy in charge. After she hurries Sophie into the shower, she considers calling Jack. Pausing in the doorway of the bathroom, gathering her wits, Peggy recalls the night she'd called Jack in Vermont. She'd been helpless, full of irrelevant worries and taxed by the simple task of finding a bottle of rum.

"Call if you need me," she tells Sophie, then hurries down the hall toward the stairwell. Ian is using bathroom towels to mop up the mess. "Thank you, Ian," she remembers to say.

Ian conveys the wet and smelly towels into the laundry room and starts a load of washing. Across the hall is the bathroom. Ian hears the spray of the shower and, off and on, the sound of his sister wailing. Ian is scared to death. He opens the door to check on her, just to be sure she's all right. "Can I do anything to help you?" he asks.

Sophie turns off the shower and extends her hand. "Can you give me a towel, Ian?"

He checks the hooks, notices that the towels have mysteriously disappeared, then remembers that he's just finished stuffing all of them into the washing machine.

"Do you think I killed my baby, Ian?" Sophie asks from behind the shower door.

He can't fathom the question, so he blurts out, "I'll be right back." He goes to get his sister a towel from the linen closet. By the time he returns he can hear her inside, turning on the sink's faucet. He knocks cautiously.

"Just hand it through the doorway," Sophie instructs. He is relieved to do just that and then scurry back to a chore he can hope to master: laundry.

He's ready to turn on the machine when his mother arrives at the bathroom door, carrying clothes in one hand, Sophie's moccasins in the other. "Sophie?" she says. She doesn't even sound like herself. Everything that comes out of her mouth has the cadence of a question. And the tenor of her voice has dropped, or else has gone flat. She's a ghost mother. "Sophie, I've got your clothes?"

No answer.

Ian stops what he's doing, goes entirely still, and listens as his mother knocks again at the bathroom door.

"Do you think her baby is okay?" he asks. The question comes out in a whisper, directed at the laundry room wall. He doesn't expect his mother to hear it, much less answer it, but she does—not right away, but eventually. For the moment, they are both distracted. Sophie has opened the door and is standing naked and wide-eyed in the yellow bathroom light. She's clutching her bulbous belly, so big now that her breasts, also large, appear to rest on it. It's a frightening, fantastic sight. His sister is the center of the universe; his sister *is* the universe. In this family right now, there is only Sophie. They are all small stars or moons or bits of debris, orbiting about her. They cast light, in the case of Ian, or they cast shadows.

He takes it all in, only to recall it later in fragments, oddly compelling bits that he won't be able to integrate into a complete picture. He sees it all, though not in any particular order: the milky-white skin, the chapped lips, the mass of black curls draped over one shoulder, those wild eyes and wet cheeks. His poor sister. Her splayed fingers grip her belly. Ian will never forget this sight, the most amazing and moving in his life thus far.

From this point forward, the sight of a woman's splayed fingers will rivet his attention, as with his ninth-grade homeroom teacher. She will start each morning with a news item, something gleaned from the *New York Times* and featuring another part of the world. The lesson includes the globe; indeed, the globe is the lesson's *raison d'être*. The one his teacher employs can be lifted from its hanger and held aloft like a soccer ball. She carries it around the room, situated in her splayed fingers to best display the country they're discussing. She wants them to learn to identify the countries. That's the whole point, though Ian is most often fixated on her fingers.

Then there is the piano teacher, the woman he'll marry. From her thumb to her pinky, she can stretch an octave. She will demonstrate it for him one afternoon in the Student Union Building at the University of New Mexico. She'll be stationed at the grand piano in the ballroom, not playing anything, just absorbing the ambience. And he will wander into the big empty room—early, as usual, for an evening lecture—and ask her to play something for him.

"Do you know how to get there?" Sophie asks when the three of them have piled into the car.

"Of course I do," Peggy replies, but she sounds more confident than she feels.

The hospitals are all on the other side of town. Peggy chooses

Presbyterian because it's easy to find. She knows it is just off I-25, at the University Boulevard exit. But the hospital is not as she remembered it, not at all. What used to be a turn-in to a parking lot has become a full-fledged street that accesses a complex of buildings, each one bigger and starker than the one before. Parking has been moved to the east side of the building, to a lot that sprawls off into the distance. It's plenty big enough to lose your car in. There's a parking garage as well, Peggy notes as she creeps down the street that runs alongside the burgeoning buildings.

She supposes it would have been nearly ten years ago now that she got a call from Candace, alerting her to the illness of one of the commune family members. He was someone Peggy hadn't seen in years, a man she'd turned to on occasion when Beau was in one of his indifferent moods. There were quite a few of those men, as she remembers now. This one's name was Derek, and he was in the hospital in Albuquerque. Candace had pleaded with her to go see him. Peggy, though dreading it, eventually did the right thing.

Once over the hurdle, once she'd reacquainted herself with someone she hadn't seen in years, Peggy visited regularly until Derek died. It had seemed to her that Derek didn't have many other visitors, maybe not *any* other visitors. He was so pleased to wake up from a deep sleep to the sight of a familiar face.

As she looks for a place to park, Peggy recalls the halting conversation they had, the one during which she'd inquired as to how he had contracted the virus. It turned out that he had been an IV drug user. Wasted his life, he'd said, tears in his eyes. *Wasted it.*

The lot is only about half-full, and once they've found a spot and are out of the car, Peggy follows a sign pointing the way to the emergency room, which is in the midst of a renovation. "I think we should start out at the emergency room," she says to Sophie. She leads her daughter past a temporary fence, erected to keep people from trespassing on the construction area. Peggy has a hold of Sophie's arm.

"Don't tell them," Sophie says.

But Peggy is concentrating. She doesn't see well in the dark. In her whole life, she's never had to wear glasses—something she's always been vain about—but now she needs them. It occurs to her that she shouldn't be driving around town without glasses. Everything is blurry. Why didn't she realize that sooner? Distracted, she asks her daughter, "Don't tell them what?"

"Don't tell them I wet myself," Sophie hisses. She shakes loose from her mother's grasp and stands her ground in the parking lot. Ian has been trailing the two of them, and he stops a good ten feet away, as though to offer a modicum of privacy. Not that he can't hear every word that passes between them.

Peggy's hesitation isn't meant to broach argument. She's simply a little befuddled by her daughter's request. Is that what Sophie thinks this is about?

Sophie begins to cry, and the words that follow come out in a wail: "I didn't mean to!"

"This really is hard, isn't it?" Peggy isn't so much commiserating as she is looking for validation. "When exactly was it that our lives went to hell?"

Sophie knows. She supplies an answer immediately. "When Jack had his heart attack. Nothing has been right since."

They are getting somewhere with this discussion, but it's not the time or the place for it, as evidenced by an ambulance that turns the corner and bumps over the curb. The lights aren't flashing; it's not a genuine emergency. The patient has been in a car accident and has broken her leg. She's a teenager, too, as it happens. When Peggy and Sophie don't move out of the way fast enough, the ambulance driver blasts a warning, a honk so loud and obnoxious that it all but lifts mother and daughter off the ground. Ian scuttles around them and disappears inside. Peggy will find him later in the waiting area, watching cartoons.

The emergency room entrance is temporary, erected hastily and without any real attention to detail. It reminds Sophie of last year's Valley High School haunted house, which also had a twisting temporary entrance, perhaps assembled with the same sort of plastic panels. These are nailed at intervals, and the seams are sealed over with red and blue tape, layer after layer. While Sophie recollects the haunted house, Peggy is reminded of the packages Sophie used to wrap, all the tape she used, layer after layer applied haphazardly. "Good lord," she says aloud. "Do you suppose this was constructed by children?"

Sophie doesn't answer. She doesn't really register the question. A pair of stretchers beside the wall has captured her attention. "I guess we're in the right place," she says. As they round the corner, the two suddenly find themselves in the thick of things, nurses and doctors hurrying in both directions, signs shouting TRIAGE and *REGISTRARSE*/CHECK IN.

"What do we do now?" Sophie asks.

They are standing, obvious interlopers or strangers, in the middle of a linoleum intersection. The worker bees in colorful scrubs—periwinkle, purple, and pink—pay them no mind. If Peggy and Sophie have an emergency, it isn't apparent, which gives them a boost of confidence. At least they don't look like a disaster. Others elsewhere—hidden behind curtains and doors—are worse off.

Peggy is expecting a glass window with a round hole for communication, the sort of thing you see in banks and prison visiting rooms. This check-in station is really nothing more than a Dutch door, open on top and closed on the bottom. A clipboard rests on the narrow counter, and near it is a pen with a stem that's clearly been chewed. Peggy hesitates, then fishes in her purse for a pen of her own. She'd just as soon not grip a surface that's been gnawed by a stranger. Perhaps that's fastidious of her, but she feels justified.

She bends over the clipboard and begins to form the letters, and as she does so she takes note of the fact that her hands are shaking. She registers the symptom but isn't sure what it's caused by, whether she's frightened or hungry. Probably hungry. She can't remember when she last ate.

A female voice inquires, "May I help you?"

Peggy raises her head and comes perilously close to burying her face in the biggest bosom she's encountered in years. She forgets to straighten and address the nurse face to face. Instead, she directs her response to the woman's chest, which is covered with dozens of tiny hot air balloons floating every which way in a blue, blue sky.

"What if I don't have my insurance card?" Peggy asks.

She hears the woman sigh. "Well," the nurse says. "Do you have means for payment, then? If you don't have a means for payment, we're going to request that you go over to UNM Hospital. Do you know where that is?"

Ordinarily Peggy would straighten and look the woman in the eye. Ordinarily she would be indignant at the insinuation that she might be indigent. She had her fill of those interactions during her years in the commune. Now that Peggy thinks of it, she recalls going to the hospital with Jimbo and Denise when their baby was sick. It was humiliating the way they were treated. "Are you just going to let my kid die?" Jimbo ended up asking.

Of course, they hadn't. The doctor and nurses had treated Banshee's ear infection, and later on they'd set his broken leg. And if they hadn't looked happy about it—and they hadn't—at least they didn't take out their frustration on a helpless little boy. The disdain they felt for the grimy parents was fairly evident, but they were kind and caring to the child. Peggy remembers this and takes heart.

"I do have insurance," she is quick to explain, "but I'm not sure I have my card on me." She reaches around for her purse and pats at its sides, hoping to ferret out something with the dimensions of a wallet. Now she worries that she left that at home. But she's in luck. She has both the wallet and, tucked away inside, the insurance card.

"Be glad you're insured," the nurse says.

"Oh, I am," Peggy replies.

The nurse flips a page on her clipboard and gets down to business, asking Peggy a series of questions. "Your daughter is nine months pregnant?"

Peggy nods. It's her turn to sigh. She has not gotten used to this predicament. She has not managed to make her peace with it. At first, around the time she read Sophie's cards, Peggy was philosophic. It wasn't real to her then, the pregnancy, so she could afford to take the long view. But as the months have worn on, her daughter has changed: she has grown heavier and slower and more serious.

"And she's sixteen?"

"Just turned seventeen."

A nod accompanied by a pursing of the lips.

Peggy feels judged, found inadequate and ridiculous. She wishes she could put aside her pride, but she can't seem to manage it. For the first few months, she was too intent on hustling Sophie to the abortion clinic. No other alternative seemed possible. Once the time for that had passed, she drifted into a depression. Did she think that if she stayed in her bedroom for a few months, the whole thing would blow over? She's not sure what she thought. Certainly she's done all the wrong things. All wrong. She wonders now whether she can resolve to do better, whether it's possible to get the ship that is this family's life moving in the right direction, whether there will be time for that.

"She fell down some stairs? And did she hurt herself?"

Peggy says, "No, apparently not. But she's worried that she might have hurt the baby." And there it is: a flood of feeling, the first real rush of feeling that she can remember in months. And along with the feelings come tears. She's standing there with wet cheeks, blubbering. It's such a relief to feel something—even fear, even shame.

The nurse is touched. "Not to worry, darling," she says, edging out of the Dutch door and patting Peggy's shoulder. "Let's go see your daughter."

Sophie is sitting just around the corner, in an orange plastic chair that cradles her body. She sits with her feet planted and her hands clasping her belly, a large mound that presses against the front of her overalls. Her hair is wild, a tangle of curls.

"Is that her?" the nurse asks. "She doesn't look like you." She quickly corrects herself. "I'm sorry. I don't know why I said that."

Peggy shrugs. "That's all right. It's true. She looks like her father."

"She's a beautiful girl," the nurse says. She strides up to Sophie, brandishing the clipboard. "Why don't you come with me, young lady?" And she leads her away, off down the linoleum hallway. Peggy sits down with one last sigh.

When the nurse returns and invites Peggy to join Sophie in the examining room, Peggy digs in her purse and offers Ian a dollar for the snack machine. He smiles up at her, says thanks, and then, suddenly remembering their purpose here, asks about Sophie.

"She's fine," Peggy assures him. "I'm sure she's just fine."

She is and she isn't. She's donned a hospital gown that shifts across her belly, has to be readjusted, and shifts again. She's perched on the edge of the examining table. It's apparent that she's been crying.

The resident leans against the wall. She looks like a tired child. Wispy blonde hair streams down her back. She's thin and pale and practically the last person in the hospital Peggy would have identified as her daughter's physician. When Peggy was Sophie's age, the show *Peyton Place* was on everyone's lips. One of the stars was a young woman named Mia Farrow. The resident resembles the actress, right down to the carefully neutral way she holds her mouth as she explains that an ultrasound is called for.

"Anyone ever tell you that you look like Alice in Wonderland?" Sophie asks.

Odd comment, Peggy thinks, but it clears the air.

"A time or two," the doctor says. She strides over to Sophie and presses a hand to her shoulder. "We should go ahead and do this now, to be sure the baby isn't in distress. I really don't want to debate this point, Sophie. Some things are worth talking about, and others just aren't."

The doctor—whose name is Betsy Sparrow—calls for an attendant, and a young woman arrives promptly with a wheelchair. Everyone, it seems, is just a little intimidated by Betsy Sparrow, including Peggy, who doesn't think to ask a single question. She helps her daughter into the wheelchair and pushes her out of the emergency room and into an elevator. Maternity is on the third floor. Even in the middle of the night, someone is on hand to smear the jelly and read the screen. Peggy stands back and watches, while Sophie looks away. She has explained herself on this point: she doesn't want to know the sex of the baby because the baby isn't hers. She is a vessel, and she wants to remain as such.

The photos are printed out on what appears to be a set of cards. Once the test is concluded and the doctor is satisfied that the baby is fine, she directs Sophie to a changing room. Peggy is carrying her daughter's clothes, shoes and shirt and panties wrapped in overalls. There's a brief flurry of activity when Peggy realizes they don't have a bra, but Sophie finally lets them know that she didn't wear one. Here, too, Peggy is perplexed. "I know I brought her a bra," she keeps saying.

She thinks she would have noticed if Sophie wasn't wearing one, but when her daughter emerges Peggy realizes that the apron of the overalls hides Sophie's breasts.

Peggy is holding the cards, five ultrasound photos that capture the little being in Sophie's belly. The technician has gone over them with Peggy, who listened carefully as the woman traced the outline of the baby—Peggy's grandchild—on the black-and-white image. Where this technology is concerned, not much has changed since Peggy was pregnant with Ian. Except for the cards. Now the images are printed on stock the size of playing cards, perhaps, or a smaller deck of old maid or tarot.

It's nearly ten in the morning when they get home. Peggy escorts Sophie upstairs, tucks her into bed, then watches over her for the few minutes it takes her daughter to drop off to sleep. By the time Peggy has fixed herself some coffee and a piece of toast, it's just after eleven. She rings Candace in Taos.

Candace is walking along the path that borders Kit Carson Park. Cell phone reception still isn't particularly reliable there, and the signal fades repeatedly. As soon as she returns to her room at the Mabel Dodge Luhan House, she rings Peggy on a landline.

"I think you should come home," Peggy tells her.

And though Albuquerque isn't Candace's home, the message is certainly clear enough. "Is she in labor, then?"

"Not yet. She's resting now, but I have this feeling that today is the day."

Candace doesn't ask questions. She simply hangs up and begins to pack. For the six days she's been at Mabel's, she has been waiting for this call, living in limbo—taking walks, looking up old friends and acquaintances, visiting art museums and the toy store.

Only once has she said anything to anyone about the reason for her visit. Mabel's is known for its breakfasts, served family-style in the dining room. One morning, Candace struck up a conversation with an older couple from England who had a fascination with all things New Mexican. They were commenting on the room's ceiling. The vigas and *latillas* are painted in a design that resembles a Navajo rug, with the traditional colors: sienna red, earth white, and lampblack. When the woman asked Candace how long she would be staying in Taos, Candace shrugged her shoulders and smiled. "I'm waiting for the birth of my first grandchild," she told them.

The wife reached across the table and clutched Candace's hand. She squeezed hard and whispered fiercely: "There's nothing like holding your first grandchild."

Candace nodded. She was certain this was true.

When she has made it to Santa Fe in her little red rental car, the cell phone buzzes. Peggy confirms that today *is* the day. "Can you meet us at the hospital?" she asks. "I'll give you directions. We haven't left the house yet. Sophie is packing her bag—very, very slowly."

They'll have visited two different hospitals in the same day. Peggy realizes that she should have taken Sophie to Lovelace to begin with. The Lovelace Women's Hospital is situated on Montgomery Boulevard, in a part of Albuquerque known as Midtown. The hospital is a four-story construction with the austerity of a courthouse and the anonymous ambience of a mid-priced hotel. The building has been recently renovated, and the stucco has been resurfaced in three different shades. The dominant color is a reddish brown the exact color of the dirt on the Sangre de Cristo Mountains outside of Santa Fe; that austere shade is offset by the tannest of tans and accented with a bold shade of blue. Candace arrives ahead of Sophie and Peggy, and so she has time to consider the face of the hospital, which reminds her a bit of the dining room ceiling at Mabel's.

She spots Laurel's beat-up Tercel wheeling into the lot, and watches as the younger woman parks, gets out, and hurries into the building. In another couple of minutes, the plate-glass doors slide open. Laurel emerges and takes a seat on a concrete bench out front. Something about the way she cradles her purse in her lap is touching to Candace, who decides to join her. She's on her way across the lot when Peggy and Sophie arrive. Peggy pulls up to the entrance, and Laurel leaps up from her seat to open the passenger door for Sophie. In the excitement, she drops her purse to the pavement. Candace collects it for her, carrying the heavy bag into the hospital and handing it over once they've delivered Sophie to the maternity ward.

They are greeted by a sedate young man prone to throat-clearing. "May I help you?" he asks, more maître d' than health-care professional. He accompanies his answers with the twirling of a stethoscope as he peers at the four women skeptically. "We're really busy this afternoon," he says, as though they ought to reconsider their timing.

Just behind the intake nurse, in the hallway outside a labor room, a large Hispanic family—father, mother, grandmother, and two women who look to be aunties—has gathered. One of the aunts is dressed in a black leotard and a long, full black skirt hemmed by a black-and-white polka-dot ruffle. When she turns and walks past them, headed for a collection of snack and drink machines, she moves crisply, with her head held high. The heels of her black tap shoes sound smartly on the linoleum.

Laurel offers to find a vending machine and bottles of water. Meanwhile, Candace and Peggy settle themselves on a window seat and wait while their charge sheds her overalls and replaces them with a blue-and-white checked hospital gown. Sophie is perspiring. Her forehead is damp to the touch, and within minutes the underarms of the gown are wet as well. Once they measure her dilation, a modest five centimeters, Sophie's hospital bed is wheeled into the hallway toward the labor rooms. There aren't enough to accommodate all the groaning women whose babies are entering the world on this bright May afternoon in Albuquerque. Sophie will have to wait her turn.

The hallway is narrow, so Candace and Peggy spend most of their time on a nearby window seat. Peggy dozes off, her head in Candace's lap, which leaves Laurel to soothe Sophie, to feed her chips of ice, and to glower at the dancing woman. The woman's short black hair is teased into an old-fashioned beehive. Two spit curls point in the direction of her red, red lips. A CD player is clipped to her waistband; the woman wears earbuds and struts to music only she can hear.

Finally, after an hour or more, the dancer takes a break and acknowledges her audience. "You must wonder what I'm doing," she says.

Laurel nods. She's clutching her cell phone, considering whether she should slip away to make the call. She has a private side, and it's a private call. Part of her is ashamed that a son she's raised, all she really has to show for her life, has run away from his responsibility. Another part is relieved for him. She wants him to have his childhood—or what's left of it—and the companionship of his father, such as he is.

"I'm scheduled to compete tomorrow," the woman explains, "in a flamenco competition."

Laurel nods, as though she's known this all along.

"It's my first time, and I'm really nervous. I have to practice. I just have to."

"Sure," Laurel says. "You go right ahead."

The woman strikes a pose, one arm snaking out in front of her, the other raised and bent behind, then sashays down the hallway.

"Shall I call Will?" Laurel asks Sophie.

"Not now." Sophie looks directly into Laurel's eyes. "Right now I need you."

"What do you need?"

Sophie extends a hand, and Laurel takes it. Sophie's grip is damp but impressive, and when a contraction comes on, the girl squeezes as hard as she can, hard enough to make Laurel flinch.

"There," Sophie says, gritting her teeth. "Does that hurt?"

Laurel yelps, "Yes."

"It's nothing compared to what I'm feeling," Sophie pants.

And Laurel agrees. "I know, honey. I know."

The woman swings back by, hardly looking in their direction. She's practicing her *floras* now; her hands are flowers, waving in the air.

"Shoo!" Laurel says to the dancer.

The woman doesn't notice, and she wouldn't be offended if she had. Indeed, she smiles down sweetly at Sophie as she whirls away. Later, in the aftermath of the birth, in those strange dreams that seem drug-induced in their intensity, the dancing woman will appear to Sophie with wings, an angel wearing a polka-dot ruffle and pouty red lips. Perhaps the dream comes from the way the woman gazes down on Sophie with the fond affection of one who has survived this particular variety of suffering, and is grateful to be elsewhere in her life.

In fact, the dancer's name is Yvette, and she has an angelic side. When she's not dancing flamenco, she's a nurse in Oakland, California. Several times during Sophie's long night of labor, Yvette will halt her dancing long enough to run her fingers through Sophie's hair. She will smooth the dark coils that spill over the end of the gurney, and when Sophie is grunting in pain, Yvette's strong and graceful fingers will knead Sophie's temples and scalp. Near dawn, Peggy and Candace will collapse in a tangled heap on the window seat, and while Laurel takes a bathroom break, Yvette will console Sophie, who is weeping from too much pain, too little sleep, and simple fear. "*Shh*, darling," Yvette will say, bending over Sophie. "Don't grit your teeth. Relax, relax now."

By morning Yvette's niece has delivered a little girl, so she and her extended family are moved to the postpartum unit on the fourth floor. Yvette speaks to the nurse on duty, and Sophie and her family are ushered into the vacated space, Labor and Delivery Room 353. As with the rest of the floor, the color scheme is green and purple—the western wall is purple, the northern wall green. For years to come, Sophie will associate that particular shade of purple, eggplant, with the third stage of labor. She'll feel vaguely uncomfortable and out of control each time she encounters it.

From her bed, Sophie can't see the view from the window, so Peggy describes it to her. Once day has dawned, the big window on the western wall lightens to reveal the city falling away toward the valley, a grid of buildings, streets, telephone poles, fences, and walls, orderly but, from this perspective, altogether ugly. Clearly visible in the distance, however, is a version of the view Sophie contemplates from her window at home: the vista of the Sleeping Sisters, those five dormant volcanoes. At some point in the distant past, all five spewed forth lava, which eventually cooled and formed an escarpment extending seventeen miles. As long ago as AD 1300, the Ancient Pueblo peoples carved their history into the dark basalt boulders.

"Peggy!" Sophie cries out, her voice cracking with anguish. "Make it stop!"

Turning, Peggy catches sight of the mounded sheets covering Sophie's quaking belly, and she wails in response. "Oh, my poor baby!"

Candace and Laurel are dozing in lounge chairs assembled near the window. They start at the sound of Sophie's plea.

"Can we do something?" Candace asks, looking groggy.

But Laurel is already doing it. Laurel is already out the door and headed down to the nurse's station.

Dennis is born midmorning. The date is May 9, a calm day during which the bees are especially busy. Because last winter was relatively wet by Albuquerque standards, the first flush of wild flowers in the Sandias is exceptionally vivid. Pink calypso orchids nod to hikers along the 10K Trail below the crest, while down in the North Valley, the purple sage grows lush and bushy.

In honor of the day, the buds along Mr. Bojangles's joints unfurl to reveal papery magenta blossoms. Although the bees are more interested in the cone-shaped flowers of the chaste tree and butterfly bushes, Mr. Bojangles certainly looks festive all decked out in his gaudy splendor. Cane cholla has only this one season, this one week in the whole year to appear showy and grand. What a happy coincidence that the newest member of the Granger family is delivered just in time to see him at his best.

The visit home is a brief one, however. As agreed to at a family meeting, baby Dennis stays in Albuquerque just long enough to get a clean bill of health from the pediatrician and to suckle at his mother's breast for that all-important dose of colostrum. Then Candace whisks him away, and the house, which was briefly full of noise and life, falls altogether silent. Thankfully Ian has his teepee to pitch, and the weather is mild enough for him to justify spending most of his time ensconced in its shadowy depths.

Though dawn arrives in central New Mexico before six in mid-May, first light doesn't penetrate the Grangers' first-floor rooms until nearly seven. The reasons are several. First, the windows are set back in thick, mounded adobe walls, and a pitched metal roof overhangs the eaves, deflecting initial rays. Too, the house was built facing the south, its wide wraparound porch protected by that expansive pitched roof. Generations of New Mexicans have learned to take into account the ravages of the sun and plan accordingly. The result is a traditional—and recognizable—architectural style. Drive through Santa Fe or Taos, and you'll pick out the contours of northern New Mexico homes mingling with the squatter Pueblo-style houses.

Over the years, Jack has developed a fondness for northern New Mexico architectural features, preferring them to the Pueblo style and the square-columned, window-trimmed territorial style, both of which feature flat roofs. His preference makes sense: the northern New Mexico home is to the Southwest what the Adirondack-style house is to New England. When he was young, Jack planned to build an Adirondack house, but now that he's made his home in New Mexico, he's had the good sense to revise that dream. He is satisfied with his current project: remodeling the fixer-upper. Concessions of this sort are necessary to happiness, and he's learned not to haggle with himself over them.

Although accustomed to the dark stairwell, Jack climbs slowly, not only because he is exhausted—it's been weeks since he's slept straight through the night—but also because he dreads the task he's about to undertake. He doesn't feel equal to it, and he is worried about making matters worse. His usual destination when he takes these stairs is Ian's room, but today he stops before his daughter's door. Just now, Sophie has the upstairs to herself. Ian has seen fit to vacate the premises.

Jack stands before his daughter's closed door. He raises his knuckles and, sighing, raps lightly on the hollow wooden surface. He doubts Sophie is asleep, though he predicts that she'll pretend to be. As recently as an hour ago, she was awake; he heard the toilet flushing and the water running in the sink. He was talking to Peggy in their bedroom, so it had to have been Sophie. Ian usually doesn't bother to come inside to piss, and when he does he skips the hand-washing. That's part of what appeals to Ian about life in the teepee. He can piss in the sage and be done with it.

Jack isn't expecting a response, not the first time anyway. He's planning to knock again in a minute, louder and longer, but in a sleepy-sounding voice Sophie calls out, "Who is it?" Jack isn't fooled. He knows she is preparing to send him away. Off and on these last two weeks, he's slept here at the house out of concern for his daughter. Again and again he has tried enticing her down to breakfast. He's offered to cook eggs or even make pancakes, but she's sent him on his way without so much as opening the door. Instead, she simply calls out, "I'm so tired. I'm so tired, Jack."

This time he says, "Cover up, I'm coming in!" Then he does exactly that. If anything, he's expecting Sophie's bedroom to be even darker than the hallway—gloomy, like her—so he is surprised by the dawn light. Already it illuminates the edges of the room, revealing the gorgeous furniture from France. Once Jack got over his indignation at Candace—money *can* buy you love, or so it seems to him—he was as awed as the rest of them by the beauty of the workmanship.

"What have you got against curtains?" Jack asks.

Sophie stirs and then sits up on the side of the bed. They had finally gotten around to buying a set of box springs and assembling the bed frame. Tam and Belinda's move provided Sophie's room with an area rug that is more Southwestern than French, but the colors—greens and blues and oranges—are good. Now Sophie's room has the sophistication and warmth that the rest of the house lacks. He doesn't begrudge her a little ambience though.

She sits up on the side of the bed. "Nothing," she replies. "Nothing at all. I used to hate them, but not anymore."

She's wearing a sleeveless floral nightgown, something that used to be her mother's. When he reaches her side she offers a wan smile, which also used to be Peggy's. Now it's Sophie's. As he kisses the top of her head, he takes in the sour smell of her hair. It's been at least a week since she's bothered to wash it.

"Good morning, darling girl. I find myself in need of your excellent guidance and good taste."

"I'm tired."

"So am I. Being tired is a fact of life, not an excuse for refusing to live it."

"Give me a break."

"I've given you a break, and now, as I said, I need your assistance. Just step into your overalls and come downstairs. I'll have breakfast waiting."

He's putting bread in the toaster when she enters the kitchen, and, turning to greet her, he's surprised to see that she has followed his instructions to the letter. She's pulled the overalls on over her nightgown, and on her feet she wears a pair of cheap orange flip-flops. She is ready for the day.

"Would you like some coffee?" he asks.

"Actually, yes," she replies. "Now that I'm not pregnant, coffee tastes good."

He pours Sophie a cup and fetches the Coffee-Mate from the fridge. He's the only one who can stomach black coffee. It's his private opinion that real grown-ups drink their coffee black. He wants to tell Sophie this: that if she is truly interested in maturity, she must strive to drink her coffee unadulterated. But the assertion sounds absurd, even to him. So he feeds the toaster a couple of pieces of nine-grain bread and gathers the tub of margarine. Once the toast is ready, he serves the slices on a plate—he's already had his breakfast—and sits down across from her, pushing the honey pot and margarine in her direction.

"Eat up," he says. "We have all manner of chores to do."

On the way down Rio Grande Boulevard, Sophie rolls down the passenger window. Like Jack, she enjoys the wind whipping through the car, and now that she's pulled her mane into an unruly ponytail, she can simply lean her head back and close her eyes. Once they're on the road, headed toward Indian School, she takes a peek at Jack, who hums to himself while he drives.

"Where are we going?" she asks.

"Lowe's."

"You need me to go to Lowe's?"

"Old man like me can't make up his mind."

"You're not old, Jack," she replies.

He snorts in response. "I'm old all right, but I don't mind being old. Being old is a privilege—it means you've outlasted all those bastards who never got a chance at life."

They are quiet then, until Jack swings into the Lowe's parking lot and turns off the ignition. He makes no move to get out, and neither does she.

The idea that Jack isn't her father, and never has been, sweeps over her again. She can't speak. What is there to say, after all? This loss, compounded by the departure of her baby son, has taken everything vital from her except breath. Sitting in the car with Jack is both easier and harder, she realizes. It's easier in the sense that she no longer worries about letting him down. Her failures are no longer his, at least not in the genetic sense. He can blame her bad traits on her real dad, a dead man. But she can't help worrying that he loves her less now. She isn't really his; he isn't obligated to love her, now is he?

"Are you thinking of Gwendolyn?" Sophie knew nothing at all about Jack's older sister until a year or so ago, when Jack revealed that Gwendolyn had been run down by a drunk driver. A drunk driver? Sophie has a hard time imagining how something so contemporary could have happened in a small Vermont town more than fifty years ago.

Jack stares through the windshield. He's wearing sunglasses, the wraparound kind that only men his age are willing to be caught dead in. "Gwen's a good example, sure, but I wasn't thinking of her in particular."

"Who were you thinking about, then?"

Sophie thinks now of a girl named Bethany, who was killed by a drunk driver during her sophomore year. Bethany was in Sophie's French class. On the first day she'd been absent, none of them had thought much about it. But then, at the beginning of the next class, the teacher had cleared his throat and made the announcement, choking up a little as he said her name.

Now Jack clears his throat. "If you want to know, I'm thinking of Dennis Jackson. You did a brave thing, carrying him to term and giving him up for adoption. You could have done something easier. God knows I was all for the abortion option. But I'm proud of you for seeing the matter through, Sophie."

She squeezes her eyes shut and blindly reaches out with her left hand, groping for his hand, which he gives her. She manages to say, "Thanks," then grips his hand tightly, maybe as tightly as she gripped Laurel's during the labor and delivery.

Jack regrets having missed the birth, but he'd like to think that he is here with her now, seeing her through something that might be every bit as hard. When Sophie has her emotions under control, she whispers, "I love you, Jack."

"I love you, too, Sophie." As he watches, she presses the button to raise the window again, but nothing happens. Jack has already turned off the ignition. Sophie turns and gives him a questioning look.

Her face is losing the moon shape it took on in the latter stages of her pregnancy, yet he doesn't expect her ever again to resemble that curly-headed vixen who opened her mouth to a hive full of bees. That girl is gone for good, and he didn't even know enough to bid her farewell. He faults himself for not seeing what should have been perfectly obvious: his daughter was trying to get his attention. He failed her once, but it's his express intention not to do so again, not to let her down or leave her to the indifferent intentions of her mother. Peggy means well, but she is busy closing up her shop. She seems distracted, even disoriented.

"Work is healing, Sophie," he says, and for once she doesn't argue.

She gets out of the car and heads directly for the main doors, arriving there ahead of her dad, who stoops to pick up a flyer from the street in front of the store. If he leaves it, the flyer may be in Gallup by late afternoon. This golden, tranquil morning will give way to what Jack likes to call a "blow storm." Before getting in the car that morning, he took a stroll out to the field and warned Ian that the teepee might be blown away during the afternoon. He'd be wise to strike it. "Just to be on the safe side," he said. Ian didn't argue. It's his natural inclination to play it safe. He has to be nudged into taking risks, whereas Sophie has to be deterred from them.

Jack's one reservation about turning the paint selection over to his daughter is that she'll opt for deep, dark shades of red—that she'll insist on painting the interior to resemble a blood bank or a brothel. Jack wants to sell the casita, the quicker the better, and that means appealing to the tastes of the common man.

Recently, the kids from the house in front of the casita have dragged a picnic table out of their yard and into his, the better to clear a space for softball. When she gets out of the car, Sophie plops down on the bench and spreads the paint cards in front of her on the table. Jack stands and peers over her shoulder; he is relieved to see that only a few of the twenty or so cards are red. He says the paint names to himself: "'Hibiscus' and 'Cherry.'" Then he muses aloud, "I can read those from ten feet away, but I can't read them from ten inches away." He shakes his head.

But Sophie isn't listening. Her attention is on the color chips. She has picked up cards from more than one brand of paint. Some are small squares; others are rectangular, with rounded corners. Sophie is intent on dividing them by color—greens go in one pile, blues in another, and yellows in a third. When she has finished her rough classification, she's ready to head inside and survey the house.

It will take a good deal of hemming and hawing, another trip to Lowe's, and two more trips to the casita before Sophie makes her selections. For each room—the bedrooms on either end of the house, the kitchen, the original entryway, and the bathroom—she decides on two complementary colors, one for the walls and another for the sills and floorboards. The overall color scheme has logic to it as well. She explains to Jack that the "Lemongrass" she uses on the kitchen walls will be complemented by the sage green called "Summer Field," which she plans to use for the accent. And then in the bathroom, she will repeat "Summer Field" on the walls, but use something even a little greener—"Inchworm"—for the sills and floorboards. Once she's made her decisions, she tapes the color chips to the walls of each room.

She wants to do the work herself, too. "Any moron can paint a wall," she assures Jack. He isn't so sure, but they're way too far down this road to turn back now. Although Tam has invited Sophie to fly to Dallas for a weekend of fun in early June—the tickets are Belinda's treat—Sophie postpones one week, and then another, to complete the painting job.

After giving her a few tips and hovering in the next room for the first hour or so, Jack relaxes. Sophie is good at painting, so Jack is able to devote himself to landscaping. He starts with the front yard, which is bordered by the coyote fence. He decides to lay a flagstone patio the size of a lily pond next to the front door. He can only hope that he'll be as good at laying flagstones as Sophie is at painting.

In the larger of the two bedrooms, Sophie uses a milky shade of blue for the walls, something called "Cassiopeia." The sills she covers in "Milk Sugar," but the shade is so light that she is forced to layer on four coats in order to get the necessary coverage. Her plan was to use "Milk Sugar" on the walls of the smaller bedroom and "Forget Me Not" for the accent, but she has second thoughts after her experience with the sills of the master bedroom. She's already put off her trip to Dallas twice, and she wonders what Jack would think of a last-minute change of plans.

"I don't want to let you down," she tells him.

They're sitting at the picnic table having bologna sandwiches, bread-and-butter pickles, and potato chips. Once they scooted the table closer to the coyote fence, they got another hour or two of shaded comfort.

Sophie is drinking a Dr Pepper, and Jack is drinking water. Since coming to work at the fixer-upper, Sophie has insisted on stocking the refrigerator, something Jack never bothered to do. Now they can stop for lunch whenever they have a mind to, and it's not necessary to get in the car and drive to Taco Bell. Sophie still has some pounds to lose; Jack could stand to drop a few, too. In this way they've managed to have some good talks. Jack has explained his troubles at work and why he no longer wants to serve as an administrator—"It just isn't worth it!" And Sophie has shared some of her experiences at New Futures. A week or so into her work at the casita, she even manages to tell him that she doesn't think she can return to high school in the fall.

"What about going to back to Valley?" he asks. He's finished his sandwich and is fishing in the bottom of the sack for potato chip crumbs.

Sophie shakes her head vigorously. She can't, she tells him. "I'm not that person anymore, that high school girl."

They eat in silence for a moment. Or rather, Jack eats. When the neighbors' dog wanders over for a handout, Sophie feeds him the rest of her sandwich, then explains to Jack that she doesn't want to answer questions about Dennis Jackson and Will. She's afraid she'll cry, and the idea that she'll be sobbing in those dark Valley hallways, well, it's just too depressing to contemplate. Not to mention that Tam is gone. Jack nods. He drops the sack and reaches across the table to cover one of her hands with both of his, all ten salty, oily fingers. He understands, but she has to graduate, doesn't she?

Sophie has thought it through. She wants to get her GED, then go to college back east.

Jack sighs and goes silent.

"What is it?" she asks.

"That's an expensive proposition," he tells her.

She replies that she wouldn't ask him to pay for it. "I'll sell my furniture," she jokes. She looks away, to the empty swing set on the edge of the neighbors' property. The kids are off swimming. As they climbed into the backseat of their parents' car, the boys were making whooping noises and fighting over an inflatable shark.

His hands still pressed over hers, Jack takes the opportunity to gaze directly into her eyes. "I couldn't love you more," he says. "You know that, don't you?"

And then she surprises him. She meets his eyes and says: "If I were your daughter, you mean?"

"What?" he sputters.

And she goes right on looking at him. "You couldn't love me more if I were actually your daughter?"

In spite of himself, he straightens, draws back, and reviews her with the greater clarity that distance provides him. "You are my daughter, Sophie," he says.

"Not your flesh and blood."

"My heart and soul." He leans toward her again, arms crossed over his chest, hands curled into fists. "My heart and soul, Sophie. I wouldn't trade you."

She leans across the table and presses an index finger to his lips. "Ditto," she replies.

When Tam calls to confirm the weekend plans, she is full of excitement. "We can't wait to see you!" she says. It's the "we" that gets to Sophie.

"Who's we?" Sophie asks, but Tam just rushes past the question. She has all kinds of news, most of it about her job at the ice-skating rink, and she talks and talks until Sophie gives up on making a smart remark.

Tam wants to take Sophie ice-skating. It's her newest enthusiasm. Evidently working at the rink is not enough; she spends her free time there as well. She has athletic ability, as Sophie remembers from their softball days. Tam didn't hit the ball any more often than the rest of them, but whenever she made contact, the damn thing was likely to sail right over the fence. Even so, Tam would still put her head down and run the bases twice as fast as any of the rest of them.

Tam tries to be reassuring. "We'll have fun, Sophie. Our apartment building has a pool, so be sure to pack your suit."

Much as she wants to be good, Sophie can't help but say what she is actually thinking. Tam is her best friend, after all; if not to Tam, then to whom? "I'll bring my bikini. That way I can showcase the slew of stretch marks that crisscross my big, baggy belly."

And before she knows what has happened, Sophie is sobbing. Lately she gets ambushed by her emotions, and at the oddest moments. Only a few days ago she wept while removing the painter's tape from the casita's bedroom windows, and last night she found herself screaming at Ian because he ate the last of the vanilla ice cream. When she registered the stricken look on his face, she slapped a hand over her mouth. And, predictably, started to cry. Then, and now.

To her credit, Tam stays on the phone. She sits silently and waits while Sophie gets control of herself. "I'm sorry, Sophie," she says. "It's just that this is the best I can do, the best I can be. I wish I could think of all the right things to say, but I can't."

Sophie sniffles. It's her fault, and she knows it. "Do you still want me to come?"

Sophie has flown a few times in her life, but this trip is her first time flying alone. On the Friday morning when Sophie is scheduled to depart, Peggy has a doctor's appointment, so they leave earlier than is necessary. Mother drops off daughter, but before letting her out of the car, she clasps Sophie's face in her hands and kisses her smack on the lips. "Allow yourself to have a little fun," Peggy admonishes, and, once again, tears spring to Sophie's eyes. This time she has the forethought to lift her chin, which keeps them from leaking out and betraying her.

Pronto, Sophie is out of the car and grabbing her overnight bag from the backseat and her canvas tote from the floorboard. "Bye, Peggy!" she calls over her shoulder. She turns her back until Peggy's car has safely pulled away. Then she puts her head down and allows the tears to drip onto the pavement. She can feel them raining down on her bare toes. She's wearing flip-flops and a shift dress that disguises what's left of her baby belly. The dress is cotton, and the white background is splashed with pink and yellow daisies. Because the armholes are too large, she wears an orange camisole underneath. Sophie likes the bright colors, and when she ducks into the restroom to wipe her eyes, she does what she always does when wearing the dress: she studies the flowers on her chest. In this way, she avoids her own gaze.

As she leans over the sink to wash her hands, the ends of her hair sweep across the bowl. She has to catch hold of a handful, then wedge the tail of her hair into her armpit for safekeeping. She meant to braid it, but she ran out of time. Only months earlier, plaiting would have been out of the question. But those corkscrew curls, once tight as a baby's fist, have relaxed into finger curls, and now Sophie's long locks cascade in waves over her chest, occasionally catching in the zipper of her jeans. In another hour or so, when Tam catches sight of her old friend, she will actually gasp. "Are you straightening your hair?" she'll ask. Sophie will say no. She'll shrug away her friend's surprise, then toss the bulk of her mane over one shoulder. "I'm thinking of cutting it," she'll say. "It's a pain in the ass."

"Don't you dare!" Tam will reply.

Sophie has brought along a baggie full of paint chips. She plans to show Tam the color scheme she worked out for the casita. In addition to the paint chips, she has photos of each room on her cell phone. But Sophie will never get around to sharing them, at least not with Tam and Belinda.

On Friday night they go out to eat barbecue. Then, under cover of darkness, Sophie and Tam take a swim in the apartment pool. Belinda reclines nearby on a lounge chair and drinks a beer while Tam and Sophie revert to early girlhood, turning flips in the deep end and taking turns doing cannonballs off the narrow diving board. At ten o'clock Belinda wryly notes that they need to leave some water in the pool for others. She stands up and offers each of them a towel.

On Saturday morning Sophie accompanies Tam to the skating rink, which is tucked inside the Galleria Mall. "You've roller-skated, right?" Tam asks as she prepares to open the rink. They both know the answer. They used to go in-line skating together on the Bosque Trail, back home in Albuquerque. Somewhere in the shed at home, Sophie's skates are waiting for her, but Tam sold hers in the massive garage sale a few months back. "You'll be fine on the ice, Sophie. I was. You should see me now. I can pirouette!"

For the first hour, Sophie has the rink to herself. She falls a couple of times—she takes a quick dive forward, which she breaks with her hands, and has another, more comical fall flat on her bottom. That one Tam happens to witness, and she makes a loud hooting noise, then calls out, "You're okay, aren't you?" Mostly, though, Sophie manages to stay upright.

She is feeling pretty good about her progress when she takes a break at ten to assist Tam with the opening rush. Not that Sophie is anywhere near being ready to twirl, but she has her balance and a clean stroke going. So much of what she remembers about roller-skating applies to the ice—stopping, for instance. She's managed to stop a few times with a graceful dip of the knees. When she takes off the skates and joins Tam behind the counter, her cheeks are rosy and she's worked up an appetite. Fortunately Belinda pressed granola bars on them as they went out the door, and Sophie scarfs down one and then another as Tam shows her the ropes.

On the way to the mall, Tam had explained that Saturday mornings are a zoo. She had predicted a line of chattering, squealing pubescent girls by the time the rink opened, and sure enough, they are waiting in full force. For nearly an hour the two of them stay busy, ringing up tickets and passing out skates, and when the rush finally dies down, Tam hugs Sophie. "Could you visit every Saturday?" she asks.

Because Tam has another three hours left in her shift, Sophie decides to return to the ice for another few laps. Then she'll go get pizza for the two of them and bring it back. She tells herself that she can skate off the calories in advance, so she won't need to feel guilty about eating a second or third slice. To be back to her pre-pregnancy weight, she still needs to lose nearly twenty pounds. Sometimes the prospect seems hopeless, but not today.

She stays close to the railing so she can reach out and catch herself, should that be necessary. She's also avoiding the girls who skate in tandem, sometimes holding hands—two, three, even four abreast—and the boys, who zip past at a rate she finds downright alarming. Several are actually talking on cell phones, though the rink rules prohibit it. "Slow down," she mutters as a boy about her age flies past, imitating the bent-over posture of short-track skaters. "Ohno wannabes," Tam called them. The reference was lost on Sophie, who'd never heard of Apolo Anton Ohno, but then Tam hadn't heard of him either—that is, until she began working at the skating rink.

The boy who plows into Sophie isn't talking or texting; he just isn't looking where he's going. He dashes onto the ice from one of the entrances, and Sophie simply doesn't have the wherewithal to avoid the collision. He doesn't see her, and she gets only a glimpse of his red ball cap before they collide and then collapse in a violent embrace. Sophie doesn't remember trying to break their fall with her left hand, but she must have, because the x-rays reveal a broken wrist. Her left knee is banged up as well. She spends a couple of hours in urgent care with Belinda. Tam can't leave work to go along, although she's waiting when they get back to the apartment, and she is distressed to see that her friend is wearing a cast.

Well after midnight, Belinda gets up and discovers Sophie asleep on the couch, emitting small moaning sounds. Rather than leave her to this nocturnal misery, Belinda kneels down beside the couch and shakes the girl awake. "Are you in pain?" she whispers.

Sophie is hard to wake. Belinda has to reach out and stroke the crown of her head, softly and then more firmly, pressing her fingers into the curling masses of hair. Sophie stirs, then makes a complaint, something unintelligible. Belinda asks her question again, and this time Sophie answers by saying she doesn't know.

"You're moaning."

"I'm sorry," Sophie replies.

"Don't be sorry. Is there something I can do to help?"

As it turns out, there is. "I don't want to go home tomorrow," Sophie whispers in the darkness. "I want to change my ticket and fly to Boston instead. Please, Belinda, can you help me?"

"I don't know if I should," Belinda replies, but Sophie is insistent, reminding Belinda that this is an open adoption, that Candace is practically a member of the family. Eventually Belinda relents.

The flight is nonstop, and Sophie sleeps for the duration. She has Candace's address memorized, so it's really only a matter of finding her way from the arrival gate to the baggage claim area, then out to the taxi stand in the median between westbound and eastbound traffic. Because Tam slipped her forty dollars, Sophie has money for a cab.

She has the sympathy factor going for her, too. Her left wrist and hand are wrapped up tightly in a lime-green cast. She uses her right hand to drag along a cheap weekender. If she didn't know better, she'd swear the damn thing had square wheels. Over one shoulder she schleps a canvas bag full of incidentals: her sandwich bag of paint chips, an extra pair of shoes, and a whole handful of granola bars, courtesy of Tam.

Sophie has on her sixties shift dress again, with the orange camisole underneath. Wearing flip-flops on the plane was a bad idea—she was seated by the window, and the air-conditioning vent blew directly on her feet. But she was asleep most of the flight, and she didn't really register the discomfort until she woke up and realized that her toes were actually numb. She tried burying her feet under the canvas bag, which was stowed beneath the seat in front of her, but it was far too late for half measures. Briefly, it occurred to her that she might have done actual damage. She imagined hobbling up to the brownstone where Candace lived, her wrist and arm in a cast, her pinky toes blackened with frostbite. Wouldn't any decent person have to take pity on her?

Now, queued up in the line for a taxi, it's her arms that feel cold. Her feet have only just begun to thaw, so it's no wonder that she begins to shiver. The breeze smells of brine. Boston feels downright chilly compared to Dallas, where all weekend the temperature hovered near one hundred. The woman in line in front of Sophie sounds just like Candace: "You have no idear!" she exclaims to her friend. "Pahking is impossible!" Sophie listens to the two women talk, their Boston brogues so thick that she has trouble following the course of their conversation.

She hugs herself for warmth. The sleeve of the cast presses against her breast, and she thinks about what a relief it would be if both arms were covered in plaster. At least she wouldn't be so cold. An older man behind her clears his throat and asks her a question, though it doesn't occur to Sophie that the words are directed to her. The man tries again, louder this time: "Are you cold, deah?"

Sophie nods repeatedly, then watches as the man squats and unzips the leather duffel he's been kicking along the sidewalk in front of him. He rummages for a minute before he teases out a brown hoodie, which he holds up to her. She takes it gratefully, then struggles to put it on until he reaches out and touches her arm. "Shall I assist?" he asks, and with an odd, closed-mouth grin, he helps her negotiate the sleeve over the cast. He takes her canvas bag and waits while she fiddles with fitting one half of the zipper into the other half. Ultimately she has to give up the attempt, because the line begins to move. The women disappear into a cab, still talking companionably.

It's Sophie's turn to grab a taxi, and when she's confronted by the stern young man with a whistle in his mouth, she is ready with the address. She has memorized it. Speaking it aloud to the young man in front of her and the older man behind, Sophie is exhilarated.

"The Commons," the older man repeats. "Not so far from my alma mater." He taps her on the back, but it won't be until later, when she is finally warm enough to remove the hoodie, that she will register the lettering on the back: HARVARD. For years to come, she will hold onto this hooded sweat shirt, pulling it over her head and wearing it—regardless of the season—whenever she needs a reminder of this day and all its gifts.

She's in the cab and reciting the address yet again when she takes note of the driver, a young man in a turban who nods to her in the mirror. "Excellent!" he exclaims, and, as though to underline his approval, he stomps on the gas so that the vehicle lurches forward and into traffic. What Sophie can see of the sky is hung with dark clouds; an occasional large drop splats on the windshield. "It's raining," Sophie comments.

"This isn't rain," the cabbie corrects her. "Not at all." Then he asks her what brings her to Boston.

She leans forward, straddling the hump in the rear floorboard, one leg on either side. "My baby boy brings me here," she tells him, suddenly breathless with anticipation. It's funny. While she was painting the walls of the fixer-upper, Sophie had pined for Dennis Jackson. She did her best to remember every square inch of his seven-pound body. Everything curled from his time inside her. Even his toes were curled inward. She isn't sure that she ever saw him straighten his legs. They were bowed up around his abdomen, bent at the knees and splayed. His pouty little rose-colored lips amazed her, pursed together to suckle and then spread wide to scream. He knew just what he wanted, if only he could have told her. But he did tell her, she reminds herself. *He told me. I just steeled myself not to listen.*

The cabbie has been chattering all the while she's been lost in her memories of Dennis Jackson. Is he telling her that he has children of his own? She thinks so. She wants to ask him a question. She wants to establish a back-and-forth, something she knows is required in polite discourse. But when she opens her mouth to inquire after his children, she instead blurts out news of her own child. Later she will tell Tam about spilling her guts to this gentle man in a turban. *He kept nodding*, she'll say. *He steered the cab through traffic and he listened carefully to every word I uttered.*

Occasionally the cabbie interrupts the flow of words to point out a sight. Sophie is nearly breathless with urgency. She has to finish before they arrive, and he must sense as much, as he gives up interjecting and simply allows her to explain herself.

"Have you ever wondered who you really are?" she asks as they near their destination.

"Many times," he answers.

"And what have you concluded?" Before they arrive, she should ask at least one question, and this is the important one.

He doesn't disappoint. "I've learned this," he says softly. He pulls the cab to the curb. Here they are. "I've learned that the answer changes every time I ask the question. Who are you today, Miss Sophie?"

She is ready with her answer. "I'm a mother," she tells him. And then she remembers to inquire of him. "And who are you?"

"An admirer of Miss Sophie's, of course."

As she stands before the ornate, arched double doors—carved and painted a rusty orange with teal panels—as she grasps the knocker to make her presence known, Sophie hears a familiar sound. Since her arrival, nothing about Boston has been the least bit familiar—not the temperature, the winding streets, or the accents of those who've spoken to her. But now, at last, she is confronted by something she recognizes: Dennis Jackson is crying. He is a loudmouthed baby who opens his mouth and wails indignantly. He is Sophie's son.

She is ashamed to be standing there, abashed and anxious, lest she be sent away. But the woman on the other side of the door has rarely ever turned anyone away. Even when it was in her own self-interest to do so, as it had been when she chose to shelter Peggy, who was prettier, who had a Texas drawl and a shy smile that she'd soon turn on Beau. Even then, she chose kindness over envy.

"Look who's here!" Candace exclaims to the baby in her arms, who is red-faced from crying, so much bigger than Sophie remembers, and entirely bald! "It's your mother, Dennis Jackson! Your mother is here." And then Candace, still in her bathrobe—which is the same milky blue as the walls of the casita back home—stands aside and ushers a sobbing Sophie through the door.

"Are you okay?" Candace asks, gesturing to Sophie's cast. "How did you break your arm?"

"Ice-skating."

"Did you say 'ice-skating'?"

Sophie nods, then breaks out in a peal of laughter, which first startles and then delights Dennis Jackson. The grinning baby reaches for and grabs a fistful of her hair. A weary Candace chuckles gamely while the baby snorts and sniffles.

Dennis has his first cold and his first stopped-up nose. For several days, Candace has tried all manner of remedies. The bulb syringe made him furious, and Candace never did get the hang of it. Saline spray frightened him into a bout of the hiccups, and the humidifier made a whistling noise reminiscent of a teakettle. Whenever it started or stopped, Dennis would wake and wail. And getting his fill of formula was all but impossible—each time he took the nipple in his mouth and began to suck, he panicked because he couldn't breathe.

"Thank god you're here!" Candace exclaims. "I could really use a good night's sleep." And before Sophie has to ask, Candace thrusts the baby into the younger woman's arms.

Of course, it won't be the first thing she does, or even the second or third, but when Dennis is down for the night, Sophie will recover the canvas bag she's dropped in the entranceway. While Candace is getting their tea—she drinks chamomile before going to bed, and she has convinced Sophie to try it—Sophie will dig around in the bag and pull out the sandwich bag of paint chips. By the time Candace has carried the two steaming cups and the saucers to the table, Sophie is spreading the cards on the table.

Candace is so tired that it's all she can do not to fall asleep in the chair. But she sits down and smiles absently as Sophie arranges "Summer Field," "Lemongrass," "Inchworm," "Milk Sugar," and "Forget Me Not" in front of her.

"What's all this?" she asks, reaching out and running a finger over "Forget Me Not."

Sophie has her answer planned: "I want to show you the colors I painted your house."

She feels quite sure of herself, at least until Candace heads off to bed upstairs. Dennis is dozing in a cradle in the guest bedroom, an arrangement Candace and Sophie have agreed on, both because Sophie can't bear to let him out of her sight and because Candace is, as she puts it, "one of the walking dead." She wants nothing so much as an uninterrupted night's sleep. Once the older woman has retired, Sophie is finally able to take stock of her surroundings. For hours on end, she's been drinking in the sight of her baby, completely oblivious to anything else.

The apartment is posh, like a movie set. As Sophie tells Tam in a hushed whisper, "I feel like I'm staying with Oprah. You can't believe how beautiful this place is! Wall-to-wall French country furniture and original paintings."

The rooms are all so white, Sophie thinks as she wanders into the kitchen, cell phone pressed to her ear. The countertops and cabinets are white, and so are the appliances. Even the floral arrangement in a crystal vase is white. "But are the flowers real?" Tam asks. That's the test, she tells Sophie. Oprah doesn't decorate with fake flowers.

"Neither does Candace," Sophie says, and she's got a handful of petals to prove it.

"What about the walls?" Tam asks.

"What about them?"

"Are they white, too?"

"Yeah," Sophie replies, and then it dawns on her why Tam is asking. "Oh my gosh! I showed her the paint chips. She didn't say a word."

"It's not a deal breaker, Sophie. If she wants white walls, you'll paint them white, won't you?"

"Yes." But she says it grudgingly.

"What else?" Tam asks, and Sophie proceeds to tick off the telltale signs of an opulent lifestyle: grand piano, grandfather clock, parquet floors in the living room, oil paintings on the walls. "Wow," Tam breathes. "At least little Dennis will have the best of everything."

This remark sets Sophie off on a new round of weeping. As soon as she manages to check her tears, she heads back down the long tiled hallway to the guest bedroom, stopping just long enough to shush her friend. "Don't say a word," she warns. "You could wake him up, all the way from Texas." To which Tam murmurs, "*Shh!*"

The cradle is large and deep—it's a slatted wooden basket hung from spindles—and when Sophie leans over to see inside, she inadvertently presses the bulk of her cast against the slats and sets the cradle rocking. Dennis doesn't wake. Instead, he reacts by settling more deeply into slumber and signaling his satisfaction with a ragged sigh. From the very beginning, he has luxuriated in sleep. It comes easily to him; he doesn't fight slipping off the way some babies do. Candace has already shared as much. Standing over him, Sophie realizes that her son slept just as easily when he was still in the womb, that he rarely woke her at night by tossing and turning. Other girls at New Futures yawned off and on throughout the day. Even before they made it into the world, those babies were waking their mothers with kicks and pokes. Not little Dennis.

The rug under Sophie's bare feet is soft; she curls her toes into it and peers down at the tiny, tucked body. "I wish you could see him," she whispers to Tam.

"Me, too," Tam replies. "I bet he's beautiful."

"Doesn't cover it," Sophie says. "His little lips are making sucking motions! Do you think he's dreaming of eating?"

"Well, yeah. What else would he dream about?"

The moment is perfect. If only Sophie could stop time now, she thinks. She wants to tell Tam that *this* is the future. It's here now, the instant when everything is exactly as it should be. Just as Sophie is about the register the thought, Tam yawns into the receiver and expresses her own need for sleep. She is due to open the skating rink at nine in the morning, which might as well be the crack of dawn. "I have to get up at seven," she complains.

But Sophie has stopped listening. She is tiptoeing out of the guest room, saying her goodnights to Tam, and, once she hangs up, wondering what she did with her canvas bag. Her arm aches at the elbow. And it will, off and on, for the rest of her life, a not-unwelcome reminder of the time when she was mowed down and then she picked herself up.

She wonders whether the pain will keep her from sleeping, but she knows she should try to rest while the baby is down. They taught her as much at New Futures. It's a cardinal rule for new mothers. Sophie wonders whether Candace knows how important it is to nap when Dennis naps. She will have to remember to share that particular bit of wisdom.

A good night's sleep puts Candace back in working order. She's up by eight. After putting on the coffee, she pads down the hallway to the guest room. The door is open, and the glow of the nightlight reveals Sophie stretched out on her back, the arm in a cast propped with pillows. Candace finds a throw on the rocking chair; she covers the girl with it. By the time she's done, Dennis is stirring in his cradle, and Candace quickly scoops him up and carries him away—before he can decide he's both wet and hungry, and therefore unhappy. He doesn't cry often, but when he does, it's a loud and demanding wail of indignation.

Candace closes the guest room door behind her. She hums as she goes about cleaning Dennis up. Now that she's rested, she knows exactly what she wants to do.

By the time Sophie gets up, Dennis is back down again, and Candace is packing two overnight bags, one for herself and one for the baby. She calls and makes a reservation at her favorite bed-and-breakfast in Brattleboro, for two adjoining rooms, one with a baby bed.

"Are you hungry?" she asks Sophie.

Sophie is, and she complains that her arm is aching. She rubs at the cast, wanders into the living room, and then returns to ask if Candace has seen her canvas bag. "The doctor gave me some pain pills," she says. "I think they're in the bag, but I couldn't find it last night. I didn't want to turn on all the lights and wake everyone."

They find the bag where Sophie left it, under the dining table. Candace offers to fix the two of them breakfast. As she puts raisin bread in the toaster, she wonders aloud whether Sophie wouldn't like to take this opportunity to see her grandmother. "Vernie's just a few hours away, you know."

Sophie has seen Vernie only a few times in her life, and she has no memory whatsoever of Jack's father, who died of a heart attack when she was just a toddler. She does recall several Christmas visits, made while Vernie was still living in her tiny, two-bedroom clapboard. Peggy, Jack, and baby Ian slept in the room that had once been Jack's, and Sophie shared her grandmother's high bed. Sophie recalls the smell of talcum powder, as well as waking to her grandmother's tight-lipped hum. As she dressed and brushed her hair, Vernie made a small, melodious sound—something between song and sigh, melody and moan.

During the Christmas when Sophie was six, they made a snowman in one corner of the small backyard, and Vernie got out her camera and caught Sophie standing with one red-mittened hand on the snowman's potbelly. The photograph is in a scrapbook. Sophie pages through on the second day of their visit to River View Manor. She feels shy and oddly out of place, not because the facility is unfamiliar or because she is so young and the residents so old. Her sense of unease has more to do with the uncertainty of her role. Who is she now? What is her role in the proceedings? Is she a granddaughter? She is and she isn't. Vernie doesn't recognize her as such, and Sophie is painfully aware that, strictly speaking, she is more stranger than kin. Nor is she a mother. Not really.

When it comes time to show off the baby, Candace tucks Dennis into a striped sling, which fits snugly around her shoulder and chest, and sets off down the long hallway with Vernie at her side. Vernie introduces Candace as "my daughter, Gwen," and sidles in close to nuzzle at the impostor's shoulder.

"You're not really her daughter, you know," Sophie complains when the two have returned to the bed-and-breakfast, a two-story with a wraparound porch and a bathroom that reminds Sophie of her childhood soaks in Vernie's claw-foot tub.

"She doesn't know me. . . ." *Her own flesh and blood*, Sophie is about to say, but she doesn't because she isn't, not that Vernie knows or would remember even if she did. "But she does know you, and *you're* the one who's the stranger."

Candace is sitting on the bed, about to change Dennis's diaper. She wants to say, *You're your daddy's girl, all right*. Beau was always the center of attention, and on the rare occasions when he wasn't, well, he could pout and snarl with the best of them. Instead, she smiles patiently and bends to the task of stripping the wet diaper from the baby's bottom. "Family is as family does," she says quietly. "If you behave like a daughter, most often you'll be treated like a daughter."

"And like a mother?"

Candace shrugs. "I wouldn't know for sure, not yet anyway." She reaches down and covers Dennis's penis with a cloth diaper. His timing is impeccable. In the short time Sophie has been changing him, he's managed to spray her twice. "But I'm guessing same, same." She reaches for the wet wipes. "You know what the Rolling Stones say, don't you?"

Sophie shakes her head.

"Well, I don't remember the words exactly, but the refrain is about how even though you might not get what you want, you can get what you need. No truer song lyric was ever written, if you ask me."

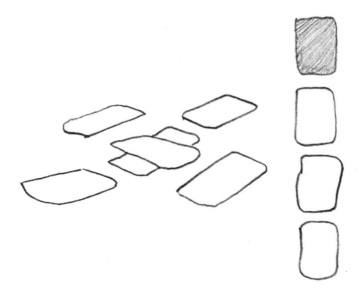

Position #10—"The Outcome"

Given the forces in motion at the time of your reading, this card represents the most likely outcome.

~ The Empress ~

The Empress is passionate and generous, and she represents all aspects of motherhood. She wears a flowing gown befitting a pregnant woman. She is surrounded by nature—a field of corn unfurls around her, fed by a waterfall and bordered by a grove of trees. The Empress nourishes our bodies and our souls.

ON A GOOD day—and Candace has chosen a brilliant early summer afternoon—the drive from Albuquerque to Taos takes all of two and a half hours. Most travelers can make the trip without stopping, but if need be, the journey can be neatly divided into thirds. Having made this trip several times in recent months, Candace has already preselected their rest stops, places where Dennis can get a little breather from the restraint of the car seat.

Candace likes to brag that he's a "good little traveler," but it's only true for the first forty-five minutes. Then he begins straining against the belt. "Want out!" he calls, and if he doesn't receive a response, he asserts himself with a warning: "Not kidding!" He learned this phrase from Sophie, who quit saying it as soon as Dennis picked it up.

Sophie's precursor to "I'm not kidding" was, "You're going to hurt yourself!" Dennis loves to run. If confined, he will dash around the edges of a room, around the perimeter of the coyote fence, down the aisles of Lowe's, and across the park. Candace and Sophie jog along behind to make sure he stays safe; Candace moves more slowly than Sophie and sometimes slows to a walk. Dennis motors along, his arms outflung. The shriek he emits may sound like a sign of distress but is, in actuality, the articulation of pure joy.

For his elders, happiness is a car in motion. Without consulting one another, Candace and Jack both bought new red vehicles. And in the months since making those purchases, they've received a fair amount of ribbing for being copycats. Most afternoons, Sophie bikes to the casita, and one day recently she arrived to find a shiny Beetle parked next to the coyote fence. While she was stowing her bicycle out of sight on the side of the house—wouldn't you know it, the neighborhood is sketchy—Candace wandered out, carrying Dennis on one hip. She looked a little dreamy and pleased with herself, as though she'd just been screwed, which was more or less appropriate. She'd paid more for the car than was strictly necessary, just because she doesn't like to bargain.

Sophie rushed to tell her that Jack had just bought a big, hulking truck—it's "the same exact color! Swear to god!" Jack's vehicle has been dubbed "Also Red," because that's what Dennis shouts each time he sees it. He points out the window and calls out, "Also Red!" This morning, Also Red is carrying lodgepoles and the rest of the teepee. It's Ian's idea. Candace is building a house on her land, and they're going to pitch the teepee next to the site.

Leaving Albuquerque, Sophie has a view to the east. From this vantage point, the Sandia Mountains dominate the landscape, casting a shadow that seems to extend for miles. Cacti-covered foothills give way to a jagged limestone and granite face.

The first leg of the trip, from Albuquerque to Santa Fe, covers a little over fifty miles. The road climbs steadily except outside San Felipe Pueblo, where a long, steep drop is followed by an even more precipitous incline, a roller-coaster ride in the middle of the desert.

Just outside of Placitas, the Jemez Mountains come into view off to the west. Depending on the light, the mountains can appear reddish—their true color—but in the afternoons and evenings, they are tinged purple and slate blue, a series of peaks and mesas that blend and bleed into the distance. The sheer immensity of the view leaves Candace awestruck. Even the ocean doesn't look this big, not to her anyway, but Jack sees fit to disagree. Nothing looks any larger or grander than the ocean. He misses New England, although even now he says he won't return for more than a lengthy visit.

"Awesome, isn't it?" Sophie remarks as the Jemez Mountains come into view. "They look like a painting, don't they?"

"They do," Candace agrees. "Maybe you'll have a chance to paint them someday."

Sophie laughs. "Yeah, I can just see myself setting up an easel on the side of the highway."

"I've seen stranger sights." And that's when Candace tells one of her hippie stories, this one about a trip to Albuquerque. The driver had insisted on stopping the car beside the freeway, the better to explore what was left of the Santa Fe Trail. "We were jammed in like sah-dines," she says. "I'm thinking we were in the back of a pickup, and someone in the front seat got a wild hair to hike up and see the ruts left by the wagon trains."

Candace was wearing brand-new moccasins, and she wanted to tread carefully, bring up the rear, get a glimpse from a distance, and then head back to the truck. "I was so goofy," she confesses. "I was such a go-along." Because she sees the questioning look on Sophie's face, Candace pretends to concentrate on the road, but she goes on talking, describing the breakdown of the truck, which refused to start when they got ready to go. There was nothing to do but take off walking to the next exit, a hike of several miles. Everyone kept yakking about how lucky she was to have on the moccasins, but the heat of the asphalt bore right through the suede bottoms and burned the soles of her feet.

"Was my mom with you?" Sophie asks.

"I don't remember," Candace admits. She was fixated on the toes of her pretty beaded moccasins and then, as they trudged one mile after another, the tender soles of her feet. She wishes it had been otherwise, that she'd paid closer attention, that she had a better memory, *something.*

Dennis is quiet, and Candace assumes he's dropped off to sleep. A glance in the rearview mirror confirms it. She loves the way he goes limp when he snoozes: his head droops, his mouth hangs open. He looks less like the littlest angel and more like the littlest drunk.

They drive in silence for a few miles, passing one after another laboring semitruck. The road ascends, dips, then ascends again. Because she's lost in thought, Sophie takes a while to notice the quiet backseat. "He's asleep, isn't he?"

Candace nods.

"I guess we can make good time after all," Sophie remarks.

"More time to spend at Twirl!"

Candace is anxious to share the toy store she discovered in Taos. She's told Sophie a little about it, but she doesn't want to say too much. Once or twice recently, she's built up Sophie's expectations, only to disappoint her. She has promised what she couldn't deliver, and now, even regarding the inconsequential, she is careful to be measured.

The store is situated at the heart of the plaza. It's in an adobe building that has been occupied by a succession of artist types, Dennis Hopper and painter Agnes Martin among them. Over the 150 years since it was built, eccentric occupants have put their stamp on the space, adding a pyramid skylight on the second floor and an indoor fish fountain in what used to be the dining room. During the building's newest incarnation as a toy store and kids' space, the owner has put a muralist to work; the walls of the entryway are now painted to resemble a jungle, and a secret staircase is watched over by snakes and grinning dragons. Candace, for one, is enchanted by the shop.

The 599 Relief Route funnels traffic around Santa Fe—nicknamed "The City Different"—and directs it back onto US 84/285. From the juncture, Candace cranes her neck, hoping for a glimpse of the partially open-air structure that houses the Santa Fe Opera. The first structure was built in 1968, the year Candace arrived in New Mexico, but she hadn't heard about it until she was back in Boston, and then it was from a friend of her aunt Agnes. "Did you make it to the opera while you were there?" the woman had asked. Beau had snickered, and Candace had probably done something like kick him under the table. But he'd been undeterred: "We saw *La Bohème*, didn't we, darling?" And she'd nodded more times than was necessary. Even now, all these years later, the memory brings a smile to her face.

Candace is relieved to note that sandstone rock formations still outnumber houses, but she knows it's just a matter of time before commerce calls from both sides of the highway. While Candace was away, living life in Boston, the pueblos had erected casinos beside the highway, each one the size of a small shopping mall and surrounded by an expansive asphalt parking lot. Surely not, Candace thought the first time she had laid eyes on all the parking. No betting person would ever wager that the lots would all be full by nightfall. Not out here in the middle of the desert. But every night, the headlights of hundreds of cars light up the desert. Visitors headed to Taos can take the High Road at Chimayo, but the fastest route is straight through Española, where 285 intersects with State Road 68. Española is the home of the lowriders. "Low and slow" is their motto, and their vehicle of choice is the Chevy Impala. Not everyone can drive an Impala, though, and Candace ends up behind a lowrider SUV. She is tempted to reach over and shake Sophie, to get her to explain why it is that perfectly sane men would want to drive down the road with a chassis inches from the asphalt. Sophie would be grumpy, though. She would complain about men, which would wind up being a complaint about Will.

So Candace contains her incredulity. She knows from experience that *vatos* take advantage of frequent red lights to demonstrate their custom hydraulic suspensions. Show the slightest interest, and they will put the vehicle through its paces—they'll raise and lower the front and rear, dip and raise the sides of the car and its four corners.

The SUV turns in to a Walmart, and Candace is able to accelerate. She's looking forward to the last part of the journey. It's the shortest in terms of mileage, just under forty miles, but 68 is a narrow, winding two-lane road that follows the path of the river. For many years, Candace had assumed that the Rio Grande Gorge, which is nearly eight hundred feet deep in some places, had been carved out by the river over eons. But Jack has done a little reading on the subject, and he discovered that in this case, the rift came first. It was a fault line created by shifting plates.

Eventually the snaking low road finds its way upward, passing orchards and vineyards along the way. The horseshoe pass, a looping dive and ascent—one last flourish—brings the traveler up to the summit, where the overlook is magnificent. There the vast Taos Plateau extends in every direction, marked by the chasms of the Rio Grande Gorge, which undulate across the valley floor. The play of color changes depending on the sunlight and the season, but the view is always spectacular. To the north are the distant mountains of Colorado; to the east lies the often snow-covered Sangre de Cristo Range. And most prominent is that gentle giant, Taos Mountain, El Monte Sagrado.

"Wake up, Sophie," Candace says quietly. "We're here."

Stretching, sitting up, Sophie turns to look past Candace to the immense valley floor spread out below the road. "Immense" is not too big a word; "magnificent" is not too grand. "Wow," she says as she reaches up and rubs her eyes. "Who could ever do that view justice?"

"No one except God," Candace replies.

When Sophie first laid eyes on the Empress, when Peggy tapped the card and whispered, "What will come," Sophie saw the feminine figure and thought: *That's me*. She was the Earth Mother, a field of corn ripening before her, water flowing around and beyond her. The Empress was Venus—the goddess of love—and so Sophie thought of herself. She was just that "full of herself," as Tam would chide her.

It would take all this time before it would occur to Sophie that the Empress was actually Candace. The mistake was understandable: when the reading took place, she didn't know Candace, didn't even know *of* Candace. It made sense that she would make a wrong attribution, that she would see herself where she *should* have seen someone else. And then there was the fact that Candace wasn't, and never has been, Venus. But she has been, and still is, an earth mother. That's the way the old hippies who still live in Taos remember her—she bought beans and rice for the multitudes. She fed the hungry and sheltered the homeless. She never turned anyone away. That isn't true, of course. She had to say no, at least occasionally.

By the time they park in the square and make their way down the boardwalk—Dennis insists on being carried, as he's still too groggy from the long nap to propel himself to the store—it's nearly closing time. The store is rather cramped and mysterious, a series of tiny rooms that weave in and out of one another in a way that reminds Sophie of *Alice in Wonderland*. She wanders slowly, ducks through doorways, picks up this and that.

The lack of natural light and the smell of adobe remind Sophie of her mother's store. It is too soon for those memories, early childhood snippets from when Sophie was a toddler. She used to stay in the store all day, playing hide-and-seek among the clothes racks, Peggy pretending not to see, allowing Sophie to win this game, all games. So she is relieved to have a reason to leave the toy store. She needs to go to the bathroom. It's urgent, this need. They've driven straight through from Albuquerque, after all. She shifts her weight from foot to foot and watches Candace, who holds a small plastic dragon that Dennis has thrust into her hands. He likes to share the things he finds. Candace can play with the dragon, and he will play with the knight.

Wearing an absent smile, Sophie asks Candace about the bathroom. "I think there must be one here," Candace replies, "but I know there's a public restroom as well. Take the boardwalk there on Kit Carson. It's just past the Kit Carson Home." Sophie nods and departs, pleased to be outdoors, bathed in the golden light of late afternoon.

The tourists are thinning out, heading back to their hotels to freshen up for dinner. No one wants the day to end; if it were possible, they would hold their breath in unison and stop time altogether. No one is in a hurry, either. No one except Sophie. The glow of impending evening graces the world around them. The heavy, knotted trunks of the cottonwoods appear etched as in a woodblock by, say, Gustave Baumann. Tall spires of hollyhocks nod against the adobe buildings, tissue-paper flowers of red, pink, white, and a splendid lavender.

Sophie wishes she'd brought a sketchbook and colored pencils. She would have tried her hand at rendering the scene. More and more, she seeks to remember Dennis's babyhood through drawing. Tucked away in a drawer at home are dozens of sketches, some of his pudgy fingers, others of his eyes, his ears, his toes. There are even one or two of his "little snail," which is what she calls his penis. Sophie manages to do some justice to her son when she relegates herself to one feature at a time, but she can't begin to render the whole of Dennis. He overwhelms and astounds her. "He makes me drunk," she has admitted to Candace. "He makes me dizzy!"

They have that in common, the two of them: their reverence for this boy.

During those last days of Peggy's life, Sophie drew her mother, too. She sat in the chair beside the hospital bed and tried again and again to capture Peggy's face. In the space of only a few days, the Peggy Sophie knew all her life had disappeared. She had been replaced by a wax figure of a mother, someone who vaguely resembled Peggy, who had her hair—a wiry woven mass of gray and brown—but not much else. She kept her eyes closed throughout the last two days of her life, never even saying good-bye to the rest of them. "She's just too tired," Candace kept saying. "We have to let her sleep a bit."

Sophie brought Dennis to the hospital, thinking that Peggy would surely wake for her grandson, but she didn't. She couldn't.

Sophie, Ian, Jack—they all had tricks they played to bring her back to them, but nothing worked. Ian had a little song he sang, something he said he remembered hearing when he was little more than a baby. Jack never told them what he said when he leaned over the bed and whispered something in her ear. Jack's whisper made Peggy sigh. She turned her head toward him. Her eyelids fluttered. They were all there: Sophie, Ian, Jack, Dennis, and Candace. One and all leaned toward the bed and waited, as they say, with baited breath.

But she slept on. And then, she died. Sophie was puzzled by her mother's departure, so abrupt and unforeseen. Peggy kept her illness a secret for as long as she could. Of course she did. And it made Sophie furious.

Only a few months back, Sophie had reason to visit Old Town and the space Everyday Satin had occupied. Jack had sold the property, and she went with him to help with the final cleanup. That's when she met Donald, a scarecrow of a young man. He wept when Sophie revealed that Peggy was gone. Evidently Peggy had befriended him, and he wanted to thank her. Sophie shook her head grimly. "Not even the family got a chance to tell her good-bye." There are regrets, and then there are regrets. It will be another year before Sophie receives her mother's instructions, the reading notes Peggy compiled at Everyday Satin and carried home when she closed up the store. A letter to Sophie, notes on tarot card reading, and the deck itself: all these are secreted away under Peggy's side of the bed, and they won't be discovered until Jack decides that it's time for a new mattress.

During Sophie's senior year at New Futures—when Candace returned to Albuquerque with Dennis, allowing Sophie to think rationally again—she went back to seeing Ms. Jimenez. It was a luxury of sorts, to go and sit and talk about her feelings, and she made good use of the time. In one of her more emotional sessions, Sophie had a revelation: her whole future had been determined by Tam's careless vacuuming. If Tam hadn't run over the cord of the vacuum, if Belinda hadn't grounded her and sent Sophie home, where she met Candace—no, where Candace met her—well, then, she'd have proceeded with the abortion.

No Dennis. That was unimaginable. But then there was this as well: "Will wouldn't know his father!" She practically shouted the words, so surprised was she by the revelation. "He wouldn't have gone to Lubbock."

Ms. Jimenez smiled. She rarely had sessions as satisfying as this one. She reached over and patted Sophie's knees, and as she did so, Sophie closed her hand over the counselor's. But that wasn't the end of it. Ms. Jimenez wondered whether Sophie could understand something of Peggy's dilemma. "She was so happy to have you. To have *you*. She didn't want to rock the boat. She had her marriage and her darling baby, Sophie. You may not approve, Sophie, but surely you can understand."

But Sophie shook her head fiercely. No, she could not, *would* not understand. She could not extend herself that far on her mother's behalf. She won't be able to do so for many years. Not until she is nearly thirty and has a second child—so different from the first—does it really sink in that she is the child of Beau and Peggy, raised by Peggy and Jack. She would have been someone entirely different if she'd simply been the child of Peggy and Jack. Much as she adores her second son, she can't help but notice that he lacks the devotion of his older brother. The devotion came from Will.

One of the central regrets of Sophie's adult life will be the loss of her mother, losing her before Sophie could properly forget and forgive what was certainly a transgression, but perhaps not a betrayal. The leukemia took her quickly, coming on like a flu with a vengeance. Ian had come home from school and, inexplicably, found his mother curled up in the backseat of the car. He'd had some practice driving; both Sophie and Jack had taken him out a few times on rural roads around Albuquerque. Ian is so cautious, so responsible. Jack couldn't imagine that he would abuse the privilege, and he hadn't.

It was such a good thing, they all agreed later, that Ian was able simply to slip into the driver's seat and convey his mother to the hospital. Perhaps because he had visited the hospital when Sophie had her mishap, he didn't hesitate or second-guess himself. All the way across town, he spoke reassuringly to his mother in the backseat. She didn't respond, but he continued to talk to her, and when he turned into the hospital parking lot, he called back to her, "We're here!" Following the signs to the emergency room, he pulled the car right up to the curb in front of the sliding glass doors.

He jumped out, strode directly to the counter, and commanded the attention of the nurse and orderly on duty. "My mother needs help," he told them.

Later the nurses would be confused—they didn't register his age. He seemed like a young man when he entered the hospital, but later, when a whole clutch of nurses came in search of him—mainly because he'd left the car in the middle of the emergency drive, had just forgotten all about it—they didn't recognize him. There he was, standing in front of the snack machine, staring through the glass at the offerings: Doritos, Fritos, Snickers, Twix, Doublemint, Juicy Fruit. He wasn't hungry. He didn't have coins to feed the machine. As Sophie would have said, he was shit out of luck on both fronts. But he needed to direct his attention elsewhere, and so he repeated the names of the products aloud: "Lay's Potato Chips, Peanut M&Ms, Hot Tamales, Honey Roasted Peanuts."

In the space of a couple of hours, he'd gone from looking like a young man to looking like a young boy. When they called his name, he glanced up, scared, the nurses agreed. Scared and so pale. Like a ghost.

The playground at Twirl is dominated by a series of colorful tunnels of the sort Candace most often sees at McDonald's. Dennis is drawn to the tunnels, to crawling through the passageways, which eventually emerge at the toddler slide. (He's amazed by the tunnels because he has never set foot in a McDonald's.) The owner of the store has been thoughtful enough to provide several plastic Adirondack chairs, complete with footrests, and Candace stretches out on one of these—but only after turning it to face the giant caterpillar-like apparatus into which her dearest has disappeared.

Occasionally he calls to her, "Are you out there, Candy?"

"Candy's here," she replies. "Don't worry, sweetheart."

She's not sure why he began calling her Candy. She suspects it was Sophie's doing, but of course the little vixen isn't about to fess up. And the truth is that Candace will answer to anything if it's Dennis calling. It helps, of course, that Dennis calls Sophie "Soapy." Soapy and Candy answer gladly to their nicknames, and they have even begun to refer to one another as such.

When the back door to the store opens, Candace turns her head, planning to speak to Sophie. *Are you hungry yet, Soapy?* she is going to ask. Candace herself is starving, and she's trying to decide just what sounds the most delicious. Like the scenery, the food in Taos is fabulous. But two little girls appear, instead of one young woman.

Dennis has emerged just in time to welcome them. He's sitting at the top of the blue plastic slide, and he shrieks joyfully at the sight of new play pals. The two little girls run straight for Dennis. One is older than he is, three maybe, and the other is a toddler like him. The toddler wobbles and teeters as she attempts to shadow her older sister. Both are dressed in embroidered jeans and tiny tube tops, pink for the younger girl and orange for her sister. Occasionally, one girl or the other wrestles with her top. They have a tendency to slip down, relinquishing the position of blouse to assume the post of belt. The girls do their best to keep the tops in place, but sometimes they end up rushing about more or less topless. Not that it matters to either of them. It certainly doesn't matter to the gray-haired gentleman who accompanies them. The older girl is named Maisey, and she refers to the man who follows her as "Pops."

Candace gets up and finds a spot on the bench closer to the man. She hopes he doesn't think she's coming on to him. Wouldn't that be embarrassing and unfortunate? Still, she has to find out if she's right. "I knew someone named Maisey when I lived here."

He grins broadly and slaps his hands on either knee. He's wearing jeans, which look to be pressed. Surely this is no one she knew, Candace thinks.

"Was she beautiful?"

She nods.

"And did she work as a waitress at Joe's Restaurant?"

She nods again.

"My wife," says the man, nodding. It makes perfect sense to him. "That's her granddaughter." He points in the direction of the little girl disappearing into the tunnel.

Now Candace is mighty curious. Is it possible that she *does* know this well-groomed individual? She still can't picture it. Who could this man be, then?

He is more than ready to start with the introductions. "Name's Hank," he says, thrusting his hand in her direction. "And you are?"

"Candace Cuzak," she replies.

The sound has barely left her mouth when he shouts, "Whoa!" And then he adds the diplomatic rejoinder: "Of course, you haven't really changed *that* much."

"I'm sorry," she says. "Do we know one another?"

Hank grins broadly and starts to reply, but Dennis interrupts. He wants Candy to watch. The grown-ups halt their conversation and turn their attention to the much-younger generation. "I can go fast!" Dennis calls out. He looks impish and full of himself up there. When Candace turns back to Hank, she sees that he is intent on Dennis's descent down the slide. The two little girls are waiting at the bottom of the slide, and while they have a minute, they adjust their tube tops.

"*Whee!*" Dennis shouts, but the slide isn't particularly slick. He descends haltingly. When he gets to the bottom, the girls jump up and down, which action lowers their tops, like flags going down.

"Good job, Dennis!" Candace commends him.

Hank has returned his attention to Candace. "You don't remember me, do you?" he teases. His chambray shirt is tucked into his jeans.

"We met?"

"We lived in the same house—your house—for months and months."

"How can that be? How can that possibly be?"

"That be," he jokes. "That certainly be. You might have recognized my voice—that is, if I had ever spoken. But I didn't, you see." He does have a big voice, a baritone, and Candace can imagine him singing, in a church choir perhaps.

Because he is so clean and pressed, it takes her longer than it should to make the connection. Candace claps a hand over her mouth. She gapes at him and only reluctantly says, "Hermit Henry?"

And he chortles appreciatively. "That's me." Ever the attentive grand-dad, he glances over at Maisey and her sister Myra and watches as they clamber into the tunnel maze. They follow Dennis, who is motoring uphill on all fours and shrieking loudly. He didn't know he liked girls, but he has decided that he does.

If you haven't heard it before, Dennis's shriek is just a little discon-certing. So Candace offers a brief explanation: "He's happy. He's delighted."

Hank shrugs. "I'll take your word for it." First he crosses his long legs, then he crosses his arms over his chest. "Anyway," he says, "I'm so glad I ran into you. I want to thank you, Candace. You took me in when no one else would have. I had to get that asceticism out of my system, and I did it at Morningstar, there in a safe place with people who . . ." He hesitates, searching for the word. "With people who tolerated me."

"Wow. You communicate very clearly now."

"Made up for lost time where the talking is concerned."

He goes on to tell her how he ended up going home to Oklahoma and getting a nursing degree. All the while, he and Maisey wrote letters to one another. Eventually he returned to Taos, and they married and had three children.

When he finishes his own story, he inquires of her, "Do you still own land here, then?"

She nods. "I do, in fact."

"Thought I heard that Kevin Costner made an offer on it."

It's still a small town. Candace remembers the way it used to be, how she had to drive all the way to Santa Fe to get a pregnancy test, because she didn't want the rest of the commune to be in on her secret. They weren't supposed to have secrets back then. Evidently that's still the case.

She laughs loudly. The children pause in their play to glance her way. Then they disappear into a climbing tunnel. "You know more about it than I do. The agent was so hush-hush; no one was supposed to know anything about the buyer. . . . But wait a minute." She stops and thinks for a moment. "Did he win an Oscar?"

Hank shakes his head. "You got me. Never did keep track of that sort of thing, and now . . ." He spreads his long arms in front of himself, indicating the playground, his granddaughters, and beyond. "Now I've got so many more important things to keep track of. Can't remember the last time I went to see a movie."

Candace nods and waves at Dennis as he pops up in the center of a tire swing. At times like this, when he is intent on his own happiness, Dennis looks most like his grandfather. And perhaps Hank sees it, too, the ghost of Beau past. In any case, he chooses this moment to state what would seem to be the obvious: "So, Dennis must be your grand-child. He resembles Beau. He sure does."

Candace has prepared herself for this moment. She has made a sol-emn promise, unspoken but no less binding for that. "Dennis is Peggy and Beau's grandchild."

"Is that right?" Hank smiles absently.

Her friend's name brings to mind the well-wrapped box in the trunk of the car. On the last leg of the trip, as Candace maneuvered the car along the twisting road, the box slid the length of the trunk and then back again, down and back, each time they took a turn. If you didn't know what it was—a box of ashes—the sound was hardly noticeable. But Candace did know, and for maybe half an hour, she concentrated on driving and tried studiously not to cry.

Once or twice she managed a glance in Sophie's direction, but the young woman was dozing. If Sophie had recognized the source of the sound, she'd decided not to mention it. Candace spent the rest of the drive wishing that she'd stowed Dennis's stroller in the trunk rather than in the backseat. Or that she'd had the presence of mind to wedge the box into a corner or, better yet, to buttress it between the two small suitcases.

Hank's brow furrows. He gazes off into the past, trying to sort out the entanglements. But it's all so long ago now. He really isn't quite sure. Perhaps it was Peggy who married Beau. Perhaps he's remembered all wrong.

"How is Peggy doing, then?"

Candace sighs. "She passed away this spring, very unexpectedly."

Hank shakes his head and offers his sympathies. Candace thanks him. It's surprised her, really, how quickly they've all accepted the death, though what choice do they have, after all? Entrances and exits are simply part of the stage drama known as Life. Dennis's entrance was every bit as unexpected as Peggy's exit. They had scarcely more time to prepare for one than to brace themselves for the other. While Dennis's arrival had nothing to do with Peggy's departure, the one did make the other a bit easier.

Sophie appears in the doorway just as Candace is trying to think of what else to say. Sophie's hair is cut shorter now; a cascade of curls bounces around her shoulders.

"There she is!" Candace reaches over and grasps Hank's arm and smiles. Sophie is wearing those scuffed cowboy boots, a cutoff denim skirt, and a snug red T-shirt. She could take this town by storm, Candace thinks. Perhaps she already has.

"Sophie, come over here," Candace calls. "There's someone I want you to meet."

At the sound of his mother's name, Dennis slips out of the tire swing. "Soapy!" he shrieks.

"Wow!" Hank says, "I'd know her for Beau's daughter anywhere."

Candace smiles. "Yes," she says. "Me too."

He's not a dimwit, Hank. He sees the secretive curve of her smile. "It was all so complicated back then," he says genially.

"No more complicated than it is right now," Candace replies smoothly, watching as Sophie heads over to the swings to give Dennis a hand. He wants to hang from the monkey bars, but he needs Soapy to spot him. She turns back to Hank and finishes her thought. "Family is *always* complicated."

Acknowledgements

The black-and-white tarot cards used in this book are taken from *The Pictorial Key to the Tarot*, a book by Arthur Edward Waite originally published in 1911 and now in the public domain. Devin Alan Warner drew the illustrations of the Celtic Cross, taking his inspiration from the diagrams on Joan Bunning's website, www.learntarot.com. I encourage anyone interested in tarot to visit this informative and free website.

While writing this novel, I referred to many books on tarot, including *The Complete Illustrated Guide to Tarot*, by Rachel Pollack; *Jung and Tarot: An Archetypal Journey*, by Sallie Nichols; *The Pictorial Key to the Tarot*, by Arthur Edward Waite; *The Complete Idiot's Guide to Tarot and Fortune-Telling*, by Arlene Tognetti and Lisa Lenard; *Mastering the Tarot: Basic Lessons in an Ancient, Mystic Art*, by Eden Gray; *The Mystical Tarot*, by Rosemary Ellen Guiley; and *Tarot for Writers*, by Corrine Kenner.

For introducing me to the lives of honeybees, I am grateful to two beekeepers: Les Crowder and Matt Allen. In addition, I have benefited from several excellent books on bees. My favorites are *A Book of Bees*, by Sue Hubbell; *A Keeper of Bees: Notes on Hive and Home*, by Allison Wallace; and *Beekeeping: A Complete Owner's Manual*, by Werner Melzer. Recently the plight of honeybees has become a matter of deepest concern to many of us on the planet. To help save the bees, I refer readers to the Xerces Society for Invertebrate Conservation at www.xerces.org.

Two moving memoirs offered me insight into the psyches of pregnant teens: *Without a Map*, by Meredith Hall, and *Waiting to Forget: A Motherhood Lost and Found*, by Margaret Moorman. I should also mention an inspiring book on the inner lives of teenage girls: *Reviving Ophelia: Saving the Selves of Adolescent Girls*, by Mary Pipher. My thanks go to Christine Cooney Martin for sharing her experiences as a nurse-midwife.

I am indebted as well to Albuquerque Public Schools English teacher Nancy McGovern, who invited me into her creative writing classroom at New Futures High School. I taught several writing workshops at New Futures and came away a real believer in both the school and its mission. One of the first schools in the nation devoted to the education of pregnant teens and teen parents, New Futures offers these young women a way to earn a high school diploma. With child-care facilities onsite, the school provides new mothers—and a growing number of young fathers—with a stable, nurturing educational environment.

Although my sons enjoy teasing me about my hippie days, I decided not to rely on what I still remember about hitchhiking cross-country, for instance. Instead, I did additional reading on the 1960s, and particularly on the commune movement in Taos, New Mexico. Three books I found both inspirational and informative are *New Buffalo: Journals from a Taos Commune*, by Arthur Kopecky; *If Mountains Die: A New Mexico Memoir*, by John Nichols and William Davis; and *Scrapbook of a Taos Hippie: Tribal Tales from the Heart of a Cultural Revolution*, by Iris Keltz.

Sophie's House of Cards grew out of several short stories, and I am indebted to *Prairie Schooner* and then-editor Hilda Raz for publishing three of them: "The Object Lesson," "Signs of Life," and "Sweetness." A fourth story called "Love Child" appeared in the *Laurel Review*; for that I thank then-editor Rebecca Aronson. The novel's progress was advanced by two writing residencies. For those, I am grateful to novelist Jim Crace and the Atlantic Center for the Arts, and Karen Young and the residency program at the Mabel Dodge Luhan House in Taos.

Debra Monroe, Minrose Gwin, and Valerie Kinsey read drafts of the novel and provided commentary, criticism, and encouragement. I particularly appreciate the message from Debra with the subject line "I Dreamed About Your Characters Last Night!" The book took a long time to write, and over the years, I had the benefit of feedback from several seasoned editors: the late Carol Houck Smith, Anika Streitfield, Jane von Mehren, and, finally, the University of New Mexico Press's Elise McHugh. Particular thanks go to Elise for championing Sophie and bringing her story to print. My agents at Inkwell Management, Kimberly Witherspoon and Alexis Hurley, have also been a consistent source of support and counsel. And I want to express my gratitude to Grace Labatt—copyeditor extraordinaire.

Thanks to my tarot buddy, Joy Harjo, who saw me through trying times and an actual trial, and to Greg Martin, Diane Thiel, Daniel Mueller, David Croft, Eva Lipton-Ormand, and Jonis Agee for their love and friendship. Above all, I am deeply grateful to my family: my *darling* husband, Teddy; my *dear* father, who was this novel's first reader; and my two sons, Corey and Devin. Whatever I know about family I began learning in my earliest years from all *six* of my siblings: Sonny, Lisa, Debbie, Robin, Chris, and Ronnie. I love and appreciate all of you.